Oaths
&
Old Gods

OATHS
&
OLD GODS

ANDER LEVISAY

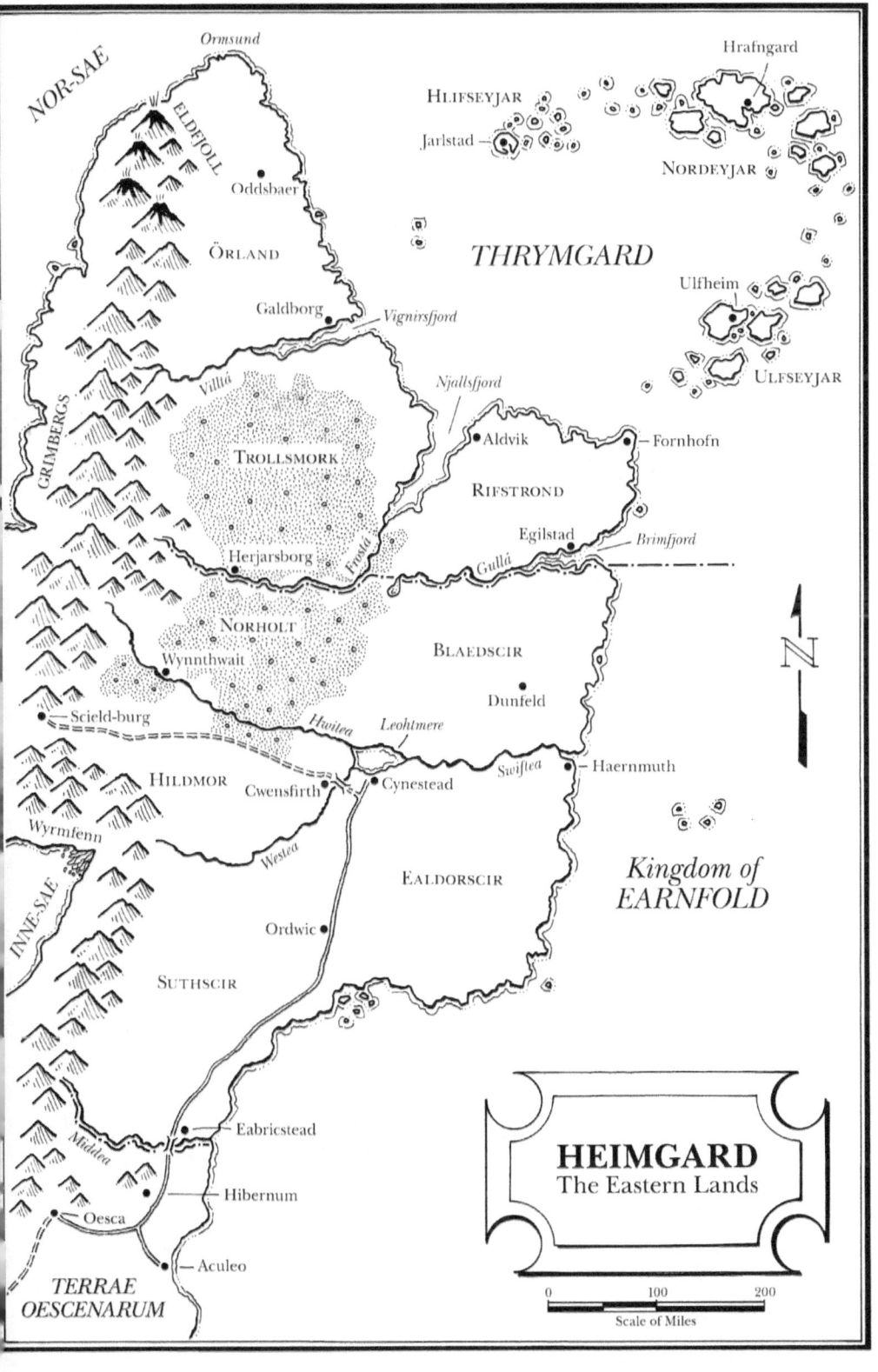

NOR-SÆ

Ormsund

ELDFJOLL

Oddsbaer

ÖRLAND

Galdborg

Vignirsfjord

CRIMBERGS

Villá

TROLLSMORK

Herjarsborg

Fraud

NORHOLT

Wynnthwait

Scield-burg

HILDMOR

Cwensfirth

Hwitea

Wyrmfenn

Westea

INNE-SÆ

Ordwic

SUTHSCIR

Eabricstead

Midtea

Hibernum

Oesca

Aculeo

TERRAE
OESCENARUM

HLIFSEYJAR

Jarlstad

Hrafngard

NORDEYJAR

THRYMGARD

Ulfheim

ULFSEYJAR

Njallsfjord

Aldvik

RIFSTROND

Fornhofn

Egilstad

Brimfjord

Gullá

BLAEDSCIR

Dunfeld

Leohtmere

Cynestead

Swiftea

Haernmuth

EALDORSCIR

Kingdom of
EARNFOLD

N

HEIMGARD
The Eastern Lands

0   100   200

Scale of Miles

PROLOGUE

"HAIL, FRIEND. I mean you no harm." The woman held up her bandaged hand in greeting.

Wigmar could not have run if he had wanted to. The mud in the pigsty was ankle deep in the best of spots and uneven. There was a fence between him and his hut. The wolf dog would be on him before he crossed half the distance. And then the axes at the men's hips would make short work of the boards and rope he had fashioned into a door.

There were five of them, counting the woman, all mangy and ill favored. The hound made six. They had come from the tree line while he was sinking fence posts, and he had not noticed the birds had gone silent until too late. He still clutched the maul in his right hand. The men kept their eyes fixed on it, so he took care not to so much as twitch. One of the axemen might have been a woman, now that they had come a little closer, but there was too much dirt and matted hair and he did not have time for study. By the way they all shadowed the bandaged woman, one wrong move would be final. Sweat ran down Wigmar's wrist and dripped off his knuckles.

"Aelfhild is my name," she said.

Her accent had all the crisp, stilted condescension of Cynestead, which told a different story than her gaunt cheeks and the rags that hung off her shoulders. Folk from the capital were skilled in all manner of conniving and backstabbing, but outright banditry was unusual for them. Too close to real work. Wigmar grunted. The stake in her left hand, all the more intimidating for its crudeness, said he could not be rude, but Gods damn the whole lot if he had to be polite to his robbers.

She continued, "My friends and I were wondering if you could part with some supplies."

He risked a glance over his shoulder. No one was coming. No one ever did. That was the price of solitude. Being undisturbed was the sole benefit of this benighted frontier—no one cared who you had been, what you had fled. The handful of local homesteaders knew as little as possible about him, in case anyone from the old days came seeking, and the Eorl's guards never came out this far. A pair claiming to serve the Eorl had come through last fall asking for "the lord's tithe," but Wigmar had fair little faith that those pigs had ever found their way across the mountains to Thrydwulf's court. Such was the price of lawless lands. Was a day when he could have had such ruffians tossed from his hall and driven from his lands, when he did not have clay caked under his fingernails and crusted around his face. Was a day when he did not have bruises left by surly pigs, scrapes from chasing wayward swine through brambles, or sweat stinging the blisters on his palms. Was a day—but the Gods had seen to all that.

How great their bounty. Praise the Four.

"Just what you might be able to part with," she was saying.

Wigmar tensed for the demands. First, she will be wanting this and wanting that. Then another thing, and oh, what bother, they left their purses at home. He could have spat if the men standing by his fence would not have cut him down simply for moving. But how it made his nose itch when the thieves pretended to be other than they were. Get on with it and be done.

Then she lifted a braided arm-ring from her belt pouch. It was tarnished, the workmanship shoddy, but Wigmar knew silver when he saw it. He might not have been a deft hand at farming, but some talents never faded.

"We can offer something in return, of course." She smiled.

Wigmar lifted his free hand to wipe the phlegm from the corners of his mouth. The men glowered at him. He did it slowly.

"Hah." His voice failed him at first.

Her smile never faltered. The men's eyes stayed on him, the dog's, too. Their hands never moved toward their axe handles, but they did not have to.

"Hail, friends," he said, mirroring her words and her smile. He bowed his head slightly. His shoulder was throwing bolts of searing fire down his back, but he kept that maul held steady.

Who said a man's luck could never change? That silver, paltry as it was, that was a start. A turn for something bigger, something better. Maybe he could return home sooner than he had planned. One piece at a time. The smile felt unfamiliar as it curled up his cheeks. There had not of late been much cause for mirth.

"Yes," he said. Wigmar suspected he might just be able to turn this to his advantage.

1

"**ELA.**"

A hand touched her shoulder and called Aelfhild back to herself.

It was the scream that haunted her most. One moment, Ceolwen suspended in the light, drawn up above the Oath-Stone that they had strived and suffered to reach; the next moment, a blinding flash and that dying wail. Everything gone. Nothing but ash coating the skin, choking the nostrils, forming a chalky sludge at the back of the throat. The urge to retch at the memory was not as strong as it had been in the immediate aftermath, but was still not gone.

Aelfhild cleared her throat. The feeling caught her at odd moments. She squinted at the ground. "It looks like a puddle."

"You can manage better than that." Kolbrun knelt and pointed along the edge of the depression. With anyone else, Kolbrun's voice had a bass edge that could strike sparks off flint. It was softer for Aelfhild—these days at least. "See how this one is deeper than the last? A second man, a fat man, met the other one here."

"How do you know he is fat?"

Kolbrun took a moment to flick the rain from her face before answering. "Is the track longer or wider? No, so he must be near the same height. Is it deeper? Yes, so he must weigh more. I have told you all this before."

Aelfhild nodded along. She was not a tracker. She was not from the countryside. And she did not much appreciate the deliberate tone the shieldmaiden used to answer what might, admittedly, have been a foolish question. But her companions had all turned sour when the drizzle rolled in to spoil the tracks, so she decided not to push her luck further.

"Anything over there?" Onund, with nothing but a dripping grey beard protruding from the wrappings of his tattered cloak, squelched toward the kneeling women.

Kolbrun gestured to the ridgeline. "Embla lost the scent back here. Eyvind took her up on the rocks to see if they could pick anything up."

The Grimbergs loomed around them, snow-streaked slopes disappearing into pregnant clouds. On the far side, to the east, lay Earnfold—home—all green summer pastures and babbling brooks, but first they had to contend with a line of peaks, glaciers, and crevasses as impenetrable as any Oescan citadel. Part of her hoped that this Wigmar they had come across had been wrong about the path. He had seemed a shifty one and was most certainly not from these parts. Maybe he had lied about the hidden path just to get them to clear off.

Maybe they would never have to return home. There were worse fates.

She tightened the knot on the bandage swaddling her hand. The rune never pained her; there was only ever a pinprick tingling that could as easily have been a trick of her mind. But it did make her feel like a thief of the lowest sort. The diamond traced in glowing gold, cut in half by a bright line that ran from her middle finger to wrist, was meant to be on the hand of the future queen. That had been the plan. Instead, Ceolwen was dead and the Oath-Stone had marked her nobody of a maidservant by mistake. Looking at its glow made Aelfhild queasy, and she kept it covered at all times. Better to hide the shame, from herself and from the stares of her friends. A figure above caught her eye. "Is that him waving?"

Kolbrun grunted. "About time that mutt earned her supper."

Pebbles skittered underfoot as they pulled their way up the landslide. It might have been summer below, but the mountains were only just warming to spring. As the ice gave way, boulders and whole banks of rock and mud came sliding down to blot out the few goat paths and narrow trails that edged out along the sheer granite, and most of the footprints that might lead them through. They had spent frigid days following puddles into dead ends and rockfalls. Today, at least, driving wind had given way to lazy showers.

Kolbrun gave Aelfhild a leg up onto a ledge, and Eyvind hoisted her up after.

"She caught a scent," Eyvind said. "There is a canyon not far ahead; looks like it could lead somewhere. And a stand of trees so we can catch a little shelter.

"Small mercies," Jarngrim said, coiling their last surviving length of rope around his shoulder.

Eyvind grinned. "Wait till you see the ledge before you say that."

It was rare, but Aelfhild did occasionally appreciate being built more for work than for show, as the old maids back home would have called it. Shorter and wider meant better balance, so she and Kolbrun had some advantage crossing paths that only mountain goats and wanted brigands would be mad enough to set foot on. Embla snuffled along the sliver of a ledge in front of them, pausing occasionally to nose through goats' leavings, while the rest clambered along behind in single file.

Aelfhild kept one hand on the rock beside her. She could hear packs and shoulders scraping the cliffside behind, as the men had to turn sideways to shuffle across.

Cracking like thunder echoed from above, somewhere high and out of sight through the sagging grey. It shook down through the rock; she could feel the vibrations through her palm. They froze.

She held her breath. The lower ice fields, down from the everwhite peaks, groaned and split as they warmed. Sometimes pieces broke loose and careened down, bringing the mountain with them. Sometimes. So far the crew had been lucky.

Nothing came through the clouds but rain. They shuffled on.

Aelfhild exhaled as the trail widened, dipping down into a stand of gnarly, yellow-needled firs. She breathed deeply and blew into cupped hands as she waited for the others to catch up. This high, it always felt like being down half a lung, and her fingertips were perpetually blue and numb. Her toes had been prickling since she had awoken.

They stood in a circle in the lee of the trees, stamping their feet and trying to shake some life back into their limbs. Kolbrun fussed with her hair. No Thrym raider worthy of a place at the oars went in for trailing locks. It gave foes too easy a handhold. Months in the wild had left them all shaggy, but Kolbrun bore it worst. She was at war with her matted, sunbleached tresses. It dawned on Aelfhild why the farmer had stared so; they all must have looked hardly human. Rags, grime, sunburned brows. Eyvind's ears, baked to a livid pink by long summer days, were the only contrasts with the earthen red dust that had leached its way into his, and all of their, skin, hair, and remaining clothes. He had tried to bring a bit of civilization to the tangles of his ruddy beard by tying it off with a piece of vine. Jarngrim's skin had fared better, given the walnut complexion of his southern heritage, but the curls on his head and face had snags that would yield to nothing less than sturdy shears. Onund had managed to keep his long, silver whiskers in something close to order, but the once-blue cloak wrapped tightly about his shoulders looked as though it was only held together by the man's unyielding belief. And Aelfhild feared her own turn in front of the looking glass. Puddles reflected a windbeaten crone. It was the stuff of nightmares.

In the middle of their little circle, Embla pawed lazily at the back of an ear. The hound's tongue lolled out over her jaws. Her silvered coat was thick and luscious as ever. Not all of them were in such lowly state.

Jarngrim stretched. His head was even with the tops of the scraggly trees. "Makes you wish we had not complained so much about the heat. Someone was listening."

Everyone ignored him. Kolbrun asked, "How close do you think we are?"

"We must be past the Scield-burg by now, but if we keep looping back, we may have to spend another night up here," said Onund.

"The farmer said the bandits camped closer to the Earnfold side. If we find them, we find the way down," Eyvind said.

"*If,*" Kolbrun said.

Jarngrim was squeezing his hands into fists. He was the biggest and seemed to be struggling with the thin air. "Could have taken the pass, but instead we fool around up here."

"And what, you think the guards would have just bowed and unbarred the gates for four Northmen and an enemy of the King?" Aelfhild asked.

She had argued hardest for going the long way. Her Thrym companions tended for a more straightforward, hands-on-axes approach. Even though Ceolwen was not with them anymore—the passing thought of her panged—Aelfhild still wanted to avoid anyone who would ask hard questions. She was not explaining her hand until it was unswervingly necessary. And besides, the men guarding the pass below were still her countrymen, even if they pledged themselves to the wrong liege. Eyvind had taken her side, in the end, and among the crew that counted for at least as much as her mark. Even without a ship, the captain was the captain.

"We could handle a few poxy Earnfoldings, eh?" Jarngrim nudged Kolbrun with his elbow. "Eh? We faced stronger."

Aelfhild saw Onund wince as he readjusted the strap on his rucksack. They all tried to give the elder due respect, but it was clear that the journey had extracted a heavier toll from him. His knuckles were swollen into whorled knots by the damp, and Aelfhild suspected that his back had taken more of a beating in the shipwreck than he let on. None of them was spry—sleeping on the hard earth with maybe a spruce bow for a pillow took its toll even on young bones—but his every movement was deliberate, his steps ginger. Not that he would admit to it, of course.

"Let me carry that for you, old friend." Eyvind kept his voice low as he leaned over, as though they did not all know. Kolbrun and Jarngrim were suddenly quite interested in the rocks by their feet.

Onund barked the driest of laughs. He cinched the strap tightly. "I am not ready for pasture yet, youngling."

Jarngrim giggled.

"As you say, greybeard." Eyvind caught Aelfhild's eye. "Ready?"

Aelfhild nodded. They shouldered packs and pressed on.

The canyon ahead was narrow and tall enough that the upper edges seemed to bow in above them. Rain and snowmelt trickled through the narrow gap overhead and pooled underfoot, the water numbingly cold and black enough that it was hard to judge depth until you were knee deep in it. Embla took the lead, as always, and then Jarngrim with axe in hand.

Wherever folk settled, there were bandits. And bandits, like any predators, needed safe havens near hunting grounds. If Wigmar had spoken true, there was such a nest hidden in the mountains, away from the Eorl's garrison in the pass below. "They rob us blind, they carry off our livestock, pluck up our crops!" the sweaty farmer had ranted. "They hide right under the guards' noses, and what does the Eorl do about it? Naught! You tell me what the difference is between the lot of them." Once Wigmar was sprung, Aelfhild could not have stopped the torrent of curses and finger-pointing that followed. He had still been spitting when she had led her companions back into the woods. Nobles had a way of drawing that out in folk.

Ice and water had carved the mountainside into an interlocking mess of winding, fluted channels. Jarngrim's broad back blotted out all the light ahead, and the thin ribbon of sky above was no help. Aelfhild lost complete track of direction. They had to cross mirrored lakes of icemelt in some of the lower dips, but the walls were so close together that she could shimmy across without having to stretch.

Embla whined.

"Hold!" Jarngrim threw up a hand. He crouched.

Kolbrun and Eyvind followed suit, and Aelfhild behind them.

"What is it?" Onund hissed from the rear. Aelfhild passed along the message in a whisper. All she could see was Jarngrim rooting around in the gloom. She squinted and shaded her eyes from the half light above. There was a nub on the rock—nothing she would have noticed—but Embla had stopped dead in front of it. Jarngrim ran his fingers across the gap. Aelfhild saw a thread, gossamer-thin, snag and break.

With a snap, something arced across the trail and splashed into the water along the canyon floor. Sharpened teeth whistled as they cut the air.

"Good girl, Embla. Good girl!" Jarngrim turned back to the group after tousling the hound's ears. "Traps. Easy now, and quiet as you like."

Aelfhild saw the snare as she stepped over. It was a branch, drawn tight to the shadowed wall of the canyon and tied off, with fishhook barbs bound along its length. *If that had caught one of our legs*, she thought. She stepped as carefully as she could with frozen feet in sodden footwraps. They went silently, but it cost them speed; the day bled away.

Traps meant humans, at the very least, and something ahead worth guarding. But they had not the faintest idea what they were walking into. Despite the cold, Aelfhild's hands were slick with sweat. Eyvind must have been thinking along the same lines, because she heard his voice from ahead: "Axes out."

They had only two axes left among the whole crew, and Aelfhild's skill did not rate one, but she kept her makeshift spear handy.

There were a few false starts in the dark. Jarngrim paused and checked a gap, waving his axe through thin air before motioning them on. It seemed to be getting darker above, but it was hard to tell if that was not just nerves.

Embla growled.

Aelfhild smelled it, too. "Smoke," she whispered.

They crept onward. The walls of the canyon widened. Aelfhild could see more of the world to either side of the figure in front of her, and the space ahead caught a shred of feeble light. She strained up to see what was beyond.

Eyvind's shoulder hit her face, driving her lower lip into her teeth. She tasted blood as she fell back against Onund. Pebbles and grit skittered off the rocks around them. She had one arm around Eyvind's bony chest and was trying to push herself off the ground with the other without dropping her weapon. They were all scrabbling to get back on their feet and tripping each other up in the close confines. She could not see which side the attack had come from. Onund pressed up from behind with his spear raised.

"Easy!" said Eyvind with a hiss.

"Something in the water," Kolbrun was whispering. Either Jarngrim had toppled back onto her or she had yanked him backward.

Once they got their feet untangled, Aelfhild stood on her toes to peek over the shoulders ahead. Her breath echoed off the walls and hammered back in on her. She could just make out white points down in the dirt. Water trickling from the canyon pooled in the bowl of a ledge before running down the rocks below. Someone had sharpened wood stakes and sunk them into the silt along the bed of the pool. Forunately, the whittled tips had caught Kolbrun's gaze before Jarngrim's foot. He had been focused on the clearing beyond, it seemed, and not watching his step. There was a fresh rip in the back of his tunic where Kolbrun had latched on. He did not complain, not even a little jest, which told Aelfhild that he was shaken.

Eyvind's eyes were wide as he turned to face her. He patted her arm.

She gulped and nodded back. Her lip was hot and swelling, but the bleeding seemed to have stopped.

They skirted the pool and lay out on the ledge at the canyon's mouth.

Huts jostled against one another in the dell below, crammed end to end to take up every spare bit of ground. Wisps of steam rose from several roofs. Mixed with the campfire smell were notes of overripe meat and thawing midden, all the usual signs of human habitation. It was a fair spot for a camp, Aelfhild had to admit. Sheltered by the peaks on all sides, hidden from the world, and a real chore to find—the bandits had chosen well. Even in the unlikely event that the Eorl's guards took an interest in clearing out the nuisance, the fight up the mountain would have been a punishing one. And the crew's only way down was on the far side.

"Any dogs?" whispered Eyvind. "Watchmen?"

No one could spot either. The bandits were likely confident enough in their seclusion, in the local guards' laziness, and in the farmers' fear.

"How many, you think?" Onund asked.

"Could be five, could be thirty," muttered Jarngrim. "If we are lucky, they all left this morning."

To that, Kolbrun had one word to say: *"If."*

2

EYVIND WAS NOT one to rush. Aelfhild could feel him tensing, even from a distance.

"We need to move," Kolbrun whispered. "Cannot linger in the open."

There were no guards in sight, but they would not know till they were down there. The same for dogs, the same for traps, the same for foes. Aelfhild gripped her spear tightly.

"Forward or backward?" Kolbrun whispered. "But we need to move."

"Losing the light," added Onund. The sun was in the lee of the mountains by now, and it was only going to get darker. They had made it through to the eastern slopes of the divide, at the least, but the final stretch was always roughest.

Another thunderous rumbling up the mountainside, and this time gravel came trickling down from above. Ice was shifting above the clouds. Aelfhild did not want to be in that canyon when it made the trip down.

"Forward or backward?" Kolbrun whispered. "Now."

Eyvind exhaled. "Forward. We take the left path, there, stay low and quiet. Sneak where you can. Kill if you have to. On me now." He shimmied down the ledge and dropped onto the path below.

Embla landed alongside and pressed against her master's leg. How the dog understood them all so well, Aelfhild could never fathom. It was eerie to watch the hound mirror human stances at just a click or a whistle. Now

Embla's tufted ears swiveled from side to side above unblinking yellow eyes. Muscles bunched below bristling fur.

All the Thrym held their weapons at the ready and unslung shields from their backs, if they had them, but Aelfhild focused on her steps. The others were warriors; she was not. Not yet, despite the Thrym's efforts at training. For now they could focus on keeping watch, and she would focus on not tripping and giving them away. That seemed fairest.

The huts were jumbled together without pattern or plan. Two lanes cut haphazardly through to the other side of the camp. A pair of sheep in a tight corner paddock chewed straw and stared glassy-eyed as the newcomers approached. Eyvind crouched at the fork between the paths, listening. He pointed down the left-hand lane, which looked less trodden, and they set off again. It was just light enough for them to see where they were going, but that meant it was still light enough for someone to see them as they went. They had to be silent but swift. And hope no brigand felt nature's call at that same moment.

Aelfhild stepped wherever Kolbrun did. She could feel Onund behind her, bringing up the rear, but heard nothing save her own rising pulse. She guessed they were halfway across the clearing, maybe more. The midden smell was swirling strong, and that was on the far side of the camp.

Then things started to go wrong.

The flap of one lean-to flared open and a figure stepped through. Eyvind and Jarngrim were already on the other side and lunged forward, but Kolbrun, Aelfhild, and Onund were stuck behind. The man sagged out into the lane, flagon in hand, followed by a whiff of moonshine strong enough to drop a mule. He leaned heavily against the wall opposite his hut for support. After a few deep breaths, he proceeded in the same direction the crew meant to go. Drink had done enough to dull the bandit's senses that he did not mark Eyvind's silhouette slipping into a side alley ahead.

Dead silent, Kolbrun motioned for Aelfhild and Onund to follow. Empires rose and fell with greater speed; the drunk's legs could scarcely be convinced to go in the same direction. A few paces in he let forth a rattling belch that left him flailing for support against a nearby fence. He was still for a moment, doubled up as though he might be sick. Kolbrun stopped. She raised the axe from her side.

The blow would have to be perfect. The slightest yelp or scuffle could betray them. It would leave a body behind—anyone could find it. Aelfhild bit her tongue and watched the blade.

The bandit chose that moment to rediscover his voice and burst into song. His tongue was in no better shape than the rest of him, though, so it came out a wordless caterwaul. "O'er the mountain dew" seemed to be part of the first bars.

They might as well have stirred up a guard dog. Or, as Aelfhild's mind raced, it could be a distraction. Who bothered with a drunk? "Kill if you have to," Eyvind had said. If the singing stopped, someone might notice. No one needed to die. They could disappear without a trace. No more dead bodies. Aelfhild watched Kolbrun's hand. The axe lowered. The shieldmaiden heeded her captain.

The drunk lurched onward and was lilting through some garbled praise of meadows either green or grand when Jarngrim's knotted arms flashed from the shadows and dragged the singer out of sight. Evidently the other Thrym had chosen a different tack. Just as Aelfhild feared, jarring silence rushed to fill the sudden gap. The door of another hut swung open beside her. Wide, bloodshot eyes met hers.

Kolbrun had reflexes that would put a serpent to shame—she was on the second man in the blink of an eye, axe darting as she dragged him back into darkness. Aelfhild heard the wet thud of iron on flesh. The shieldmaiden emerged, dripping. There was growling ahead, and Aelfhild took off at a jog with the others in tow.

Embla had her teeth in a bandit's flank and was wrenching back and forth as Eyvind pressed the shaft of his spear across the writhing foe's throat. Kolbrun ran in swinging, while Jarngrim and Onund spun to watch the rear.

Things were cascading out of hand—and fast. Aelfhild knew if she could hear the din over the pounding of her heartbeat, anything else in the clearing with a pair of ears could, too. Confusion was their friend for the moment, but that advantage would quickly fade.

She could not bear another death. Not another scream to haunt her.

A hand on her shoulder. "Aela, grab fire," Onund said, "make smoke."

Simple words, spoken with the ironclad calm born of a lifetime in shield walls, lanced through any hesitation.

Grab fire, make smoke.

Jarngrim kicked in the door of a nearby hut. Aelfhild followed. Someone stumbled up from a nest of rags on the dirt. Jarngrim's axe put him back down. Blood spotted the walls.

Embers smoldered down in the hearth. Aelfhild kicked them around as she yanked a piece of cloth off the floor and grabbed the end of a smoking branch, swinging it as she ran back to fan some life into the flames. As soon as she cleared the door she hurled the brand at the nearest roof, and Jarngrim arced his toward another tent. Onund followed with a third. Aelfhild heard a slight hiss of breath as he let fly.

"Run! Move!" shouted Eyvind, back on his feet.

Aelfhild bounded over a bandit's body and sprinted after the others across the clearing. There was yelling on all sides now. A man stepped from a door in front of her, sleep still plastered across his features, and she swatted him with the butt of her spear. Her hands went numb with the impact. The bandit dropped but the blow would not keep him down long.

Something whistled past her ear, ruffling her hair. She hunched and veered to the side. They had almost reached the far edge of the clearing. Onund's hand rammed her back, pushing her down and forward. Another arrow buzzed past, then a third. Up ahead, Eyvind stumbled but found his footing again.

The path opened before them and they never slowed from a sprint. The huts were behind, all the smoke and the clamor, but Aelfhild could hear the skitter of arrowheads on stone closer than she cared for. She rounded a bend in the trail and gasped as Kolbrun grabbed her, dragging her behind a raised shield. The shieldmaiden stood shoulder to shoulder with Jarngrim, their shields blocking the path. "Help him!" she screamed into Aelfhild's face.

Embla was howling frantically beside Eyvind, who kneeled in the path. The shaft of an arrow stuck from his heaving back. It had sunk deeply, all the way to the fletching, and shook with each breath he took.

"Take him down the path. We will hold whoever comes," called Jarngrim.

Onund, long since grown used to battlefield commands, rushed to lift Eyvind over his shoulder. Aelfhild was still reeling. She gawped at Kolbrun.

"What do I—" She never finished the question.

Kolbrun kicked her back. "Go now!"

The shout brought her senses back enough to get feet moving. The world seemed washed out, colorless, as she ran to catch up to Onund and Eyvind. She felt impossibly light on her feet. Eyvind looped an arm around her neck and they surged forward.

He got heavier as they ran. At first he carried his own weight, but as more blood dampened his tunic, he began to sag. Aelfhild and Onund dragged him along until Onund called for a halt.

"We need to stanch the bleeding. Lay him down," said the greybeard between gasps. They tore Eyvind's tunic in two around the arrow and bound the wound as best they could. Aelfhild's hands slipped in the blood smeared across his clammy skin.

"I can . . . keep moving," Eyvind wheezed.

"No talking," said Onund, pulling the binding tighter.

Eyvind groaned. "Keep . . . moving."

"The more you talk, the faster you die, boy, so still that tongue. I give the orders now."

Onund nodded to Aelfhild when he was ready to move again. They heaved Eyvind upright once more and he stumbled along between them.

We can still save him, Aelfhild said to herself as they ran. *We have to. We have to. I will not let another one die.*

She ran on, and her legs burned, her back was a knot of agony, and it was nearly pitch black along the path. The sun was long lost and any moonlight they might have gleaned was blocked by cloud. Eyvind's breathing grew increasingly ragged, and Onund's was not far behind. She could feel more weight shifting onto her shoulder as they ran.

"Do you need to rest?" she called.

"Not done yet," Onund hissed. "Go!"

It was easy enough to follow the cliffside by the echo of their movements, but the path was uneven and every time they jostled Eyvind, he sputtered in agony. Embla was useless as a guide; she trailed behind her master and whined. If there were any pitfalls in the trail ahead, Aelfhild feared they would fall in headfirst.

We need light.

Hand. The rune!

She had spent so much time hiding the mark, so much time denying it, hating it, that the thought had never crossed her mind. With her teeth she yanked the bandage off her palm. The glow from the mark was anemic, a thin patch of chalky light no more than a pace ahead of them, but it helped. Progress was slow.

Heavy footfalls came from behind them. Aelfhild had dropped her spear to carry Eyvind and could not see if Onund still carried his. If anyone but Kolbrun or Jarngrim was coming, all this had been for naught.

"We have to stop," she whispered.

They propped Eyvind against a boulder. His breathing was shallow, his body soaked with sweat and caked with half-dried blood. Embla licked at his chin, but he made no move to respond. Onund slid down onto the ground beside him. The old man was trembling, wheezing with pain of his own. Aelfhild turned to look up the path. She folded her hand in what remained of her tunic to hide the glow.

There was a raspy whisper in the dark. "Onund? Aela?"

Kolbrun had survived, at least. Aelfhild felt her eyes welling and fought back the tears. "Here," she called softly.

"And Jarngrim?" Onund asked the darkness.

"Here," came the warrior's voice.

Aelfhild bared her hand once more to give them what light she could. Both Kolbrun and Jarngrim emerged covered in steaming red, but with shields and axes still in hand.

"Are either of you hurt?"

"Nothing serious. Eyvind?"

"Still alive," Eyvind muttered. He gobbed pink foam into the dirt.

The Thrym clustered around their captain. It was hard to inspect the wound in the dark, even with Aelfhild's rune, but they all knew something needed to be done.

"We must get the arrow out," said Kolbrun.

Onund had other concerns. He spoke between gasping breaths. "Did the bandits not follow you?"

"We caught the ones that followed around a bend in the path. I think they know not to give more chase. They ran back to put the fires out," Jarngrim answered.

The greybeard pressed on. "What if they went to fetch their bows?"

"Then we die." Jarngrim shrugged. "As will he unless that arrow comes out."

Kolbrun turned to Aelfhild. "Do something."

"I can help get the arrow out," Aelfhild began. "What else is there?"

"Your hand glows," she said, her voice rising to a frenzied pitch. "You are touched by the Gods. Do something." The shieldmaiden rounded on Aelfhild and grabbed her neck. "Do something. Do something!" Jarngrim had to pull her away and stifle her.

Aelfhild recoiled. The calloused fingers around her throat, the flash of madness in Kolbrun's eyes beneath spackled gore—that was not her friend. That was not the same woman who had saved her, trained her, consoled her. She trembled and suddenly felt very much alone. "I will try," she whispered. "Let me try."

They put a scrap of leather between Eyvind's teeth before snapping the arrow, then pulled. He screamed through it. Every muscle in his body wrenched. It was the work of a moment, though, and then the bandages were pressed back on. Aelfhild knelt beside him, palms still tacky with his blood, and prayed. She could think of nothing else to do. Her marked hand hovered over his wound as she turned her mind skyward. *Please, O Gods, look down upon us in our hour of need. Ivar, Solveig, Hakon, and Halla, give me your gifts and save my friend.*

Nothing happened. The words rang horribly false and fake in her mind. She could feel nothing but the stares of her companions. No heavenly light split the darkness, no divine fire, nothing but the cursed rune, glowing sullen and ugly and useless.

Miracles were reserved for those truly chosen. Not for ungrateful little thieves.

She pushed the bitter thought aside. There had to be some trace of power. Even stolen power would do, if it could save her friend. She pressed her fingertips against Eyvind's chest. She felt his weakened heartbeat, the rise and fall of his breathing. He was dying. He had sat like this over her body after the holmgang in Jarlstad, what seemed like ages ago. He had been there to rescue her and Ceolwen from the slavers. She could see that day so clearly. She could smell the rotting straw in the bottom of the boat's hold. She remembered a song, just a few disconnected notes.

There was a thunderclap beside her head. She fell backward. The ground came up fast and hard below her and emptied her lungs as she struck. She lay there gasping, until hands lifted her up.

The first face she saw was Kolbrun's, the madness vanished from her eyes. "Thank you, thank you." Kolbrun gripped her face with vicelike hands. "Forgive me."

Aelfhild's eyes refocused. Smoke curled up from Eyvind's wound. The binding on his chest crackled and glowed at the edges where it had burned away. His breathing seemed steadier, but Aelfhild had not the faintest idea whether she had helped him or harmed him further. The Thrym stared in awe.

"What happened?" Her ears still rang from the thunderbolt, but it seemed to only have touched her. The others showed no sign.

"The Gods helped you heal him," said Onund, "we all saw the light. Praise the Four!"

"Praise them," Kolbrun whispered. She was bent over Eyvind, wiping his face.

Aelfhild worked her jaw up and down in an attempt to ease the ringing in her ears. She wanted Eyvind to say something, to open his eyes at least. But he did not stir. Jarngrim remained in the moment. "Unless your prayers can turn arrows, we need to be far gone from here when the sun rises."

Onund began, "We were just witness to—"

"Arrows are arrows, old one," said Jarngrim. "Pray later. Now we go."

Kolbrun helped him lift Eyvind's limp body and they followed Aelfhild's light down the path. Onund limped along in the back, leaning heavily on his spear, but yelled at them anytime they slowed on his account. Aelfhild focused her eyes on the path and kept her lips sealed lest the madness leak out. First she had stolen the destiny of the rightful Queen. Now she had stolen the very fire of the Gods. She had no right, and the Gods would turn their eyes to her before long. The pain her friends had endured thus far would be trifling next to the vengeance wreaked upon her, as it would doubtless spill onto their heads, too. It was her fault. Her doing. The Thrym followed, just footsteps and heavy breathing in the dark. But she could feel them watching, as sure as she could feel the baleful, seeking gaze from above.

3

"HIS HEART BEATS, but no sign of waking." Onund held two fingers to Eyvind's pallid throat. "Still, praise the Gods!"

"Praise the Gods!" said Kolbrun.

They were well away from the bandits' roost but had kept running through the night. They slowed only to trade carrying duties and catch half a breath. There was no sign of pursuit. Indeed, they had seen not one solitary sign of fellow humans, hostile or otherwise. The foothills of the Grimbergs slid down into balding grassland speckled with boulders and jumbled till, the remnants of the glaciers that stretched from the mountain peaks during colder spells. Farming was meager in that shallow soil, scraped as it was by aeons of the ice's ponderous back and forth, so settlement was sparse.

Kolbrun shaded her eyes as she scanned the horizon. "We can risk a break. You two get some sleep." Jarngrim and Onund nodded. There had been no vote, but neither raised objection to Kolbrun's stepping into the gap left by their captain. "Aela, with me."

Aelfhild followed. She stole a glance back at Eyvind, lain out on the ground with arms folded over his chest as though awaiting the funeral pyre. Embla curled up at his feet, equally still. The only movement came from wind flickering through their hair. He must have been cold. They had an old cloak to pad the ground beneath him but no blanket to cover him. Aelfhild's mouth was dry. She did not know what Kolbrun wanted.

There were few good hiding places on these high plains. A teardrop hunk of mottled-grey sandstone, tall as a mainmast but narrow and listing hard to port, screened them partly from the men. Kolbrun sat back against the stone, and Aelfhild settled beside her. In the silence Aelfhild thought, *Maybe an apology would smooth things over. I could have done more, acted faster. I could have begged the Gods' forgiveness, made sacrifices, offered up myself if I had not been so callous and selfish. If I had really believed, I could have healed him. Believed hard, like Onund and Kolbrun, like decent folk did.*

Kolbrun broke the silence first. "I need you to know that I never wanted this." Her whisper barely rose above the breeze.

Aelfhild's lips worked as she flailed for a response.

The shieldmaiden continued, "I did not want to lead. I did not wish for this to happen to him."

Aelfhild let her head fall forward. So that was it. Kolbrun was not after an apology; she sought absolution. "I know you did not," Aelfhild said. She looked down at her covered palm. As the sun had risen, the bandage had gone back around her hand. The rune was still there, though. "And I know just how you feel."

Kolbrun rubbed a filthy sleeve hard across her face. The stiff cloth scratched pink streaks below her eye. For the shieldmaiden, no evidence of such shameful, feminine weakness could be allowed to linger. "We head northeast." The bass edge returned to her voice. "We go to Jarl Harald. He will want to see his son. We make for Herjarsborg and pray for speed."

Harald. Aelfhild could have spat at his mention. The Oath-Stone had been his plan, one of the Jarl's many schemes to spread his borders and swell his coffers. Ceolwen was—had been—his blood, but he only ever used her as a pawn. Instead of any of that, Aelfhild said, "That is a long way to carry Eyvind." Which was true. They had just barely crossed into the lands of Earnfold, and Herjarsborg was well to the north, guarding the border of Thrymgard. There were rivers; forests; and many, many leagues between them.

"We cannot trust the folk here. My oath is to the Jarl. If my captain cannot give orders, I go to my liege lord. This is my duty."

"These are my folk," Aelfhild replied, "and I say there are still some we can trust."

"No."

Aelfhild shifted to face Kolbrun directly. "No, what?"

"You belong with us. You are of the Thrym now. Nothing ties you here. I am sworn to go to the Jarl. He will want to see his son and he will want to see you."

There was no chance whatsoever that Harald even remembered who she was, and Aelfhild knew that. What he would want to see, what Kolbrun meant, was the rune on her hand. That would pique the Jarl's interest mightily. And as to her ties, her parents were Earnfolding. Her father had died for Earnfold. She had served the old king until his death, and had intended to serve the rightful queen, Ceolwen. For the moment, though, she tried to flatten her bristling pride and speak reason through clenched jaws. "But we are closer to Wynnthwait. Once we get to Norholt, we can go to Eorl Cuthbert and he will protect us," Aelfhild said.

"If your Cuthbert yet lives. We have been gone long enough for Osric and his Oescan masters to make that a question."

At the mention of that name, Aelfhild did spit. Backstabber, pretender, puppet of the southern dogs. Osric was a false king on a stolen throne as far as she was concerned.

Kolbrun continued unfazed. "And the Eorl will be expecting Ceolwen, not you. Not with four Thrym behind you, either."

"He knows me. I trust him."

"I do not. I cannot. And I will not be so quick to put our lives into the hands of a man I have never met."

The thought did make Aelfhild falter. Cuthbert knew her only as a maidservant. He knew Jarl Harald, but not Eyvind or the others. His cousin, the would-be Queen of Earnfold, was dead, lost on a fool's errand that he never even knew of. If, indeed, he still lived. And Osric could claim royal blood. He was Ceolwen's half brother, after all. Was that it? Had they already lost, and Aelfhild had just been too slow to realize it? The weight of the last day, month, year caught up with her and she felt suddenly bone tired. Her shoulders sagged. Had it all counted for nothing?

Perhaps it was better to let the real warriors lead the charge. Better to leave the scheming to the Jarls. She was only a maidservant. A maidservant without a mistress. "Herjarsborg, then. As you say," she whispered.

Kolbrun seemed to toy with the idea of reaching out for a moment. Her fingers flexed by her side. In the end she merely nodded. "Good."

Ceolwen's ghost was not so easily shaken. Aelfhild stared eastward across the plain, toward her old home at the kingdom's heart. She would go along for now, but she could not let go yet.

Eyvind was getting worse. For days he had hardly stirred from his torpor. The most they had managed was to force him to drink broth of scavenged herbs mashed in water. The fever rose, slowly but unerringly, until he started to mumble and thrash. It was impossible to carry him across their shoulders with his squirming, so they cut boughs to make a stretcher. He drooled between nonsense syllables as they lashed him to the wood.

Kolbrun was strong. Her voice was steady when she gave orders. She never flagged as she urged them on over the next hill, past the next copse, through every evening until they lost all light and could go no farther. They took turns mopping Eyvind's brow and stole what sleep they could.

But it was not enough. The going was tortuously slow. They covered a few leagues a day and progress grew harder to mark as they passed into the deep forest of Norholt. The stretcher snagged on every exposed root and they had to shunt it up and down through the slipping loam of a thousand ravines. Such a crawling pace put days between them and the Hwitea, the mighty river that drained the distant mountains and cut the great wood in two; then they had to somehow ford the roaring water and face weeks more on to Herjarsborg. There was only so much light in a day, only so much speed they could squeeze from their legs, and precious little food they could snag from branch and bramble. Aelfhild could see the same conclusion in the grimaces the others wore around each night's campfire.

Never once did she speak contrary to Kolbrun in front of anyone, though. It was easy, disconcertingly so, to fall into the old servant's habit of nodding along to get along. But she knew that would not save Eyvind.

She marshaled her words for the argument that was brewing. *Of course, it is a risk to seek out Cuthbert's aid, but what is this whole cursed journey but a work of wild fancy? We all know he cannot last much longer.* She glanced over at Kolbrun. *No one faults you for any of this.*

The shieldmaiden was plucking berries from a prickly shrub, working fast in the gloaming light. Aelfhild had stuck close to her as they went out on evening forages in hope of settling things out of earshot of Onund and Jarngrim. Even alone, though, Kolbrun's thick forearms were imposing, and Aelfhild decided to further refine her points.

I swear to go with you to Harald after we get to Wynnthwait. What are a few more days to the Jarl if it saves the life of his only son? She bent down over some puny-looking morels in the leaf litter and sneaked a look back at Kolbrun. *No, put the axe down. No need to get angry. Please, please, do not break my legs.* She worried those might be necessary as well. Reaching through the ferns, her fingers grazed cold flesh.

She lunged back, swearing. Kolbrun was at her side with axe drawn before she could recover her balance.

"What was it?"

Aelfhild pointed a trembling finger into the shadows. "Something in there." It had felt smooth as skin, but cool and dewy. She peeked out from behind Kolbrun as the shieldmaiden parted fronds with her axe blade.

Down among the leaf litter and moss there was a hand. More ferns moved aside to reveal an arm, a torso sporting arrow shafts, and the booted foot of a second body piled astride the first. Aelfhild turned away as Kolbrun went to prod the corpses. She took the opportunity to check that they were still alone in the wood. As far as she could see, they were, but then she had nearly tripped over the bodies. "Who were they?" she whispered.

Kolbrun shook her head. "But look at the tabard. Purple, and that's a sunburst beneath the blood."

Oescans? But they should not be this far north, thought Aelfhild. Theirs were the lands to the south of Earnfold. None of the realms got along overly well, but Thrymgard and Oesca had spent generations either outright warring or picking at one another with raids and knife-edge politicking. The usual arrangement was that the two rivals would compete for influence over their shared neighbor Earnfold's court from a distance. Oescan soldiers would not be here unless—and Aelfhild found that it was possible for Osric to fall even further in her contempt—someone had invited them in.

That spelled trouble for Eorl Cuthbert, who ruled over Norholt. He was no ally to either Osric or the Oescans. The pair of corpses said someone at least was still fighting for Earnfold's dignity.

Kolbrun tugged at her sleeve. "Back to the others," the shieldmaiden whispered. "Need to douse the fire."

Aelfhild had not even thought of the fact that Eyvind was lying trussed atop a board and helpless as a babe not but a hundred paces away, amid a for-now quiet battlefield. Side by side, the two women slithered along the forest floor. The carpet of mossy slime and rotting fronds made for soft stepping. There were countless wells of shadow between trunks or under deadfalls, though the sun was fast fading and sound was their main concern. Kolbrun had her axe in hand as she peered over a fallen log. Aelfhild had lost her stick, but plucked up a hefty, rounded stone during the crawl.

Eyvind was just as they had left him, dribbling and sweaty, but Onund and Jarngrim sat in silence on their knees before the fire. Two strangers, each armed with a bow, stood over them. Hooded and backlit by the fire, neither's face was visible from where Aelfhild crouched. Their posture, though, was decidedly hostile. One of the men slung his bow and bent to tie Onund's hands. The second stood back to cover the prisoners. Every move brought a fresh growl from Embla, who stood between the intruders and her unconscious master with hackles high and frothing jaws.

Kolbrun's lips nearly kissed Aelfhild's ear. "I will circle to the right. Give me to the count of thirty. Hit the one nearest you until he stops moving." She faded into the ferns.

Aelfhild licked dry lips. One. Two. Three. She took a step forward, conscious of every twig and pebble.

The first man had finished binding Onund and moved toward Jarngrim. He called to his companion, "Shut the mutt up, will you?"

Four, five. She had understood him. They were speaking Earnfolding to each other. They might be Cuthbert's men. They might be bandits. She had to signal Kolbrun. Six, seven. If these two were the ones that had killed the Oescans, they were at least near the right side.

"I am not going near that mouth," the bowman said. "You handle it."

Another silent step. Kolbrun was invisible if she wanted to be. Aelfhild could signal her only if she could find her. Fifteen, sixteen.

"Thought you could sneak through, eh?" the first man said as he wrapped Jarngrim's wrists. There was an unmistakable Norholt twang to his words, but Kolbrun would not be able to pick up the nuance if she were even listening. Aelfhild had gotten into the habit of speaking with her Thrym companions in their own tongue, so they were out of practice with hers. "Would think you bastards might have learned not to try this route by now."

Twenty-eight, twenty-nine. She had to do something. A bush behind the kneeling stranger, just at the edge of the firelight, twitched ever so slightly.

Aelfhild stood and shouted. "Do not kill them!"

The bowman drew back his string as he spun. Aelfhild threw her rock. He was quick but she had the drop on him. This close, she could hardly miss.

4

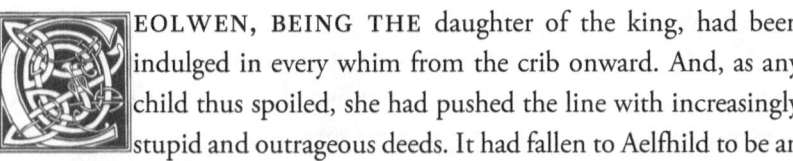EOLWEN, BEING THE daughter of the king, had been indulged in every whim from the crib onward. And, as any child thus spoiled, she had pushed the line with increasingly stupid and outrageous deeds. It had fallen to Aelfhild to be an accomplice, willing or otherwise. Petty theft, unsupervised forays beyond the keep's cloistered walls and down to the rougher parts of Cynestead, spying on courtly rivals, she had failed to talk her mistress out of everything. As the stone traveled the short distance from her hand to the assailant's forehead, one particular memory popped unbidden to her mind.

After one of those burning late-summer days when the lakeside air congealed into a suffocating carpet, Ceolwen had wanted to go swimming. They had slipped their guard, despite Aelfhild's best efforts to give them away, and sneaked down to the docks. One of Ceolwen's great delights in life was making Aelfhild strip, because the queenling shared none of her servant's insecurities and delighted in causing embarassment. And, of course, some wag had stolen their clothing off the dockside as they swam. Aelfhild would not have put it past Ceolwen to arrange it herself. Ceolwen had traipsed back to the keep, knowing full well it was everyone else's duty to avert their eyes and caring little enough if they failed. Aelfhild had set the city's entire population of dogs to barking as she tried to pluck a kerchief off a washing line to at least make herself decent. The blush had not left her face for months after.

It was, looking back, perhaps the foolhardiest thing she had ever done, with no small competition for that particular honor. Throwing the rock eclipsed it.

But Aelfhild's stone found its mark. She was already in motion as there was a thunk and a yelp and the snap of a bowstring. Jarngrim's elbow found the other stranger's knee and Kolbrun landed atop him a heartbeat later, and then there was the scrum. Embla's howling punctuated a blur of feet and foreheads and fists. The two men had secured the Thrym's weapons before Aelfhild and Kolbrun had returned, which was lucky for the interlopers, because it kept the beating that ensued from turning at once into an execution. Kolbrun did still have her axe, but opted for her hands instead, either because she had heard Aelfhild's cry or just because she was Kolbrun.

In short order, the two bowmen were cringing where Onund and Jarngrim had previously knelt. Embla, coat and tail puffed to nearly twice her true size, bared yellowed fangs at the intruders. The hound had never moved from beside Eyvind's stretcher.

Jarngrim's eye was swelling and his lip split, but he grinned at the women. "What kept you?"

Kolbrun had her axe out now and pointed it at the campfire. "Came back to warn you to put that out. I suppose we were slow."

When the warrior realized that was the full extent of the explanation, he mumbled, "Well, no use falling over yourself apologizing." But the others were moving on.

"Bows." Onund flicked aside the offending objects with disdain. "Never cared for bows. No honor in hiding at arrow's range, I say."

"Save them. Can use them to hunt," Kolbrun said. "What do we do with these two?"

"We have no time for prisoners." Onund waved his fingers across his throat. "Quickly and be done with it."

"Wait," Aelfhild said. "They are Earnfolding. They may be on our side."

"Is that what you yelled?" asked Kolbrun. "I thought you were just being . . . " She trailed off.

"What?" Aelfhild stuck her chin out. "Being what?"

"Soft. Meaning no offense."

Offended, Aelfhild turned to the prisoners. The bowman whom she had pegged with her rock still looked dazed and would be for a good while if the goose egg on his forehead was any sign, but his companion broke into the conversation. "We will tell you nothing!" he cried in Earnfolding.

The Thrym all turned toward Aelfhild.

"He has a Norholt accent," she said. The voice tugged at her memory; something about the wheezy pitch took her back to a night long ago. Memories of a burning hall and a long, black tunnel, when she and Ceolwen and Cuthbert had fled Osric's assassins. She pulled back the man's hood. "I know your face. What is your name?"

"Immin. I serve Cuthbert, Eorl of Norholt," he replied. Immin cleared his throat and made a stab at bravery. "And you foreign thugs are trespassers on my lord's lands. Let my friend and me free and I can promise you mercy from the Eorl."

Whether it was his hoarse delivery or the crooked nose oozing blood, his display did not have the desired effect on the Thrym. Just the opposite. Kolbrun stepped forward and pressed the head of her axe against his lips. "Nothing more from you, little one," she said, and smiled. A shieldmaiden's smile was not a reassuring one. "You know him?"

Aelfhild nodded. "He is who he says. I met him in Cynestead before we fled. He serves Cuthbert. At least, he did back then. He was with us the night me and"—she still found that the name caught in her throat— "Ceolwen had to run."

"Why did he not recognize you?"

Because I was no one—am *no one*, Aelfhild thought. Her entire life had been spent behind Ceolwen. Everyone had recognized her mistress's fair-haired elegance, and Aelfhild had been so much furniture behind the future Queen. Much had changed since that night in Cynestead. Everything. Aelfhild from that night would not recognize her now, either. "It was a long time ago," she answered.

Kolbrun pulled back her axe slightly. "Who is your friend?" Her accent was strong, but the Earnfolding and Thrym shared common ancestry, and their languages were not far removed. And the prisoner had reason to listen closely.

"No one," Immin said, swallowing hard.

Jarngrim laughed. "Wrong answer."

Kolbrun kneeled until she was face-to-face with her prisoner. To Jarngrim she said, "Which fingers do you need to draw a bow?" He held up a forefinger and middle finger, the knuckles purple beneath his dark skin.

The shieldmaiden leaned in. "I ask, you answer. Who is your friend?"

Aelfhild raced for the right words as she watched Kolbrun run the tip of her axe ever so slowly down the length of Immin's right arm. She would not tear Kolbrun down in front of the others. If she spoke out of turn, it might look like she was vying to lead. Not in front of the men. She realized she was rubbing her thumb against her forefinger hard enough to blister skin. They were all on the same side. Mostly. Everything had just gotten confused. But the Thrym knew what they were doing. The Thrym always knew what they were doing. They had to. Someone had to.

Immin did not hold out for long. "Sabert."

Another name Aelfhild recognized. "Cuthbert's son, Sabert?" she asked. A nod from Immin, and Aelfhild raised her eyebrows at Kolbrun. "I think we owe our guests an explanation."

The Thrym were not quick to trust, nor was Immin after that beating, while Sabert was still blinking in surprise from the rock. But the two Earnfoldings had water and trail rations, which were passed around as Aelfhild set about telling Immin their tale. Parts of it, at any rate. She checked the cloth binding her palm to make sure no light was leaking out. It went smoother when the man finally remembered that they had, in fact, met.

Then it was Immin's turn for answers. "You picked a bad time to pass through Norholt, I fear. After we escaped Cynestead, those of us that did escape, anyway, we made straight for Wynnthwait and waited for the Eorl there. Not long after, Cuthbert returned. Then, piece by piece, we heard tell that Osric threw open the gates and let the Oescans march two full legions into Earnfold. To keep the king's peace, they said." He spat into the fire. "How many wars did our fathers fight with the Oescans to keep those borders? A hundred years of fighting, good men dead, and he invites them in, soft as you like. Lays on a royal welcome. Now a legion sits in Cynestead, babysitting the young King, and a legion sits outside

Wynnthwait, starving Eorl Cuthbert. Never thought in my life I would see a king sell off his own kingdom."

"Wynnthwait is besieged?" Aelfhild asked.

"Aye. One wall to keep Cuthbert in, another wall to keep help out. Not that any of the rest is rushing in to help. Blighters cut down half the forest to do it, too. A few of us were able to sneak out and we harry the Oescans where we can." He stared into the flames. His puckering cheeks said there should have been a "but" at the end of the last sentence.

"We found bodies in the woods," said Kolbrun. "That was you two?"

Immin's back straightened and his chest puffed out before him. "Aye, we do our part!"

Jarngrim spat crumbs onto Immin's straining tunic as he talked around a mouthful of oilcake. "How long does your man have?"

"Hard to say. Last harvest was a fair one, but this winter was right bitter. He has more than a hundred men left inside so I doubt they could make it through to harvesttime. We sneak in a little by river, but the Oescans nab most of that."

Aelfhild was hopeless when it came to matters of war. "How large is a legion?"

"More than a thousand of them in Norholt, now," Immin said, and deflated.

Military strategy had not greatly featured in Aelfhild's world prior to this. She asked, "If they have so many, why do they not just take the city?"

Onund hummed to himself before he launched into an explanation. He was a skald of the old tradition, a tale-teller, and took to any talk of shield walls and last stands as a wasp to spring nectar. "A few men can hold off many if they have proper defenses. Think of the turtle"—he modeled walls and ramparts with his gnarled hands as he spoke—"hiding in its shell. And if the Oescans are in no rush, then why waste men cracking it? They can wait until Cuthbert and his warriors are too weak to even put up a struggle, or up and stick their neck out of their own mind."

"Just so, what Osric wants," Immin said. "He wants Cuthbert to walk out of his own accord and swear to him. A merciful king hardly wants to be seen hacking up his own folks."

"What about the Jarls?" Aelfhild asked. "They must send help."

"We sent messengers early on. Who knows what the Northmen will do?" The bowman received a warning glower from Jarngrim but shrugged. "For now, we stand alone."

Aelfhild stood up to stretch and clear her mind. She walked over to Embla, who was still at her master's side and growling at anyone who dared approach. Gently she spread her hands and let the hound smell. The dog's hackles never went down. The growl shifted to a low whine.

She knows he is getting worse, Aelfhild thought. And she knows there is not a thing she can do. Just like us. And Eyvind did look worse. His skin was blotchy ash-grey and his eyes sunken pits. They had little time.

She felt someone behind her and heard Kolbrun's voice. "I know what you want to say. Save it. I see it, too."

Aelfhild sighed. "I cannot sneak anything past you. Is there aught you do not see?"

"A way out." The shieldmaiden slumped at the foot of Eyvind's stretcher.

The sag in Kolbrun's shoulders made Aelfhild's own heart drop. "What more did Immin say?" she asked.

"The Oescans have scouts all along the northern bank. Two fewer now, and how proud he is of that, but they would snatch us up trying to drag this damnable stretcher. Going around would take time we do not have. Even straight through I think there is little enough chance he would make it to Herjarsborg."

"But we cannot get to Wynnthwait, either."

Kolbrun nodded. "No way out."

No. It was the single thought that had kept Aelfhild pushing forward for months. Maybe her whole life; stubbornness was a family trait, her only real birthright. No. I will not let them win. She sat in silence and tugged at Embla's ear. Then there was a spark. "Did Immin say they sneaked supplies in by river?"

"THE WORST THAT could happen? Where do I start?" Onund planted his feet wide. With his silver beard and arms crossed over his chest, he was the eternal father lecturing delinquent children. "You all drown, or the Oescans fill you with arrows, or you surprise the Earnfoldings and *they* fill you with arrows, or you get captured and trooped in front of Osric and all this has been for naught. Is that not enough? I say no. Pure foolishness. I will not do this."

"No one is asking you to," Aelfhild said. She was certain the greybeard would like the second part of the plan even less. "You and Kolbrun will head north to ford the river and on to Herjarsborg to get word to the Jarls. I will go with Jarngrim and we take Eyvind with us." She left Onund to stammer and turned to Jarngrim. "Only if you say yes. It is your decision, and yours alone."

Jarngrim waved the question away. "That decision I made years ago. But why me and not the *skjaldmaer*? A band of giantkin could not part her from that stretcher."

He was right; Kolbrun had liked this part of the plan even less than Onund. "Because you are stronger and I may need you to carry him alone," Aelfhild answered.

The giggle always took Aelfhild by surprise. Jarngrim was a man prone to scaring children and more than a few adults, but his laugh was pure, delicate music. "I knew being bigger than you would come in handy one day, Kolbrun!"

This only served to inflame the shieldmaiden further. "I still cannot see why I need to go north. Three of us will do better."

It was not vanity; not exactly. But Kolbrun was as proud as she was prickly—she had to be, a woman at war in a man's world. Aelfhild knew why she was still putting up a fight. "And if Onund falls, the Jarls will never hear of us. Double the messengers, double the chances."

Kolbrun's eyebrows were nearly pressed together by her scowl. "You could go. I could still take him."

"Cuthbert knows me, not you. It has to be me." Aelfhild twitched her bandaged palm. "And if worse comes to worst, I have this to show."

Immin cleared his throat. "Is all, ehm, well?" He still watched the Thrym with unveiled suspicion and had not grown accustomed to the northern style of disputation. Earnfoldings cultivated an almost florid politeness in their forms of speech. Finesse and elocution were held in highest respect in the court of Cynestead. It was less ritualized in outer lands such as Norholt, but no less appreciated. The Thrym dispensed with such fluff.

"Well enough. You can show us the river crossing?"

"I can, and I can take the others to a crossing farther north and away from the legion's scouts. But this is a mad plan."

"So I hear."

"The Oescans catch most of what comes downriver. They have skiffs and chains and archers. How will you get through them all?"

"Pray," Aelfhild replied.

Onund still had not shifted. "You speak too lightly now."

She took one of the greybeard's hands, pulling it away from his chest. "I meant it. If the Gods will not heed your prayers, old friend, then I say they will heed no one. And if we have not suffered enough for them already, then I say there is no hope at all."

Onund squeezed back with surprising strength. There was fight yet in the stiff fingers. "Prayers you will have," he said. Before releasing her hand, he pulled her a step closer and spoke so that only she could hear. "The Gods have great plans for you, little one. I know it." Louder, he said, "Mark my words."

Aelfhild found herself agreeing with him, but for a different reason.

Onund's eyes had glittered at the thought of some wild glory that would be her, and by extension all the crew's, reward. For the moment, Aelfhild's thoughts were preoccupied with divine retribution. She had tempted the Gods' wrath once more. It seemed as though she could scarcely stop herself. Whether she had meant all the talk of prayers or not, she hoped that did not matter. She hoped the result was what carried weight above. She hoped Eyvind would have approved, had he been conscious. Be bold, she imagined him telling her, and take the fight as it comes.

Immin led them along the overgrown banks, kicking here and there with his foot as he searched. Among some outwardly undisturbed cattails, his foot struck hollow wood. A small raft and pole were masked by a masterfully woven net of reeds and leaves. Cuthbert's outriders had been hard at work during the siege. Caches of food, quivers of arrows, filled waterskins, and coils of rope were stashed in every knothole and rabbit warren in the forest. A week's supply of rations hung in the beams of a beech; flint and tinder were buried beneath a line of pebbles, daggers under a knobbly oak root. Any Earnfolding that knew where to look could find succor, and Aelfhild could only imagine that any Oescan who strayed from the legion's cover would find themselves quickly outmatched in the woods.

"We are just west of the first pickets. The river narrows through here"—Immin pointed toward the rapids—"but opens up at the next bend and flows smooth and true through to Wynnthwait. Downstream to Eorl Cuthbert, downstream to the Oescans. This raft will take one's weight, but no more than two. Hwitea, she runs cold, so keep kicking and your legs should still have some strength when you get bankside."

Should loomed in Aelfhild's mind. *We knew it was a mad plan*, she reminded herself.

"Push off toward midnight. Air is damp enough today that you may get lucky with the fog; hard to say. Keep an eye peeled for them southern curs and the Four smile on you." With that Immin gave a curt nod and led Sabert off, leaving the Thrym to take their leave of one another.

The crew untied Eyvind from his stretcher and shifted him atop the raft, then stood over their captain in silence. Onund pulled at the long hairs of his chin as he whispered to himself. Every so often, his eyes flashed skyward. Jarngrim tested the heft of the barge pole. Kolbrun looked to be grinding her teeth.

"Good to see waves again," said Jarngrim. The Thrym were seafaring folk and these four had been too long landlocked. Hwitea roared by in white-capped grandeur. He inhaled deeply. "No salt. Shame, that." He grinned at Kolbrun. She did not return his good humor. He went back to staring at the water, flexing the barge pole until the wood creaked in protest.

Aelfhild bent and picked up the rope that had held Eyvind down. She passed it to Kolbrun. "Embla will not want to leave him." It was suddenly very hard to get the words out. She wanted to tell the others that she loved them as she had only loved one other before. She wanted to tell them that they were her family, and that they all had to live, and it was not up for discussion. She wanted to say that she was sorry for not being as good to them as they had been to her. That she wished to be the person they imagined she was whenever they stared at her hand. But she did not want to embarrass the warriors with such soppiness.

The hound growled as Kolbrun looped the cord around her neck. Without looking up, the shieldmaiden spoke. "I expect to see every one of you in Herjarsborg when this is done. No laggards on my watch."

The men grunted. Aelfhild looked from eye to eye and saw the glimmer of tears. It was not the first parting on their journey, but each one grew harder. She sniffed. "See you all in Herjarsborg, then."

Onund nodded. "Agreed." He squeezed her arm. "The Four will be at your back. I know it." He turned and followed Immin's trail. Kolbrun lingered a moment longer. She knelt beside Eyvind and mouthed a few words into his ear. What the words were, Aelfhild never asked, but she wished she had turned away. There was a closeness to it that made her cheeks burn. Then Kolbrun disappeared into the rushes at the edge of the clearing, tugging a reluctant Embla behind her. The hound gave one last bark, then was pulled from view.

It took a few tries for Jarngrim to clear his throat before he spoke. "I pity any Oescans that try to stop her."

Aelfhild scoffed. She rubbed away the lines on her cheeks and settled back into the reeds. The sun was just nearing the western horizon, so midnight was a dauntingly long way away. More time for soul-searching and contemplation than she currently cared for. She lay back and spoke to the sky. "Now we wait."

6

OLD" WAS NOT the right word for the water. Immin had been charitable. The Hwitea was born of countless streams of glacial runoff converging at the foot of the mountains, so "bone-chilling" would not have been misplaced.

Eyvind was heavy enough on his own, so Jarngrim and Aelfhild both had to trail their legs in the water behind the raft. There was nothing but starlight to warm their backs. She kept Immin's advice in mind and kept her legs kicking. The initial shock of the water was enough for her to clench every muscle in her body to the point that she worried about breaking a tooth, but the gradual loss of any feeling up her calves was even more worrying. Neither moon was up that night, which was lucky; reflections on the water were their enemy. There was no fog, which was less fortunate. Just the gentle rocking of the river accompanied by the incessant gnawing cold. It was meant to be summer, but even the air was chill.

She could feel Jarngrim churning away beside her. They both took care not to break the surface with their kicks. The barge pole rested across their forearms, which were in turn threaded through the bindings of the raft. "Paddle as much as we can," Jarngrim had said. "Push if we have to work against the current." She wished for a larger raft. She wished there was more meat on her bones to keep the cold at bay. She wished for fur blankets and sealskins and a roaring fire.

The Oescans were warm. Dozens of merry little dots in the darkness, to the east and west of the unlit gap that was Wynnthwait, twinkled in decadent, dry comfort. As far as Aelfhild was concerned, they could have Earnfold if she could have one solitary moment by the bonfire.

Hwitea's strong current saw to the eastward drift, so they focused on paddling north. Aelfhild's mind grew foggier with each labored kick, and the river was implacable. They were drifting too far east. At this rate they'd come ashore at the far end of the Oescan lines. She kicked harder.

Whether it was from a drop of cold water that splashed up between the beams of the raft, or just a turn of the fever, Eyvind groaned. It was not a loud noise, but the night was still, and sound carried. Aelfhild heaved up alongside him to slap a waterlogged palm over his mouth, which meant Jarngrim had to slide farther back into the river.

"Take the pole," he said with a grunt.

She hoped he was having an easier time than she was with the cold. He was Thrym; surely that stood for something. The barge pole hit bottom and she put her full weight behind it. The raft spun to the side and nearly pulled Jarngrim under.

He spat river water. "Easy!"

Gentler this time, she pushed again. It was better in the open air than the water, but not by much. Her muscles were dead heavy and slow to answer, as though she had downed an entire cask of mead. She tried to get into a rhythm with the punting, sliding up and back without stirring the surface overmuch.

From her kneeling pose she could see dots in the river ahead, black on black in the water but bobbing along the surface and breaking the reflected starscape. "Chains," Immin had said. Aelfhild shoved again as the raft drifted toward one of the blotches.

"On the right," she whispered, then remembered herself. "Starboard."

Jarngrim had gotten it the first time. As they passed, he prodded the offending object with a toe. There was a faint jangle of metal, what sounded like chains or tinny cymbals.

"Buoy," he said.

Clever. The Oescans had put noisemakers onto some kind of puffed-up bladder, so they floated in the current and made sound for the sentries to track if anything bobbed past. Aelfhild pushed again. She could see more in their path.

"Left. Aft." She quickly abandoned the navalspeak. "Right." They cut past another trap. "On the right."

Jarngrim shushed her. They were closing in on the far shore, near the lightless middle section of Wynnthwait, but they still had as much to fear from Cuthbert's guards as from Oescan patrols. Arrows were arrows. They pressed on in silence, and she hoped his night vision was better than hers. They were nearly to land. She could smell the runoff from the town's defenders along the riverbank. It grew steadily more overpowering as they approached. The siege had been a long one.

There was a thrashing of chains to the right, cut short by a splash as Jarngrim dove overtop of the buoy. The noise echoed in Aelfhild's ears even after he smothered it.

She cursed. The bank had been so close, she had been so focused on land, that she had not paid enough heed to the water. She pushed into shore and grabbed handfuls of reeds to pull them in. She held her breath. Jarngrim shivered in the tall grass. They were silent. Stalks rustled gently as the water lapped the bank. There was the night chorus of frogs and crickets. Hints of song from the distant Oescan camp. Aelfhild exhaled. She motioned to Jarngrim, but he did not shift. Blood pounded in her ears. Something skittered through the reeds, splashing lightly into the river. Her legs prickled with pin-and-needle bursts. She tried to rub some life into her arms. Jarngrim lay quivering, a dark shadow among the grass.

He heaved onto one side. He latched onto one of Eyvind's arms.

Eyvind was a rag doll. They had to inch his body up the fetid bank, though the exertion along with his feverish warmth did take the edge off the chill. Her chill, anyway; Jarngrim still quivered like a plucked string. Inch by inch, they closed in on the wall of Cuthbert's stronghold. The Oescans were dug in between two barricades in a rough circle around the town proper. Wynnthwait likewise sprawled around the footprint of the Eorl's inner keep and its thick walls of Norholt spruce.

Now they had to get over that wall. "Stay here," she whispered to Jarngrim.

He was holding fast to Eyvind. "Cannot . . . go . . . far." His teeth drummed.

The cattails grew thick, full of sawtooth leaves that scratched through the thinner patches of her clothing. She limped her way to the wall. The outflow stench burned her eyes; she tried taking shallow breaths through her mouth, but that was little better. It only worsened farther up. She was at the wall. She could feel splinters along the grain of the wood beneath her fingertips. There was a rotted-out knot here and there, but no gap big enough for a toehold. The logs were flush and squared off at the corners, the joinery faultless. She had a half length of rope but no grapnel. She kneeled and dug at one of the knots with her belt knife. A few sandy specks of dry rot fell away. At this rate, the sun would be up before she had made it halfway up the wall. A breeze rattled the tops of the nearby reeds. A gentle breeze, the lightest kiss of air, and only to one side. It almost sounded like grass stalks sliding across fabric.

There was a hand over her mouth and a blade at her throat before she could flinch. She dropped her knife without protest. Another pair of hands slipped a sack over her head. The material was coarse on her skin, likely burlap, and smelled of goats. The blade by her throat never wavered, but the hand moved from her mouth to the small of her back. The hand pushed. Aelfhild marched.

7

They did not go far; that was the first good sign. Or the second. Aelfhild was still standing and thankful for the fact. The wind shifted around her, what felt like a door opening, and the hand marched her forward. Stagnant air greeted her. It smelled like people, many of them pressed together. Pressure from behind slackened and she came to a halt. The knife fell away but the sack stayed over her head. She felt a droplet of blood inch down the skin of her throat from the pinprick beneath her jaw. There was someone close by; whoever it was, the breathing they were failing to muffle gave them away. The watcher inhaled sharply before speaking up.

"Who are—"

She took the initiative. There was, in her estimation, only one way things could get worse and many ways they could get better. Be bold. Do not let the fear control you. Eyvind had said that, or something like it. So she interrupted. "I am Aelfhild. I serve Eorl Cuthbert. I bring news of his cousin, Ceolwen. Take me to him."

It produced the desired effect. She was not immediately killed, and her erstwhile captors held a hastily whispered conference.

"How would the Eorl know you? What proof have you?" A softer voice this time. He spoke Earnfolding with the proper accent. The Oescans would not have needed all this secrecy.

Her knees were shaking from the rush. The air was so close and foul in the bag she feared she would stifle before they finished questioning. "The last time he saw me he rode away in a cart with an old man with one arm. Before he left, he made me swear to guard his cousin with my life." *And I failed her. But I will not fail Eyvind, too.* She could picture him and Jarngrim lying in wait, freezing and not knowing where she was and fearing the worst.

More whispering. One last push was needed. "The Eorl will want to know I have arrived. Soon." It was the very tone and pitch that Ceolwen had used to get her way all too often, and as good as a boot to the rear of a man accustomed to taking orders.

Footsteps faded away. There was only the wretched bag and her aching legs.

Heavier footsteps returning—a band of them, judging by the quivering floor. Then she heard the old bear's voice and nearly wept for joy. "Take that damned rag off her head, you simpleton. How can I know it is her if I cannot see her face? You think I recognize feet?"

The swish of burlap and there he was, thinner than she remembered, his untamed hair wispier around the temples, but alive. "Aelf . . ." He peered at her. He never could remember her name.

"Aelfhild, lord." Tears were running down her face and her nose was dripping. All the strength was gone from her knees and she dropped. One of the Eorl's men grabbed her.

"Gentle now, set her down easy." Cuthbert moved in closer. "What happened to you, lass? Where is Ceolwen?"

"Two of my friends are outside, lord. One is hurt. They need help," she had to whisper. The walls pressed in with the weight of her nerves, cold, hunger, fear. "They are Thrym but they are friends."

"Thrym here? What? Tell me of Ceolwen!"

"Harald will come for us." Sleep overtook her with its glorious, balmy embrace. "Harald will come."

Aelfhild dreamed of snow.

Her dreams were exhausting. Sometimes it was a premonition. Once it had saved her life; on another occasion it had warned her about her companions' plotting. But it was a frustrating way to talk to the Gods. To maybe talk to the Gods. When she thought about it as Eyvind would have, it might not even be any sort of godly meddling. It was all stuff she might have known without knowing, as it were, little tidbit clues that her waking mind missed but her sleeping mind was able to cobble together. Or maybe mystery and doubt were just the currency of the divine. Maybe this was their idea of punishment. A lifetime of unanswered questions. A lifetime of cuts on the inside of your cheek that never fully healed, of unreachable itches.

Occasionally the dreams were bound and guided. She would be compelled to look a certain way or see a certain thing. Mostly, though, they were lucid and she could do more or less as she pleased. Tonight it was a blizzard.

Wind howled around her. Snow cloaked anything more than a few feet away. There was no horizon, no sky, and only the slightest shadow to her footprints in the snow before they were plastered over by spotless white. She could not feel the cold, though she was clothed in the same pitiable garments as in the waking world. As she looked at her fingers, though, the wind seemed to be stripping away at her very being. The line between skin and air shimmered with energy, and every gust tore away a trail of flickering essence. It was wearing her away.

There was no pain, but something told her that she had only as long in the dream as her body lasted.

As she walked, she raised an arm to block the snow from her eyes. It made no difference. She could see a glittering halo around her limb, and on the lee side of her body, as the wind carried off her dreaming form. There was no direction in the blizzard. She simply walked.

The snow thinned ahead to reveal a wall. As she drew closer, the size and breadth grew clearer. It was not a wall in any human sense. It was a face of ice, glassy blue but fogged by hoarfrost, that stretched into the white in every direction. The blizzard hemmed in her sight, but Aelfhild felt the scale of it through her pores. Up into the sky and to either side it stretched infinitely. To even consider its weight would be as senseless as measuring an ocean in drops. Wind howled along, but found no purchase on its rippled surface. Unlike Aelfhild, it held fast against the onslaught.

The ice was cloudy. She could make out vague shapes inside, though. Hard lines, something that suggested workmanship, dark in relief to the feeble white light that strained through from the outside. Towers, arches, blocky and brutal in construction, were frozen within the wall. They dwarfed Aelfhild, looming higher than any human structure she had heard tell of, even in stories, but they were in turn encased in only the tiniest fraction of the wall's footing.

Her body was fading fast. Her limbs hardly had any profile, and the loss only quickened near the ice's face. The wind seemed to drive at the barrier all the angrier because it resisted.

She moved along the wall, unsure what she was missing. There were no clear features that the Gods should want her to see, just silhouettes buried in timeless calm. Outside, snow howled past.

But she was wrong. Steps ahead, there was a chink in the ice. Tiny, irrelevant, a chip the size of a gnat's wing made on the side of a mountain range, yet from what she had seen, unique. Behind it, a spiderweb crack. And a shadow in the ice, a new shape. A blur she could not make out.

Her legs dissolved beneath her. It was not an unpleasant sensation. There was elation in that final surrender. Her body, by now just a husk of rapidly unbinding motes, gave out. Aelfhild whipped away on the currents of the gale.

8

THE FURS WERE warm and soft; Aelfhild had not slept on anything so luxurious since they left Jarlstad. There are few greater pleasures in life than soft bedding. It had taken a whole lifetime, but she was slowly learning true priorities.

Cuthbert dozed on a stool nearby, head pressed into one of his calloused palms. Clothes tailored to accommodate the old paunch spooled off his shoulders into his lap. The rose-cheeked merriness was gone, but that might simply have meant he was sober. She could still make out the lines of old smiles around the corners of his eyes, though, and she was heartened that even a long siege had not been enough to stomp out his hair's rebellion against any imposition of order. It was a kindness to see him once more. She was, however, in no rush to wake him for the inevitable conversation.

A pair of candles guttered on a central table in the room. There were four long lines of beds like hers, furs piled atop boards, and each one was occupied. One other soul was awake, and he was bent over, ministering to Eyvind. She could only see the man's back, but it seemed Eyvind at least was still living. Aelfhild peeked under her cover. They had taken her overclothes. That was no great loss; what she cared about was the bandage on her hand. It was filthy, but untouched. She sighed and let her head fall back onto the bed. *Small mercies*, she thought. There was no sight of other clothing nearby, so she wrapped herself in the blanket. Barefoot on the dirt floor, she picked a path among tables, beds, and protruding feet. The smells of flesh and sweat were strong. Nothing foul, just a great deal of life hemmed into a narrow space with low ceilings.

The man nodded to her as she approached. He was skinny, as they all were. She saw a great deal of cheekbone in every sleeping face, and knobby elbows sticking out from blankets. No glossy hair or pearly skin in Wynnthwait these days. The man next to Eyvind had delicate fingers, cheeks scraped clean of beard, and an impressive pair of front teeth that would have been the first casualties of any brawl. His shoulders and neck sloped forward even when he was upright, concealing impressive, if gangly, height.

"Your friends?" He pointed at Eyvind and at Jarngrim, who was swaddled in a mound of blankets and rags.

"Will they live?"

"The dark one had a mere chill; he will be fit for fighting tomorrow. This one, yes, I think he will live. The fever has broken, he just needs strength. Tell me, it was an arrow?"

She nodded.

"Indeed." There was a tiny whistle between his teeth every time he sucked in a breath. It was a distraction. "And you burned the wound?"

"We did." She did not elaborate on the how.

"I was sure of it. Indeed, an arrow through the lung and he yet lives and breathes. You are trained in the healing arts?" His teeth whistled.

"No." Aelfhild kneeled and cupped Eyvind's face in her hand. His skin was dry and warm, and there was a trace of its former pink returning. For the first time she felt the ridge of the scar that ran down his face from temple to jaw. She had pestered the others for the full story and gotten several, none matching and each outlandish. She had been working up the courage to ask him for the straight of it. She would, first thing when he awoke. But as ever he was stubborn. His eyes would not open.

The healer shifted on his seat and coughed delicately. "Well done, then. Not all have the eye. The Oescans have it, you know, they have quite the culture for it." He leaned in close. "Never tell Eorl Cuthbert, of course, but it is something to be admired. I learned much from their tomes. Your friend there, for example. It is a tonic of cow's urine, elder flower, and catswort, passed down by the Oescans for hundreds of years."

He breezed past her grimace. "Earnfoldings are happy to throw herbs in water but the distillation is certainly as important as the content—"

"What is your name?"

"Oh." It took a moment for him to find his train of thought again. "Forgive my manners, I am called Dunstan."

"Aelfhild."

"Indeed, very pleased, very pleased. The Eorl did say these two were Thrym?"

"They are friends of ours."

"Certainly." Dunstan smoothed down the front of his robe several times in the ensuing silence. "Shall I take a look at your hand?"

"No." Aelfhild clenched a fist around the bandage. She was glad to have awoken before he got around to her bedside. If she had come to with him fussing with the knot—better not to think about it. The expression on Dunstan's face called for a lighter touch than she had grown used to with the crew, though, so she tacked on, "but thank you."

His smile was wide and illuminating but sincere. "Are you hungry?"

There was soup on the hearth; it was little more than lukewarm broth, and Aelfhild was not eager to know the origin of the strings of meat that bobbed within, but it was food. Two bowls disappeared in short order. She watched Cuthbert while she ate. The conversation would grow no easier if put off.

Dunstan tried his best to putter around Eyvind's bed and look busy, but Aelfhild caught him staring more than once. Polite conversation was not the only thing lacking in Wynnthwait in recent days—there were no women on any of the cots. They would have been the first smuggled out or sent away. There were only fighters left, no shieldmaidens in sight, and Aelfhild was wrapped in little but a blanket. Being around the crew was one thing; they were family. She made sure the wrap was tight and snug under her arms.

"I need clothes," she told Dunstan, who was probing Eyvind's neck in some attempt to find further ills to heal.

"Certainly," he said, blinking repeatedly before disappearing into a curtained nook. A stiff enough breeze would have swept the man off his feet, so Aelfhild relaxed for the moment and ladled herself a third bowl of supper. Or breakfast.

The healer returned with a bundle of fabric. "Forgive me, but I found only men's garments. There is thread, er, somewhere." His teeth whistled as he cast around. "You can mend them as is necessary, of course."

"Thank you." Aelfhild got a blank smile in return and raised her eyebrows. After a pause, she had to spell it out. "A moment alone?"

"Oh. Yes." Dunstan padded off again.

She snuck a look around; all eyes appeared closed. Even in her better-fed days there had never been much to hide, but better to take no chances among strangers. It was the work of a moment to change, though she did keep the blanket up as much as possible. Handily there was a belt to cinch in the breeches, she could roll up the legs, and the fabric was of sturdy enough weave that it was not flapping anywhere. The fibers were coarse enough and the weave so thick that the tunic might turn small blades in a pinch. It scratched everywhere but it covered. And there were gloves. The bandage dropped off to reveal skin dyed almost black by riverbank silt, but she did not waste a moment to even wipe her palm clean. The gloves were on. The rune was hidden. *No one saw a thing*, she assured herself. No one could have. Safely if not comfortably clothed, Aelfhild drained the last of her soup.

The air in the room stirred and set the candles flickering. A man, strapped with a bow and armored in leather, hastened to Cuthbert and shook the Eorl awake. Whispers passed back and forth. There was a groan as Cuthbert rose, knees crackling, and yawned. The old bear noticed that Aelfhild was awake and beckoned for her to follow.

There were no torches outside the billet or infirmary, whatever the room was where she had awoken, and Aelfhild's eyes took time readjusting. She followed the shape of Cuthbert's broad back; he in turn followed his watchman. They walked silently through dark passages and clomped up flights of wooden stairs. Aelfhild was lost after the second or third turning, but they were up on the ramparts somewhere. Gaps in the wall on her right gave narrow glimpses of mist beneath the fading shimmer of dawn stars. It seemed she had not slept overlong.

A broader gap in the wall gave a full panorama of the fog-shrouded river below. Another watchman awaited them; he made his little bow to Cuthbert as the Eorl arrived. "Lord."

Cuthbert nodded. "Where are they crossing?" He kept his voice low. Aelfhild had to lean closer to hear.

"Hard to say, lord, but the signal went up as usual," the guard whispered. "This mist may help them get across."

"Not if they hit another of those floating buggers." The Eorl turned slightly toward Aelfhild. "The Oescans move their little traps around so our lads can never learn a route through. Cut the main lines all you want, you always miss one or two. And I think they just fish them out of the river downstream. Devious sons of—"

Jangling cymbals cut through the damp morning air. Aelfhild knew the sounds all too well. Whoever was trying to run the river had either gotten sloppy or just plain unlucky. Now they had a choice: press on or turn back. The mist could give only so much cover.

"Come on, lads," Cuthbert whispered to the distant, unseen ship, "come on now."

The Oescans had heard the noise, too. A flaming arrow blazed a stark trail through the fog before fizzling in the water. Another followed, then a stream of probing orange bolts. Arrow after arrow fizzled in the Hwitea— but they had to hit only once. Laughter and an occasional jeer drifted over from the Oescan lines. It was all a diversion for them, a spot of relief from the drudgery of dawn watch.

The Eorl took the whooping worse than the arrows. "Bastards," he muttered. He continued his chanted exhortations. "Come on, lads."

Three bright arcs left the Oescan lines. The first and second found nothing but water, then the third plunked home onto wood. It was doused almost immediately, but the echo was unmistakable. Cuthbert sighed and settled onto his elbows to watch the inevitable end.

Now the archers had a target. The barrage began. Entire flights of flaming barbs pierced the mist; maybe half found their mark, but it was more than the boatmen could douse. There were a few heavy splashes, what Aelfhild hoped were the crew abandoning ship, as the fire rose. The skiff burned a rectangular hole through the wisps before it eventually listed, fizzled to darkness, and settled down to the riverbed.

Aelfhild shivered. Her own crossing could have so easily gone the same. One slip was all it took.

The watchmen were impassive. This was clearly not the first time they had seen this. Nor Cuthbert's. The old bear yawned. "Took them longer this time. Young Valerius is letting his lot get sloppy. Gods willing, our lads got clear."

"Aye, lord," the first watchman answered.

The Eorl turned toward Aelfhild. "I suppose it is too much to hope that you brought your own vittles with you, lass? In my day, it was only the poorest of guests that arrived with empty hands."

9

"HE SENT YOU after the bloody *what?*"

She had not even gotten halfway through the tale and the veins in Cuthbert's forehead looked primed to burst. He had passed through red and was well on the way to puce. Aelfhild toyed with the hem of her tunic to avoid his gaze.

"Jarl Harald thought that some sign from the Gods would help Ceolwen win favor among the Thrym," she continued. This was not the first interruption.

"Heavens save us all from holy men and their harebrained bloody quests!" The Eorl ground his shaking knuckles into his eyes. Aelfhild decided that he had likely not intended to make a joke and made a point of not so much as grinning. "The Oath-Stone, of all the nonsense. What then?"

Ice, ruins, storms, shipwreck, she took him through it all. She got choked up only once: Vidar's burial. She had to explain to the Eorl that his bondsman, Bercthun, whom he had sent along as a guard, had also been lost to the waves. Geir, too, though Cuthbert had never known the man. Those names had long been absent from her thoughts; the tears came back with them. Through everything else she kept her composure, which struck her as a touch odd. Maybe she was slowly learning to live with her grief. Or maybe she was a horrible person who had not cared enough for her mistress, or maybe she had always coveted, in her darkest dreams, the queen's destiny. Maybe she was evil all the way through. It was yet another point to fret over the next time she was trying to drift off to sleep and had to look upon the faces of the dead.

"Ash? It burned her up?" Cuthbert stared at the floor as the tale came to its end. He stood and set off toward the far wall of the chamber. They were huddled in a tiny side room off the main ramparts, meant for watchmen to duck out of the weather, so he could pace only a few steps in any direction. "What did I send the poor child off to?"

She had no answer. After a pause, he continued, "So you say one of the buggers downstairs is Harald's boy?"

"Yes, lord. Eyvind."

"Heard that name somewhere, I think. Might have even met the lad—who can say? And you sent more of them off to Harald?"

"And to Hafdis, lord."

"Good thinking, good thinking. She may get here first. Harald will be busy climbing to some mountaintop shrine to dig up the runesticks of his hag-ridden great-grand uncle or some rubbish." Cuthbert was not even looking in Aelfhild's direction now. He prodded the air before him with a finger to punctuate each thought. "If both make it down before harvesttime we can catch the Oescans in a pincer. See how much they care to support little Osric with the Northmen nipping at their arses. It might be weeks. We can hold, though. We can hold."

"Ceolwen is *dead*," she said. Maybe he was in shock, too.

Cuthbert stopped. "Yes." He kept nodding. "And?"

And. The disgust must have been written across her face, but Cuthbert laughed it off. "Lass, there are one hundred and twenty-eight men in this keep that look to me to lead them. There are thousands more of my folk out in those woods right now and it is my duty to care for each and every one of them. Some of them have died. All of them have bled. Their pain is mine to carry or else I do not deserve to rule these lands. Aye, Ceolwen is dead. I will miss her dearly. But if you want me to, what, weep? Rend my clothes and fall to the earth? No! No!"

He sat across from her. His face was drained of all its swollen anger. "Ours is to carry on. Not for Ceolwen's sake; her trials are finished, Gods rest her. But for every Norholting waiting for their eorl to do right by them. For every Earnfolding who knows in their heart that Osric is not fit to rule over so much as a dung heap. For the sake of these Oescan bastards who think they can sit on our land and laugh as we all bend and scrape and dance for them."

"You look at me and see nothing but a bloody rich old fool with no love for anything so much as his own voice. Maybe you see clearer than I care to know. But today there is no time for tears. There is duty. It is heavy as can be, but I would never trade it."

She nodded. "I understand, lord." And in that moment, she did. Aelfhild had grown up knowing that she was a pawn, but since Ceolwen had been the sole focus of her world, it had always followed that everyone else's plans rose and fell with the would-be Queen as well. Not Cuthbert's, clearly. There was more to do than just slip a tourniquet around the wound of Ceolwen's passing. There was a fight yet to be won.

Cuthbert could be King. That was a pleasant enough idea. Harald could be convinced, Eyvind and the rest would see to that. And then Aelfhild could be invisible again. She could be free and rid of it all.

But. "Lord, there is one more thing."

The Eorl arched an eyebrow as she pulled the glove from her hand. He squinted as the light burst forth and the cloth fell away to reveal glowing lines beneath. Without a word he reached out to flip her hand over and back. Then over, and back again. And over. And back.

"The Oath-Stone did this?" he asked.

She nodded.

Another lengthy silence ensued. Then Cuthbert startled to chuckle. "It was a good speech I made, still, before you went and smashed all my plans to bits."

Aelfhild exhaled unevenly. "It was, lord." All the tension she had been carrying across her chest seemed to unfurl. She twitched her hand slightly. "I have not the faintest idea what to do."

A grin lingered on the Eorl's face but his eyes were unfocused. "If Harald or any of his ilk catch sight of that," he said, "they will drown the whole world in blood. And all in your name."

It became a new nervous tic, tugging at the glove. Part of her mind was always turned toward it. It had snagged on a nail. It had slipped down. It was torn. With every other breath her fingers were probing, checking, and rechecking. Cuthbert's words stuck with her because she so dreaded that he was absolutely and unavoidably correct.

Aelfhild found Jarngrim at breakfast. The night watch was funneling into the hall she had awoken in, taking the still-warm beds, while the day watch stumbled out. She followed the stream of yawning, scratching men into the central courtyard.

The Eorl had quite a home for himself. Those thick spruce walls formed a honeycomb of watchtowers and guard posts, while a web of side passages led to other nooks and storerooms. In the broad central court-yard there was a stable, mostly empty now save for a handful of skinny and nervous-looking horses, and a stone tower that cast a long shadow beneath the rising sun. As a rule, Earnfoldings were woodworkers; especially the folk of Norholt. Most stonework in the kingdom, be it a bridge, wall, or tower, had Oescan origins. The elegant, curving lines, the razor precision of the blocks, and the fact that it stood more than a few feet tall without toppling over were all giveaways. Before their storied ancestor Sigurd had led his people, the Aettir, across the western mountains, the Oescan empire had sprawled northward. Cynestead's great fortifications and this very tower were remnants of the southerners' outposts, all lost to the marauding hordes of Northmen fleeing the Thurse scourge. Aelfhild wondered if the besieging legionnaires appreciated the irony in attacking their own history.

Tables were set out in the fresh air near a row of steaming cauldrons. Surly men dolloped gruel into the bowls of the assembling line. Aelfhild bobbed her head as a bowl was shoved into her hand and filled with a ladleful of suspect porridge, but got not even a scowl in response. Curses sounded from down the line. Two guardsmen had knocked shoulders and were now squaring up to one another. A louder voice called out from one of the tables, and the pair broke off short of blows. All eyes turned back to breakfast for a time. There was no chatter, no banter; the mood was heavy and she felt acutely alone in her femininity, such as it was. Luckily, a seat was cleared for her. A rectangle of empty space had formed around where Jarngrim sat levering porridge into his mouth.

As she sat across from him, she could feel everyone nearby purpose-fully not staring. Jarngrim had to feel it, too, though it did not seem to faze him. Chew, chew, swallow; chew, chew, swallow. Porridge vanished under his assault.

"Talk to the Eorl?" he asked.

"I told him the lot," she replied. He raised his eyebrows. "That, too."

He grunted. "So when do we leave?"

"I think the Oescans may have something to say about that. How is Eyvind?"

"Sleeping. Looks a damn sight better than he did, though. Did you meet the toothy one?" Jarngrim bared his front teeth. A few drops of por-ridge remained in the crook of his bowl. He scratched and scraped until the last grain was on his spoon, then downed it.

"We did meet."

He pointed at her bowl. Before she had even completed her shrug, he had it on his side of the table and was hard at work. "Sooner we are gone from here, the better." As he spoke, a lump flew from his mouth and plopped onto her side of the table. "These outlanders make me jumpy."

That one struck a little close to home. "These are my people."

He traced the gap between them and the nearest Earnfoldings with his spoon. Then he retrieved the wayward speck of porridge.

"No one said coming home would be easy," she said.

Jarngrim swallowed a congealed grey lump. After what they had been eating out in the wild, nothing could faze either of them now. "Stick close to me. When it comes time to get you out, I will not be far. We Thrym look out for one another."

Aelfhild looked to her right, and a dozen heads quickly turned back to their bowls. To the left, the same. She patted the belt knife on her hip. They were her people—never mind what her companions said—but there was no sense taking chances.

1 0

ELFHILD CAUGHT THE blow on her shield. The crack rang out through the courtyard, but it did not numb her arm as much as Kolbrun's axe strikes usually did.

She glanced at Jarngrim. "Are you holding back?"

He waved the training sword in her direction. "Wooden rubbish. Hurts my hand more than your arm. We need a good iron edge for this."

She held one of the wooden short swords as well. It was a training *seax*, a toy model of the simple, straight-edge blade that many of the Norholtings wore in case their bows failed to finish the job. The polished oak gleamed under the sun, the balance seemed close to true, but it was a trifle compared to a trusty axe. The quartermaster, though, would hardly risk breaking a real weapon during a siege so some puffed-up waif could practice her swordplay; he had made that clear. So she and Jarngrim had been issued sticks.

Cuthbert's men had improvised an arena with a circle of hay bales and a scattering of gravel. Grass was sprouting in some of the thinner patches of sand, so it appeared no one had used it in some time. Saving their energy, Aelfhild reckoned. But she was bored and preoccupied and had been living on half rations or less for months. It was just another morning for the crew, and Kolbrun would not want her to slacken her training.

She reset her stance across from Jarngrim. "One more time."

He was half again as tall as she was and had her beaten for reach. She had to close the gap quickly. Somewhere in the back of her head Kolbrun's voice egged her on. *Watch those feet. No dawdling! Never show them where you plan to strike.* She knocked his first blow away and dodged left. Her opening stab, at his leg, found air, and then he was already behind her.

She rolled to the side as his sword came down. The point kicked up a cloud of sand as it skittered through the spot she had just vacated. Jarngrim was not holding back.

Aelfhild swung again, toward his midsection, but he was too far out. She weathered three more blows from his long arms while she tried, in vain, to shuffle closer.

Close. The. Gap. Kolbrun was losing her patience.

This was going to hurt. Aelfhild gritted her teeth. She waited for Jarngrim to swing before lunging in closer. The lower part of his blade, just above his fist, drove hard into her shoulder, but she pushed through. She hammered his shield out of the way and opened a gap around his chest. As she lunged, the metal boss of her shield rammed into his breastbone and sent him backward over a bale.

There were a few cheers from the ramparts. Some of the Norholtings had taken a break to watch the strangers fighting. A few might have even been betting, judging from one or two crestfallen faces. Aelfhild raised her seax in mock salute.

She took a deep breath. "The shield is a weapon," she said. "I think Rolf taught me that."

Jarngrim was still on his back, feet propped on the bundled hay. "Aye." He grunted and lifted himself on his elbows to meet her gaze. "Though you might be missing that arm of yours if these blades were real."

Aelfhild rubbed her shoulder. The bruise would be a champion, but it had been well worth it. She winked at her toppled opponent. *"If."*

She noticed a stooped figure hustling across the courtyard. Dunstan squinted hard against the sun. Beaded sweat glinted on his brow as he puffed along.

"Where is old Longtooth off to in such a hurry?" asked Jarngrim as he brushed straw off his breeches.

A horn rang out from the ramparts, one resounding bass blast.

There was an answering horn from outside the walls. This one was clarion, sharp, a metalwork trumpet rather than the bullhorns the Thrym and Earnfolding used. The Oescans were speaking back.

Aelfhild looked to Jarngrim, who shrugged. They wandered over toward the ramparts overlooking the main gate. The door itself was triple-barred, barricaded by carts, buttressed with wooden struts, and lined by burlap sacks filled with earth. She doubted the Oescans were coming straight for that. Something else was afoot. Warriors were gathering along the top, peering out through the openings. She pointed upward. "Shall we?"

They scampered up a few ladders until they were at the top of the wall. Armored backs lined the windows, and Aelfhild could not get a clear view of anything. Space opened up around Jarngrim, though. She stepped into a fresh gap as he waded toward an arrow slit in the wood. It was a thin slice of the outside world, but if she pressed her face against the tacky, pitch-washed spruce boards she could see both the Eorl and the procession below.

Cuthbert's voice carried over the crowd. "Fetch Dunstan. Where is he? Unless one of you lot learned to speak the bastards' language overnight. Clear a space, Hengist, you can barely speak ours." The Eorl stood among his bodyguards on a bulwark protruding from the rest of the wall. He was decked for battle, in shining mail, a shield with the Norholt green-and-black across his back, sword in scabbard at his hip. It even looked as though he had combed his hair, though to little avail.

"Here, lord!" Dunstan called. Soldiers pushed him, and not gently, through the throng toward the Eorl's side.

"Leave off him, you lot!" Cuthbert called.

Through her narrow vantage, Aelfhild got her first good look at the Oescans. There was a train of white horses, glossy braided hair shining in the sun, with riders in full ceremonial gear. The dark plates of their armor were embossed with glittering laurel patterns, there were arced crests atop their helms, and their cloaks were luxurious royal purple. Before the horses were a vanguard of legionnaires, rectangular shields locked into a seamless wedge. The well-oiled might of an Oescan legion—it was an imposing spectacle.

"Are they going to attack?" she whispered.

"No, looks more like strutting and preening to me. See the one in the front," Jarngrim pointed, "the one with all the feathers and gold chains? That is their little chieftain, sure as eggs is eggs. If it does come to attacking, you can bet he will be as far away from the front lines as can be."

"What do they want, then?"

"To jabber, no doubt."

One of the legionnaires lifted a brocade flag strung from a pole capped with a gleaming bronze sunburst. One of Cuthbert's men hefted a whiteish rag on the end of a spear. The Oescan column began to approach.

The master of the legion had the entire might of his command on display. Rows of soldiers, some with shields, some with bows, others arrayed behind twisted machines full of wheels and arms and coiled rope, lined the bank outside the Oescan siege wall. It had the desired effect. Aelfhild did not make an exact count, but there were hundreds of men set against them, each with straight shoulders and mirror-shine armor. Norholt's defenders were not even close to a match.

It was also her first chance to get a look at Wynnthwait in the daylight. She saw the normal thatch and mud-daubed walls, the chicken coops and pigpens and the shingled dome of a peasant shrine here or there, just as in every Earnfolding town. But it was completely still. No trace of smoke from the chimneys, no geese pecking through the hard-packed dirt lanes, not a single sound of life. It was as though some wrathful spirit had locked the town away in one unchanging moment. Only the Oescans moved, in lockstep over the cracked earth of the main road.

Their leader, resplendent in the bright sun, rode out from the pack as the procession approached the keep gate. His horse was tallest, his armor the most intricately adorned. Gold leaf flashed as he lifted the helm from his head. There was not a hair on his face that Aelfhild could see, save for perfectly symmetrical eyebrows that might, though it was hard to tell at a distance, have been painted on. His coif was plastered down with some paste that made him look permanently damp. He had all the signs of a man drenched in perfume. The legion was intimidating, but this man squandered all that.

Jarngrim giggled.

The fop saluted the Eorl, then spoke in a dusky baritone quite at odds with his effeminate appearance. He spoke at great length in the Oescan tongue. Cuthbert waited. Once he finished, a man in unadorned legionnaire's dress stepped out of the vanguard to translate.

"Legatus legionis Avitus Valerius of the Proud House Maro, commander of the mighty Third Hibernal Legion, bids you greetings, Eorl Cuthbert of Norholt. He wishes to parlay with you as to the state of our two formidable armies and how we might peacefully resolve this regretful misunderstanding between brothers," said the emissary.

One of Cuthbert's men, hidden in the throng of watchers, sniggered. The Eorl glared in the direction of the offending sound before responding to his visitor.

"Eorl Cuthbert greets the Legate, but wonders if we might move things along. The day is hot and we all have other matters to see to!" Cuthbert shouted.

Aelfhild was not positive, but she thought the translator almost cracked a smile. He had the face of a trained soldier, not unlike an experienced servant, that buried every thought and emotion, but she knew. If Valerius was offended, he too hid it well. He rattled off another long Oescan speech.

"The Legate asks if it might not be possible for a meeting to be convened to discuss the terms of the esteemed Eorl's departure from his fortress, with full military honors granted, of course, at the earliest convenient hour."

"It is not possible," Cuthbert answered. His warriors murmured approval.

Another speech, and a pause for translation. "The Legate wonders if there are any conditions that might induce the honorable Eorl to meet with Osric, lawful King of Earnfold, or an Oescan emissary of the Eorl's choosing."

"One," the old bear growled.

The translator perked up. "My lord?"

"When every Oescan has withdrawn from Earnfolding borders and the traitor Osric has been clapped in chains, I will meet with your Oescan master so I can tell the patricians just where they can put their meetings and terms." The Eorl's men cheered louder this time.

Again, Legate Valerius was unfazed. He made a prim half bow to Cuthbert and clucked to turn his horse away.

Some bold soul among the Norholtings shouted a parting message, "Send that puffed-up horse botherer back to his inbred mammy!"

Cuthbert sucked on his whiskers. He made no move to admonish or apologize. Avitus Valerius was already trotting off with his retinue, but the vanguard and translator remained.

"Shall I pass on that last bit, Lord Cuthbert?" the soldier called up.

"Do as you see fit, lad," Cuthbert said.

The ghost of a smile flitted once more across the translator's face before he returned to his legion.

There was no mirth when Cuthbert turned back to his men. "Quickly, now," he began rattling off orders, "anything that can burn gets moved out of the courtyard. Secure the horses. Hengist, start filling buckets. Do we have long enough ropes to dredge up from the river?"

Warriors scattered to do their lord's bidding. Dunstan remained at the Eorl's side. "Was it wise to provoke them, lord?"

"Damn it all, man, we need to remind them we still have some backbone! You want to show them your belly every time, like some whipped pup?"

"Of course not, lord, I did not mean it that way."

Jarngrim put his hand on Aelfhild's arm. She motioned him to silence. They could hear Cuthbert and Dunstan as the pair moved along the rampart, but they were momentarily screened from the Eorl's sight.

Cuthbert had lowered his voice. "Did you catch anything they said, anything that did not get translated?"

"They were careful this time, lord."

"Makes you wonder."

"You think they are planning something, my Eorl?"

"Many things, I have no doubt," Cuthbert said as he rounded the corner with bodyguards and Dunstan in tow, "but the first parlay in what, months? Makes me think something might be putting the wind up them. Oh, good lass, Aelf—"

"Aelfhild, lord." She curtsied. "And my friend, Jarngrim. Is there anything we can do?"

"Gird yourselves. I take it you heard us there. Valerius may be an overconfident fool, but he's an overconfident fool with catapults, and if my gut is any judge I just made him very cross."

11

ELFHILD AND JARNGRIM carried Eyvind between them on a stretcher. They shunted him with care up the steep flagstones set into the base of the central tower, where Dunstan was assembling his supplies. He was tearing long strips of cloth when they entered. "Over there." A long finger pointed to the far wall.

"Can we help?" Aelfhild asked.

His reply was a curt "no." He bent over a neat row of herbs and clay pots, checking the contents and ordering the poultices. Over his shoulder, he said, "But you can stay here; it is the safest place when the rocks fall. So long as you keep out of the way."

Jarngrim bared his front teeth at Aelfhild. "Thank you," she said, but Dunstan was absorbed in his preparations. She knelt at Eyvind's side. *Time to wake up*, she thought. *We need you back. Do not make me a murderer twice over. Do not make me tell your father that his son wasted away in his sleep.*

"Incoming!" came a shout from the courtyard.

"Brace!"

Aelfhild crouched with her hands over her head. It was the only thing she could think to do. If there was a hit powerful enough to bring the tower down, it hardly would have mattered. They would have been saved the need for burial, to say the least, if the floors above had come pancaking down. But she was heartened to see that Jarngrim threw an arm out over her back as well.

There was a gentle patter from outside. She heard moist, squishing thumps, like melons falling onto a hardwood floor, interspersed with a few heavier, snapping impacts that still fell far short of the great crashes she had expected. She moved to stand, but Jarngrim pushed her back down. "There may be more," he said.

But there was nothing. They waited, and waited. No explosions, no earth-shaking strikes, no careening boulders. Jarngrim lowered his arm. "Something is wrong." Aelfhild agreed; she had been jittery at the thought of rocks, but this lull had turned her stomach into an aching burl. Jarngrim moved toward the doorway, still crouching low. Aelfhild followed just behind. Dunstan beat them to it.

"Gods have mercy." He started screaming. "Leave it! Do not touch it! Put that down!" He was flapping his spindly arms as he sprinted into the courtyard, yelling all the way.

Aelfhild looked out and gagged.

The courtyard had been turned into a charnel house, coated in the slick of rotting flesh and speckled with protruding bones and half-wrapped corpses. She saw a leg, bloated oily blue and skin stretched tight by corpse rot, jutting from ruptured linen wrapping. She saw a horse's carcass, or part of it, that had split asunder on impact. There were dead animals too swollen to identify and others so decayed that they had become trailing stains on the grass.

Jarngrim was not choking as she was, but he stood transfixed. This was a man who had traveled into the unknown reaches of the world and seen nightmares, and he stood now with jaw hanging slack as he surveyed the scene.

Some of Cuthbert's men had recovered their senses and were starting to clear away pieces of gruesome debris. Dunstan was shouting at them. "Drop it! Move away! Get away!" One man dropped a sagging, oozing bundle and stepped quickly back, but others ignored the yelling and pitched meat over the walls and out windows.

A new shout broke through. "Incoming!"

Aelfhild braced again. Jarngrim did not budge; he did not so much as flinch as shadows sailed across and crashed into the courtyard. These hit harder, with the sound of splintering wooden frames. They were oval baskets, woven of braided laths, about large enough for Aelfhild to get both arms around. There was weight to them as they hit, but then nothing happened. No fire, no envenomed spines, no poisoned fumes.

One of the baskets shifted. Aelfhild took a step back into the doorway of the tower. She could hear scratching within the basket. "There is something inside!" she yelled.

Dunstan was ahead of her again. "Torches! Get torches! Burn them!" he screamed.

Aelfhild grabbed Jarngrim as she ran back into the tower. "Torches, we need torches," she said. It took a moment of being dragged before he was back to himself, searching with her. Dunstan had left candles behind on his table, but they needed torches or brands or something to kindle. Jarngrim put his foot through a wooden crate, then tossed her a slat. She wrapped a bandage around the end of it and set to lighting a fire.

As she and Jarngrim reemerged into the courtyard, torches in either hand, a flood of greasy, furry backs and worm tails streamed from the broken bottom of one of the baskets. Rats. Some had died in the fall and lay scattered around the breach, but the frenzied survivors had clawed through the thin wood and were escaping in any direction available. Men kicked and stomped, swung clubs, waved fire, but the rats were too many. They wriggled into every hole and chink, through every open door and down every stairwell. The smell of burning fur was strong; Aelfhild was hacking as she ran, her eyes streamed. She threw one of her torches against the nearest basket and kept running.

A warrior screamed nearby as panicked rats swarmed up and around his leg. Wriggling black bodies flew through the air as he thrashed. Another basket gave way with a snap and unleashed a carpet with gleaming eyes and yellowed fangs.

Jarngrim was stomping and shouting but with no words that Aelfhild recognized. She waved her fire at the beasts and they piled up and over each other in tumbling cascades as they fled.

Then the courtyard was quiet. A few rats twitched their dying throes here and there, and it was impossible to step without crunching bones or slipping on viscera, but only men remained. Flies were gathering in droves;

the sun was hot, the stench spread. Any living vermin had vanished into walls and down cellars.

Aelfhild still clutched her torch. It had burned out long since. She looked at Jarngrim. His eyes were full moons, his mouth frozen in a half-open grimace. His breath rattled loud and fast, as did hers.

"Cover your face!" Dunstan screamed. He had pulled the neck of his robe up over his mouth and nose. "Cover your face!"

It took two days for the coughing to start. Dunstan had them wrap their hands and faces and told them to use pitchforks or shovels when they disposed of the corpses the Oescans had thrown. Some listened. It was not enough. One man with a fever became two, became ten.

The healthy were piling crates at the top of the cellar stairs. Most of the barrels and sacks within the larders had already been emptied during the siege, so this particular storeroom had been designated a new infirmary. As men barricaded the exit, Aelfhild reflected that it might, with the addition of just a few bricks, be made into the new tomb. And she was on the wrong side.

Cuthbert, from the outdoor side of the wall, was thanking her. "We are fortunate to have you here, lass, and no doubt. Women's hands are made for healing, the Gods saw to that. And here you are, here you are. We all thank you." They continued piling, but left a space large enough that stretchers could still be handed over. None of them was naive enough to think that the illness had been stymied.

She had volunteered, over Jarngrim's strenuous objections. Here she could finally be of use. The women's work bit made her want to roll her eyes clear to the back of her head, especially since it was Dunstan below that was brewing tinctures and grinding herbs, but she found it hard to hold a grudge against the Eorl. This was an attack he did not know how to fend off, and she suspected his conscience was doing the heaviest work. She hoped it was, at any rate.

The stairs led down into the cool earth of the hill. The walls, ceiling, and floor were boarded up, but the smell of dirt crept through and helped

dampen the various scents of the ill. Four wooden beams rose up to but-
tress the ceiling, dividing the room into nine even squares. Dunstan had
set up a workbench, with a cauldron and candles and pails of water, in the
central square. Stretchers lined one square at the far end of the room. At
the bottom of the stairs, Aelfhild pinned back her sleeves. She took a deep
breath. *They need you*, she thought. *You can help.*

Brows needed mopping, bedclothes needed changing, herbs needed
steeping. Hands needed holding. Fevered arms needed pinning down.
There was no time in the dark cellar. Shadows moved back and forth
beyond the gap in the barricade. At some point there were harder impacts
from above. Dust shook down through the rafters. The Oescans were
throwing stones this time, but Dunstan and Aelfhild were busy. Half the
cellar was filled with occupied beds now. Aelfhild squeezed water from a
cloth. "They should have listened to you," she said.

Dunstan did not look up from his mortar. He lifted the pestle and
poked at the dust beneath. "I am no warrior," he said. He started grinding
again, putting his weight behind it now, grunting between words. "I will
never have their full respect. Still, one does what one can."

Aelfhild nodded. "Yes, we do."

He looked up at her, eyes refocusing. His nose was scrunched up at
first, then he let slip a single, dry chuckle. He began nodding along. "We
do, certainly."

More stretchers came down. The cellar filled. After how long, she
could not tell, but morning sunlight stung Aelfhild's eyes as they sent the
first body out to be buried.

1 2

RAIN LASHED TWELVE graves along the far wall of the keep. Aelfhild lay against the barricade, her head through the gap, sucking in fresh, humid air. Tendrils of steam curled up off the sunbaked wood. Summer had settled into searing days and stirless nights. There were fresh divets in the grass gradually filling with muddy water that she could see from the cellar stairs, and scorched black marks in other places. The fight carried on above; she could put faces to only seven of the graves.

"Dunstan has a fever, I think," she said, "though he will not admit to it. I keep telling him to rest."

Jarngrim stood with his back against the other side of the barrier. There was enough overhang of the entrance that he was out of the downpour, though a curtain of water fell down onto the steps and streamed past their feet. "What matters is you. You are well?"

"Well enough." She picked at the hem of her glove. Why she had not fallen ill, she could not say for sure. Men had coughed into her face, clutched at her with frenzied fingers, soiled themselves in front of her. The rune, she suspected, played some part. Luck did not linger over Wynnthwait. A yawn broke through her lips. "Tired. You should be kinder to him, you know. Dunstan is saving lives."

"There was one life I needed him to save." The boxes shook under his fist.

Thunder rattled through the pause. The storm was dousing the forest as it galloped through to the Leohtmere and Cynestead beyond. Aelfhild had fond memories of watching from the distant southern shore as such storms crossed the lake. It felt like an age ago, and a different world, though she had been gone fewer than two years. She remembered some of the worries of the girl—the child, really—who had watched those storms. Ceolwen's dress, Ceolwen's hair, Ceolwen's lessons, Ceolwen's secrets. Not one had been for herself. A tiny, bounded world. Now her world was, if anything, too big, and that brought with it a new order of worries. "Eyvind is not dead." She said it for her benefit as much as Jarngrim's. Out of some stupid, dogged hope that the answer might be different this time, she asked, "Still no change?"

"I would have said."

Aelfhild stomped down the urge to apologize. Someone could try to cheer her for a change. At least he could walk under open sky. At least he could sit at Eyvind's side.

After a longer silence, he cleared his throat. "Do you ever think about what you would be doing now, if you were not here?"

She leaned back and rubbed her eyes with the heels of her hands until swirling stars appeared. This softer topic was by way of an apology. None of her Thrym companions was much good at making amends. Diplomacy happened to others. If you did not learn how to read their bashful tells from their taunts, you could spend a lifetime in fistfights. It was not their most endearing trait, but she played along. Eyes still closed, she replied, "Combing hair. You?"

"I was always rubbish at anything outside the shield wall. Weaving baskets, I expect." Jarngrim gave a half giggle, but Aelfhild left the joke to die in the air. Sincere Jaringrim was something new, and she was curious. After another silent stretch, he picked back up.

"Did I ever tell you"—his voice drifted gently over the barrier now—"that I have six sisters?"

She responded that he had not.

"What a sigh the old man must have breathed when I popped out. Six marriages to arrange, you can imagine how that is. And only one boy to carry on the name. I begged him to send me off to the Jarl. He was glad to farm, but not me. Eyvind was the first to give me a chance there. You see the way folk here treat me. That is nothing new. Harald gave me a place, but it was Eyvind that brought me into something. Me and Kolbrun. I heard someone say once he has a weakness for strays."

Aelfhild sniffed. She had heard that, too.

"My father gave up everything to marry my mother. He could have been high up in the Jarl's council by now, real power, but that never bothered him. Marrying a slave, though, none of them could stand for that. Oh, no. Bed as many as you like, but marry? Madness. He never looked back. He told me I would understand someday."

"Do you?"

"I always thought he said it to make me feel better, honestly. Who gives that up, and to dig in the mud? No. I am going to win it back before he goes. First you get fame. Then you get gold, then you get land. Then they start to listen when you talk. That was the chance Eyvind gave me. I will win my father's name back and take care of all of them. He just has to wake up."

She had heard a little of Jarngrim's background before. Something had always intrigued her, moreso lately. "Did your mother ever want to go back to her people?"

He was slow to respond. She feared she had somehow offended. His voice held no trace of anger, though. "I only heard her talk of it once. There was a feast day and we were all in our cups. For the life of me, I cannot remember how we got onto it. It was her own people that sold her. She never said why. I never did ask. But there was not even a hint of 'back home this' or 'back home that.' We were it, for her. That past was dead."

Aelfhild pressed on. "Do you ever think about it?"

"No. Thrym is all I ever knew, all I ever will be." She could feel him shrugging through the barricade. "All I ever needed to be. Eyvind gave me that, too, I reckon."

She pressed her forehead into the crate in front of her. "He will wake up."

"He damn well better."

Aelfhild snorted. She stood and looked down the stairs. Her eyes had adjusted to the meager outside light enough that it was pitch black below. She did not want to go back down. But she would.

"Before you go"—Jarngrim's face appeared in the gap—"a messenger made it across the river yesterday. I followed him into the tower, made like I was going to check on Eyvind, and tried to listen in. Cuthbert's guards are not keen on eavesdroppers, though, and my welcome has been wearing a little thin of late. Those boys are restless. I dared not push it. But something is afoot. The Oescans know it, Cuthbert knows it, I can feel it."

"Harald?" Aelfhild asked. Hope of rescue had long since been supplanted by pure survival instinct, but even this slim piece buoyed her.

Jarngrim shook his head. "Cannot say. But hold fast."

HE RATS DID the work the Oescans sent them to do. They got everywhere, no matter how diligently Cuthbert's men plugged holes and set traps. It was a slow attack, but constant. Every night—nibble, nibble, nibble. Morning revealed the wastage. A sack of oats gnawed through here. A box of wheat cakes soiled there. Each one too dear to waste. Aelfhild found a dead rat bobbing atop the last of their soup. It pained her to pour it out, even though the rat had barely lowered the quality, but some standards had to be kept. She stared at the empty cauldron. "Only in dire need," the Eorl had said when first allowing her out of confinement. She had used poorer excuses than this.

"I will watch over them, certainly," Dunstan said. The red rings around his eyes clashed with the rest of his bloodless face. Even his lips were pale.

She had to try. "They will survive an hour. You should rest."

He listed to the side as he spoke. "Someone must keep the vigil."

She left him to it, and prayed he would at least pass out away from the fire. Beyond the barricade there was sunlight. For a moment she forgot the cellar completely. She closed her eyes and turned her face to the sun. The warm rays felt better on her skin than the most richly scented bathwaters in all the world's kingdoms ever could.

"Stand like that long enough," said Jarngrim, "you will grow roots."

She did not open her eyes. "I will risk it."

He waited in the shade. Even when she felt her skin starting to burn, she tarried a moment longer. The dark of the cellar was clinging. She fanned herself as she joined him. "How is the mood today?"

Even the best of men will lash out when hurt. It was an excuse Aelfhild had heard often. She half believed it herself. Every man had a limit. Women did, too, but they tended to lash inward when pushed to theirs; men, less so. It was easy enough to see through the eyes of the Norholtings. Everything had been fine until the strangers arrived. They had been slowly starving in a wooden prison, granted, but that had been manageable. Now more than a dozen of their friends, their brothers, were in the ground. Anger was fair. When Jarngrim told her to watch herself, she understood. "No rocks today, at least," he said. "The Oescans are moving their machines again."

"Why?"

He shrugged as they stepped around an anvil-shaped boulder that had not been present on Aelfhild's last foray. Across the courtyard men were shoring up a roof that sported a gaping hole in its thatch. The hammering was slow and steady. Every defender measured their steps these days. The rocks sticking up from the grass were another sign. They only bothered removing the ones that really got in the way.

The quartermaster could wait. He would grumble before parting with a half-stripped bone or a lump of suet, maybe some turnip peelings if they caught him in a giving mood. Aelfhild wanted to see Eyvind first. He did not speak back, but she found that telling him everything, be it the pang of a patient lost or the fleeting joy of one sent back to the fight, made it easier to return below. Sitting by his side for just a short time was enough to bolster her through another string of sleep-starved nights. They made for the tower.

"Hengist," Jarngrim whispered through the side of his mouth.

Some of the men were worse than others. Hengist was not a bad man or evil, but rather a natural leader. The other men liked him. They looked up to him. He was one of Cuthbert's ealdormen, which meant the Eorl turned to Hengist with the tougher or touchier tasks. So he had respect, he had charisma, and he felt the added pressure to set an example. That was not a combination Aelfhild wanted to see in the current mood.

Hengist glowered at them from one of the crowded breakfast tables in the tower's shadow. That much was normal. Grumbling among the men was normal. But today did feel off. Cuthbert had ordered rations cut once again. It was just a fraction, hardly noticeable, but even the tiniest of symbols had a way of puffing life into embers.

"We need to go around," said Jarngrim.

"Right behind you."

As they swerved off there was a clatter behind that suggested benches moving. *Bad.* The back of Aelfhild's neck prickled. Footfalls in their direction. *Worse.*

"You two!" Hengist called.

Jarngrim did not turn. "Keep walking," he said out of the corner of his mouth.

"We want a word," Hengist insisted. "Stop!"

As Aelfhild and Jarngrim rounded the corner of the barricaded gatehouse, two watchmen were coming out of the nearest side passage. They looked at the strangers with surprise at first, rising to alarm when they saw the men approaching from behind.

Stuck, thought Aelfhild. *Here we go.*

"Stand behind me," said Jarngrim.

Aelfhild said, snorting, "You stand behind me. You think they want to beat up a woman in broad daylight?" She was glad when he did not reply because she was not entirely sure herself.

"We want a word." Hengist was in the front of the pack. The others fidgeted behind him, plucking at their tunics or rubbing at stubbly jaws. They looked at the cornered pair, at Hengist, at one another. They were confused. Hengist was trying to lead, and Aelfhild felt a touch of sympathy for that, but he had no clearer idea than the rest of them. "We want a word," he repeated.

Aelfhild shrugged. It was like dealing with a feral dog. Show no weakness, show no fear, and it just *might* leave you be. "What?"

"We were fine till you lot showed up. You brought ill luck with you, ill luck. That dark one there, he is from the South. Maybe the Oescans sent him in."

"I am Thrym," Jarngrim said with a growl.

Someone else in the crowd got brave. "Looks like no Thrym I ever seen," he said. Aelfhild saw men starting to cross their arms and straighten.

"He hates the Oescans as much as you do," Aelfhild said. That did not get much purchase, so she tried, "And Eorl Cuthbert trusts him. Just like the Eorl trusts me."

"Stay out of this, girl," Hengist spat. His eyes were fixed on Jarngrim.

Not a chance. Aelfhild almost felt sorry for what was about to happen to Hengist.

"How dare you?!" she thundered. It was her best Ceolwen impression, conjured up from years of silent observation. "How dare you speak to me that way, you filthy simpleton! Do you know who I am? Do you? Clearly not!" It was working. The crowd's eyes had shifted from Jarngrim to her. Some were gazing at their feet now, others pursed their lips and took a step back from Hengist. This had not been the outcome any of them expected. She pressed on. *Dive right in and no dithering.*

"I am Aelfhild, daughter of Alaric of Cynestead. I have sailed through ice and fire and storm to be here. I have looked death in the eye and watched the last of my family burn. I am chosen by the Gods and I am your last hope of salvation." She was flying now, dancing along the knife's edge. "And you will *not* question me."

The finger in the chest was too far. She had gotten carried away. But she realized it too late; the words were out and the gauntlet thrown. The backhand made her teeth rattle. Hengist did what men do when cornered: he fell back on what he knew. He hit the problem.

Aelfhild heard the murmur from the crowd. They had not signed on for that. She was a small, lone woman. Some things were just not done. She could also feel Jarngrim tensing behind her. He sucked in a breath. If he threw a punch, then it would be a brawl, and nobody could pull them apart. And there were enough men here for that to end badly. So she hit Hengist first.

She was already bent over, she just had to ball her fists together and drive them into Hengist's exposed crotch. It bowled him forward, and she connected with his chin as it dropped. All the other men froze; there was no precedent for this and no form to follow.

Hengist was a warrior, born into it. His instincts took over. He threw a right hook toward Aelfhild's face.

She caught it on her shoulder, rolled, and hit his gut, right below the protruding line of his ribs. Twice she struck, fast and hard. Without air he would go down.

Her ears were pounding with blood. Little flecks of red danced into her vision.

His elbow was headed her way. She saw it and drove her forehead into his shoulder instead. They were both on the way to the ground now. She kept hitting. She may have bit something. The red was coming in fully now.

"Aela! Aela! Stop!" Jarngrim was shouting. He had both arms looped under her armpits. She was howling; that was part of the echoing in her ears.

Hengist was down. He was not staring at anything except the inside of his own eyelids. But the rest of the crowd had gotten the full show.

Aelfhild's chest was heaving. She spat a gob of blood onto the dirt by Hengist's feet.

Too far. Too far. She had gotten cocky. All the training in the world could not cure some ills.

Jarngrim followed her. No one else did.

1 4

ELFHILD LAID A damp cloth across Dunstan's forehead. There were fewer sick to tend to now; most had walked out, some had been carried. She had convinced him that she could care for the remaining handful, that he could take a moment's rest. That had been more than a day ago. He had—they both had—worked with next to no sleep for so long. There was always a price. His fever had broken, though, so he was through the worst. She flexed her gloved hand. The swelling had gone, but her knuckles still smarted.

Soup bubbled in the cauldron. Turnip wafted out to cover the sickhouse reek. The quartermaster had been more forthcoming after word of the fight had spread, and the Eorl's men took turns delivering the food.

One curse is not enough, she thought. Any notion that the rune might have dispelled her blood rage had perished with Hengist's dignity. Maybe, she considered, she had been wrong to expect the revenge of the Gods to arrive in some spectacular, definite form. A flaming meteorite was more what she had pictured, with how she piled slights onto her misdeeds. Instead it was rats and multiplying curses. Maybe the priests were right, and the works of the Gods, blessing and retribution both, were subtle. And how she looked forward to further subtleties.

She leaned back in her chair.

A blizzard howled around her.

Snow cloaked every direction in white, and wind ate away at her. She remembered this place. There had been something in the ice. She had to find it. There was no cold to slow her feet, and she knew there was nothing that would keep the snow from her eyes. There was no sense fighting it. She chose a direction and ran. Instinct bowed her head against the squall. Snow rose up to greet her, and more, and more. She feared she had chosen wrong.

The wall broke through the snow ahead, infinite and unchanged. She ran parallel to the sheer ice and looked for the spot. There had been a chip, the tiniest imperfection, she had seen it. Somewhere. *There.*

Gossamer cracks writhed their way into the fogged glass depths. It was as insignificant to the scale of the wall as the tip of a blackberry thorn in a giant's toe. But she had been meant to see it, meant to find it. And there was a figure encased within, roughly her size but the rippled surface distorted shapes beyond. Wind whipped around her, redounding off the ice and battering her, stealing away more of her dreaming body. The dust sparked and glittered as it blew away. She would have to work fast. She hit it with a fist, once, twice, three times. She tried both fists. She kicked, rammed her shoulder against the ice. No change. Her limbs grew increasingly spidery, bulbous joints connecting thin spindles, and her blows lost any force.

The rune.

Aelfhild hoped it was her own thought. There was a hunger in those whispers that needled animal instincts buried below her thinking mind and made the muscles in her thighs bunch for flight. But she raised her hand. The rune glowed in the dream just as in the waking world, and glowed on even as the hand disappeared around it. She pressed what remained of her palm against the ice, over the crack.

The vibration started low. She felt it arise within her core, roll down her arm, then transfer into the ice. Gradually the wall was vibrating like the rim of a copper bell, just barely kissed by a striking rod. The vibration grew. The cracks grew. The wall was shaking like a beach pounded by storm surf. Chunks of ice fell away to reveal the figure within. It was a man's body, covered by jagged rime, arms outstretched to freedom. She grabbed a hand and pulled. The shaking grew, the body came free. She dragged him into the snow.

She felt for a pulse, but her fingers were mostly gone. She pressed a palm against the face. There was a beard, each hair frozen to brittle crystal. There was a scar she would recognize anywhere. "Eyvind," she said, but the sound was whipped away by the gale.

The ground pitched wildly now. Aelfhild turned. A crack shot up from where the chip had been moments earlier, splitting the colossal height of the wall. She expected a thunderclap, an explosion to match the force of the rupture, but all sound seemed to be sucked back into the gap. Air rushed past her ears to fill the void. For a moment, there was silence. The wind slackened. The ice seemed to be holding. She stood and stared at the fissure stretching skyward and out of sight along the infinite sheer face. Then there was a popping sound, starting far away and building. The ice groaned, and cracked, and started falling around her in pieces. Some were small as hail and others seemed the size of continents as they tumbled down. The ground bucked under her. Clouds of ice and snow and crystalline mist swirled around so she could not see, only feel the pieces fall.

Eventually the world grew still. The air began to clear. She looked out at where the wall had been. There was nothing, only billowing cloud. White clouds above her struck up against banks of grey mist on the far side. Along the dividing line, the air crackled with energy. She could feel it spark along her body, which seemed to have ceased its decay with the dying of the wind. Snatches of black sky were visible through the opposing clouds.

A hand clamped onto Aelfhild's shoulder.

She turned to face Eyvind. It was not Eyvind. It was his face, his crooked nose, his body, but his eyes were bottomless wells of sunlight, the same golden color as the rune on her hand. Heat rippled within the endless pits. There was a glowing mass on his chest, a distorted handprint, and the veins that ran from it shone through his pale skin. The pulsing lines snaked down his arm, across his chest, and up his neck. He opened his mouth as if to speak. Only searing light poured forth. She screamed.

Aelfhild rocked forward in her chair. She could still feel the vibrations through the soles of her feet. Dunstan lay in front of her, unmoving.

Everyone on the floor nearby was fast asleep. She saw one man, though, lift his head and look around. She turned and saw the top of one of the buckets of water beside her. The water rippled as though it had been kicked.

She was up and running. She cleared the barricade with a leap and a slide. One of the night watch called out, but she did not slow until she reached the tower. There were spruce boards tacked across gaps in the circling stairway where the old masonry had given out. The planks rang out like a drum under her pounding feet, alternating with wet slapping as she leaped from slab to stone slab. There was a stitch in her side that dug into her lungs every time she inhaled, and her ankles throbbed with each bare footfall, but nothing could draw her focus from the next stair. She hit the landing onto the fourth floor. Jarngrim was rolling out of his blankets, knife drawn to meet whatever was rampaging from below.

"Is he awake?" Aelfhild said.

It took him a moment to disentangle himself from his covers, but soon they were both bent over Eyvind. At first she noticed no change. The blood started to rise toward her already sweating face. Some nightmares could be just that. She was not going to hear the end of it from Jarngrim.

Eyvind coughed. His eyelids fluttered. Aelfhild knocked heads with Jarngrim as they leaned in. The eyelids parted. She and Jarngrim yelled. Eyvind's eyes widened as they took in the sight of what must have been two mad faces, hardly a hand's width from his, beaming and shouting and clutching at him and one another.

There were tears running down her face. She could hear Jarngrim snuffling beside her. Her fingers were bunched up in Eyvind's tunic around his shoulder, and she realized she was shaking him as she rocked back and forth on her knees. She ran a hand down his face. The skin was warm, dry, stretched tighter than it should have been across the bones, but his eyes opened to reveal unchanged grey hidden almost entirely by black pupils.

They had to lean in to hear the rasp of his voice. "Drink."

Jarngrim lifted him from the bed as Aelfhild raised a waterskin to his lips. Eyvind coughed after the first mouthful, then drank deeper. He let it fall away, and looked around. He squinted.

"Wynnthwait," said Jarngrim.

Eyvind looked at Aelfhild, then at Jarngrim, then past them. "Others?"

"Alive, but not here," Aelfhild answered.

He nodded. "I dreamed."

Aelfhild leaned closer. She licked her lips. "What did you dream?"

"Gone now." His eyelids drooped down again.

She swallowed. That could wait. He was awake. She had not killed him. Everything else could wait. She grabbed his hand in both of hers.

Stairs creaked behind them. "You lot make enough of a racket to wake the Oescans," said Cuthbert. The Eorl descended from his roost at the tower's top. He was shirtless, mussed, and had a streak of drool down one side of his beard. "What is this nonsense?"

"He is awake, lord." Aelfhild nearly sang the words.

Cuthbert plopped himself onto a stool. "As are we all, now." He looked down at Eyvind. "You do not look awake, Jarlsson."

Eyvind's eyes were still struggling to stay open. He smiled at the voice, though. "Cuthbert."

"Eorl Cuthbert to you, my boy," the old bear growled. "And we have some things to discuss, you and I. Your old father, for one."

"He is tired, lord," said Jarngrim. He shifted himself to screen Eyvind from Cuthbert's sight.

The Eorl grunted. There was more creaking from behind, and a watcher peeked his head over the top of the stairs. Cuthbert gestured for him to approach, and the warrior whispered into his master's ear. With a wave, Cuthbert dismissed him, then rose from his stool. He stretched. "Get your rest, Haraldsson. We will pick this up later. And you, lass, do not go far. Some of this concerns you." He trudged his way to the stairs.

Aelfhild had already turned back to Eyvind when she heard the Eorl's voice. His bare shoulders and head were still visible past the edge of the landing. "You do not know anything about that tremor earlier, do you, lass?"

"No, lord," she lied.

"Hmm," was Cuthbert's response. He disappeared.

"Embla," Eyvind called. "Where is my lovely?"

Eyvind still seemed to be in and out. How much he actually perceived, of them or the surroundings, Aelfhild could not tell. She watched his hand slowly drift up to his chest and scratch at the scar. She tried to keep her voice flat, make it casual when she asked, "Does the wound pain you?"

"Here, Embla," Eyvind said. He gave no sign of hearing her question. Jarngrim had. He raised an eyebrow at her. She shook her head. Better to be sure before she went starting any fires. "I will fetch some soup," she said. "Maybe he will come around with a full stomach." She desperately hoped that were true.

1 5

ELFHILD STEPPED OUT of the tower. The night air was soggy enough to paddle through. Without hardly moving she was dewy all over, her clothes sucking to her frame as though she had been swaddled in rolls of soaked linen. The men were snoring above. Jarngrim could nap in the most precarious position, in the most inhospitable location, at a moment's notice. As soon as his head hit pillow, or wadded-up cloak, or a flat enough rock, he was out. It was hard not to resent his instant snores. She had not even tried to lay down. Whenever she closed her eyes, the image of Eyvind, or rather the Eyvind husk, from her dream was emblazoned on the velvet darkness. She needed to stretch.

All manner of bullfrog, grasshopper, and nightjar had come out to join the midnight chorus. Every click and croak, every rustle and ribbet melded into that primeval summer melody. Occasionally a hoot or a whistle would rise above the tapestry, one thread would fall silent until an owl passed or when a mate approached, but the ebb and wane were part of the natural, pulsing cadence. Both moons shimmered high above so the creatures were well lit in their undertakings. Aelfhild drank it in. On their own most of the creatures sounded downright frightful in the darkness, but meshed together the texture was infinitely more soothing. She tugged at the glove around her hand as she listened. A bit of light spilling out of the bottom had attracted a firefly; it flashed plaintively but disappeared when the glow did not return.

"No love there, little brother," Aelfhild whispered.

She picked her way through the craters left by Oescan catapults. Rainwater in each depression reflected the twin moons skyward and made it easy to chart a course without ending up sunk in mud. There was no clear direction to her wandering. She listened to the night song and felt the grass part around her toes. But each time, just before she could lose herself in the melody, those burning eyes popped back to her mind. She wandered on.

The gatehouse was unlit. Watchers were on the ramparts somewhere above, but it would have been a waste to kindle torches on so bright and clear a night. As she walked beneath the ramparts, she heard the creak of board against nail that told her someone was moving around.

Someone in a hurry, if the rapid pace of the footfalls was any indication.

Aelfhild squinted. A cloaked back caught the moonlight for the briefest second as it darted across a gap in the uppermost rampart, and there was more movement beyond, but it was all blurred shapes in the dark. She did not like the urgency of those feet nor all the furtive slithering about. Something was wrong. She glanced over her shoulder at the tower. The wise move would have been to go wake Jarngrim and to see if the Eorl was in his bed on the top floor. A lot could happen in that time, though, and she was closer to the gatehouse stairs.

It was a quick decision. As she climbed toward the ramparts she aimed to tread along the outer edge of each step so loose planks did not give her away. She was feeling proud of her catlike stride when she reached the top. Nary an untoward sound! Part of her success, though, was that she had neither armor nor arms. That made her quick and light, but it also made her wonder what exactly she planned to do if anything actually was amiss.

She did have her belt knife. It badly needed sharpening and it added maybe a hand's length to her range, but it was better than nothing. With her left hand she clutched the sheath as she darted around the pools of silver light cast through the windows. There was movement along the northern wall. She dipped into the shadows to watch.

A finger tapped her shoulder, and her heart nearly burst from her chest. She spun, too surprised to even draw her blade. In her haste she had failed to notice that there were already three occupants in the room she had ducked into. The man who had touched her shoulder was near enough that with a single backward step she would have trod upon his toes. He pressed a finger to his lips. Aelfhild did not recognize him, but he was dressed like one of Cuthbert's men and held a bow in one hand. His companions were similarly girded, and both watched her with wide eyes. All three, she suspected, were praying that she would not scream. And she did not, but it took a good few moments for all of the muscles that had contracted in that instant of surprise to fully uncoil again.

The man pointed with his free hand out the window and down toward the bank below. That was what all the sneaking was about.

As her eyes adjusted, Aelfhild saw more bows in the shadows along the wall. All of the night watch, along with anyone else they had been able to rouse along the way, from the look of it, huddled into every nook, perch, and corner. Though she could not see Cuthbert, she guessed he was somewhere nearby. The Eorl always was. It was a while before she heard any suspicious noise, though. The bugs and birds drowned out most other sounds; what had begun as song was now nothing but an annoyance. She strained to pluck out a footstep or a whisper from among the clamor.

Then there was a scrape below, fleetingly quick, and a low whistle. It seemed that the Oescans had not taken the time to learn the local birdcalls, because the wheedling trill was not from any native Earnfolding fowl. It was human and no doubt about it. She was well away from the nearest window but in her mind Aelfhild could picture a line of men crouched in the grass, stock still as they listened for an alarm cry, while one picked himself up from the dirt with belated care. She imagined their hands shaking just like hers. None of them knew they were already discovered. Already dead.

Cuthbert's defenders drew arrows from the quivers at their hips. It was the gentlest flutter, a moth's wingbeat, as fingers brushed along fletching. A few of the iron points caught moonlight. Aelfhild wished, or half wished—she felt guilty for the feeling but equally guilty at the thought of not feeling it—that the Oescans had heard so they could turn tail and flee. What was coming would be slaughter.

Run! Run! She could not call out to them. Part of her had hoped that when Harald arrived, as he surely must, the Oescans would see the wiser path and withdraw without a fight. She had daydreams that the legions would depart and Osric would concede to better conscience. It was stupid and pointless vanity, she knew that much, but she had to cling to the idea that the world could be, well, better. Better than it was; better than men made it. That Avitus Valerius would not throw his men's lives away callously and that Cuthbert would not snatch them up needlessly.

Two more foreign whistles from below. Her better world would have to stay idle fantasy. The Oescans would be creeping forward now, carrying out their doomed plan. One of the Norholtings pushed her gently to the side. The three bowmen advanced to the wall. There was no battle cry, no warning shout, and no quarter given. A voice, farther down the ramparts, simply said, "Now."

Bows bent and strings thrummed, followed immediately by screams and shouts from below. Oescan centurions began bellowing orders, and Aelfhild heard arrows drumming against raised shields. Gone was her soothing night chorus, replaced by writhing agony, gurgling and grunting and retching from below. Bowstrings continued twanging.

Some of the Oescan units were disciplined enough to get ladders up to the wall. No men made it to the top. Cuthbert's archers picked off anyone fool enough to break ranks, and soon the centurions were sounding retreat. Shields glinted as the attackers clattered their way downhill and back toward the safety of their lines. The Norholtings let off a few more shots before the command came, "Hold, boys, save your arrows."

The defenders broke their silence. "Need fresh quivers up here! Toss 'em up!"

"Anyone hit?"

"Run the line, lad, make sure none got through."

"Give us a hand with these ladders!" With a crash splintered siege ladders fell whence they had risen.

It was all very matter-of-fact, steady. No cheering, no remorse. Like butchers at their work, it was all so much meat. Bodies were strewn across the bank, some immobile and bristling with shafts and others yet twitching. The stench of effluent drifted up. Aelfhild recognized the smell of dying men all too well of late. Archers grabbed handfuls of arrows from the runners. They restrung bows and flicked broken bowstrings onto the dead below. Lights were appearing atop the siege wall along Wynnthwait's northern bounds. Valerius was not hiding anymore, and the legion was stirring.

Cuthbert strode the ramparts. "Brace yourselves, lads, more will be coming, more on the way now." He spotted Aelfhild. Even in the feeble moonlight her expression must have been clear enough. "Blood calls for blood, lass. Men's work, this is. And not over yet."

Kolbrun would have said something, but Aelfhild was feeling neither proud nor prickly at that moment. There was no glory here, no eloquence or honorable salutes. It was not grand and it was far from noble. The men below had not ordered the throwing of plague corpses or rats or stones. They were servants, punished for the master's sins. Pawns of men nowhere near the bloodshed. Osric, Valerius, whatever Oescan patricians pulled their strings, they had earned arrows; the bodies below had not. But she had friends to protect, and there were lives that still could be saved, so she pushed the filth from her mind and focused on the second comment. "What will he do next?"

"Young Avitus cannot let a defeat like that go unanswered, else his men will lose all their shine and vigor. My guess is he tries to soften us up from a safe distance before driving in again. Just a matter of moving his stone throwers back into range."

That struck Aelfhild as a bit odd. "Why did he not do that first?"

"Aye, crossed my mind, too." Cuthbert scratched at his beard with both hands. "Why send just a few men to sneak over this side of the wall? I had scouts at every corner and they heard not a peep, so just this wall. Even if they had managed to sneak over, it all seems a bit daft. Odd. Odd!"

"Maybe they meant to sneak over and open the gate?"

The Forl growled. The puzzle seemed to upset him more than the killing. "Without getting spotted? If the rest of the legion were outside the front gate, yes, but they are all squirreled away somewhere else." Then the old bear gave a little laugh. "Maybe it was me they were after. Get at old Cuthbert and take the fight out of the lads. Ha! Keep trying, bastards!"

They were moving along the eastern ramparts now. All was dark and quiet, no hint of movement between the fortress and the river.

"You should get down and wake that big friend of yours, Jarn . . .

something." At least Cuthbert forgot everyone else's name, too. He dismissed the troublesome words with a wave of his hand. "And get yourself something more than that butter knife, lass. There is more to be done tonight, and we can use every arm."

Aelfhild nodded and turned toward the stairs.

The whole world shifted beneath her. There was a rumble, a distant avalanche but bubbling up from below, as if the bottom had fallen out of the world. Her stomach lurched as she dropped. The massive timbers around her groaned and split as the floor pitched wildly downward. Her legs slid out from under her and she rolled until her ribs slammed into a protruding post. She curled into a ball, arms clasped behind her head, as the thatch awning above began to sag.

THE RUMBLING CEASED. The beams propping up the flimsy canopy held, though it looked like half a breath would bring the whole lot down. Aelfhild raised her head. Everything was askew; the entire section of rampart slanted steeply groundward. Cuthbert lifted himself on both hands. Every movement made the continuing creaks and groans from the wood intensify.

"Get up, lass, sharpish! Get down to the courtyard and lay your hands on something heavy."

Every fiber in the walls was stretching and twisting as the logs were pulled off-kilter. She had two choices: shimmy along the post she was wrapped around and drop to the dark ground below, or climb over to the nearby staircase that had been bent into a tortured, bulging arch. Gingerly she put a foot onto one of the stairs. It held half her weight, at least. She stepped onto it and started moving. Nails popped underfoot as her tiptoeing turned to a headlong sprint. The staircase heaved and collapsed as she bounced off the last step.

A pit had opened along the eastern edge of the courtyard. The grass had disappeared into mud below, and the back of the wall just beyond was broken into a jagged gap. It had fallen inward from both sides, leaving a ramp of rubble at the middle point between the corner towers. It looked as though some grasping titan's fist had risen from the deeps to snatch the wall down into the earth. Here was sorcery of the darkest kind, perverted foreign curses. It made the heart shrivel icy cold to even consider what further horrors awaited.

She heard shouting and saw misshapen black figures wriggling up from the hole. There was a torch on the wall beside her; even unlit it was hefty enough to make a workable club. She snatched it and charged.

The specters were not arrayed in any sort of formation. They writhed up in ones and twos, dripping and howling. Her blood was up. One muddied silhouette threw out a clawed hand as she lunged in, but she battered it aside with her club. It let out a very human scream as it dropped. Aelfhild struggled to catch her breath. Beneath all the dirt she could see the bulk and angles of Oescan armor. The hole was man's doing—Valerius's doing. The beings it vomited forth were not fiends.

Soldiers. But this was no invasion. The man she hit had not even held a weapon. The invaders coming out of the pit were panicked. Something had gone wrong. The Oescans had blundered.

Other Earnfoldings were sprinting into the fray now, swords and knives drawn. A few had the foresight to kindle torches and waved those in front of them. Everyone was yelling.

"Hold!" Aelfhild hollered. Everything was out of control. It was too one-sided to even call it a battle. "Norholt, stay your blades!" She lowered her makeshift club. A few of the intruders had put up a fight, some had been cut down on the spot, but most were kneeling and lifting empty hands toward the onrush of watchmen. "Hold back, take prisoners!" Her throat tore under the strain of shouting.

Other voices started to take up the call.

"Hold!"

"Seize them, bind them!"

"Bring light here!"

Cuthbert came down from the ramparts with a troop of his men, bristling with nocked arrows and blades behind a wall of shields. She waved at the Eorl. "Mercy, lord, they are not fighting!" she yelled. Wynnthwait's defenders formed a circle around the dazed Oescans. Ringed by swords, the legionnaires made no moves to either attack or flee.

"What in the name of all the bloody Four is happening here?!" Cuthbert bellowed.

"Something went wrong and none of them are fighting back!" Aelfhild cried. "None of them even have weapons!"

"Check them, check each one of the bastards! If any move, stick them in their cursed throats!" The Eorl beat a fist against his shield. "I want watchmen at each wall. If this is some trick I will kill every man in that pit. Someone get Dunstan;, he knows their blighted tongue."

Men ran in every direction. The defenders hemmed the Oescans into a bunch, pressed them back against the stricken wall, and patted them down for any trickery. Some of the foreigners were blank, still reeling from the shock, some boggled wide-eyed at the torchlight, others jabbered and pointed back at the pit. One Norholting defender pulled a blade on an Oescan that was trying to grab him with pleading fingers.

"Off me, you filth! Back!"

His assailant spouted forth syllable after screeching syllable, none of them intelligible.

"Easy!" Aelfhild threw up both her hands. She had dropped her stick when it became clear it was so much deadweight. Now she was wondering if she might need it to keep the Eorl's warriors in line. "Let him go! Move back!"

Every nerve was taut. Earnfoldings swept from side to side with their bows, trying to cover the entire line of prisoners. If one let fly, chances were good the others would start loosing arrows as well. The Oescans conscious enough to realize their position cowered with hands over heads or in front of faces. Both sides were yelling, but neither understood.

Dunstan dragged himself into the ring. He was still unsteady on his feet, leaning to one side, and she imagined it had taken some shaking to rouse him. Jarngrim and a handful of others followed. "Quiet," Dunstan called, but he had a scholar's voice that could never cut through the commotion.

"Silence!" Cuthbert thundered. His men obeyed and the Oescans soon followed.

The man whose jabbering had nearly cost him his life became the spokesman for the legionnaires. He and Dunstan fired back and forth.

"Well?" asked the Eorl.

"He is very upset, lord, and I am used to *reading* Oescan and, certainly, not the vulgar speech—"

"Dunstan."

"Yes." He rubbed at his red eyes as he mouthed words to himself. Then he said, "They were digging and it fell in on top of them. All the rain, lord, it would have bogged down the soil, and drainage so near the river would already be poor."

"What else?"

"They were meant to take you by surprise, then more would come over the walls."

"We dealt with those already."

"Er, indeed, lord."

"What else?" Cuthbert asked.

Dunstan spoke to the prisoner once more. "He is very insistent about one thing, lord, he says something like 'they are down,' over and over."

Aelfhild's breath stopped. There were men buried beneath their feet. Her mind flashed back to that underground trek in Cynestead, running blind through a tunnel with all the weight of the world overhead. She had dreaded it then and it still made her skin crawl to think back.

"Any response, lord?" asked Dunstan.

"Tell him to be silent," Cuthbert said. And that was all.

Aelfhild stared. Dunstan stared. The defenders were still tense. One man, and Aelfhild could recognize Hengist from afar, arrow still nocked along his thumb, spoke up. "Do we let them have it, lord?"

The Eorl grunted. He stared at the prisoners. "Hold."

"What?" Aelfhild whispered. He could not just leave them. She moved to take a step forward. Jarngrim had found her and barred her way with his arm. He shook his head at her. Softly, he said, "We are not at home here."

Dunstan must also have marked her movement, though. He looked at Aelfhild, then at the ground. He took a breath. He righted himself and said to the Eorl, "Lord, we cannot leave them."

"Do not tell me what I can and cannot do in my own keep!" Cuthbert rounded on him. "These men are enemies and they will be treated as such. If you have no stomach for this then you can piss off back to your herbs and never gainsay me again!"

"Let them have it, lord!" cried Hengist. He loosed his arrow. There were more screams. Some of his fellows let fly as well. Oescans dropped, some hit and others seeking cover on bare earth.

Aelfhild strained against Jarngrim's hold. "Aela, come away," he was saying, but the sight tore a hole above her stomach, and it felt as though her heart and guts were wrenched taut to fill the gap. Breathing grew impossible. They were her people, and here they behaved no better than their foes. "No," she whispered. "No." She met Cuthbert's furious gaze as he swept the crowd. His eyes stopped on her. The old bear was not so hard to read. Cool reason was grappling with battlerage, all tangled amid the lazy hate spawned from generations of feuds and mistrust and shared contempt. All it took was one little push, from either side, to tip the balance. "Hold!" he yelled. "Hengist, damn you, hold!"

Dunstan cleared his throat. He stared at his feet as he asked, "Lord?"

Aelfhild never knew just what it was that made up Cuthbert's mind. She never found the right moment to ask. If she had to guess, it was the fact that Dunstan would not look him in the face. But that was a guess. Whatever the reason, Cuthbert blinked. "Fetch them spades and digging bars. Let the Oescans dig their own out. And I want them under guard— you men, one wrong move and you drop every one of them."

Hengist shouted, "Aye, lord!" His fingers flitted across his remaining arrows.

The Eorl turned as he gave more orders. He sent watchers to the surviving ramparts, others to the armory, the rest to see about barricading the breach. Without glancing back at Aelfhild he headed off toward his tower.

"I hope that was wise," came Jarngrim's voice from beside her. There was no grin, no trace of mirth.

"We should leave them to die?"

The Thrym shrugged. "We have many enemies and scarce few friends to risk."

"Cuthbert will come around," Aelfhild said. "He knows. He has to."

"As you say."

The Oescan's self-appointed leader was trying to stir his surviving fellows into some sort of action as Dunstan explained the situation in stops and stutters. The legionnaires began to dig frantically as soon as

Cuthbert's men returned with armfuls of tools. Aelfhild grabbed a broad-bladed shovel from the pile.

Jarngrim cleared his throat. "We should save our strength." The "we" was suspicious.

"Save yours if you want." Aelfhild did not look back. In truth, she could feel bone-sapping weariness just around the corner. She was riding high on nerves, but those would soon fizzle, leaving her with no sleep and an empty stomach. But she was also right. Nothing would take that from her, not even an aching back. "Some of us can spare it."

1 7

THE SELF-APPOINTED LEADER of the Oescans called himself Publius. That was the only name he offered. Dunstan said it was a common enough name in the South. Beneath the coating of dirt, Publius had olive skin and the weathered, thickly set features of a peasant, so Aelfhild felt confident enough that they had not unwittingly captured some grand dignitary. There was no time for any interrogation, regardless. They dug. Or everyone but Dunstan dug. He translated.

"The Legate is cautious. He keeps many plans. They started digging the tunnel when they first arrived. It was a final resort, I suppose. In the last days they started to rush. At first it was slow and they were careful with their supports and whatnot. Publius takes care in his craft. They are a very learned people, you know, builders of the finest tradition, certainly."

Aelfhild rubbed phlegm from the corner of her mouth. She could see Dunstan out of the corner of her eye, sitting cross-legged on the grass in his immaculate robe. Apparently eagerness to practice his Oescan had overtaken his fatigue. He was enthralled. She, on the other hand, trailed sweat, and her clothes would never be rid of the oily, black mud.

"They dug it wide enough for two men to stand beside one another. It goes out into the village, hidden in some hovels. His word, not mine. I judge him to be some sort of miner. He has all these phrases for struts or drains or something that I cannot place. Nothing good to say about Avitus

Valerius, though. Indeed, no true craftsman likes to be rushed. I know the feeling well myself."

Aelfhild groaned. Her arms burned and splinters pricked wickedly even through her gloves, but her ears were most exhausted. "Enough, Dunstan! How many more are down there?"

"I think many. This was meant to be, well, the end."

They were able to free seven men from beneath the wreckage of the wall but found nearly as many corpses in the process. However many more were buried nearby, it was impossible to tell, and even Aelfhild was not willing to let them dig past the sundered ramparts. Mercy had limits. Any men trapped on the far side would have to pray the Oescans affected a rescue of their own. And Aelfhild had to pray that was what they were doing.

Cuthbert never did return to the courtyard to make apologies, so she relied on Jarngrim to scout for her. He said there was movement along the enemy lines, but nothing advancing past the wall. The Legate could have been digging, or he simply could have left his men for dead and set about building some new and terrible siege machinery. It was impossible to tell.

Dunstan came up as she was wiping mud from her breeches. "Thank you. The truth of it is, I was afraid to speak. But I saw your eyes and . . . thank you, anyway." He added, "I said that part, not Publius."

She patted his shoulder, leaving a stark print on the clean cloth. "It was the right thing." In truth, she was beginning to feel less sure. The handful they had saved brought the total just shy of twenty. A score of Oescans in the courtyard and hardly more than one hundred defenders. Even if the prisoners never got uppity, it was a lot of extra bellies. She turned back to Dunstan. "Now we need to find a way to get them out of here."

"Yes. Yes, agreed." He bobbed his head. His reedy neck and bent posture lent every movement a birdlike quality that was not flattering.

Aelfhild sighed. "I need to speak to the Eorl. Stay here and make sure the guards do not kill anyone. Please?" She was tired and only thought to make it a request at the very end.

"Yes, certainly. Er, Publius did ask about you. How shall I deal with the subject? He is curious why a woman holds sway here among the warriors. We all are, most certainly, but he did ask."

She pinched the bridge of her nose. Part of her wished she had listened to Jarngrim and stayed out of it. She had not really spoken up, but nor had she needed to. Dunstan and Cuthbert had not been the only ones to notice her. The reason she felt so conspicuous whenever she left the cellar, so exposed, was precisely that she *was* conspicuous, she was exposed. Either the men were staring at the sole female occupant of the keep or making a point not to do so. After her fight with Hengist, the stares had grown less bold, less probing, but they had not stopped. How could Publius not wonder? "No doubt he did. Tell him to be glad he is alive. Tell him not to ask questions. Tell him nothing. You decide. I leave you in command!" Dunstan's narrow chest swelled as she strode away.

In his chambers atop the tower, the Eorl seemed to shrink. She had noticed before how he had aged, a touch more white here and there, but he had not shown the full burden of his years then. Now he looked sapped and shriveled, hunched over half a bowl of broth. He glanced up as she crested the stairs. "How goes the digging?"

"Finished, lord," she said. It was the first time she had come up this far. There were no comforts in the Eorl's chambers. There were pallets laid out for his ealdormen to sleep on and a few moth-bitten tapestries between the windows. Anything edible had been eaten, anything fit to burn long since smashed for kindling, anything valuable smuggled out and buried.

Cuthbert pushed the remaining soup around with his spoon. His bushy eyebrows bunched together. "I forget how long it has been since we sent everyone away." He pushed the bowl back. "As soon as the Oescans crossed the river, we packed all the women and children off, most of the villagers, too. It has been just us warriors for such a while. When everyone around, day in, day out, looks at the world with hard eyes, you cannot help but do the same. You forget, until someone calls you back."

He looked up at Aelfhild. "I am glad the pair of you were down there." The Eorl chuckled. His shoulders rose, his brow slowly straightened. It felt as though he had expanded, ever so slightly, to fill up a bit more of the room.

Aelfhild sat on a stool opposite him. "I hope you will go easy on Dunstan, lord. He means well. Better than such as Hengist."

"I bear nothing but love for Dunstan, and the old boy knows it." Aelfhild was not sure about that, but the Eorl carried on. "Every man has a time and a place, lass. Dunstan's was by that ditch, talking mercy. Yours, too, I reckon, though I have yet to suss you out. But today or tomorrow, whenever the Oescans come, that is Hengist's day."

That does not mean I have to like the man, Aelfhild thought.

Cuthbert was watching her frown. He reached across the table and clamped one of his great paws atop her wrist. "Listen to me now, Aelfhild. I had hoped Harald would come and even the odds. That hope is past. But we will get you clear, no matter what comes. If I can teach you one thing before the end, let it be this. I pray you will not need it. I fear you will once the Jarls set their hooks in you. Leading well is not about choosing the good over the bad. Fools manage that every day. To lead is to weigh one bad turn against another, then make the hard choice."

She nodded. "I understand."

His grip tightened. "Do you? Your choice here was to save unarmed men or let them be cut down. Forgive me for saying, but that seems an easy one. Here is the choice before me. I can surrender to the Legate. That will save the lives of my men. Maybe not my life, but Osric will want to toy with me first, so I might buy a little time. But it will doubtless save my men. If I fight, my men and I face our odds in the shield wall, but we show the folk of Earnfold just who Osric is and what he is willing to do. I see in your face time and again how you want to save every little life that crosses your path. But what are a few lives compared to the soul of a kingdom? Then again, what does it matter to the widow which arse sits on a throne? See the real price of power, my dear."

"So tell me," he asked, "as the Gods' chosen messenger, what would you choose?"

Aelfhild opened her mouth, then closed it again. She told the truth. "I do not know, lord."

He let go and patted her hand. "A good start. Remember that."

"For now, I know we need to send the Oescans out of here."

"Now you think of that." There was the old twinkle in his eye—Cuthbert as he had been of old, fainter now but still kicking.

Aelfhild spread her hands in front of her. "I am just trying to choose right, lord."

They fell silent. The sound of knocking and hammering came up from the courtyard below, faint through the windowslits.

"Tell me true, this time," Cuthbert said. "Was it really you that set the earth to shaking?"

She toyed with the idea of fibbing again. The edge of her glove was starting to fray under her constant plucking. It was stuffy up in the tower, the air pressed in tight and still. He deserved to know. She suspected which path he would choose, and a lie seemed a poor way to leave things. The secret sat heavily in her chest as she went to speak. Her voice squirmed out as a whisper, "I think it was."

The Eorl gripped the edge of the table with both hands. He blew out a long breath. "I was sure of it, but it is another thing to hear you say so."

"I do not know how, lord. I cannot control it. Any of it." She rubbed her dripping nose on the back of her glove.

"Hmm," said Cuthbert. After a beat, he asked, "So I suppose any further miracles are too much to hope for?"

She sniffed. He still held firm onto the table, but a smile folded up the wrinkles around the corners of his eyes. Aelfhild laughed, for the first time in as long as she could remember, a deep, doubling belly laugh. She rubbed away a few more tears, but these were welcome. "I think so, lord."

Cuthbert harrumphed. "Some messenger you turned out to be." She could only agree.

1 8

"**B**IND THE BLIGHTERS'** hands!" shouted Hengist.

They took the Oescans to the gap in the sundered eastern wall. The Norholtings had piled tables and broken beams to barricade the newly formed opening. They were knocking in a line of sharpened stakes now. Attackers would have to approach up a ditch of sinking soil and in narrow file—the spruce logs had splintered into thickets of sharp fibers that punished any careless movement. But there was no escaping the fact that it was a gap in Wynnthwait's armor.

"We will be seeing these filth again ere long," Hengist said to Aelfhild as they moved past. "Hope you know that."

Aelfhild heard but did not reply.

Cuthbert's men grumbled as they shifted debris. If saving the Oescans had been unpopular, letting them go without reprisal seemed a downright disgrace. The men did as they were told, though.

Publius was the last to go. He seemed decent enough, for an enemy and a southling. He was diligent in looking after the legionnaires he had taken command over. Dunstan said the man had few kind words to say about Avitus Valerius, which was further merit. The Oescan gave a little bow before he waded into the muddy wreckage after his fellow soldiers. He spoke once more to Dunstan and disappeared.

Dunstan sniffed. "He seemed normal. But please do not tell the Eorl I said so."

The defenders began restacking the barrier. Aelfhild watched the prisoners go. They limped their way back to the siege wall and were met by a troop of horsemen just outside their own lines. She watched as they disappeared behind the palisade; the already flimsy hope that she had made some difference for the better here faded with them. Hengist's words were hard to put out of her mind.

"Aela!" Jarngrim's voice rang out from the courtyard. She turned and saw him walking over with a bundle slung over his shoulder. "Time to get you gone," he said as they met. "Cuthbert's orders. He said you would know."

She repeated what the Eorl had told her earlier. "There is a raft where we came ashore. I ride that downriver, then head north. Either I find Harald, or I find Cuthbert's men and they take me to Harald. I can do it."

He dumped his burden out onto the grass. There were two hardened leather jerkins and matching bracers, two shields and short swords, and one full waterskin. "I tried to find you some food. No luck." He was loosening straps on the armor as she tightened hers.

She pulled the cord bindings of one of the bracers tightly with her teeth. "I need to say good-bye to Eyvind first. And there are still a few men down in the cellar; Dunstan will need a hand moving them." As she threw a shield over her back, trumpets sounded from the Oescan lines. Many trumpets and from all sides. Aelfhild shivered. Then from the ramparts and across the courtyard a cheer rose from the defenders. Jarngrim turned, and Aelfhild shaded her eyes against the morning sun as she looked up. The Eorl had brought out his battle standard; the flag of Norholt, spruce green cut by black bars with a rearing silver bear in the middle, streamed from atop the tower. The old bear himself.

"Quick as you like," said Jarngrim. He slipped a short sword through his belt, and they started moving.

"Do you think there is still a chance Harald could get here in time?" Aelfhild asked as they jogged.

"When was our luck ever that good?" Jarngrim replied.

The keep was abustle. Runners hefted buckets of water to and fro, delivered quivers of arrows to the ramparts, and stacked stones atop the gatehouse. Every remaining sack of supplies was hauled into the tower and stowed for the final defense. Cuthbert emerged from the tower door as Aelfhild and Jarngrim approached. His oiled chainmail glinted. The longsword at his hip and emblazoned shield across his back fit him naturally. They completed the Eorl and made him look exactly as the Gods had meant him to be: ready to act, to crack skulls, not to scheme or flatter or negotiate. Aelfhild hoped there would come a day when she would find such a fit. She also hoped her leather armor would provide even a jot of the protection that mail gave to the Eorl.

"Time to go, lass!" Cuthbert bellowed as they passed him and his retinue.

"Aye, lord!" she yelled back. *Just one more thing*, she thought.

Dunstan bent over a steaming iron cauldron on the bottom floor of the tower, sprinkling powders and stirring. As Aelfhild entered, he called out, "I could use a hand here; none of the others will help. Indeed, just a moment's work."

She slowed to respond, but Jarngrim pushed her from behind. "Not now, little man," he said to the healer.

They left him sputtering. More trumpet blasts rang through the windows as they climbed. Horns answered from the keep side, overlapping and competing for volume as the Norholtings sounded their raucous defiance. She had known that Cuthbert was not going to surrender. Now Valerius did, too. Aelfhild listened for war cries in the distance. She had a vision in her head of the Thrym arriving, Jarl Harald and Jarl Hafdis resplendent at their head, to break the back of the legion as the Oescans left their fortifications. So far, though, there was nothing.

They reached Eyvind. He had propped himself up on his elbows and was staring out the windowslit across from him. He squinted as they came up the stairs. "What is happening?"

"Oescans," Jarngrim answered.

"My father?" Eyvind asked. Jarngrim shook his head.

Aelfhild kneeled beside him. "I have to go." She put her hands on his shoulders. He still felt so frail. There was no meat on any of them, but his weakness ran deep into the bones. Any dream of them all escaping together would have to stay that way. "Jarngrim will stay with you."

"He should go—" Eyvind began. He did not finish the sentence, but settled into a fit of wet, racking coughs.

"You need someone to see to you." Aelfhild thumped his back until he began to still. She tried to snatch a look at the wound on his chest through his flapping tunic, but it was hard to see anything in the poor light. "I can do it. They will not be watching the river now. You all taught me well."

Rocks were falling outside. The floor shook, but only gently this far up.

Eyvind looked for a moment like he might argue. Few could match his stubbornness; mules were yielding as willow boughs compared to one born a jarl's son and risen to captain longships. But he nodded. "Go safe. Do not worry about us."

She leaned in and pushed her forehead against his. "I promise I will see you again." His bony fingers wrapped her arm.

Jarngrim touched her shoulder. "It is past time."

She readjusted her armor as she headed for the stairs. There were still no horns from outside the siege lines. This could not be it. She turned back to them. "I will find Harald, and we will come back for you. I swear."

"Go!" Jarngrim's voice was raised now. He bounded to her side and pushed her toward the stairs. Softer now, he said, "Fast and safe now. Go."

The haze of tears was clearing as she reached the courtyard. Sunlight glinted off the Eorl's silvered helm on the ramparts above. She could pick him out at a distance. The catapults seemed to have stopped, but there were scattered boulders and fresh trails of debris to avoid. Mixed in were wooden bolts, the thickness of her forearm and fixed with carved wooden fins, that stuck up from the earth to about waist height. The thought of one screaming home into a human target made her blanch.

"Help me, please!"

She saw Dunstan on the stairs to the gatehouse. He had both feet braced against the stairs as he strained to lift his cauldron off the landing. There was a rut in the ground where he had dragged it through grass and mud. Warriors ran past him without slowing as they hastened up to the walls or off to the eastern breach.

Gods have mercy. Aelfhild looked to the left, toward the riverside wall, her path out, and the raft that waited in the reeds. She looked to her right, at Dunstan's struggling figure. She knew where she should go, where common sense told her to go, where Cuthbert and Jarngrim and Eyvind would tell her to go. *Eyvind is not the only one who can be stubborn*, she thought, as she turned right.

The gate shook with enough force to knock back some of the sandbags piled against it. Hinges groaned and wood splintered, but the door held. It was braced and blocked and buttressed as best as the craft of Norholt could manage, but it would not hold forever under such an assault.

She grabbed the cauldron's handle and heaved. It bounced onto the next step as Dunstan changed his grip. The stench of rotten eggs was profound. Aelfhild covered her nose and mouth with her free arm. "What did you do?"

"From the Oescan's own ammunition." Dunstan grunted as they made the next stair. "I made my own blend." Another grunt. "Should work well against that testudo."

They heaved their cargo into the gatehouse. Archers stood at the window, firing at the machine below. Aelfhild could see a boxy wooden frame set atop reinforced wheels, standing just a few paces from the door. There was a gaping black mouth at the front of the housing, which she suspected would not stay empty long. The sound of chanting was audible over the din.

Arrows bounced off the roof of the ram, which was plated with some sort of dull sheet metal. One of Cuthbert's men managed to put an arrow through the gap in the front of the housing. There was yelling from inside, but the machine soon lurched to life once more. Another warrior threw a rock; it must have made a deafening racket beneath the roof, but it rolled away without stopping anything. She heard the swish of the battering head and felt the impact against the gate quiver up through her feet.

Dunstan tugged on the edge of her tunic. "Heave!" He had to shout over the noise from all sides now, trumpets and horns, bowstrings, screaming, splintering beams.

The ironwrought cauldron was heavy enough that they both had to grasp the handle with two hands. The sludge was too thick to pour; they had to swing the entire kettle out and over. "One, two," Aelfhild counted it out as they swung back and forth to build up some arc, "three, now!" The cauldron bounced along the top of the ram, putting some sizable dents into the plating. Its contents spilled out and trickled down toward the wooden sides. Dunstan pointed down and yelled, "Light your arrows!"

The ram boomed once more and the gate screamed.

The archers drew a few shafts with clothbound tips. They kindled them from a brazier of coals on the floor and let fly.

Aelfhild held her breath. Most of the shafts had bounced off, but a few stuck in the tarry liquid. She watched as the fire guttered slowly out. The cloth binding on the arrows shriveled away. The gate shook again. There was a change in the sound, louder, sharper, as the doors began to give way.

She exhaled. She had wasted time for this.

"The gate is lost! Move to the Eorl! Shore up the side!" One of the defenders called to his companions. They all ran over toward the northern edge of the battle.

"Wait," said Dunstan. He was flat on the floor, peering at the ram below.

"Dunstan!" Aelfhild screamed. He pulled his neck back into his shoulders. It was not him that she was angry at, it was the stupid girl that had so needed to be of use, just one last time, but there was no way he could tell that from her voice.

"Wait." His voice was pleading, he pointed down at the ram. The light was flickering on the far side of the machine. In the bright of day it was hard to tell if or where there were flames. The metal roof of the machine still was not burning, but it looked as though whatever had trickled down to the plank siding had ignited. Dunstan cried, "Smoke!"

Whatever was mixed into Dunstan's concoction, it took its time igniting—but ignite it did. The entire length of the battering ram's side was soon licking ghostly blue flames. A few of the operators ran out with buckets. Aelfhild grabbed a stone from one of the nearby piles and chucked it at them, but the Oescans were out of range.

"Leave them," Dunstan said. A grin spread across his face. "Let them spread it."

With each splash, the flames danced and moved but would not quell. The fire grew. There was shrill shouting from inside the ram now. Another strike against the door, but this one halfhearted and it did not shake Aelfhild's knees like the previous battering. The drivers were in trouble. Flames started to appear even along the plated roof as the inferno along the ground grew. One man sprinted out of the back of the construct and headed for the distant siege wall. Screams grew from within as the heat rose.

Aelfhild licked her lips. The rest of the ram crew broke from their posts and fled. Flames engulfed the machine and kept spreading. "How do we stop it?" she shouted. Dunstan's face was blank as he looked back at her. Fire shimmered along the gatehouse walls now. *Of course he did not think that far.*

The walls shook once more. The sill of the window beside them exploded. Aelfhild threw herself onto the floor. She lifted her head to see one of the bolts, still quivering from the impact, lodged up to its fins in the far wall. She grabbed hold of Dunstan and pulled him out of the gatehouse. Splinters from the window stuck from the skin of Dunstan's cheek. She felt some along her own brow. A finger's width to the side and they would have found her eye. Her hand tightened around the thin man's bunched robe. There was no taste in her mouth, her heart raced, and he seemed light as a feather. She yanked him along behind her.

The courtyard below the ramparts was clear, but not for long. Wynnthwait was close to lost.

1 9

"FALL BACK!" THE Eorl and his men sent a sundered ladder tumbling back. Cuthbert's once-bright mail was drenched in blood. His sword was drawn and flashing over the grapnels and laddertops. Around him was his vanguard, their arrows spent, hacking away with blade and spear. "Fall back!" the old bear howled. One of his men raised a horn and blew. Shields raised to cover the rear, they all locked together to retreat down the stairs. Aelfhild, holding Dunstan up by an armpit, ducked into their formation. They rattled their way into a square formation once in the courtyard.

"Rally to the east!" shouted Cuthbert. It looked as though the shield wall at the dike was giving way.

The Oescans scaling the ramparts did not give pursuit but took the opening to secure the northern walls. Some of their own archers began firing down. Judging by the smoke from the gatehouse and rising along the western flank, they would not enjoy their new position too long.

"Shields!"

Aelfhild got Dunstan to stand on his own feet. She unslung her shield, joining the press of bodies as it shuffled eastward. The Eorl must have spotted her. Aelfhild felt a mailed fist clamp onto her shoulder as she heard his voice. "Damn your eyes, girl, are you still here?"

The right time had come and swiftly gone. She was in no position to argue. Here were the fruits of blind hope. They very much resembled the costs of profound stupidity. Arrowheads slammed into her shield and sent pains shooting along her elbow. Two more blasts rang from the horn right beside her ear. She was deaf on one side now, and the press of bodies moved the other way. It seemed they had rescued whatever was left of the eastern line and were retreating to the tower now.

Cuthbert shouted in her good ear, "When we get towerside, get yourself to the south wall! Move your arse!"

The smoke was swirling thicker now, which made her feel less like bait. But if the eastern wall had fallen, the Oescans would be pouring in. Everything had turned sour. Her watering eyes stung and her ears echoed.

A mailed fist grabbed her shoulder and wrenched her out of the line. "Run!"

She sprinted away from the shield wall, past the tower, and toward the hidden riverbank door. Shapes moved in the smoke to her left, but she ran on. She was deaf and nearly blind in the acrid haze, so her feet had to trace their way by memory. Shoulder first, she rammed against the inner wall of the lower southern rampart. That meant a left turn, a short hallway, right into a guardroom, then downstairs and she was out. She turned left and immediately flattened herself against the wall.

Men were moving along the hallway she needed to pass through. They were all looking toward the inner keep and no one had spotted her, but it put them between her and an exit. She spun and slinked in the opposite direction. Her mind raced.

Up these stairs, double back, right turn, and there should be a window to shimmy out of. Rubbing her eyes against her shoulders did little good. Her one arm was still tied up in the shield and her other hand clutched the seax. She needed more hands. The smoke was thicker this way.

She turned right and ran into an Oescan archer who was emerging, equally watery-eyed, from a side staircase. The fortress was a warren of the bastards now. He held a bow but no arrow. As he shook off the impact, his eyes widened. His hand went for his quiver. She had the advantage. Her sword was drawn. But this was different than training with the crew. Sweat traced lines across the man's smoke-stained skin. A tarnished copper amulet, the pattern on its greening surface rubbed down to vague, blunted shapes, hung out over the collar of his tunic and onto his breastplate. She could see the man running his fingers over it as he whispered prayers before leaving the safety of his barracks. Aelfhild stomped on his ankle and slammed the rim of her shield into his nose. Bone and cartilage crunched under the blow. He went backward, down the stairs. He would live. She ran.

Left turn. *No! Straight, then left.* Her ears were still ringing but she could feel the floorboards shifting as other feet drummed against them.

Window. No hesitation, no thought, she dove. It was only two flights up—or possibly three, there might have been a third set of stairs in the mix somewhere. She knew she had to roll when she hit the ground, but her eyes were still streaming.

Her ankle snagged the bank first, then she rolled. The shield came off her arm on the trip to the bottom, her sword was long since dropped, and she managed to get both hands up around her face as she went careening down. Reeds whipped past her and she was in the water.

The Hwitea was still bitterly cold. It was a blessing against her burned skin, though, and soon she could see again. But she was heavy. The cured leather of her armor was slightly buoyant, but the wool lining and her thickly knit clothing were very much not. She gasped a quick breath as her head went under.

Her belt buckle had been crooked to begin with and seemed to lock up in the icy river. She kicked her shoes away and wrenched at the clasp around her waist. Pumping her legs could only keep her from sinking further, though; she was not rising. Something snapped; it was murky and hard to see, but the belt came free. Then the breastplate was off, and she was up above the waves.

She sucked in air and kept kicking. The river was fast, but she wanted to be a moving target in case anyone on the bank had arrows and the wrong inclination.

Swimming was not as natural for her as it was for her Thrym companions. They were born for the water. She was bred for the shore. She paddled, not unlike Embla would have, with both arms and legs to stay afloat.

Once she felt that a safe enough distance had passed, she risked turning over onto her back. It was awkward and she got a few mouthfuls of chalky river water for her trouble. She looked back at the pillar of smoke rising over Wynnthwait. There were more figures advancing up the hill from the siege wall, encircling the fortress. It was over or soon to be. Cuthbert would hold the tower long enough to do his lads proud, but he would not sacrifice every life under his command for naught.

She had forgotten to say good-bye to Jarngrim.

Her back struck some sort of rock or submerged log, and it drove the breath out of her. She decided to turn attention to the river. The siege wall disappeared from view as the river dipped and turned downstream. She could feel the cold sapping her strength. Her fingers and toes were dead, her arms leaden, and her legs did not have much left. She struck out toward the bank.

Face-first, she pulled herself through the muck, grasping at cattails and rushes on the marshy shore. Just above the bank was a broad, flat rock warmed by the sun. Aelfhild dragged herself onto it. "That could have gone better," she whispered to herself.

Water rushing over stones—there was no more soothing sound in all the world. Reeds rustled in the breeze. A fat dragonfly clicked its way over the river. Aelfhild opened her eyes. Her eyelids were sticky; it took added effort to break them open. She lifted fingers to her face. It was caked in mud, then all the way down to her belly button, and had hardened into a brittle cast under the sun. She rolled over and groaned.

Where the bruises ended, the welts began. The ankle on her right leg, which had taken the force of her dive for freedom, felt about double the normal size. Walking on that would be trouble. She lifted herself on hands and knees and crawled, infant-like, toward the water's edge. It took a great deal of splashing and scrubbing to shift the muck. She had not chosen the spot for its beauty, but as she leaned back from her bath and took a glance around, it was hard not to appreciate. The setting sun danced regal pink hues along the rippling flow of the river. Across the way, willows stooped to trail their fronds into the water. All the gnats and dragonflies had attracted a pair of riverbirds, maybe kingfishers—but Aelfhild was hardly an expert—that flitted just above the surface and snatched up their dinner on the wing.

Upriver there was still a column of smoke rising above Wynnthwait. The color had changed from black to a pasty white plume. She hoped her friends were still alive. Eyvind was hardheaded but also too weak to be any real threat, and the Oescans would have to see that. Cuthbert was important. They would want him as a trophy. For Jarngrim, she could only hope.

Driftwood gathered in an eddy by the rocks she slept on. Most of the sticks were flimsy, but she found one branch that would make a passable crutch.

She lifted herself to a crouch first and jammed the broad end of the stick under her right shoulder. *The first step will be the worst*, she told herself. *Deep breath*. She stood. The pain was tolerable. She adjusted her makeshift crutch.

Her jaw clenched as the ankle rotated. It was a bright, insistent pain, a procession of boiling needles jabbing one after the other into the bones of the joint. After another deep breath she continued. At the top of the bank she had to rest. Either the ankle grew less swollen as she stretched or her mind blocked out more of the agony, but the going grew slightly easier as she limped into the tree line.

"Run north, as far and as fast as you can." Those had been Cuthbert's words. Running was out of the question. Walking was uncertain. But north she could do. She kept the sunset on her left and picked a painstaking, tender path through the brush. Every time her crutch skidded off a stone or snagged a root—and there were many roots—her ankle delivered a fresh bout of tooth-crunching pain. She had a direction, though. North—simple, clear, a driving purpose. Her teeth might be ground down to nubs by the time she got there but she was going north, and nothing, save for steep hills, would stop her.

2 0

ELFHILD FACED A dilemma. There was a towering oak tree, long dead and with a pair of gaping holes on one side where limbs should have been, and she was certain she had seen it before. Almost certain. It was an easy landmark with its creeping vine cape and crown of naked twigs. She was also almost certain she had gone north past the tree, but here it was again. The sun was climbing higher now, but it was vaguely on her right, and that was where it ought to have been. Unless more of the afternoon had gotten away from her than she thought.

Sweat beaded along her eyebrows. She tried to find a clean patch on her tunic to wipe her brow but had to settle for the least soiled section of sleeve. The river was behind her. Probably. Possibly. So that meant north was past the dead oak, even if she had already tried that route before. She sighed and hobbled on. Her armpit was going to have a kingly bruise from the rough end of her crutch.

This time, whether she was headed north or otherwise, the forest disgorged her onto a path. It was little more than a pair of cartwheel divots, and the woods were well on their way to reclaiming the gap, but it might as well have been the Imperial Way. No roots grabbed at her stick, no rabbit holes threatened to swallow her feet, and her view was blessedly clear of leaves and trunks. She took a quick glance at her shadow. The sun was straight overhead. There were no signs on the path. Nothing made one direction more appealing than the other. She picked the way that looked flatter.

If Kolbrun were here, she would know what to do. As it turned out, the disadvantage of even ground was that she had to focus less on her footfalls. The niggling little thoughts started to seep back in. Onund would remember some old wives' tale about moss and the sides of trees. Eyvind would have a trick with sticks in the dirt or shadows or whatnot. Kolbrun would hit someone until things became clear.

Aelfhild scuffed her right heel against the ground. It was fleeting, but the fresh, sparking pain burned away the expanding web of self-pity. It gave her eyes a real reason to water.

My friends need me, she thought. *They need me and I am lost in the woods. We need each other. I need them.*

She thumped her foot again and gritted her teeth.

Around a bend in the path, she found horses. There were two, long-legged and glossy even in the shade, each saddled and hung with barding. Riders were nowhere in sight. Aelfhild ducked into the ferns along the path's edge. She wriggled back into cover, dragging her useless leg along as quietly as possible, until she could peep out at the beasts without fear of being spotted. The horses showed no alarm.

Indigo paint flaking from the leather trappings and the golden embroidery along the reins meant that these animals belonged to the legion. Outriders from the main body of the Oescans, Aelfhild suspected. It made sense that the only spot of luck she had so far, finding the path, would just be a way to lead her into a column of marching legionnaires. The Gods did so love their little japes. She was most concerned, though, with the riders.

She raised her head as far as she dared. There was no outrunning anyone with her deadweight ankle. Just beyond the nearer horse she could see the tip of what might have been an Oescan helmet, with the arced crest and dyed horsehair. It was not moving very fast, whatever it was. The scouts were in no hurry. That much was clear.

Aelfhild relied on the horses to tell her if anyone approached. The pair nibbled grass. They swished away flies with their tails. Once, they nickered back and forth. It made Aelfhild perk up and crane forward in her hiding spot. She thought the scouts would be returning, or waking, or doing anything to stir up the horses, but she was disappointed. They were as bored as she was. She settled back into her watch.

And woke with a snort. Her chin had knocked against her chest and there were conspicuous dribbles down the front of her tunic. A few hard blinks and she had a bead on the horses once more.

The riders had reappeared at some point. Definitely Oescans. They wore light armor with their crested helms, and each had a sword at his hip. One of the men was stretching. Aelfhild was not the only one who had been napping. *Deserters?* Aelfhild wondered. *Or shirkers?* Either way they did not seem to be a grave threat. She slithered farther into the ferns just to be on the safe side. One Oescan heaved himself into the saddle. His companion was still flexing and yawning. The tired man waved off his companion, who nudged his horse into an easy trot down the road and straight toward Aelfhild's hiding spot. She held her breath as the rider approached.

The man was trimming bits of mold off a crust of bread. He never once looked up. If the horse caught scent of a strange human in the bushes, it gave no sign of caring. Rider and mount were soon around the bend and moving out of sight.

There were two damp thumps. Arrows sprouted in the rider's neck and chest.

Aelfhild stifled a gasp.

He toppled slowly out of the saddle. His body threw up a cloud of pollen as it struck ferns below. The reins were tangled around his leg or foot and pulled the horse to a sidelong halt. It stood, head down, and waited patiently for its master to rise.

The second scout never made it to horseback. He was fussing with the blanket beneath his saddle, oblivious to his companion's fate, when the arrows took him in the side. His horse gave a nervous whinny as the man crumpled, but stood its ground. These were warhorses. A warhorse that bucked and ran from blood or battle was no good to anyone.

Then there was silence. Aelfhild stayed perfectly still. She kept both hands over her mouth and focused on breathing through her nose as gently as possible. On the one hand, enemies of the Oescans were likely friends of hers. On the other hand, she was a stranger.

The ambushers took their time emerging. There was the gentlest rustle of leaves as they stepped out of the shadows. Each figure was daubed in mud and wore dappled, mismatched clothing, all uneven lines and shapes that the eye slid right over. Four of them left cover. Aelfhild guessed more might yet be hiding. All carried bows. Each had an arrow nocked in case of Oescan deceit.

The first rider had died immediately. The bowmen stripped him bare and tossed the naked corpse into the woods. One man took the time to rearrange the bent fronds around the body; only someone probing deep into the undergrowth would spot anything amiss. The dead man's horse shied away from the strangers as they approached, but one of the ambushers was there with the reins, stroking the animal's face and cooing as he led the beast into the woods.

The second rider was less lucky. He crawled some ways off from the spot he had fallen. Aelfhild heard the faint gurgle as one of the attackers finished him off with a hooked knife. She winced.

And then the path was left empty.

No bodies, no horses, just a touch of blood spatter that would be a chore to spot in the tangled grass. No ambushers, either. They all had vanished, melted back into the thicket whence they came.

It was a while before Aelfhild lowered her hands from her lips. She waited for the grip on her shoulder or the blade at her throat. They might have seen her arrive. They might have watched her as she watched the Oescans. An arrow could be pointed straight at her heart, awaiting the wrong move.

She stood, slowly. She considered raising her hands but decided against it. What little dignity she had left, she could at least take with her to the grave. With the crutch under her armpit she felt a touch safer. Only a true rogue would shoot a cripple. A crippled woman, at that—she would gladly have someone disdain her abilities this once.

Oescans one way, assassins another. Neither option appealed to her.

The ambushers had not left a trail, but the horses had. They were well fed and iron shod, so the tracks were clear enough that she could follow.

Kolbrun's lessons had not been entirely wasted. Aelfhild kneeled at the edge of the path, clutching her stick with one hand. Somewhere down the path was the legion, with her friends held captive. At the end of the dimpled trail through the loam was a horse to ride and a band of warriors that might not kill her. They might even be made to help her. She cocked an eye skyward. "If I am to get an arrow, at least make it quick."

2 1

SHE FELT THE eyes on her early. It could have been nerves, but there was a stillness to the woods that made her think she had more than one shadow. Bird and bug alike were laying low; far too many feet were tramping through their forest. She never caught a hint of movement. They were clearly master woodsmen, while she risked falling any time she looked up for more than a heartbeat.

It was impossible to be stealthy with only one good leg. There was nothing for it. She had to scrape and bang her way along and left even more trail signs than the warhorse ahead of her. A blind man could have tracked her; a deaf man would have marked her passing. Aelfhild decided that making herself obvious was the wiser approach. Surprises had a way of setting arrows aflight.

The ground sloped down toward what smelled like a peat bog. Sawgrass and moss carpeted the drier patches, broken by the odd stringy spruce. Aelfhild paused. One of the horses was ground tied on a little knoll toward the clearing's center. All on its own, too, no human in sight. It was clearly a trap. Though, as she considered it, was a trap still a trap if the prey recognized it? That might have been nonsense, as she considered further. It did mean that they had seen her. If they wanted to kill her they could have without fuss, so the Four might have to wait on their vengeance for a touch longer. Aelfhild turned one final warning glance to the heavens.

The horse watched her limping approach. Its round eyes were sweet if a little dull—spirit was likely not high on the list of requirements for a battle steed. It seemed happy enough to have Aelfhild stroke its face, and nuzzled the side of her head in return.

"Who is a good . . ." She peeked under the animal's barding. "Good boy. Nice boy." The gelding seemed satisfied that she had no food to give. He returned to nibbling at the abundant bog myrtle.

Aelfhild decided to raise her hands. The crutch made it a little complicated. She had to wedge the stick under her elbow and it threw her balance off, but a little pain in the ankle seemed a fine trade-off for continued life. "I am not armed," she said. "And I am a friend of Eorl Cuthbert."

There was a pause. It lasted long enough to make her feel foolish for teetering in a deserted clearing and speaking to empty air. Then there was a voice.

"Turn around."

She hopped a half circle.

"Again."

Aelfhild grunted as she turned back.

"One move, you die."

She nodded clearly enough for all to see.

A few of the men broke cover. One had been settled into the tall grass only a stone's throw away. It was obvious when he moved, but Aelfhild would never have spotted him in time. Their bows were at the ready. Sunlight played off of arrowheads.

"Who are you?" The man farthest back was speaking; the rest were advancing.

"Aelfhild. I am a servant of Eorl Cuthbert. I was at Wynnthwait when the walls fell. The Eorl sent me away but I hurt my leg escaping."

"I do not know your face."

That was a good sign. That implied he was from Wynnthwait himself. But it also meant he had every reason to be mistrustful of newcomers. Familiar names always helped. "My friends and I arrived just days ago. We met Immin and Sabert across the river."

She could see a grey-tinged beard beneath his hood; mud obscured the rest. He looked like a swamp creature, from where she stood. She probably looked similar, though; the dirt in Norholt was persistent. They were still quiet, so she added, "and I hit Sabert in the face with a rock."

One of the men nearby snorted. It was the best sound Aelfhild had ever heard. She could have said a thousand prayers. "Did I not tell you that those two were lying? Fought off a whole Oescan patrol, my soggy feet! A twig of a girl hauled off and hit him with a pebble!"

Aelfhild wiped the sweat from her wrists onto her breeches. Hands were easing off bowstrings and she could see arms and shoulders relaxing around her. She tried to look as harmless as possible.

The leader still looked unconvinced. "None of us can vouch for her."

"Lighten up, Bertwald, for Gods' sakes. You can see she is hurt. What is she going to do to us?"

Rude, but forgivable in the circumstances.

"We can bring her back campways and Immin can say aye or nay. Go on!"

Bertwald, the mistrustful leader, made a rumbling in his throat like distant thunder. His scowl was uninviting. But he voiced no protest as they set off toward the far end of the clearing. The matter seemed to be settled.

The joking man cupped his palms to offer Aelfhild a leg up onto the horse. "Hand on my shoulder, there. Looks like you could use a rest."

She winced as her right foot struck the saddle. It took a moment to get settled into the stirrups. Her new friend helped tighten straps and cinch buckles. He muttered as he worked, more to himself than to her, "Hit Sabert with a rock. Champion!" Then he grabbed the reins and led the horse after his companions. "Quiet now, or else Bertwald will turn real sour."

She never had a chance to get a word in, anyway.

"Yes, she is who she says," Immin said, though he did not look thrilled about the admission.

Aelfhild's newest friend, on the other hand, was overjoyed. "You lying buggers! We knew it!"

"Piss off, Godwyn." There was still an angry-looking mark on Sabert's forehead where Aelfhild had pelted him. She felt a little guilty about that, and for the fresh grief the pair were getting from their compatriots. But she was glad to see them alive and said as much.

Immin nodded. "You as well. Made it downriver, then?"

"We did. I was with Cuthbert until, well, everything. Did you get my other friends to a crossing?"

"Aye. We left them soon after. As agreed, mind you. Cannot speak to any more than that."

The camp around them was sparse. On the ride in, Aelfhild had pictured a hidden fortress among the trees, with rope ladders and trapdoors and secret byways. A haven to spark a new campaign of resistance against the Oescan invaders. What greeted her was a handful of threadbare canvas tents and tree branch lean-tos. Off to one side was an outpit crowned with a wheeling gout of gnats. The two Oescan horses brought the mounted strength of the woodsmen to three. The lone Earnfolding horse took a tentative sideways step as the fat, glossy southerners arrived in its patch of grass. The creature's backbone and haunches jutted sharply enough to pose a greater threat to any would-be rider than battlefield foes. That was the visible extent of the Norholt uprising.

"How long have you been here?" she asked.

"Just since the walls fell," Godwyn said, dumping an armful of kindling next to the campfire. "Have to keep moving. Even the Oescans catch on eventually."

"Are there any more of you?"

"Could be. Hard to know." Immin left it at that.

A handful of bows, a few horses, and some mud-daubed, ill-fed warriors. It was a start—or could be. Not a grand beginning. Some of the best stories did start humbly. It took every shred of stubborn, desperate hope that Aelfhild had left, but she tried to fan that little flame back to life. Then she could start putting a little fire back into the others. She hopped over toward Bertwald. The crutch made her look weak. She tried to compensate by straightening her shoulders and speaking with all the warlike rasp she could muster. "What is your plan of attack?"

The old man rumbled again. He was sorting through the supplies and sundries lifted from the slain Oescans. He picked through bulging saddlebags, tossed away crinkled vellum, and sniffed at pouches of herbs.

"You do have a plan?" She watched as he moved edible items into one pile and anything metal to another.

He grunted once more. There was a ring, more goldish than gold, which he tested with his teeth. Disappointed, he tossed it into the shrubs.

Aelfhild knelt to keep her words between them. "We must rescue the Eorl. We owe it to our friends. We owe it to Norholt!"

Bertwald sighed. It was clear the girl was not getting discouraged, so he had to answer. "The Eorl is lost, and Norholt with him. That is done. Finished. Now my men and I must take what we can"—he held up a silver chain gleaned from the bottom of one saddlebag—"and buy back the Eorl when Osric is done with him, if he lives. That is the *plan*."

He offered her a piece of grey-tinged Oescan hardtack as consolation. She declined and left him to his dour accounting. If that was the best that the blood of Norholt had to offer, she would need to do better. It should have been reason enough to take her leave, thank them kindly for their help, and go north. To follow the original plan. She knew that she should find Harald and let him sort things out. But she could help. There was time left to get Eyvind back, and Jarngrim. And Cuthbert, she reminded herself, best to lead with that one. The plan would survive one delay. She played with the hem of her glove. It seemed wiser to save that to the last in case push came to final, desperate shove. There had to be another course.

Aelfhild looked around at the warriors. Bertwald was not alone in his attitude. One man scuffed his way past the horses, not looking up even as the animals knickered at him. Another hunched over a pot hanging above the campfire. He stirred rhythmically, back and forth, back and forth, as the porridge within gave occasional noisome plops. His eyes were fixed, unseeing, in the middle distance. Immin sat on a fallen log with his arms crossed over his knees, curling in on himself, as if that might keep the wafting scent of defeat at bay. Who could make something of this lot? Eorl Cuthbert had, but now buzzards circled around the column of smoke rising from Wynnthwait. Maybe the Jarls could. Jarl Harald would preach and goad until each one was battle hungry and eager for death. Jarl Hafdis would be among them in a flash and pummel them one by one to put some spine back into the lot. Jarl Sindri would make bribes of gold and glory. But none of them was here. Aelfhild was alone.

She pictured her friends. Advice was not forthcoming; it served only to make her feel lonelier. Thinking of Onund, though, gave her pause. The skald, the tale teller and song spinner—now, *he* could stir weary hearts. He could kindle and spark souls with the best of them. It was a godly gift—literally, if the legends were to be believed. Aelfhild remembered most of his stories. All of them, in truth, word for word, because she could never get enough.

It was the best she could offer. She knew just the tale.

2 2

ELFHILD SPREAD HER hands. "It all begins with mighty Sigurd, the great warrior—the hero!"

It was far from difficult to find a gap in the conversation. Silence reigned over the campfire. One of the logs might shift and crackle or a man might cough on a bite of dried venison, but that was the extent of the evening's entertainment. Hardly any of them spared her a glance, which was a kindness, as her cheeks were already flushed. The gestures seemed unnecessary with no one watching, so she focused on pitching the words to hook her audience. How Onund did this for a lark was still beyond her.

"This was after his fateful battle with his brother, Breki, but before he led the Aettir across the mountains to our lands."

Godwyn perked up. He seemed impervious to the mood that had infected the others. "Who are the Aettir?" Godwyn whispered to Sabert, loud enough that Aelfhild had to pause.

"The old tribes," Sabert said with a hiss. "Shut it—I want to hear."

Aelfhild resumed. "Sigurd's heart was broken, for he was a kinslayer, cursed and cursed again for spilling his brother's blood. He wandered far into the western reaches of the old realms, through forest and cave, upriver and over lake. He fought and he drank, but no amount of glory or silver or mead could drown his sorrows. One day, he awoke to darkness. Now, this was odd for it was summertime, and dawn should have long since broken. There was a clamor all around—foxes keened, roosters crowed, owls hooted, and all at once, as though none of the beasts knew what was what. Something was afoot, and Sigurd knew mischief when he saw it.

"There was a village nearby, so Sigurd set about finding the cause of all this murk. The peasants were in their own frenzy, for if the sun failed to shine, then their crops could scarce grow. And if the crops withered, then the rest was soon to follow. They had all manner of fanciful explanations. Each man blamed the next for the troubles.

"That man is too pious, one said, the Gods grow sick of his whining! That man never makes sacrifice, said another, the Gods are punishing his laziness! They blamed the rich, the poor, the old, the young, and turned on one another like starving curs. Sigurd had to wade in with the haft of his axe just to get them talking sense. But the blacksmith in this village was a level-headed man. He kept his wits about him as every man ought, and he told Sigurd what he knew.

"A wyrm lived in an old iron mine atop the mountain. The monster had come to their lands long ago in his father's father's time. It had been small at first. It stole the odd chicken and the farmers cursed it, but the loss was never so keen that they gave chase. But the serpent grew. It began to take sheep. The villagers gathered their scythes and cudgels and chased the beast into its lair, but the wyrm slipped into the deep cracks and crevices in the mount and always eluded their hunts. So they grew used to its thieving, for it took only one sheep at a time.

"But still the serpent grew. More sheep it ate, and it swelled to greater and greater size until it could swallow a man in one snap of its fanged jaws. By the time it turned to devouring the cows, the wyrm was too great for the villagers to fight. It spouted rotting venom, and darkness rolled off its back like the blackest mist. They named it Nótt, for it was night terror given form. Every fortnight the villagers led a fatted cow to the foot of the mountain and left it for Nótt and prayed that the serpent would but leave them be.

"And so they had done for a generation. The villagers thought little of it. That was just the way of things. The wyrm left them to their farming, and they learned to leave the wyrm well enough alone. But still it grew.

"The blacksmith feared he had the right of what had happened. So great and so greedy had the serpent grown that it had plucked the very sun from the sky. And there it sat, curled in its mountain lair, the sun melting away in its scaled belly.

"Sigurd feared no evil. Some say he sought death for all his deeds and misdeeds, but never had he met one mighty enough to give it. It was a worthy challenge. He did not shrink from it. The people needed him, and he could never abandon them. But his axe was old and rusty, a pauper's weapon in truth, and the serpent's hide would be thick and hard as solid stone. He needed a blade that could pierce it.

"The blacksmith knew all the secrets of coaxing iron. The men worked over the forge together as the moons rose and set and rose again. Sigurd pumped the billows and swung the sledgehammer. The blacksmith cut and folded and quenched, and a gleaming sword was born from the embers. Sigurd swung the blade from side to side and marveled at the perfect weight and balance. He tossed a rag skyward and cut it to shreds before it touched earth. He nicked the wings from a passing blackfly in two neat strokes. He listened to the blade's whisper as the very breeze split upon the edge. With that, he thought himself ready.

"The peasants laid their hands on what weapons they could find and followed Sigurd with his bright sword up and up the mountain paths. Sigurd's resolve was steady, his will unbreakable, but the farmers were made of flimsier stuff. Bones littered the foot of the mountain. Some turned back at such a sight. The farmers had to return and tend to the harvest; the shepherds had to return to their flocks. Farther up the mountain came the stench of the great wyrm, all rotting meat and poisoned blood and acid bile. More turned back—the rich man had to live on to guard his silver, the poor man to care for his children.

"Only three souls made it to the summit: Sigurd, the blacksmith, and a young maiden born of a poor family. She had no title, no land, and awaited no inheritance. Her father wished to marry her off to a fat merchant, but she kept her own council and had her own plans. She had taken up shield and spear and meant to fight. Fjola was her name.

"Sigurd said nothing to his companions. That they had come this far told him everything he wished to know. He walked to the mouth of the cave, Fjola one step behind. And they saw the wyrm within.

"Darkness wafted in clouds out of the burrow. Inside, midnight blue on pitch black, were the coiled scales and rippling skin of the great serpent. Fell green light glowed through the thin slits of her eyelids. Nótt's belly was swollen with the bulk of the sun, and she dozed content in the knowledge that none would dare strike at her splendor. Bones were scattered on the floor among the cast-off scales and shed teeth from the wyrm's dripping maw, each tooth longer than a grown man's arm. It was here that the blacksmith, whose courage had held for so long, lost his nerve. He wept as he ran from the summit and left Sigurd and Fjola to face their quarry.

"Sigurd drew his sword. The blade drank of the starlight until it appeared to glow from within. Fjola hefted her spear. Her hand never shook, for just like Sigurd she had little to lose and death scarcely troubled her. They circled the sleeping wyrm.

"Sigurd's first blow was mighty and swift, his aim was true, but his sword clanged off the serpent's scales. Though unscathed, the beast's fury was terrible. Even gorged and fat as she was, Nótt was deadly quick and full of venom. She thrashed from side to side in her cave as she tried to crush and bury the stinging pests.

"Rocks fell atop the heroes, and the wyrm's coils whipped forth and back again, each strong enough to strangle the life from puny human hearts. Sigurd and Fjola danced around the cavern, darting here and striking there, but no blows could pierce that terrible hide. Fjola's spear shattered against the scales. Nótt spat forth a gout of poison vapor, and Sigurd's grand sword bubbled and melted down before his very eyes.

"But the heroes did not despair. Everything was lost, the entire world would shrivel and freeze, unless they could save the fiery sun from its prison. Their lives were a trifle next to the weight of all creation. So they fought on with fist and foot.

"It had been a generation since Nótt had hunted. Safe in her lair and with tribute laid upon her doorstep, her indolence had grown apace with her belly. Writhing and thrashing took its toll. She tired quickly. The little humans danced through the gaps and jumped out of reach, they dodged and rolled and shifted before she could snuff them out. She grew exhausted and turned to flee.

"Her warren of cracks and crevices proved smaller than she remembered. She wriggled into a gap, but her distended gut held her back. Sigurd laid hold of her tail and wrenched with all his might to stay her escape.

"But he could only hold her. It fell to Fjola to find a way to slay the beast. She cast about for any weapon. Her spear was in pieces, Sigurd's sword a lump of useless slag. There were serpent fangs all around, though, and each one needle-sharp.

"Fjola lifted Nótt's own fang, yellow and pocked by the beast's poison, and drove hard into the skin drawn taut around the wyrm's belly. Nótt screamed fit to shake the mountain to its roots. In the village below, folk quailed in their homes and buried their heads to hear such evil. Again and again Fjola stuck, and each scream from the serpent threatened to bury the heroes in rockfall. But lo did the golden light begin to trickle forth from the scar—first a pinhole but growing with every blow. Scales cracked and hide split. The wyrm writhed agony and cleaved the earth with her heaving, but sunlight poured forth.

"As the great orb burst out anew, Sigurd and Fjola dove from the mouth of the cave. The fire scalded them all, blackening skin and burning cloth, but none worse than Nótt. The serpent writhed and wriggled its way to the bowels of the mountain and lingered there evermore. So great is the torment of light in Nótt's memory that she only ever stirs from her depths in deepest winter, when the sun is long gone from the sky.

"Sigurd and Fjola lived. They bore the scars of that battle for the rest of their long lives. The villagers held a great feast and gathered together the riches they could spare, a hoard of gems and furs and gold, but the heroes were nowhere to be found. They had done what was needed. It was not the end of their adventures, for both had many trials ahead, but it was perhaps the grandest of their victories.

"The battle with Nótt taught Sigurd two lessons: first, the sword is worth a damn sight less than the hand that holds it. Second, a lone warrior is a weak warrior; a companion more than doubles his strength. And so Fjola became the first of the Shieldmaidens, and her deeds ring nearly as loud as Sigurd's through the ages."

Aelfhild added that last part. It was not, strictly speaking, true, but she wanted to live in a world where it was. If she repeated it often enough, maybe she could. Her audience had other concerns, though. She could hear their disputations.

"Are we Sigurd in the story? Or are we the woman?"

"Watch your tongue, I am no woman!"

"You really are a simpleton, Godwyn, you understood none of it. We are clearly meant to be Sigurd. Right?"

"Was it meant to be, you know, word for word?"

"I think we are Sigurd."

She settled back into her blanket. They seemed to have swallowed the lure, so now she would just have to work out how best to pull them in. It would have to be a cunning plan. The horses might be useful; she stewed over that one.

"If we are Sigurd, and she is the woman, then who is the wyrm?"

"Go to sleep, Godwyn."

2 3

THE BARGE LURCHED shoreward, driven on by rowers who were mere specks at this distance. It was too far to hear, but Aelfhild could see the shudder of the collision as the prow rammed against the makeshift dock. Antlike figures scrabbled about gesticulating at the bargemen and their clumsiness.

A midge bit at her temple. Aelfhild swatted the side of her head for the hundredth vain time. The tops of her ears were chewed raw and itched furiously. Anywhere that was not concealed by mud, as Bertwald and the rest had shown her, was liable to be stripped bare by the swarming gnats. She tried to focus on the scene below but was constantly having to either swat or scratch.

Bertwald had left a man watching the lake. The scout reported skiffs and rafts crossing for days. The Legate meant to sail his legion across rather than take the long journey over the Hwitea and through the roadless countryside beyond. Barges stretched a bobbing line from the shore, tied one to another in a sort of rudimentary quay, with a motley assortment of rowboats and ketches tied alongside. These boats were the chink in the armor, the gap in the shield wall, and under far lighter guard than captive Eorl Cuthbert himself.

So Aelfhild lay, slathered in muck once again, atop a bluff overlooking Leohtmere's shores. Immin, Bertwald, and a few others were with her. They had led the way through the tangled marsh along wobbling planks over oily bogs that looked deep enough to swallow horse and rider alike.

Norholt's forest stretched from hill to swamp to hill, always thick with trees but some groves grew on firmer ground than others.

It was a good plan. Aelfhild was certain of it. The best any of them could muster. She just had to work out the particulars. "How many days out is the legion?" she asked.

"Three at the outside," Bertwald replied.

Immin was left to furnish details because their leader was terse at the best of times. "Valerius is too scared to leave his siege toys to us heathen northerners. He has his men turtled up around them and his precious self right at the center. They are safe as can be, but a child on foot could outpace their oxen."

"Are the prisoners with them?"

Bertwald gave an affirmative rumble.

Aelfhild knew that she and a band of bowmen could not go at them headlong. The fighting had been bitter enough, but there were still hundreds of legionnaires marching toward Leohtmere and the boats moored along the lake's edge. But the rebels, as Aelfhild preferred to think of them, had speed on their side.

"More riders." Immin pointed. Bertwald grunted.

Horsemen galloped down one of the lakeside paths toward the Oescan camp. The southerners had either only brought up their summer gear or were more used to desert fighting. Their tents were of gauzy cotton that billowed and swayed in the lightest breeze. The encampment mirrored the ceaseless rippling of the nearby water. Luckily for the Oescans, the siege had broken before Harvesttide, or else they all would have found just how bracing an Earnfold winter could be. The patrol slowed to a canter and disappeared into the swaying rows of tents.

"The horses are our way in," Aelfhild said. "We can use the pair you captured yesterday."

Bertwald's rumble sounded negative this time. "Still too many down there."

It was harder than wheedling coins from the King's bursar. Every time she thought there might be a crack for hope to seep in, the man pushed his dour little chin down onto his dour little chest and would have none of it.

Immin had more to contribute. "All that wood down there—one spark would send it all up."

"We have Oescan armor. We can send two men in," Aelfhild said. "Or a man and a woman, as it might be." So the pieces were falling into place. Her heart was certainly stirring.

Bertwald stared down at the camp. He grunted; this time, there was a hint of possibility there. "Needs a distraction."

"All we have to do is slow them down. Then the Thrym can do the rest when they get here." Aelfhild could see it all unfolding. A few could pass where many might not, after all. It had just the right ring of heroism to it. It could work.

There was no hint of eagerness on Bertwald's face. At his age, a bit of stodginess had to be forgiven. He rumbled assent. Aelfhild grinned.

She shifted in the saddle. Either her legs were too short or her torso was too long but she could never balance right on horseback. She tipped and sagged from side to side like a top-heavy sack of turnips. Someone had told her once that she needed to relax her back and sway with the motion, but that almost ended with a quick trip out of the saddle. She vastly preferred her own two feet.

On the horse beside her Immin looked more at home. He bobbed back and forth with one easy hand on the pommel. He looked comfortable, even strapped down in stolen Oescan armor. Aelfhild did not appreciate it.

She was armored as well. The previous bearer had been at least a head taller than she, so the gorget atop her breastplate jabbed into her chin with every bob of the saddle. With armguards up almost past her elbow, it looked as though either the armor had magically expanded or the wearer had suddenly shrunk. Her right greave acted as a rigid splint for her ankle, at the least, and that was a blessing.

"What is the word again?" Immin asked. The helmet over her ears made him sound like he was trapped at the bottom of a well.

"*Valete.* Or wall-ey-tey," she replied.

"And that means hello?"

"That is what Dunstan said." She was not willing to take full responsibility. That whole mess was still a bit of a haze.

Immin growled. "Damned Oescans cannot even speak proper. Wall-it-ey. Wall-eyt-ey." He practiced a few more variants until he seemed satisfied, though not happy.

"Look sharp," Immin whispered.

There was an Oescan picket ahead. Two spearmen slouched behind a barricade of sharpened stakes. They stood at attention as the horsemen approached and raised a greeting hand. One of them said something in the southern tongue; the other was squinting at Aelfhild as if he did not fully trust his own eyes. Part of her face was visible past the helmet's cheek-guards. Even the Oescans were not that effeminate.

"Wall-it-ey," said Immin, raising his hand.

Arrows whistled from the tree line beside the picket. Aelfhild had been expecting it but still flinched. The one guard had been staring straight at her. The blank surprise on his face as the shaft passed through his neck lingered when she blinked. Bertwald and the rest had the bodies off the road in a flash. It was a moment's work, and two new legionnaires emerged from the brush. One had blood spattered across his shoulder guards, and both had a strip of black cloth tied around their right arms, as did Aelfhild and Immin. Now there were four in their fledgling legion. They set off down the road.

The hope was that the Oescans would be too confused to react—harried on all sides, and with men, or women, in their own uniforms attacking them, they would barely be regrouping by the time the boats were put to flame and the Norholtings were away. There was, admittedly, a great deal left to luck, but nothing in life was certain. Aelfhild knew that fact all too well.

She heard water lapping the lakeshore. Leohtmere, the great mirror. And Cynestead, her home, just across it. It had been a long time. Her throat swelled at the sound of those familiar, gentle waves. She nudged her horse onward.

The tents, and the guards reclining within them, were on the far side of the beachhead from Aelfhild and her companions as they came down the path. Skiffs had been dragged prow first onto the sandy scarp at the water's edge. The barges in their makeshift dock extended well out into the lake.

Here was Avitus Valerius's escape plan. It all had to burn.

Aelfhild and Immin kept their horses at a slow trot. No need to draw attention until the very last moment. Bertwald's man had said messengers or scouts came and went regularly, so no one would be fussing about new arrivals. They had tried to time their arrival with the afternoon meal. All the movement in the tents suggested the plan was rolling along smoothly.

Immin clucked to his mount. He pulled to the left and let the horse bend to drink from a puddle near the shore. "Here is close enough," he said. "Godwyn, hold the horses."

The drop made Aelfhild wince. Her ankle was better after a night's rest and with a tight wrapping, but it still crunched with every step. She held her hand out to Godwyn. "Spear," she demanded. He frowned but handed it over. Now she had a walking stick. She made for the skiffs. That was her assignment. There was flint and tinder in her belt pouch and a saddlebag filled with wood shavings and dried leaves to ensure the flames would catch. Her pulse was drumming as she ducked behind the hull of the first boat. She, at least, had cover.

Immin and his companion headed toward the shorebound barge. It was the bridge that led out to all the others; that was their target. The companion, and Aelfhild had already forgotten half her rebels' names, headed out along the line of connected ships. He stooped now and then to check a mooring or coupling, which was smart. It made him look natural.

She dropped her flint. Aelfhild's fingers were trembling. *Focus.* She took a breath. *Let them mind their task. You mind yours.* A pinch of tinder, then she started striking sparks.

There were voices. She looked up from her sprouting flames. An Oescan was walking toward Immin. The Oescan did not look alarmed, not yet, but Immin could neither understand nor answer without giving away the ruse. Rebels thought fast, though. Immin was sitting on the edge of the first barge and his companion had dropped from sight at the first sign of trouble, so he stretched out his foot and groaned. He mimed some sort of injury, too painful to speak. The Oescan moved closer.

Aelfhild's fingers burned. Her fire had caught, and it was spreading.

She kindled a brand from the bag slung over her shoulder and moved toward the next boat.

When she glanced up, Immin had the Oescan on the ground; Immin's knife flashed, once and again.

There was a pile of sailcloth in the next boat, Aelfhild dropped her brand and moved forward. Smoke would be rising soon. Bertwald needed to make his move.

Shouting on the far side of the camp said he had. Immin was out on the barges with his companion, scattering embers. They were screened by the tents, but Aelfhild could see legionnaires scrabbling for weapons and running toward the far barricades. Bertwald and his company would be picking off marks from the bushes.

She emptied her bag into the hull of the last skiff. More sparks and smoke started to curl up. She puffed the flames into greedy life.

A scream split the air, too close to be Bertwald's work. Aelfhild peeked around the boat's prow. An Oescan bowman had dropped Immin's companion. Immin dove across the gap and put his knife into the attacker's belly. The two rolled across the sand. The fight did not last long. "Run!" shouted Immin, and took off toward their horses. He dragged one useless leg in the sand; a snapped arrow protruded from his thigh.

One of the Oescans was either cleverer or better trained than his fellow legionnaires. He burst through the tents on horseback, sword drawn, and bore down on Immin. Aelfhild was already halfway to her horse and there was nothing she could do. The sword dipped, the hooves trampled. Immin fell.

"Spear!" Godwyn yelled. Aelfhild tossed it to him and dropped to the sand.

His aim was true; Godwyn lifted the man from his saddle with a heaving cast of the spear. The horse kept running and kicked sandy soil over Aelfhild's head. She heard the patter of stones against her helmet.

Godwyn pulled her up, and they ran to the horses. "Ride! Ride!" he called.

There were hoofbeats behind them, but Aelfhild was focused on one thing: staying in the saddle. She kicked at her mount and hoped that the gelding knew the path, because her helmet flopped down over her eyes and she could only clutch at the saddle. Up and down the hard leather hammered her innards as the horse's hooves tore the ground. They came to a bend in the track. Aelfhild could not see, but she did feel it. The horse dipped or leaned or shifted somehow as it scrabbled for footing around the curve and she lost her long battle with momentum. She hit the ground with her shoulder. This time she remembered to roll. The loam and her ill-fitting armor took the brunt of the hit.

She knocked the cursed helmet off her head in time to watch from the bushes as another Oescan horseman galloped past. Godwyn would have to deal with his pursuer. Aelfhild's horse had not lingered to see what befell its rider.

Smoke billowed up over the treetops. They had done what they set out to do. The day was won. She swallowed. Victory felt decidedly hollow when she knew each face that paid for it. Maybe that was why Sigurd never stayed for the feast.

2 4

ELFHILD WAITED FOR the others at their camp. She tried to eat. Her stomach was not up to task and her hands were still jittering too much to get a morsel to her lips. It was a long wait. Toward sunset, Godwyn returned. He was on foot and shed of his Oescan armor. He grinned at Aelfhild, but the mirth never made it to his eyes. "We showed them, eh?"

She smiled in return but knew it would look equally empty.

He broke off a piece of venison from his pack and offered it to her. When she refused, he tried to buoy both their spirits. "The Oescans will need to do more than that to spoil my appetite, I say." Neither of them had the heart for it, though. He trailed off and ate in silence.

Dark had fallen when Sabert came trudging through the thicket. He carried another rebel over his shoulder; both were doused with blood. Godwyn helped Sabert lay the wounded man down, but two fingers to his throat and Aelfhild knew there was nothing they could do. She shook her head at Sabert. His shoulders fell. He walked to the edge of the wood and bided there for a time.

When he returned, Aelfhild asked the question she had been dreading. "Is this all of us?"

"Likely," he replied. "I saw Bertwald fall myself. He took a band of them with him. The rest . . ." He flicked his hand out into the night.

"We saw Immin fall," Aelfhild said, "and . . ." She still could not recall the other man's name.

"And Raedwald." Godwyn supplied it. He likely had not meant it as such, but the words had the sting of a rebuke.

The tears started to build, hot and with more to come. Her stomach clenched into a throbbing knot. Godwyn had to look away to hide his own watering eyes. He was still young. Not all youth's sensitivity had been burned away from him yet.

Though he did not look much older, Sabert had a better hold on himself. He looked angry, instead. His lips drew down into flat, pale lines. "Every man here wanted to fight. They wanted to fight for Norholt and for my father—for the Eorl. We all knew what was at stake. We have been one step from death in these woods since long before you got here," he said, staring down at her. "They died fighting for their home. They died on their feet—"

"They died *for* something." Godwyn broke in, scuffing at his cheeks. "You gave us that."

Aelfhild swept tears away with the edge of her tunic. Words would not come out, so she nodded her head and snorted. The men fidgeted; consoling women was not something they had expected or practiced, clearly. Eventually they left her to sort herself out.

It was all a tangle. Sabert was right, but only partly. All the Norholtings were their own men, no question, and men of war. She respected that. She remembered a speech she had given to Ceolwen ages ago when she had felt young. She had believed it herself then. But now? Everything she touched fell to pieces. In her wake were pain and death, so much that they made the few good deeds pale. There had been a plan. She had ignored it and wrought this instead.

And she had thought it was fun. Exciting—an adventure. She had even had a cute little name for them: *rebels.* Now they were dead and all for nothing. It was time to grow up and put stupid, childish dreams aside. The stories stayed stories. The endings were grim. No heroes and no gods were coming to save them.

Godwyn, much to his credit, tried to keep things light the next morning. He walked just ahead of Aelfhild and peppered jokes into his stories. Sabert was somewhere out in front with his bow and no inclination for small talk.

Aelfhild envied him.

She mostly tuned her companion out. He seemed to need no replies; he must have been used to such a reception. There were other things on her mind. They had burned the boats, though at such cost. That hindered the legion and thwarted Osric for a short while, maybe a fortnight, but it solved nothing. Not really. If she could sneak in among the legion at night, though, perhaps she could get to the prisoners. Free Jarngrim and Eyvind at least. She could slip in disguised as a servant.

And get them all killed trying to escape. Her plans were getting worse. She hated that her brain would not stop with them. Sabert and Godwyn had given enough. She had taken enough. Cuthbert told her to go north. It was past time to listen.

Something Godwyn said finally registered. "What did you say?"

The question broke his flow. "When? About the goats?"

"What? No, you said Bertwald had a son."

"Oh, aye," Godwyn fell back into his cadence. "His name was Bercthun. Good lad but not the best thinker, if I were honest. He got snarled up in all that business with the Eorl's cousin and Osric. I heard tell that he went on a grand trek up to the realms of those Thrym beasts and never returned."

It hardly mattered now, but she could have said something if she had known. Bertwald might have heard about the man his son had become. Or where his son came to his last rest. Maybe it was for the better he had never heard that part.

Mistaking silence for interest, her guide resumed his previous story about the family goat farm.

Poor Bercthun. *I made it home for you, old friend. For all of us. And then I got your father killed.* This was about as far from piety as Aelfhild had ever felt; it was hard to see any mercy, let alone kindness, in the workings of the Gods. Bercthun had deserved a homecoming. His father had deserved a proper burial. The good seldom got what they deserved. Across the lake,

Osric still reclined atop a throne. She was still walking free. Maybe this was another subtle punishment. Maybe it was just the way of things.

Sabert put an end to the banter. He whistled from up ahead and Godwyn motioned for Aelfhild to follow in silence, as though she were the greater risk.

They had circled around behind the legion and stood now on a spruce-crowned hillock overlooking the Oescans' progress. There was a vanguard ahead, a bristling wedge of heavy infantry, then a long column of wagons pulled by ox or mule teams. Valerius and his glittering command staff, all riding, naturally, followed the last cart. The Legate was surrounded by marching ranks of shields and swords. Nothing was getting through to him. Though, on closer inspection, the legion did not seem so hale. Legionnaires dragged their tower shields in the dirt. Bandages peeked out from under armor or swaddled helmless heads. Their shoulders were bent and their ranks passed in loose file; the Oescans had lost as much spirit as blood during the siege, from the looks of it.

Prisoners brought up the rear. The guard was surprisingly light. At this distance Aelfhild could not pick out faces among the captives. They were all chained together, and each man was bound hand and foot, so the risk was small and the watchmen sparse. Cuthbert would have been under heavier guard. Aelfhild guessed that the Eorl rode up with the Legate; likely still in chains, but honors where honors were due and all that.

Sabert said, "I can see your thoughts, lass, plain as the ears on those jackasses down there."

"Planning again." Godwyn smirked.

Aelfhild's cheeks burned. "No. I was just looking."

Sabert pointed toward Valerius's party. "I reckon my father is down there with the fancy ones."

Aelfhild shook her head. "There is nothing we can do. I have to go north and find Jarl Harald."

Godwyn sucked his teeth. "Here I thought you were one for the fight."

"Leave it," said Sabert. "She knows her business. Sometimes it is better to leave the decisions to those that know about such things, lad."

Godwyn turned back toward the woods they had wandered through. "Do you hear barking?"

Sabert continued, turning to Aelfhild, "But if we can pick off a few guards quiet-like, we can get the prisoners free and fighting. Wait till the main body is across the river and they will never turn back for that. It will be bloody work. But none of us goes alone. What was it you said? A companion more than doubles the warrior's strength?"

She had said that. Now the words crumbled to ash. Life was not that romantic.

"I thought I heard barking," said Godwyn to no one in particular.

"What?"

"What?" Aelfhild listened. She heard it, too. It sounded familiar. She hated to let hope get her in its snares once more.

2 5

ELFHILD TORE OFF in the direction the baying had come from. Her ankle was still stiff and swollen purple, though, so Godwyn and Sabert had an easy time keeping up.

"Careful." Sabert kept his voice low as he jogged along behind. "Could be trackers." He kept an arrow in hand and nudged Godwyn to do the same.

Please let it be her. The barks were few and far apart, but each one was a few paces closer. Aelfhild chanted as she half ran, half limped. *Please let it be her.* She had resisted hope's pull at the start but now it was too late and she was lost to those dreamy depths. *Please let it be her.*

Everything could be forgiven between her and the Gods for this one moment. She would sacrifice something big. Someday.

Another bark, downhill and deeper into the forest, away from the legion. It came from the north. All the signs were right. If it turned out not to be Embla barking, then Aelfhild would be angry enough to take on the entire legion herself. The Oescans would have to turn and flee her wrath.

And there she was, crooked silver tail wagging madly, tongue lolling from her jaws, and golden eyes agleam.

"Embla!" Aelfhild screamed. Her dragging foot snagged at the last moment, and she tumbled onto the hound. Embla seemed happy enough with that outcome. She was wriggling and slobbering over every bit of Aelfhild's face.

"Wait! Easy now! Back up!" Sabert and Godwyn were shouting. They did not share Aelfhild's joy.

"It is fine," Aelfhild said between gasps, "she is my dog. It is fine."

"Tell your friends not to shoot me." There was Kolbrun.

Aelfhild pushed Embla aside. The shieldmaiden had followed the hound out of a stand of trees, hands spread before her. She wore a studded hauberk with leather trimmings, satchel and shield slung over her back, an axe at her hip, and red war paint. "She is a friend," Aelfhild said to her companions in Earnfolding and stood to face Kolbrun. They embraced. Aelfhild dribbled a little on the shieldmaiden's shoulder, and was only slightly ashamed of it.

Kolbrun, for her part, thumbed at her nose as they parted. She inspected Aelfhild. "Embla caught a scent. I hoped there would be more, but one is plenty. You look like I thought you would."

Aelfhild let herself laugh. She felt a thousand years younger. The grime and grief rolled away; the world was, for a fleeting, solitary moment, better. "So do you."

A nervous cough came from behind. They were not alone. Aelfhild turned. "Sabert, you met Kolbrun."

"I, uh, did not recognize you. Many apologies."

"With that hit you took the last time I saw you, it would be lucky if you remembered aught." Kolbrun snorted.

Godwyn sniggered.

"And this is Godwyn. Godwyn, Kolbrun." Aelfhild pointed to the younger man. The shieldmaiden grunted. "There is so much to tell you! Eyvind is alive, but the Oescans have him, I think. Jarngrim, too, I think. We fought in the siege, but I had to jump out a window. Cuthbert was there but now the Oescans have him. Are you with Harald? Is Onund with you?" Aelfhild was babbling, partly in Thrym but with bits in Earnfolding as well. She could not stop. "We burned the boats yesterday. I thought you would never come, but you did. Why did they take so long? If they were not so slow, everything would be good and they would all be alive! Why were they so slow?"

Kolbrun grabbed her arm as she sagged forward. Her eyes had gone misty now. She lowered Aelfhild to the ground. "Easy now. I am here. Easy. Forgive me."

In Aelfhild's imagination, the reunion had played out with a good deal more grace. Even with her head between her knees, sweating and gasping for air, she felt lighter than she could ever remember. Kolbrun would not make things worse. Kolbrun was strong enough to set things right. She reached out and clapped a hand on the shieldmaiden's shoulder. "Tell me you brought more."

The grin on the Thrym's face was feral. "I brought plenty. Follow me." Kolbrun led them downhill. Embla trailed behind, licking Aelfhild's fingers. The hound growled if either Sabert or Godwyn got too close. Aelfhild was hers and hers alone.

Whistles preceded them. Kolbrun put fingers to her lips and blew, and the replies fanned out across the wood. Aelfhild and her friends were not the only ones watching the legion move. The Thrym were here. A shadow shifting behind a tree or twigs shaking on a bush—those were all the signs Aelfhild could see of Harald's skirmishers. They would need more than that and she almost said so, but Kolbrun led on.

They crested a ravine and looked down on the might of the Thrym. Two hundred men, maybe more, sat or sprawled on the ground, waiting. They rested on shields, sharpened axes, or cinched belts tighter around ringmail coats. Each man was strapped with half a dozen blades and bore the red and silver of the Leifings on their shields. The crimson of Trollsmork against the purple of Oesca. Aelfhild shivered. She saw burnished helms with their broad faceguards, and remembered the first one she encountered. Faceless warriors. Blood specters.

Eyvind and Jarngrim were coming home. Today.

"Did you find them?" Harald shoved one of his bodyguards out of the way as he spotted Kolbrun.

She bowed. "Just one, lord. He is down with the legion."

The Jarl kept his face placid. Aelfhild thought his shoulders dipped, ever so slightly, but he knew how to maintain the royal mask. "Well done, skjaldmaer. We shall have him back soon enough. The others, too."

"Aye, my jarl. This is Aelfhild, of whom I spoke."

Jarl Harald was decked in fur-trimmed splendor. There was a splash of mud on his boots and brambles snared in the hem of his cloak, but he shone from every iron link and plate. In a few places, among the white, his hair retained the same ruddy hue as his son's. Aelfhild saw the familiar broad cheekbones and grey eyes there, though Harald's nose had a proud aquiline cast that Eyvind's headstrong living had cost him. How she looked forward to seeing that mashed, lopsided nose again. "Lord." She bowed low. She hoped Kolbrun had not told him too much. Better to shift his focus elsewhere. "Jarl Harald, I present Sabert Cuthbertsunu and his man, Godwyn."

The Jarl spared a nod for the serving girl and breezed past to greet Sabert. "Young Sabert, welcome and well met. I have heard much about you from your dear father. We have so much to discuss, you and I. Come, I imagine you are famished." And with a twirl of ermine and brocade, Harald and the Norholtings were away down the ravine to tour the assembled army.

Aelfhild leaned over to Kolbrun as she watched the men depart. "How much did you tell him?"

"Enough," Kolbrun replied. "Not *that*. I leave that joy to you." The shieldmaiden crinkled her nose as she leaned in. "Come now. You need fresh clothes. And an axe."

Aelfhild did not argue. "Some food, too," she said.

2 6

ER HANDS WERE shaking. She wanted to be as steady as Kolbrun, who stood beside her the picture of pristine calm. She pressed her palms against her thighs to steady them.

The shieldmaiden must have noticed. "Fear keeps you sharp. Do not run from it."

Aelfhild nodded. Embla could sense her nerves as well. The hound nuzzled against the back of her knee. Even the dog was more battle-tested than she was.

"Stay on my right. This should be light work. We make for the prisoners at the rear column. Leave the heavy lifting to the Jarl's brutes up there." And brutes they were. Harald had a company of huskarls with him, armored in scale from head to toe and each bearing a swept-blade greataxe as tall as Aelfhild herself. They were the line breakers, the shield splitters. A human—or mostly human, anyway, some of the hulks must have had giant blood in their ancestry—battering ram. Valerius would never know what rolled over him.

She bent to pick up her shield and tightened the strap around her forearm. She checked the buckle twice. And a third time. No risks today.

"Ready?" Kolbrun whispered.

Again, Aelfhild nodded. She scarcely trusted her voice not to quaver, so she saved her words.

"On my right."

She followed the shieldmaiden up the leaf-strewn slope.

The forest rustled and clanked as the Thrym advanced. There were no horns yet. Hopefully the Oescans did not even know an army was upon them; now was the time for positioning. The charge would come, and right soon. Aelfhild clamped the helm down on her dripping brow. The world was focused into two half-moon slits. Someone else was doing the planning. Someone else bore the weight. Her world consisted of keeping Kolbrun's sword arm and shoulder in her left eye without faltering.

Harald was at the far end of the line with Sabert and, probably, Godwyn. The Jarl would be in the shield wall at its thickest. There were a few things to dislike about Harald. On that point Aelfhild would not quibble. But just as with Cuthbert, cowardice was not one.

"Breathe, Aela." Kolbrun sounded so cursedly calm.

Aelfhild let slip a shaky breath. Nothing to hide behind but her shield. No wall. No gate. No stealth, no surprises. She knew exactly what lay on the other side of the trees.

"Stay on my right. Pay no mind to the battle cries. Find Eyvind. Find Jarngrim," Kolbrun repeated.

There was a rattle, from up the line and proceeding down as men raised their shields. Embla growled low and constantly.

The drumming started. Axe heads against shields. Clang. Clang. Clang. Aelfhild drummed along with the rhythm. Clang. Clang. Clang. Clang. It began to quicken.

Then they were hammering fast as could be. Red flecks began to dance into her vision. *Here we go.*

The warhorn blew and they broke through the tree line at a sprint. Branches whipped at her helmet. She kept Kolbrun in her left eye, though the bloodlust was swirling, rising around her. The line breakers collided with the Oescan formation, which had not even managed to deploy fully. There was a palpable crunch. Screams, cracks. Blood's metallic scent in the air.

An Oescan in front of them. He was on the back foot and only just hefting his weapon. Kolbrun turned the pilum with her shield and split the man from shoulder to chest with an arcing blow. Aelfhild heard the patter of liquid against her faceplate. The shieldmaiden kicked the man free from her blade and they ran on to the line of carts.

Someone lunged up from behind a wagon. He thrust a bill hook at Aelfhild's head as he sprang; she heard the swish of air across the tip as she barely turned the blow with the top of her shield. Before she could recover, the hooked blade was swinging back around. The long shaft of the polearm gave him greater reach. She skipped back a step. The blade scythed past. Frothing at the mouth, he advanced and screamed southern curses. His only protection was momentum. He wore no armor, and both hands gripped the shaft of the weapon. Her hand tensed around the axe handle. She knew what had to come next. She threw her shield forward. The descending blade struck her shield boss and rebounded. The man's arms flew skyward. She swung her axe. It found his ribs.

Spurting flesh drew her blade in deeper, pulled her closer. Froth around his mouth turned from white to pink as he sagged. His eyes were fixed on her until he struck the ground. She imagined the blank faceplate, broken only by two bottomless pits, reflecting back to him his last ragged breath. Her axe pulled free on the second try. She wished the red spots were thick enough to cloud her vision.

"On my right, Aela!" Kolbrun cried. Another body lay at her feet. "Go, Embla, seek! Seek!" The hound loped off, muscles bunched and still growling.

Aelfhild's limbs were numb as she followed. Her heels dragged on the ground. In the distance the Thrym shouted to one another. She could catch fragments of that. Oescans babbled. Donkeys brayed and mixed the smell of panicking animals to the dust and sweat.

Most of the fighting was down the line, but the battle had never been more than one-sided. The Oescans broke at the first hit. A few mad souls stayed to die, but as Valerius and his horsemen fled so did the legion's backbone dissolve. Some cast themselves down to surrender. Most dropped arms and sprinted for the river.

Embla was howling. "With me, Aela!" Kolbrun yelled.

A man loomed in front of Aelfhild. She froze with axe raised. He lifted chains before her. She struck, knocking manacles loose, and followed after the shieldmaiden.

The war horn was blowing again, many peals this time. Exaltation. Aelfhild pulled the bloodied helmet from her head and tossed it into the path muddied by thronging feet. She wanted it away from her. Red still ringed her vision, but not enough to blind. She could breathe, though her chest heaved and chafed against the iron armor.

Kolbrun was ahead with Embla. The hound was wagging, even more than when she had found Aelfhild.

Eyvind was there, trussed in irons. He leaned on Jarngrim for support, though the latter was bandaged over one eye and wore a sling about his shield arm. Both men sported toothy smiles.

Aelfhild wiped at her face. Her hand came away bloody. Along her cheeks and chin, where the faceguard had not covered, was a slick, crusting smear. She turned away from her friends, welcome sight though they were, and emptied the contents of her stomach onto the path.

"Strip the carts! Keep anything worthy and burn the rest!" Harald strode down the line shouting orders of his own. "Get those men up, you! Cuthbert's lot to one side. Oescans down lakeward. Knock his chains off, you fool. We came to save these ones."

Some of Cuthbert's men tried to follow the Oescans in flight. The Thrym breaking through the tree line was a sight fit to freeze the boldest man's blood, and axes were hardly smart enough to tell ally from foe. A few of the Earnfolding prisoners cowered, knees tucked against chests and hands over heads. Others legged it for the river alongside their captors. Even in chains, a chance with the rapids was better than being trampled beneath some raging savage's hobnails.

Sabert was shouting from farther down the line. "Norholt to me! Stay your running! Hear me, Norholt!" It did little good. He lacked his father's booming voice.

The yelling only increased as the tumult of battle faded. Men had crawled under siege wagons to escape their attackers, some of them Oescan and some Earnfolding. Thrym raiders yanked them out and threw them to the earth. All the sides shouted at one another in different tongues. One of Harald's brutes raised his axe over a cowering prisoner.

"Friend!" Aelfhild stepped into the warrior's face to yell. Spittle flew in every direction. The Thrym brute backed away and went in search of another outlet for his fury.

Aelfhild had seen her friends for just a moment between bouts of retching, but the chaos billowed around them all. She had no choice but to jump in. "All Earnfoldings stand your ground! Show them your chains!" she yelled. "Your chains!"

The Jarl leaned over to one of his grey-bearded followers. "How many of ours lost?"

"A score wounded, my jarl. One may die tonight; the Gods will decide. Three already dead."

"Anyone I should know?"

"One boy was Sveinn's grandson. Died well, lord, so I am told."

"Fat Sveinn?"

"Aye, lord."

"He is an old stalwart. The boy died with honor. Sveinn will understand." Then Harald spotted Aelfhild. "You, girl! Where is my son?"

"Just here, lord." She led the way.

"Eyvind! My boy!"

"Father!"

It was easy to scorn Harald from a distance. His scheming, the self-serving piety, the way he used folk just to cast them aside when they were spent. He had every symptom of nobility and Aelfhild respected him only as one might respect a serpent—amazingly apt in form and purpose, but too slippery and venomous by far. Up close, though, his tears were real.

"My boy," the Jarl whispered as he clutched his son. "We feared the worst."

"You taught me to handle the worst, old man," Eyvind replied, thumping his father's back.

"Ha!" Harald held Eyvind at arm's distance and inspected him. "You look well enough after all the skjaldmaer told me. Born for the fight, you are, fit to make our ancestors proud. Come now, come! Everything to see to."

Eyvind looked back as the Jarl half dragged him away. "It was them that saved me, Father. My friends." He fell into another coughing fit, though his hacking was not nearly as wet or as wrenching as when Aelfhild had last seen him.

"You need a good meal, my son, and a rest. Everything to see to still, plans to be made. We did not manage to nab our cousin Cuthbert. But as fate would have it, his son is with us. We can sort your friends out after the rest." Harald drifted off into a crowd of his huskarls. The warriors were flocking in to their lord to hear new orders or to show off looted treasures. Legate Valerius had left a wagon of his personal stores behind. Word of gold and stones spread through the Thrym quickly.

Aelfhild watched them go. "That was the thanks we get?"

"Seems about right," Jarngrim said. He was massaging his wrists. The sling had vanished and the eyepatch had gone to reveal a perfectly intact eyeball beneath. He noticed Aelfhild's consternation. "That was all the toothy one's idea. He thought if I slapped a few rags on they might not look too close."

"Toothy one?" Kolbrun cocked an eyebrow.

"We have much to tell," Jarngrim replied. "But first, tell me you brought mead."

The shieldmaiden grunted. She craned her neck, staring farther along the muddle of Thrym, Earnfolding, and cowering Oescans. "He will want to move out soon."

"Grab what you can, then." Jarngrim clapped a hand on Aelfhild's shoulder. "Anything metal is worth keeping, you follow?" He lifted a pilum abandoned by some legionnaire and snapped the long iron point from the wooden handle. "Make a bundle. Iron, copper, bronze. They will have stripped any gold by now."

It was like watching ants working over a carcass. Everything not nailed down was fair game for the raiders, though some were even levering up the bolts and flanges in the wagons. Aelfhild was still unsteady on her feet. Her thoughts were skittish and slippery, sounds from the outside world were muted and bent as though she were listening from underwater. Trudging around, she managed to snag a broken sword, some iron points, and a notched copper knife from the strewn spoils. She was staring at an overturned wagon when a brawny raider came and shoved her aside. The man bulged and bristled, he was fat but clearly had muscle beneath.

Hair sprouted from every knuckle and earhole. He did not look keen to discuss sharing rights, so Aelfhild left him to root through the wreckage unchallenged.

Sabert had a cluster of his father's men gathered along a ditch off the path. Those that had recovered from their shock shifted nervously as they watched the Thrym at work. Aelfhild passed a group of raiders who were tossing corpses down the far bank. It was the limp, flapping arms as the bodies rolled into a pile at the bottom—it made her heave again. She looked away and moved on but could still hear the impact as each Oescan landed.

Kolbrun and Jarngrim had a trove spread out on a raggedy cloak when she wandered back. "Throw it in, sharpish!" Jarngrim rolled up the bundle, tied it off, and slung it over his back. Anyone who dared approach got a scowl.

Aelfhild watched a fistfight break out over a roll of silken cloth. "I thought we were on the same side?"

Kolbrun shrugged. "Fighting Oescans is one thing, looting is another."

It was all too familiar. She surveyed the battlefield. Here was the rescue she had so eagerly awaited. And such grand heroes they were, carrying off armfuls of boots and bulging sacks of shattered blades.

"Moving out!" came the cry, passed down along the remains of the caravan.

"Moving out! Burn the rest!"

They left smoke behind and blood crusting in the dirt. Oescan prisoners were set loose, stripped bare but alive. Fast and light, the Jarl said. This was no slave convoy. Sabert and his men joined in. The Eorl's son took pride of place alongside the Jarl at the front. The path led back toward Wynnthwait and along the river, though Harald had them on it for only part of the afternoon. They cut north into the woods at a turning and made for Thrymgard.

Aelfhild fell in with her friends at the rear of the marching order. She loped along beside Jarngrim, who was hard at work explaining all that had unfolded to Kolbrun while she had been away. Every time he waved his hands the bundle on his back would jangle. "So the wall fell in, like the earth just gobbled it whole, and the Oescans were crawling up out of the pit like ghouls. You never saw such a thing. But you know who was first to get stuck in?" He jerked a thumb toward Aelfhild. "This one."

He was embroidering the story with a heavy hand. Aelfhild was not keen. Kolbrun would think it trifling if she believed it at all. It was too much. There were more important things to focus on, besides. She tried to change the subject.

"How far is it to Herjarsborg?"

"A week, maybe a tenday. The wounded will slow us down." Jarngrim broke from his story just long enough to answer, then he was right back to the tale. Worse still, Kolbrun seemed to be paying heed.

"It seems we would go faster without the oxen," Aelfhild said. She might not be able to stop his gabbing, but she could at least break up the flow of the story. "We could have left them."

"An army needs to eat." Kolbrun chuckled.

2 7

THE OESCANS WERE an enemy shared by both the Thrym and the Earnfoldings. The Oescans were not, however, present. That meant the Thrym and the Earnfoldings had to make do fighting one another. Aelfhild spoke both tongues, so she got to play translator and peacemaker. Many of the gathered men spoke their opponents' language at least as well as Aelfhild did, but in the presence of their fellows and spoiling for any trifle to fight over they had all conveniently forgotten. Sabert and Harald were Gods only knew where, so it fell once again to Aelfhild to step in.

"Bugger that," Godwyn replied. "It is my knife. Tell him he is a rotting sneak thief and a liar."

Aelfhild did not. The Thrym in question was not the same man that had pushed her aside a few days earlier but could have passed for his twin. A worrying number of Harald's men shared that same boar-like quality: pockmarked skin bristling with coarse hair and ink. This one had forearms that bulged like cured hams.

"It is mine. It has my mark on it." The man did not have to raise his voice like Godwyn. He towered over both of them.

"Your mother never learned you to write, Knut, come off it." Jarngrim sat cross-legged atop a nearby fallen log, Kolbrun at his side. Both still held their breakfast.

"Mine," Knut repeated.

Godwyn clearly did not know when to give ground. He glowered up at the would-be thief. "Mine."

Out of the corner of her eye, Aelfhild thought she saw Jarngrim nudge Kolbrun with his elbow. This was all good sport to them. She sighed as more men began drifting toward the confrontation. She made one last stab at peace. "Godwyn, you are going to lose more teeth if you keep this up."

"What is mine is mine!" This got a cheer from the assembled blood of Norholt.

Aelfhild stalked off to join her friends. By the time she reached the stump the scuffle was under way. Kolbrun handed her a strip of pale meat. The Oescan mules had disappeared yesterday evening. It was not unpleasant—a tad dry.

"I tried," Aelfhild said through a full mouth.

Jarngrim whistled as an Earnfolding drove a haymaker into a Thrym brawler's chin. "You can try to stop the tide next, if you want a simpler task."

Dunstan's birdlike figure, all knobby knees and elbows, was picking its way through the flailing legs and scattered packs. He had survived the siege as well. It turned out there was more grit to the little man than his form suggested. He bobbed up to Aelfhild.

"Fair morning." He pointed toward the fray. Godwyn was head-butting the porcine thief, who had tried to smother him in a bear hug. "Should we—"

"Better to let some fights happen," Kolbrun answered. There were barbs fixed to each word, and not aimed at Dunstan. She proffered him a side of mule. "Breakfast?"

Dunstan paled. He was not at home. The Oescans had not allowed him to fetch his precious tomes before they marched him off. The southerners had proved far less enlightened than the sage might have hoped. Legionnaires were not interested in his thoughts on herb lore. His fellow Earnfoldings were not either, and as far as the Thrym warriors were concerned Knut was one of their nimbler thinkers. Dunstan needed a friend. Aelfhild knew what it was like to be a stray.

"March with us today, Dunstan?" she asked.

His smile shone bright around the gaps. "My privilege, certainly."

"Enough! Break away, you lot!" Sabert came in with the flat of his sword. "You, too, Godwyn." The brawlers had all swung themselves tired by that point, so the anger had passed. There was the requisite finger pointing and blame passing, but Sabert paid no mind. He drove his men off with kicks and curses.

Shaking her head, Kolbrun said, "All the hounds have pissed on their little trees for the day."

Knut sat up and pressed sausage-thick fingers against his dribbling nose. He seemed used to that outcome. He trundled off with his Thrym brothers.

Jarngrim looked up from his meal. "Who got the knife?"

No one knew.

Eyvind limped his way through the field of flattened ferns and crushed pinecones. He shook his head at the mess. Behind him Embla sniffed for any spilled morsels. She stopped to nibble a suspect twig.

"What news from the Jarl, O master?" Kolbrun called. She held out her fork with its joint of skewered mule. "Breakfast?" The shieldmaiden shrugged as he waved it off.

Eyvind moaned when he sat. "I cannot take any more. I march with you today. If he tells me that the Gods have great plans for us one more time, things will get bloody."

"They have the horses up there. You should ride while you can," Jarngrim said and hefted what was left of a rib. "Rest up."

"I am done resting."

Divided loyalties seemed to be weighing on poor Embla's spirits; Eyvind was in one place, but the rest of her pack was lagging behind. She thrust her shaggy muzzle onto Aelfhild's lap and whined. The hound's full-moon stare said that only abundant ear scratches, or maybe pieces of roast mule, could lift her from despair. Aelfhild obliged with both. No one could deny that pouting, silvered face.

Kolbrun slung her satchel and bedroll across her back. Jarngrim dropped the bundle of looted goods into Dunstan's arms. "Carry this." The healer scuttled after the pair as they joined the assembling column.

Aelfhild offered a hand to Eyvind. He wheezed as she pulled him to his feet. "Never mind all that," he said. "I can keep up."

Out of the corner of her eye, she marked him scratching at his chest again. "Does it still bother you?"

"What?"

It took all her patience not to grab hold of him and yank back his tunic. Instead, her answer was serene as a mountain glade, as only years of being a servant could teach. "Your wound."

"The skin just pulls a bit tight, is all."

That left Aelfhild chewing the inside of her lip. He might be lying to her. Or it might be spreading inside him and he just did not feel it yet. She remembered the glowing veins in the dream. The thought that her vision might have been wrong did not find any purchase. That earthquake had been real enough and, as Jarngrim had said, when had their luck ever been that good?

"Did I ever say thank you?" Eyvind asked.

"No, you never did."

"I will."

She caught his grin but struggled to match it. Kolbrun was waiting up ahead. She motioned for Aelfhild to join her. The shieldmaiden ran her thumb up and down the leather-sheathed edge of her axe as they walked. Aelfhild found herself sympathizing. They marched in silence until Eyvind, Jarngrim, and Dunstan were a few paces ahead and wrapped up in conversations of their own.

Kolbrun cleared her throat. "I did not tell the Jarl about your hand, but I cannot keep it from him forever. Truthfulness is part of my bond to him. My holding this back breaks that."

"I am not asking you to lie," Aelfhild started.

"Are you not?" The edge was back in her voice. "Aela, you understand as well as any other that what little I have, I must work twice again as hard for. I should be off bearing some man's children by now as far as they are concerned. Eyvind can lie to his father. You can lie to his father. I cannot. My oath is all I have, bought with all the strength my body can muster."

Aelfhild stared at the ground in front of her. She picked at the glove covering the rune. "Just a while more," she said. Eyvind's back was to them, but she watched him walking. She was charting a blind course, and with rocks all around; she needed to talk to him alone.

"Sort out what you must," Kolbrun said, "but I cannot lie for much longer."

An endless plain of snow stretched out before her. Where once there had been a driving blizzard, there was now a slack breeze. A few flakes drifted by, sometimes a gust rose enough to kick up an eddy in the white, but it was nothing compared to the earlier storm.

Aelfhild turned and saw the wall of clouds. She was right under them, close enough to see starless void through gaps in the billowing grey on the far side. Storm clouds above her swirled up and dashed themselves against the invisible middle barrier between the two skies. Chunks of ice stood out of the snow in either direction. Some reached just above her head; others were large enough to crush all of Wynnthwait beneath their towering expanse. She remembered how her last dream had ended and looked back over her shoulder. There was nothing but snow.

As the wall of ice had fallen, it had freed more than just Eyvind's twisted form. What had been blocky outlines before were now soaring towers, arches, and spires of hewn stone raised along the border line. It was no style Aelfhild could recognize. Each spire came to a brutal pyramid point, and jutted at unsettling angles from the larger towers. There was no grace in these arches; the sides rose too high, and there was a bulging capstone in each that looked as though it would fall inward with the slightest push. Stairs, carved of the same dark, crystal-specked rock, ran down from the mouth of one arch.

Aelfhild peered down into the darkness. She shivered. Her dreams had never before posed a threat, but that did not make her eager.

The steps were set so deep and wide that she had to slide herself over the edge of one to drop down onto the next. They continued into the deep until she reckoned herself to be on the night side of the barrier. There was no noticeable change to the air.

At the foot of the stairs, the stonework changed to lighter marble. This white stone had its own soft glow, providing the only illumination. There was no ceiling in the gloom. The walls were pale hints in the very distance. A lump stuck out of the marble a few steps ahead. It stood out, all lopsided and gnarled, against the perfect angles and level blocks. Aelfhild bent and felt it. A thorn pricked her finger. Fingerling vines rose from a few cracks in the floor and ran back into the hall. The outer rind was hard as aged oakwood, veiny, and covered with hooked points. She followed them along.

The vines thickened as they furled and ran into a tangle of others, arising from all directions along the stone, and cascaded down as an entwined curtain into the pit of an amphitheater set into the marble. From the central, sandy bowl rose a swollen, thorn-speckled knot that pulsed with inner light. It reminded Aelfhild of the light on her palm, but a redder sunset hue.

Drub. Drub. A heartbeat came from the burl. *Drub. Drub.*

She paused. There was no other movement. No viney tentacles whipped at her legs. No bark-wrought guardians arose to protect the root. It was clearly an invader in this otherwise pristine edifice, but there was no sign of struggle. She lowered herself down the tiers of the amphitheater, ducking around thorns grown to dagger size and glimmering sharply. It was impossible to tell if the roots sprang forth from a central node within the heart, or if all the thousands of tendrils had wriggled in and converged to form a tumor within its marble host. There was no discernible age to the vines; thicker and thinner, they were all the same petrified brown hue, streaked by suppler green along the curves and bulges.

Drub drub. Drub drub. Little by little the beat quickened. The heart slowly stirred, but it was still at a snail's pace compared to her own feeble, human pulse. It was stirring, though, unmistakably, stirring to life or wakefulness or to some unknowable purpose.

Aelfhild dropped onto the bottom tier and stepped in the sand. The heart held her full attention. Both her arms outstretched would cover maybe a quarter of the knot's surface, though the thorns would never let her close enough. On each downbeat, light pulsed brighter through the cracks. Something jabbed into the skin of her foot. She skipped back onto marble. Looking down, it was a bird's skull. She bent to pick it up. A meat-eater, most definitely. Hawk, eagle, buzzard. The delicate bone was spotless, but yellowed by long years, and ran down to a black, hooked beak. Sand trailed from the empty sockets and glittered in the nostrils. Now a speck of blood darkened the point of the beak.

As her attention shifted to the pit, she saw the bones. The curved horn and long spine of a bull's skull, half a hollow eye staring back over the sand. The knobbled end of a thighbone too large for humankind. Ribs, shoulder blades, bird and beast, upright fragments of claws and finger bones that made it look as if their owners had died scrabbling in vain against sinking sand. Some she recognized, others she could not. It was hard to tell which had come first, the sand or the bones. Perhaps the sand was all the remained of bones that had been left aeons to weather. Vines grew over and through the boneyard.

Aelfhild watched the thorn heart. *Drub drub. Drub drub.* She poked the point of the bird's skull into her palm, and watched as shadows cast in red flickered around her. As with all things of late, she suspected that whatever this was, it was her fault.

2 8

THE FOREST WAS still. Dawn arrived a perfect calm, and there was enough mist clinging to the spruce trunks to make Aelfhild feel alone. There were others out there, gathering firewood or tending to their morning needs, but they were obscured by the fog and easy enough to ignore. She stretched.

To the north was Herjarsborg. All of Harald's plotting would come to a head there. War would come to her homeland. It would be waged in her name, if not for her sake, if he found out about the rune. To the south was home. Or what once had been. Now Osric was there and Ceolwen was not. Her only friends were a few paces away now, but each of them had loyalties that would pull them elsewhere. To the west were mountains. She could not see them through the trees, but she knew ice white peaks broke through the clouds a few leagues distant. And then, beyond that, the wilds—empty and free.

There were a few scraps of food in the sack she had snatched up when no one was watching, along with a flint striker and a knife. She had armor, she had an axe. Hunting would be a challenge, but she was lean, and Kolbrun had taught her much. Summer would last a few moons longer. Once she was across the Grimbergs she could cut south and avoid the worst of winter.

Running was a plan. It would be a while before anyone missed her. Aelfhild looked back over her shoulder. She was alone but she kept check-ing. Her legs felt stiff. Her feet felt heavy. The first westward step took immense effort; her boot might as well have been shackled to the earth. She was betraying her friends. She was saving them. Back and forth she went in her head. The second step was easier.

Embla caught up to her after the twelfth. She was a stone's throw from where she had started, and that much had taken more time and effort than she cared to admit. The hound sniffed Aelfhild's leg before sauntering onward to mark a clump of moss as her own. If the dog was here, the master would not be far. Aelfhild counted a few heartbeats before she heard the footfalls.

"Running away?"

She turned to face Eyvind. "I tried. It did not take."

He leaned with both hands on a freshly whittled walking stick. There was already sweat on his face just from the gentle slope beneath their feet. "You could never have outrun Kolbrun anyway. She would not have been gentle fetching you back."

"You are never awake long enough to talk. I had to make a plan on my own." Each day had followed the same pattern; Eyvind claimed he wanted to talk but then marched himself ragged and dropped unconscious every night. Aelfhild might have taken it personally.

"Only because I had no better ideas," he replied. "Besides, you waited too long. *We* waited too long. Walk this way."

She offered him a hand when his leg slipped out from under him on some dew-slick leaves, only for him to yank his arm away and snort. He got the walking stick back under himself and limped forward. There was a gap in the trees ahead.

"I thought this place looked familiar last night. Turns out I was right." He pointed with his stick. They stood looking out over an evergreen valley that snaked in lazy curls eastward. Rising sunlight turned the mist in the vale a deep lilac, while the wisps rolling up past Aelfhild and Eyvind shimmered argent pink. It was a view worth remembering.

"What am I meant to see?" Aelfhild asked.

"Below all that fog? That is the Frostá. One step over that river and we are in Thrymgard." He swept his stick down, toward a crook in the river. "And you see those lights down there?"

She had to squint. It would have been easy to dismiss the glimmer as a glint of the morning light. "I see them."

"Herjarsborg. Home. You are stuck with us a while longer."

They stood looking out over the river.

"If I go down there," Aelfhild said, "more will die. I do not want it to be for me."

"You think they will live if you run? There will always be a reason for killing, whether you go or stay." He traced a circle, around and around, on the morning air.

"And if I make it worse?"

He scratched his chest. "Then try your best to fix it. Like the rest of us mortals do."

She dropped her sack of supplies onto the ground. Even her unconscious mind had not judged running a real option, it seemed. Embla sidled up to her thigh and put an impossibly cold, damp nose against her wrist. "Time to go back?" Aelfhild asked the hound.

The army was faster to rise that morning. There was none of the squabbling that had plagued them since the battle. All the Thrym knew they were close to home, close to sleeping in their own beds, and downed their morning rations in a gulp. They marched at full pace under the mild sun. A few even took up song.

Herjarsborg followed the riverside for what must have been nearly a league. It was a narrow strip of city that hugged the bank, and Aelfhild felt nothing but pity for those poor folk who lived at the downstream end. The water surely would have been well used by the time it reached them. But the Thrym were waterbound people, after all, so apparently being close to the river was a more pressing concern than pleasant air. There was a grand hall perched on the lip of the valley at the far western end—no man built upstream of the Jarl—and Aelfhild could see the earthen walls of several ring forts rising among the roofs. Every time Herjarsborg had grown too big for its old walls the residents had just built more downstream. Palisades popped up at random between rows of buildings, protecting nothing but standing as reminders of the former bounds of the city.

A covered bridge led from the Norholt side over to the Trollsmork in

Thrymgard. There was a trading post hamlet around the Earnfolding end. Villagers assembled to greet the Jarl and cheer his warriors.

"Hail the Jarl! Hail the Leifings!"

They looked just like Earnfolding peasants. Wool tunics, linen caps. Sturdy dresses. Faces flushed by days of backbreaking toil, and fingernails black with dirt.

"Onward Thrymgard!"

"Forward the Leifings!"

Across the bridge the crowd turned from farmers to tradesmen. Smudged with soot and wearing leather aprons or slung with market baskets filled to spilling, they waved to their sons and brothers. Aelfhild could see a few more paunches on display, more color in the clothing, an odd bead braided into hair and beards. Harald was at the head of the column of soldiers, on horseback and thoroughly combed. He beamed at his subjects, magnanimous in victory, and lifted a triumphant fist. His people drank it in and howled exultations.

"Hail the Jarl!"

They passed through more of the queer half walls. The crowds would mostly disperse by the time the army's rear guard was passing, so Aelfhild could get a better view of the town. All the buildings around the dead-end walls were built of logs and stones suspiciously similar in color to the dismantled fortifications. The Thrym were not wasteful, at least. The thatch roofs and sunless, muddy lanes could have put them in any town or village in Earnfold. Some things were constant. She marked struts propping up walls and fresh boards that clashed with weather-stained neighbors in more than a few places. It was widespread such that she wondered if there had been a spot of trouble recently. Then they came to the nobler halls. Those here were a little more staid in their wealth. Tunics were darker in color but the fabric was fine enough to catch the light when they turned. A trimming of silver here or fur there sufficed to show who had risen above, or been born above, in life. These folk were as well fed as they were scrubbed.

"Jarl Harald has returned, praise the Four!"

"Victory for us all!"

Outside the Great Hall was an august greeting party—the greyest of the greybeards, the holiest of the holy men, all bedecked in enough rings and chains to fill a longboat. This was the true power of Herjarsborg. Even Harald made a short bow to this assembly, although they bowed first and foremost to him. Aelfhild picked out Eyrun in the back, a flash of ruddy-red locks against all the grey. Their eyes met, but Eyrun looked past her. She was looking for one face in particular, and Aelfhild's was not it.

The army clattered to a halt. A servant ran over with a wooden step and laid it down before the Jarl. Harald stood and looked out over his men.

"Brothers, I called you to fight, and you have made me well proud. This was not our war, but every one of you held brave and held true. You are the blood of this land! I name you the pride of Trollsmork!"

Eyrun's eyes still swept the crowd. Her head bobbed impatiently. Her father's speech did not hold her interest.

Aelfhild elbowed Eyvind. "Your sister," she said from the corner of her mouth.

Kolbrun shushed her.

"But for now, our task is finished," Harald continued. "Go back to your homes. Go back to your plows. Go back to your wives!" There was a collective rumble from the army.

"Another time will come, another chance for glory and gold, but for now brothers—you are free!" The Jarl threw up his arms with the rising cheer.

The column scattered in every direction. Sabert and the Norholtings were left fidgeting beside Jarl Harald. He waved them in to meet the nobles of his court. Dunstan stood in the back of the crowd, forgotten and straining to get a glimpse over the shoulders of his bulkier companions.

Jarngrim looked to Kolbrun. "Mead?"

"Mead," the shieldmaiden agreed. The pair melted into the crowd of departing warriors. Every inn and tavern within walking distance would be abustle tonight if Aelfhild was any judge.

Embla keened as Eyrun broke through the crowd. She had the same air of brittle elegance about her as before, pearly white and slender, but the young woman nearly tackled her brother when she spotted him.

"Easy on the ribs," Eyvind whispered but squeezed back just as hard.

Suddenly Aelfhild found great interest in her toes. Her new position was an awkward one: not quite common enough to drink with the rank and file but not nearly noble enough to merit introduction to the lords. So long as Harald knew as little as possible, anyway. For now she was acutely alone.

There was a delicate hand on her shoulder. "Aelfhild." Eyrun's smile said she actually remembered the girl behind the name. It said everything Aelfhild wanted—needed—to hear. Not for the first time she was left to marvel at Eyvind's sister and how much could be accomplished with a wise word and gesture. "It warms me to see you alive."

"Thank you, lady," Aelfhild replied.

Eyrun turned back to her twin. "I saw Kolbrun and Jarngrim. What of the rest? Rolf? Ceolwen?"

With a sigh, Eyvind took his sister's hand. "For that tale, you will want to be sitting down. And I need to be." The pair departed with Embla in tow. The hound's tail was a blur to see all her favorite people in one place. Aelfhild hung back. She had not been invited. She was not family. Embla turned and barked.

"Come on, Aela, no dawdling!" Eyvind yelled over his shoulder. "Part of this is yours to tell!"

2 9

HE LEIFINGS' COUNCIL was only one or two swords short of a gladiator's arena. There was even sawdust on the floorboards in case of spilled blood. Harald did not care for a mess.

The Jarl's Great Hall was actually several longhouses built at catercorner to form an enclosed compound. One of the halls was the Radhus, the Council House, lined with benches and the banners of every tribe and noble branch in Trollsmork. Today it bulged to overfilling, packed with flesh and humid as a bathhouse. Harald brought his thanes, freemen, and huskarls together to recount his victory and to discuss future plans. What exactly those plans were, Aelfhild had not the faintest clue. There was so much yelling. The floorboards flexed and bounced as the men hollered and menaced each other with raised fists. The Jarl sat on a wooden throne in the center of the room. Feet perched on a fur-covered stool, he was the picture of serenity. There was an order to the seating in the rest of the hall; the beards nearer to Harald were longer and snowier and the hair sparser, while youth was shunted to the back. There was no such order to the selection of speakers.

Aelfhild had not had to tell the Jarl her secret yet. Kolbrun was missing at the bottom of a barrel with Jarngrim somewhere, so the shieldmaiden's threat was not currently in force. Eyvind and Eyrun had both taken a more generous position toward informing their father. Eyvind had an allergy to all things religious, while Eyrun had a spider's patience. It could wait as far as they were concerned. To illustrate how Harald had other things to occupy his time, Eyvind had brought Aelfhild along to the council. It earned him a few sideways stares. That sort of thing was not done, apparently, but Eyvind did seem to revel in chafing the traditionalists.

The Jarl's hand rose. It cut through the clamor remarkably well, though it did take some of the men farther in the back and out of eyeshot a moment to catch on to the change. "Sveinn still has the floor. Speak, my brother."

Fat Sveinn, indeed, thought Aelfhild. The man had chins in abundance. Even his wrists wobbled. He rose with the aid of a thick, copper-shod cane; Fat Sveinn had only one leg. "You lot turn my stomach with all your moaning," the man thundered. "I lost a grandson in this last battle and dear he was to me, but in my heart lives only the glory of Thrymgard! Cowards, the lot of you! You shrink away from a fight like startled jackrabbits, I say!"

There was a fresh eruption of disputation. Aelfhild leaned over to Eyvind. "Was he a warrior?"

"Aye. A right terror on the battlefield in his day, if you can believe it. My father was there to save him when he earned that peg, so he loves the old man dearer than kin."

"What are they even arguing about? I can only make out pieces." Aelfhild had to speak with her lips almost on Eyvind's ear.

"Where we go with the spring thaw next year. Some men want to raid farther south as usual, needle the Oescans a bit. Father has sown the seeds for other ideas. He will not say it himself, mind, but others will take pains to say it for him."

A brave soul in the back perked up his courage to shout Sveinn down. "It is not our fight! Let the Earnfoldings put their own house in order! The omens are against us. One day the ground shakes, the next my thralls gibber of wisps in the shadows."

"What mewling nonsense!" Sveinn jiggled his free arm, and the old man's sons were up around him now, flashing choice gestures at the challenger and his supporters. The back and forth continued without discernible progress. Jarl Harald sat in the center of it all. He flicked a chicken bone to a wolfhound stretched out beneath his chair. How the dog stood the noise, Aelfhild could hardly fathom. The poor beast must have been long since deafened.

Aelfhild dripped sweat. The room was horribly close. Summer beat down upon the shingles above, and every body in the room was a well of rank heat. She leaned over to Eyvind once more. "I have to step out." He nodded but stayed behind.

Fresh air was the Gods' own reward. Between the Jarl's longhouses was an open courtyard where the servants tended a herb garden and summer kitchen. Honeybees droned along a bed of musk thistle blooming in vibrant purples, and down lines of dillweed and fennel. There was a bed teeming with mint stalks; Aelfhild walked over to break off a sprig. She crushed it and held it to her nose—the perfect, crisp antidote to the smell of sweaty men with aging bladders.

The weather was far too hot to have fires burning in the longhouses themselves, so the servants cooked atop firepits in the courtyard. Pork sizzled on skewers. Bread crisped up on the stones beside glowing coals. An endless trail of women came and went through the garden, carrying jugs or baskets, appearing suddenly from one curtain, then disappearing into the opposite hall. Aelfhild felt at home. Though she never would have been still for this long in her old life; idling fetched you a wallop upside the head.

There was a rhythmic scratching noise from behind her back of what sounded like nails on wood. Aelfhild turned, both gloved hands and mint still pressed against her face. On a stool beside the Council House door sat Eyrun with an overflowing sack of raw wool. She worked her combs back and forth, slowly and patiently, getting at the snags and muck caught in the threads. After thorough inspection she transferred the clean wool to a reed basket. Voices swelled in the hall anew. Eyrun paused, cocked an ear, then returned to her combing. It might have furrowed brows for a woman to sit in on men's council, but none of them would spare a glance for a woman combing wool. That was what Thrym women spent about half their year doing, from the first shearing through to wintertime. It was as natural and unremarkable as breathing. So Eyrun sat and heard every word the men said through the door without having to endure the closeness of the hall. And the menfolk were none the wiser. She caught Aelfhild's eye and smiled.

Aelfhild grinned back; it was not a secret they shared so much as a recognition of just how absurd their world could be. She dropped her sprig of mint. "How do they get anything done?"

"Rarely. But always with great ceremony." Eyrun's hands never stopped from their work. The task was by now instinct and required none of her focus. Another ball of wool went into the basket, quickly replaced by a wad of raw fiber. "Father and I do much of the work. They get their chance to yell and feel better about the whole thing. Never forget how easy it is to convince folk to do something they never meant to do so long as you let them complain about doing it."

So that was the source of Harald's placid smile and grinning eyes. He could sit there watching, listening, and knowing it was all so much empty theater. The Jarl was a slippery one and no doubt.

Eyrun must have spotted Aelfhild's grin. "You should take note, if you are to be a queen."

The last word landed like a punch to the gut. "What?" Aelfhild snorted. "Me? I am not *that* foolish."

"Who then?" Eyrun's combs paused. She peered up at Aelfhild.

There was nowhere to deflect the question, no one to hide behind. Aelfhild stammered as she ran through a list of possible answers in her head. "Er. You, maybe?"

Eyrun sniffed. She put down her combs. She stood and walked over to Aelfhild. With a deft hand she straightened the shoulders of Aelfhild's dress and brushed away a piece of thistle fluff that had snagged on the wool. "No," she said. "I will be just behind you, telling you the right thing to say and the wiser thing to do."

Aelfhild stared. The conversation had gone from amusing to gut-rending in a heartbeat. There was not a hint of jest in Eyrun's eyes. No grin tugged at the edge of her lips. She was dead serious, and that terrified Aelfhild more than anything. The fancies of old men were one thing. Eyrun had a mind to match her patience. Her plans might actually come to pass.

"You promise?" she managed. It was weak, but the alternative she considered was turning and sprinting for dear life.

"I do." Eyrun turned back to her seat and picked up her combs. She leaned against the door and picked at the rough brown wool. As though nothing had happened, as though they had not one breath earlier been plotting a new regime.

The Council House doors swung open. Aelfhild stepped to the side, out of the path of the emerging nobles and screened from Eyrun's eyes. Not one of the departing thanes or huskarls commented on the presence of the Jarl's daughter. Nary one of them noticed her. That was power and just as dangerous as all the clout the Jarl wielded. Harald could never pass unseen. Harald would always be the center of attention. Eyvind drifted through the crowd toward Aelfhild. Sveinn thumped his way past and whacked the Jarl's son on the shoulder. The fat man whispered some nonsense to Eyvind before chortling his way off across the courtyard flanked by a train of sons and grandsons.

"You look rough," Eyvind said. He reclined against one of the beds of herbs.

"The heat," Aelfhild lied.

3 0

ELFHILD KEPT A vise grip on the pommel. Boughs whipped past in pastel blurs, loose hair streamed across her face, and the saddle jerked up or careened down without the slightest trace of rhythm. Her horse was in control at this point; Jarngrim and Kolbrun rode ahead, though they were nothing more than two distant, flapping cloaks. Aelfhild's horse followed theirs for lack of better ideas. The reins she held clutched in one hand but did not dare draw them back at this speed. A sudden stop would spell broken bones at best.

Spiderwebs crisscrossed what must have been a quiet and seldom-traveled road judging from the overgrowth. The other horses tore the webs to shreds and left gossamer remnants adrift on the breeze. Aelfhild caught another tangle of webbed insects to the face but had no time to claw it away from her mouth and eyes. Her thighs burned from clenching the saddle. Still the hooves thundered beneath her. The hunt was on.

Kolbrun started to slow, and the two other horses fell into a trot alongside. As the pace slackened Aelfhild was able to take one hand off the pommel to pull some of the spidersilk away from her face. She had tied back her hair but it had been no match for the speed, and now the sticky threads were mixed in with the whole tangled mess. She was left to just bat at her face with one free hand.

"Here, see the spoor?" Kolbrun pointed to gaps flattened through the brush on either side of the path. "Not many animals big enough to make that. Should be our beast."

Jarngrim nodded farther down the path. "West, you think?"

"Aye, stands to reason. If it came down from the mountains it may range back that way." The shieldmaiden looked over at Aelfhild. "Still with us?"

Those three little words were nothing but bait. Aelfhild did not deign to respond. She grunted and massaged the small of her back with clenched knuckles.

The common folk had lately been on edge. There was talk in the Herjarsborg barrooms of livestock savaged and smokehouses raided out in the hinterlands, of smashed graineries and ruined stills. Rumors were a constant in any city, but the mood built like a thunderhead. Such tension had a way of earthing itself in mobs of torches and scythes. A farmer from one of the outlying steads had brought in the remains of a sheep to the Jarl. He and his fellows had hemmed and hawed, afraid of confronting their lord outright. If it please your lordship, if it were not too bold to say, clearly his highness needs no telling, but neither wolf nor bear could leave such marks, the men had said. Harald had been patient—indulgent, even. The men had left well pleased, bowing down to the floorboards, even though the Jarl for all his speaking had not actually committed to action. Superstitious bumpkins jumping at shadows, some counselors said; it will be a sow come down from the mountains with her cubs; or a new pack with a young, bold leader. But old Harald had not held his seat for so long out of blind luck. He had called for a Great Hunt, made it an occasion for revelry and a contest among his warriors. There was a purse for any that fetched a trophy befitting the Jarl's hall. The roads out of Herjarsborg had flooded with pounding feet and hooves. Jarngrim, Kolbrun, and Aelfhild were some of the first through the gates.

Not that they needed the silver, really, but it was a chance for Kolbrun and Jarngrim to garner a bit of glory and for Aelfhild to get away for a day or hopefully more. That was worth enough. Harald, and even Eyrun of late, scared her more than any woodland beast.

"Do you hear that barking?" Jarngrim asked.

Aelfhild strained up in her stirrups. "I hear them." It sounded like a whole pack of hunting dogs to the north. "Sounds like we may still be ahead, though."

The shieldmaiden was not as optimistic. She growled. "I said we needed that blasted hound."

Embla had been bitterly torn but had decided not to leave Eyvind's side. Eyvind had not been happy, either, when everyone had insisted he was still too weak to ride. Words had been exchanged. Then his sister gave a ruling. That was the end of discussion.

"West it is." Kolbrun clicked to her horse and galloped off. Aelfhild was left grappling with the saddle once more. The bundle of spears slung alongside cracked up against her thigh.

It will be a *jarfr*, Jarngrim had said, come down from the highlands. He had seen one in his youth, but they were rare enough that the farmers would not recognize the signs. Someone had tried to translate that for Aelfhild and came up with "stink bear," but that was not overly helpful. Beastlore had not figured into her city upbringing. Others, with more hunting experience, had argued and made their own guesses, but they all agreed that spears were the best choice. Whatever it might be, better to keep a distance.

Her horse did not have a name, or no one had bothered to tell Aelfhild what it was. She was a sorrel mare and sweet enough at a standstill but unsympathetic to her nervous rider. As the path disappeared under the mare's feet, Aelfhild decided to name her Sorg. It meant sorrow. That was what Aelfhild knew she would feel the next time she got a chance to sit.

There was a limb down ahead. Kolbrun's horse leaped. Jarngrim's followed. Aelfhild braced herself as the muscles in Sorg's haunches coiled. There was a brief moment of weightless serenity, a welcome pause in the jolting, then a teeth-rattling impact. They rode on.

The Trollsmork was as dense a forest as Norholt to the south, though they were really one and the same great wood. It made slim difference to the trees which side of an imaginary line they grew on. In scattered patches a homestead was either burned or hacked out of the evergreens. Kolbrun eased the pace as their path spilled out into a clearing. Turnips stretched in tidy rows to the north and south. A distant lump in the sod was the farmhouse roof. Along the length of the plots and pastures ran a spindly fence. It looked to be more ceremonial than all else. To the west, as Jarngrim had guessed, was a freshly splintered gap in the line and tracks through the field. Rain the previous night had turned each track into an indistinct puddle, but whatever it was had heavy paws.

"Less than a day," Kolbrun said.

Jarngrim raised a fist. "We have it! Ride!"

Sorg was off again. This time they were off the road and the pace was slower. Branches slapped at Aelfhild's cloaked shoulders, spruce needles scratched the skin of her face when she dodged a moment too slowly. She was glad not to be as tall as Jarngrim; he was nearly doubled over and still getting the worst of the boughs. The tracks ended at the bank of a stream cutting through the wood. Kolbrun glared at the ground as she rode up and down in silence. The shieldmaiden had a competitive spirit, without doubt, and the mud was not cooperating. She swung her horse back around. "Anything?"

Jarngrim shook his head. Aelfhild shook hers.

Kolbrun spit. "We split up, then. I ride upstream, Aelfhild rides downstream, Jarngrim keep straight. Got it?"

"That sounds—" Jarngrim broke off. He must have caught the look on the shieldmaiden's face. He shrugged and spurred his horse across the burbling water.

"Be ready with your horn," Kolbrun called over her shoulder as she bobbed upstream. "Call us if you find a trace."

Sorg dipped for a drink of the crystal waters. Aelfhild fumbled around behind herself. Each had a hunting horn, but hers had drifted around behind her back with all the bouncing and jostling. She kept a grip on it as she nudged Sorg forward.

The pace was blessedly easy. Sorg picked her way through the stones of the streambed and ambled up onto the far bank. She seemed content to trot. Aelfhild leaned from side to side, scanning for marks. It was all moss and pinecones; each bit was as lumpy as the next. There were puddles in abundance but none looked patterned enough to be tracks. Her nose began to burn as she rode farther downstream. There were the normal loam and sap scents of the woods, but underneath those, a musky tang. The smell grew stronger with each pace. It started mild as wet dog but built into an eye-watering stench like a tannery in summertime. Something meant to mark its territory; if that was stink bear musk, she was not eager to meet the bear itself.

Sorg twitched. The mare did not much care for the scent either. She nickered and pushed back as Aelfhild tried to urge her forward.

"Just a bear, my girl." Aelfhild leaned up and rubbed circles on the horse's neck. One hand stayed glued to the pommel—she was not taking chances. "Just a bear." Though the word "just" did strike Aelfhild as a tad ridiculous, the crooning tone worked.

Stepping forward, they found the source of the musk. A pine tree had been ripped from the earth and cast down. Muddy roots, snapped and frayed, clung to the base of the stricken trunk. The taproots were thicker than Aelfhild's calves in places. Such a tree would not have come up easily. Viscous amber fluid dripped off the bark. It made Aelfhild's head spin just to get within a few steps. She pulled Sorg away and fumbled for her horn. Her lips were dry and she had seen it done only once before. She pursed and tried to keep her mouth tight, but blowing at the end of the horn with all the air she could muster produced a reedy, flapping noise. A few more attempts left her without breath or any audible progress. "Kolbrun! Jarngrim!" she called. Her voice cracked. The woods were thick here.

She traded the horn for a spear from the bundle by her foot. It felt good in hand. The balance was true and the weight reassuring. Its razor point gleamed. She pushed her ankles in. Sorg trotted on.

As good as the spear felt against her palm, it did mean she only had one free hand. She had to hold the reins instead of the pommel, which left her rocking less steadily than she would have preferred. Some of the trees on either side had scratches on them that she was not keen on. There were three long, deep claw marks. Bears had some number of claws, she knew that, and three did not seem correct. She remembered seeing a bear claw necklace once but could not for the life of her recall a count. With every passing heartbeat she was less sure that spraying awful musk was even something bears did.

"Kolbrun!" she called. "Jarngrim! Can you hear me?"

Silence.

Just a bear, Aelfhild said to herself now. Convincing the horse was the least of her worries.

There was a clearing ahead. Brush had been flattened in a circle and more trees toppled and dragged around. The trunks formed a rough cover over a burrow dug down through the moss. From where she was sitting, the mouth of the tunnel looked at least wide enough to ride her horse into.

Sorg stamped. Aelfhild agreed. "No chance is that a bear."

She licked her lips until they were good and lathered this time. She put her mouth to the horn, inhaled through her nose, and puckered. Her eyes watered and she kept blowing until her ribs creaked and sparks danced through her vision. Everyone in Trollsmork could have heard her. Sorg shook her head and sidestepped to try to escape the noise; Aelfhild's ears keened.

The problem—and Aelfhild realized with a sinking stomach that she had not thought her plan all the way through—was that her quarry was closer to her than Kolbrun and Jarngrim were. And whatever it was in the burrow could hear the horn, too. And since she had a spear in one hand and a horn in the other, she did not have a firm grip on the horse. It was not an elegant moment. She could feel the dumb grimace twisting her own face.

A roar split the air, rising from the mouth of the nest. Something broke out from the shadow—there was a hint of fur, but bone too and plentiful teeth. Aelfhild did not get a chance to look. Sorg was not waiting around to scout the situation. Rocking backward, Aelfhild managed to cast aside the horn and hook her fingers on the lip of the saddle. She clenched the spear and hung on as her knuckles popped under the strain. In a single leap Sorg was across the creek and headed north at speed.

3 1

AGS OF SILVER were far from Aelfhild's mind. Her left hand was agony. She could not shift her grip on the saddle's edge without dropping the spear in her right hand, and the mare was not pausing for anyone. Another roar from behind amid heavy footfalls said that their pursuer followed along. Whatever the beast was, it did not seem to be as fast as Sorg, so Aelfhild at least was gaining ground.

She spotted another horse in the edge of her vision. It looked like Jarngrim, headed to meet her. "Run! Ride!" she screamed.

There was no time for explanations. Jarngrim kicked his steed onward and they wove through the trees alongside one another, though Aelfhild was doing precious little steering. All the crashing behind them had to mean that Kolbrun would have a good trail to follow whenever the shield-maiden caught up. The trees parted and they were in the turnip field again. Sorg cleared the fence without slowing. Free of the woods, the horses could sprint unfettered. The farmers would not have been pleased to see their progress, as few turnips were spared the brunt of the hooves, but even the finest royal stallions would have struggled to match their pace.

"Whoa!" Jarngrim called. He was reining in his horse, looking over his shoulder.

Aelfhild dared to glance. Nothing was behind them in the field. She made a grab for the reins and got Sorg to slow. Aelfhild's chest was heaving as much as the horse's.

Jarngrim stared at her. "What?"

"Not a bear." She knew that much.

Another horn rang out within the woods. Kolbrun was still back there. She would have followed their trail straight into the beast's back. There was never even a question of helping the shieldmaiden. Jarngrim kicked his horse. Aelfhild wrapped her wrist through the reins. The horn sounded again as they rode back toward the tree line. Flattened bushes, spattered mud, and broken branches gave a clear picture of where both beast and Kolbrun had passed. Aelfhild clutched tightly to her spear. Both her mare and Jarngrim's were pushing hard. Breath steamed up between them and sweat slicked down both horses' coats. The pace was brutal. It had to be. Kolbrun was alone.

The trail led them to some sort of orchard—not wide open exactly, but the trees were spaced in rough lines and there was room enough to turn a horse. The shieldmaiden blew her horn. Aelfhild caught sight of the beast through the branches.

"On the right!" she screamed. Jarngrim split off from her and over to the next cleared lane. He had a spear in hand.

The creature's back was to her. Tufts of thick fur rose up around the shoulders and in clusters down the back, but there were thick plates of stone or bone that protruded through the hide. It had stocky back legs and hefty, bristled forearms that ended in three wickedly clawed digits. A spear protruded from its side—Kolbrun's work.

As Aelfhild approached from behind, the beast rose onto its haunches to roar. Aelfhild flinched back in her saddle. Its voice was a sawblade dragged across slate. The shieldmaiden looped around a tree, twisting a circle to shake the creature loose, and hurled a spear toward its chest. The iron point glanced off a bone plate, which the creature seemed to have in abundance, and spun back to bury itself in the ground.

Aelfhild aimed for the back leg. She leaned in her saddle, then whipped the shaft forward. The blade struck home but did no more than stick in the leathery hide. She swore and pulled Sorg hard to the left as the beast swung at the new annoyance. In passing, she caught a glimpse of the face. It was a sight drawn from the blackest depths of the deepest cave, with massive hooked ears and too many beady white eyes. A bone crest dominated the forehead above a dripping, crushed-in snout. It was a dozen creatures mashed together and stank worse than any of them.

Jarngrim put a spear into the beast's shoulder and drew its attention away. Aelfhild drew another spear as the shieldmaiden blasted a peal from her hunting horn. At first, Aelfhild thought she might be trying to summon other hunters. Then she saw the creature flinch. Each time the horn sounded it cowered and roared again. Its big ears flickered. Aelfhild pushed Sorg back around and drew a bead for the creature's throat. *Breathe. Focus. Make it count.*

Her second spear flew wide. *Useless.* Sorg was exhausted and starting to flag; Aelfhild could feel the hooves dragging. She drew a third spear while she still had time. But the horse had gotten close to the beast. Aelfhild saw the flailing arm too late.

A massive forearm struck horse and rider like a falling boulder. Aelfhild tumbled from the saddle. There was no question Sorg had survived the blow, because immediately the mare rolled up from her side and let out toward the far end of the orchard. The reins had hooked around Aelfhild's foot during the fall and dragged her along. She rolled herself into a ball, arms around her face, and tried to twist the foot free. Grass whipped by, tearing at the bare skin of her arms. She slipped her foot out of the shoe and rolled back across the path. Sorg disappeared into the stand of fruit trees. Aelfhild's cloak dripped with the rotted apples. She whipped it over her head and cast the garment aside.

Her grip on the spear had faltered during the fall. She looked around for anything. *Get yourself together. Help them!*

Kolbrun's horn was still sounding loudly. That was one good sign. The creature had spear shafts sticking from its sides, back, and shoulder, but was still very much alive. It lunged at Jarngrim, who was able to pull his horse away. The steeds looked to be at the end of their endurance.

Your horn. Use the horn. Aelfhild fumbled around her belt. The strap was tangled around her leg, and a crack snaked down from the lip of the horn toward the binding, but it had survived the fall. She put it to her lips. The creature snapped its jaws from side to side. Twigs from a nearby branch brushed its shoulder, and the beast spun and snatched at the empty air. Its claws waved, then touched the branch and ripped it from the tree.

Aelfhild ducked instinctively but the limb flew wide and far overhead. *It cannot see*, she thought. She blew her horn. It flattened itself to the ground. Its twin nostrils swelled. It could smell, though.

Lowering its head, bone crest set forth like a battering ram, the beast charged. Sorg had been doing the running all morning. Aelfhild's legs were still fresh. She sprinted behind a tree trunk and dove toward the earth. Apples dangled from every twig, and someone had staked and tied each branch to keep the trunks from splitting. The result was a fortified nest of snags and points.

The impact sent clods and splinters flying over her bowed back. She fully expected for the trunk to follow, but it somehow held. The tree lurched sideways, and the creature screamed. This was a different sound than previously—not defiance or rage, but pain. Kolbrun must have caught onto the idea. Her horn sounded from across the clearing. The beast stood and shook its head. It moved uncertainly now, stumbling on fallen fruit. This world was bright and full of stings, and the pests moved faster than penned sheep. It growled and lowered its head for another charge. Muscles bunched in its bloodied shoulders and thighs.

The shieldmaiden was on foot now. She let loose another peal.

It took the bait. Kolbrun cut and ran as the beast drove headfirst for another apple tree. Something went wrong. Instead of ramming the trunk, the creature dodged to the side and picked its way through the trees after the fleeing shieldmaiden. Kolbrun was fast, but the beast ran on four rippling legs.

The sun, Aelfhild realized. The sun had been at her back before; the creature had been charging into it. Maybe it could not see Kolbrun or the trees well now but it could make out silhouettes. She put her horn to her lips once more, but there was nothing she could do.

Jarngrim came charging down the line of trees with his final spear held high. His horse was still galloping, somehow, and he clearly meant to close on the beast before it could snag Kolbrun.

The creature swung wildly and hooked a clawed finger in the shieldmaiden's cloak. Kolbrun staggered.

Aelfhild reached out a useless hand as she ran.

At the last moment the horse tried to turn to avoid the beast's extended legs. Jarngrim yanked the reins sideways. Horse and rider collided directly with the monster, and the spear drove up through the creature's jaw. Animal and man dropped into a quivering pile of limbs.

Aelfhild was almost to them. She could see the ribs of the horse heaving up and down. The monster was still. Jarngrim was buried.

"Jarngrim!" Kolbrun was first to the bodies. "Say something! Aela, help me!"

There was muffled noise from beneath the beast's carcass. Aelfhild bent and strained at one of the massive forearms. It oozed sweat and blood and worse and it stank.

"Get it off me!" came Jarngrim's voice from underneath. "I cannot breathe under here!"

They were able to lever the arm up and kick back the torso enough for Jarngrim to wriggle loose. As they jostled the body, another arm, this one withered and pale, flopped out from along the creature's belly.

Aelfhild yelped and stumbled back. "It has six arms. Legs."

All three warriors stood shoulder to shoulder, stained and shaking. It took a while for anyone to speak.

"They were sure it would be a bear." Kolbrun seemed keen to start with the facts.

Jarngrim snorted.

The creature just looked wrong. There were clumps of pelt, but some of the hide was bare, pebbly leather. Bone plates jutted up at bizarre angles. The face was a nightmare. A serpentine tongue lolled out through rows of crooked fangs. Musk oozed off it in moldy layers.

"I would have felt bad killing a bear," Aelfhild admitted.

It was Kolbrun's turn to snort. "Soft."

"It never caught hold of *me*," Aelfhild countered.

Jarngrim kicked the dead monster's shoulder. "What do you think it is?"

Kolbrun hesitated, as though she did not want to be first to say it. "Troll?"

But trolls were just stories. Even if they were real, Onund had said they had all been hunted down and killed. She still wore the lump of "trollbone," which looked suspiciously like common rock, that Eyvind had given to her on a string around her neck. But then she did have a glove on her hand concealing a glowing rune. She had seen a walking corpse and fire from the heavens. Maybe a troll was not so far-fetched.

"Eyvind would laugh at us just for saying that," Kolbrun said.

"We can show it to Eyvind first," Jarngrim replied, "and see how clever he is then."

Aelfhild looked over her shoulder. Sorg was long gone, and Kolbrun's horse had vanished as well. Jarngrim's mount had managed to hoist itself back up and was nibbling grass down a distant row of trees. The poor thing looked knackered. "We lost our horses," she said.

Kolbrun's chest swelled. "See how fast we were? The others still have not caught up, even after all that ruckus. *We* earned our silver today."

They sat in the shade and waited. Aelfhild plucked one of the yellow fruits from overhead and took a nibble. It was tart enough to make her whole face pucker. She grimaced, but at least it cleared the stink of musk from her nostrils. She leaned back against the trunk. Dogs were barking in the distance, so help was on the way. Maybe one of them would find her horse. Against all odds she missed Sorg.

Jarngrim giggled. "Remind me to listen to the farmers next time."

RINGING HOME A boar or a stag from a hunt was cause for celebration. The people would have found excuse to make merry even if the hunters had returned empty-handed. But returning with a monster drawn straight from legends and old wives' tales was an entirely different matter. Herjarsborg erupted.

It took four horses to drag the beast on a makeshift sled through the gates. Other bands of hunters had converged on Aelfhild, Kolbrun, and Jarngrim on the way back, and each was eager to snag a fragment of shared glory, so they entered the city in dense company. Dogs were smart enough to keep their distance; all the hunting hounds stayed as far from the corpse as their leashes would allow. Children that ran up to see the corpse departed shrieking and sped off to spread rumors of fang and talon. By the time they dragged the troll in front of the Jarl's hall, the streets were churning. Harald emerged from his doors with raised eyebrows. The old man knew when something odd was afoot.

It had been Kolbrun's idea to mark their skin with the troll's blood. The shieldmaiden had an eye for that sort of show. She had a fondness for war paint. Perhaps because she was shorter than her fellow warriors she had to exert more effort to look the part. The tarry blood had burned like a wasp sting when Aelfhild put streaks on her forehead and cheeks.

"Have my hunters returned successfully?" Harald's voice boomed. He opened his arms wide to receive the victors.

"We have, lord," Kolbrun said, bowing low. "We have slain a troll for you. We return with it for your great glory."

The Jarl was poised. He was good. But Aelfhild had been around nobles her entire life. The way Harald's eyes widened at the word was a greater reward than silver and gemstones. It took him a moment to gather himself. "A troll, you say? This I must see." He made a show of inspecting, poking and prodding at the corpse. His nose wrinkled at the smell, but he did not shrink from the face. Harald grabbed the jaw and wrenched open the mouth. "By the Gods, those teeth."

He turned to his men. "We must show the Runemaster. To the square!"

Now the Jarl led the way. His huskarls pushed aside the swelling crowd and made way for noble and hunter alike. Harald pulled Kolbrun to his side. Aelfhild could hear the whispers. "Who killed it? How many of you?"

"Three of us, lord. Jarngrim struck the killing blow. I was there and Aela, too. Aelfhild, lord." Kolbrun finally had to point. "Her, lord."

"Oh, that one. Just the three of you?"

Kolbrun nodded. The Jarl leaned over to one of his underlings and there was more whispering before the minion ran back toward the Great Hall.

Downhill and just downriver from the Great Hall was one of several open squares, but Aelfhild got the sense that this was *the* town square as far as the well-born and monied were concerned. There was nothing so crude as a market stall or merchant's table here. Anyone respectable enough to be seen in this place had servants for buying and selling life's lesser trifles. There were benches and stone firepits in the square where men could meet and warm their hands and discuss matters most grave.

One hall dominated the space. Its roof was only slightly lower than that of Harald's Great Hall; its beams were nearly as well engraved, its doors almost as ornate. Ravens and stags danced across the woodwork, each one inset with garnets or amber. An effort had been made to make it the second most impressive building in Herjarsborg by only the narrowest margin. A hobbled whitebeard was making his way down the steps. The Runemaster bowed. "Jarl Harald, the Gods greet you."

Harald matched the elder's bow. "And may the Gods smile upon you, wise one. We have need of your council."

Each step was a chore for the Runemaster. Long years had turned his arms and legs into dusty twigs. He was swaddled in layer on layer of robes and wraps despite the summer heat. He shuffled around and peered at the so-called troll. There was no sign of surprise on his face. His eyes were so clouded that Aelfhild was not sure how much the old man could actually see.

"Is it truly one of the enemies of old, wise one? We must know!" Harald swayed as he spoke, and his hands came together with a crack on the last word. The entire crowd leaned in to hear the answer. No one breathed.

The Runemaster turned and shuffled his way back inside the hall. He turned back to crook a finger at the Jarl before disappearing inside.

Harald called out to the crowd, "We must consult the runes. Those that slew the beast will join me inside." A few of the other hunters stepped forward as if to join their lord. The Jarl's warning glare made clear that any fraud would be costly. The men stepped back, and quickly.

Aelfhild followed the others inside. The air within was parched. Sawdust gathered on every flat surface and danced around their footsteps. Wooden pillars lined the walls; all of them were carved edge to edge with runes and crowded figures. It was Herjarsborg's answer to the Hall of the Aettir in Jarlstad. She counted herself among the fortunate few to have seen the storied runestones there, each one graven with names and deeds reaching back to the first ancestors, the ancient granite guarded from time's wear in that stirless, lightless hall. Those before her now were the art of untold hours and devotion immeasurable, but paled, if she was honest, by comparison. They lacked the traction, the heft, the radiating permanence of aged stone.

"Boy!" The Runemaster's wheeze sent dust flying.

A pudgy lad, barely into his teenage years and dressed in a robe identical to that of the Runemaster, jogged to the old man. This was the apprentice sent to learn everything the old man knew before time took its inevitable toll. They were the priests, scribes, and historians, all in one. Fortune tellers, too, if the piles of marked bones on the floor were any indications. The Runemaster whispered to his helper for a while.

No one was watching, so Aelfhild ran her fingers across a slab of reddened oak that was chiseled with all manner of arcane marks. The tacky gloss of countless layers of resin brushed on over generations of keepers pulled at the fabric of her glove.

The boy led them to a particular pillar. The Runemaster had to run his crooked fingertips over the surface to read the runes. The hall was lit by as few windows as possible to keep out the damp. Decades spent in the murk would steal anyone's sight. But the old man found the passage he was looking for. "Here, my jarl," he pointed with a bulbous knuckle, "the last mention of trollkin."

Harald leaned in. "Read it, boy."

The poor lad was not used to such attention. His voice quavered as he read. "Torfi slew the mother of the rock-biters. In his reign did the troll fathers fall. No more will the enemies of man trouble the Eastlands."

"I was just a babe, then." The Jarl plucked at his beard. "My father was sure he had killed the last of them. Anything more? Does it describe them?"

"Rock-biter. Bone-bearer. Goat-stealer." The Runemaster was chanting in an odd cadence. His eyes were squeezed shut as he leafed through the records still left in his mind. "Night-hunter. Those are the kennings I yet recall. The bodies I never did see."

Harald bowed. "Thank you, wise one. The Gods will repay you a hundredfold for your good council." The Jarl waved for the rest to follow him out.

The crowd was still gathered. There was a space of about two paces between the troll and the front rank of onlookers. No one had to enforce the gap; it formed naturally. Hungry eyes turned to the Jarl. From atop the steps, Harald shouted to the throng, "Folk of Herjarsborg, my people! We have consulted the runes, we have heard the words of our ancestors! Not since our forefathers' time has such a beast troubled our lands, yet the blood of Thrymgard has not been found wanting!"

And the blood of Earnfold, Aelfhild corrected him silently.

There were murmurs from down the steps. "It is a sign! Grim tidings!" someone called. Others joined in.

"The Gods punish us, lord!"

"We have angered them!"

"The wilds rise against us!"

Ripples moved out through the growing mob. Some pulled at their hair and clothes, a few fell to their knees. Some jostled their neighbors or stretched their arms toward the Jarl.

"Save us, lord!"

"Darkness falls upon the wicked. Hark!"

"Gods spare us! Mercy!"

"Brothers, sisters, hear me!" Harald pushed down the crowd with open palms. "Do not give in to your worry. The Gods have sent us a test, yes, but we have overcome! What is our strength without struggle? What is our courage without battle? The Four know our hearts to be true, but they must remind us of our own mettle. Rejoice, for our people are chosen above all others, and we are blessed!"

Aelfhild shifted beneath her cloak. Kolbrun's stare burned on her back; she felt it without turning. She hid her hand away in the folds of her clothing.

"I say"—the Jarl raised a fist overhead—"it is cause for joy! It is cause for merrymaking! The folk of Trollsmork stand ready for any challenge. Trollsmork is guarded from even the greatest foe." He raised another fist. "Good folk of Herjarsborg, I give you"—a pause, long enough for the crowd to soak in the words; Aelfhild knew talent when she heard it— "your Trollslayers!"

"Father gets what he wants, always," Eyvind lisped. He should not have been drinking as much as he was. The entire town was drowning itself, though, so he had joined in. There was a row of tankards on the table in front of him, some empty and others with a lukewarm sip still at the bottom. Aelfhild was responsible for at least half. The drinking house had a name. Something to do with bees, and it was a pun on mead and honey that the Thrym warriors judged doubly clever. She could not remember.

"And he wants heroes, they want heroes, so . . ." Eyvind rolled his finger in uneven circles. Exactly what he was demonstrating was unclear. "You know: Trollslayers."

There was a little bit of a twist on the last word. A few jugs of mead could scarcely hide that one. "We did slay a troll," Aelfhild slurred right back. "You are just jealous."

Eyvind blew a raspberry. They bumped shoulders as giggles took them both.

The door at the far end of the tavern popped open. Bartender and wife were lugging in another cask of mead in hopes of staying ahead of the mood. Manic energy suffused Herjarsborg. The laughs were too loud, the back-slapping too hearty. Grins were plastered on only with the aid of much cider. It was the air of people forcing themselves through acts of happiness. Harald's skill could only tamp down the fear, not uproot it. Drink had a way of deadening such worries, though, so the innkeepers kept it aflow.

Aelfhild had a purse loaded with silver; the Jarl had seen to that. And she was feeling free in respect to spending. "More mead!" she shouted and flipped a fat silver coin onto the table. The bartender's wife was there in a flash, palming the coin and leaving a sloshing jug on the table. Her glazed smile and wild eyes matched the moment; coins were flowing, but they had already emptied casks meant to last through winter.

It was carnage across the city. Aelfhild had seen bodies in the gutters on the way here, not dead but certainly close to drowned. She remembered fragments of a feast at the Great Hall. Harald had talked and talked so Aelfhild had drunk and drunk of the free-flowing ale. They had descended on the tavern in a rowdy flock. Only a few were left standing now. Dunstan was under a table somewhere. Godwyn was meant to be minding him. Partway through the revels, Jarngrim had departed in rosy-cheeked company. Embla sat beneath Aelfhild and Eyvind's bench. The hound was chewing something she had discovered slithering on the floor. The bartender did not care for dogs but he cared more for silver, as Aelfhild had discovered.

There was a thump and a triumphant howl from over by the blazing fire. Kolbrun was arm wrestling all comers. "The Trollslayer wins again! Who is next?" The shieldmaiden was up on the table now. "Who next!" The bartender's wife was trying to talk her down off the wobbling boards, without luck.

Eyvind poured himself another helping of mead and managed to get half into the tankard. Embla snorted as the rest trickled down onto the floor. He passed the jug back to Aelfhild. "I should have been there with you."

"Next time." Aelfhild took another swig. The pain in her legs and back, Sorg's parting gift, grew a little more distant with every drink. There would be a price tomorrow. Such was life.

"Nobody kills two trolls," Eyvind said. "Two trolls," he repeated, "two troll. True tolls." He seemed to like the sound.

Kolbrun was still dancing on a tabletop. Aelfhild smiled. "If anyone can, we will."

They sat and watched the crowd for a while.

"Thank you, Aela."

"Hmm?" she said with a snort. It was dark and warm. She had been somewhere else.

Eyvind's eyes glistened as he looked over the room. The bartender watched him with a look of genuine panic. "I said thank you. You saved them. Us. Me. Thank you."

"I had." She stopped short and hiccuped. She almost said, "I had to." But that was wrong. She never had to. She wanted to. For the first time in her life, she could think about herself. What she wanted to do. How she wanted to do it. It was a novel idea. She felt light. "I wanted to," Aelfhild said. And hiccuped.

Eyvind chortled. "Lucky for us."

There had been a lot of mead, but her head felt clear enough. She leaned over and kissed Eyvind. His lips were damp, sweet from the mead. His beard scratched her skin.

He leaned back. He looked surprised but not unpleasantly so. His eyes closed. He kept leaning back. And back. He toppled backward and slid down the wall behind. His feet were atop the bench, his body folded onto the floor. The bartender sighed and went back to ladling out the drinks. Embla settled in beside her master in case anyone tried to prey upon his softly snoring form.

Aelfhild hiccuped. She stretched and settled in to finish her drink. Then Eyvind's as well. She hiccuped again. "I was there," she said to no one in particular. "I saw it."

3 3

ELFHILD ROUNDED A corner and spotted two women in the alleyway ahead of her. *Damn it all!* She choked down the urge to spin and flee. She recognized Eyrun's ruddy locks. Kolbrun was shaded by the overhanging eaves, but it took only a moment to recognize those shoulders at that height.

"Well met, Aelfhild." Eyrun's smiled never flickered as she released her hold on Kolbrun's wrist. The welt left by her squeezing lingered. *Everything is fine*, her face said. Nothing was odd about two women speaking in hushed yet clearly aggressive tones in an alleyway well outside the better parts of the city. The shieldmaiden had no skill for intrigue. Her face sank. "We were just talking about you. And having a . . . spirited debate about the meaning of truthfulness. Is that not so, Kolbrun?"

Eyrun tried to place a calm hand on the shieldmaiden's shoulder, but the gesture ended predictably. Kolbrun batted it away and spun to face her assailant. The pair locked eyes.

Aelfhild swallowed. The river was so close. She could see it through a gap between the buildings ahead. Soothing, rippling, cold as an autumn night. All she wanted was to dip her feet. The insides of her head pounded against her skull. Her tongue grated against sandy gums. There had been so much mead. Instead she had to skip aside as Kolbrun stalked past her. The shieldmaiden never looked her in the face, never said a word. Her cheeks were blotched purple as she passed.

"Will you walk with me, Aelfhild?" Eyrun couched it as a question. It was not.

Aelfhild nodded. They strolled riverward. Just one chance to dip her feet was all she wanted.

"How are you feeling?"

"Fine, lady, thank you," Aelfhild replied. She had been sweating all morning, but now she was drenched. She had said "lady" as a reflex. She had been trained well.

Eyrun noticed and laughed. The laugh was about as genuine as her smile. "You do not call Eyvind 'lord,' do you? Of course not. You may call me Eyrun. We are friends."

Aelfhild hid her expression beneath her palm as she stifled a cough.

"May I call you Aela?"

"Hmm," Aelfhild nodded.

"Well, Aela, as I said, we were talking about you. A runner came this morning from Jarl Hafdis—you remember her, of course. She is riding out with a few of her men and coming to visit my father. Now, nothing about that is odd. Trollsmork and Rifstrond are allies, have long been allies. The Jarls meet each other often. But Kolbrun has it in her head that your companion Onund has told his master everything, and that Hafdis will tell my father everything in turn, and you can gather what I mean by *everything*?"

"Hmm." Aelfhild clenched her hand.

"Yes, that. You can imagine what a state poor Kolbrun was in. Her oath is not given lightly. She wants to bare her soul to the Jarl before Hafdis arrives and before my father gets cross with her. As if he would have his precious Trollslayers stripped and flogged for one tiny secret."

Eyrun thought that was funny. Aelfhild mustered a few words. "Not so tiny."

"Well, yes and no. Yes and no." The Jarl's daughter was infinitely reasonable. "So I was trying to convince Kolbrun that the wisest course is to simply wait and see. I told her that I will take responsibility, as would my brother, if anything unexpected were to unfold. All will be well. Our father is no monster. But you know Kolbrun. She is a spirited one." At that, Eyrun began to play with one of the thin braids that trailed down from her tresses to dance across the shoulders of her dress. It was an oddly unguarded gesture from a woman who seemed in constant, determined control. Aelfhild spotted it immediately. Eyrun herself stopped as soon as she realized.

"So, Aela, there may be some raised voices in the next few days, but leave it with me. All will be well."

"I believe you," Aelfhild replied. And she did, at least as far as her own health was concerned. After all, just as Eyrun said, what could Harald really do? Beat her? Exile her? Kill her? Not impossible, but unlikely. She was touched by the Gods and he called himself pious. For everyone else, though, things were not so simple.

Eyrun stopped short and turned to face her. The smile on her face had taken its time settling in but it looked mostly real. "I must take my leave of you now, Aela. Unfortunately there are many other things that need my care. But I will see you again soon." She squeezed Aelfhild's hand and swept away.

"Hmm," Aelfhild replied.

Feet still damp from the bracing waters of the Frostá, Aelfhild walked through the market stalls. She had hoped to lose herself in the rarest sorts of Thrym treasure, in magical curios and mysterious artifacts pried from the deepest reaches of the earth. She found, instead, fish in buckets alongside frogs and eels. Herbs and roots of every sort, from burdock through to rhubarb. Iron, wrought and unwrought. Knives, cauldrons, baskets. Blankets and baubles. Tonics with smells worse than those of any troll. She could have been walking around Cynestead. Far from distracting, it made her homesick for a home that no longer existed. It was Eyrun, really, that had spoiled her mood. Or Hafdis, or Harald. Even the river had not lived up to her hopes. Her temples throbbed.

She had felt Ceolwen looking over her shoulder all morning. It had started as a niggle; she realized she had not thought of her former mistress in ages. How short a time it took to forget. To cavort with the Thrym and drink her cares away as though her happiness mattered for aught in the grand scheme. It was selfishness. Vanity. And she had not paused to consider how slim was the chance that a troll just happened to appear out of legend at the exact moment she brought her glowing rune home. As if she were not the cause of all misfortune.

Ceolwen's stare accused. Aelfhild burned with the shame of her weakness.

There was a breath of wind past her elbow. Just the gentlest puff, no more than a swallow flitting past, and the sense honed by a life in Cynestead's lanes that her belt was now lighter. She patted the sides of her dress. The belt knife was still there. Her purse, the purse that the Jarl had given to the Trollslayer whose name he could never quite manage to remember, was not. The market was empty enough that it was tough work for a cutpurse to melt into the crowd. She saw one diminutive back hustling away from her.

"Thief!" She hollered and pointed desperately.

The Thrym all stared at her. She had yelled in Earnfolding. "Thief!" she yelled in the northern tongue. The Thrym continued to stare. Evidently it was her problem and hers alone. Maybe they would have helped a local. Maybe. The word did cause the cutpurse to speed his escape.

Her dress was not made for running, but Aelfhild sprinted after him. They were her coins. Even if she did live entirely off the Jarl's generosity she would still be damned if she was just going to let some runt carry off her coins without a struggle. She felt wool tearing as she ran and tried to hitch up the skirt without slowing. *Now I know why Kolbrun wears breeches*, she thought as her knees chafed against wool.

The thief was half her size and twice her speed. It seemed unfair to steal both her coins and any remaining illusion of youth, but the lad carried on unfazed. Or lass, Aelfhild realized; at that age it was hard to tell one from the other at a distance.

She careened around a corner and knocked over a bucket brimming with foul, frothy liquid. She skipped over the mess, but the alley was empty. Another turn brought her panting into the intersection of several side streets. There was no thief evident in any of them. After a few whirls, straining for any hint, she sighed and bent to catch her breath.

The smiths had not taken the day off, it seemed. Anvils rang staccato over the walls, and Aelfhild could make out the pillar of black smoke that rose from the city's ever-burning forges. Clinker crackled underfoot as she walked down a lane carpeted with iron scale and lined with piles of slag. Past that, she could see the smiths at work. Cinders danced on rippling air belched by furnaces. Sparks flew as hammers struck glowing orange blanks. Faces broke from the shadowed recesses of the foundries occasionally, features blotted out by black soot save for white eyes and pale runnels carved by sweat. A few raised knuckles to brow in obeisance when they caught sight of Aelfhild. They could not know her, but anyone down in these lanes so dressed and untouched by grime could only come from above.

The hammers fell without rhythm, loud and insistent, and set off starbursts in her already pounding head. As she turned away, she spotted a bit of leather between some oil-slick quenching barrels. She stooped and picked up her purse. Empty, of course.

All the twists and turns of this city were unfamiliar, and she could not remember how she had come. Riverward was the truest direction in Herjarsborg, so she made her way toward the bank as directly as possible. Warehouses butted their shingled walls against one another to block her path; windowless sheds hemmed in the side lanes. There were dead ends and guard dogs on long tethers that she could not slip past. No one stirred, so directions were not forthcoming. They were all, she imagined, wise enough to be in their beds, nursing hangovers of their own. Each turning looked exactly like the last. Finally she caught sight of another soul and tried to hail her.

A heavyset girl in a black scarf and shawl pulled a goat down the cross street. Aelfhild waved, but the stranger's attention was elsewhere and she gave no response. Since she had no better plan, Aelfhild followed.

There was a crowd gathering in a courtyard overhung by outhouses, log-buttressed shanties, and one of old Herjarsborg's abandoned walls. Someone had built a shrine there, just a five-posted awning over a firepit, but folk were gathering to listen. The girl led her goat through the line of onlookers. Aelfhild's curiosity got the better of her. She stood on tiptoes in the back and peered over.

Smoke drifted up from coals in the firepit to stain the awning and the sacrifices hanging from ropes beneath. There were chicken and geese, hogsheads and lamb hocks, most dripping fresh but a few shriveled and shedding feathers. Aelfhild was glad the charcoal smoke covered any other odors, though it did not discourage every fly. The goat was being trussed against a wooden block by a pair of cowled men. Its slitted eyes spun as it wriggled against its bindings. It gave a panicked bleat, but then one of the men brought down a cleaver and left the blood to drain into a bowl. Sacrifices were the language of the Gods, according to the priestly class, and Aelfhild had seen such work before. An old man sat on a stump in front of the fire pit. He wore a black cowl like the others, but his eyes were bound with cloth as well. His shriveled cheeks collapsed inward under the weight of years. When he opened his mouth to speak, she saw only one solitary tooth.

"More of you come today than have come in years. I smell the fright. Where was your devotion when your bellies were fat and your harvests were good? Where were your sacrifices then?" He cackled, revealing knobbly gums. "Never mind. The Gods see all. They tell faith from fear."

One of the sacrificers lifted the bowl of blood and held it before the old man. He wet his fingertips, then ran both hands down his face, leaving stains from his blindfold to his wattled neck. The carrier took the bowl around the crowd, putting a thumbprint of blood onto proffered foreheads. His fellow came after and draped amulets over the necks of those marked. None in the crowd spoke. There were no thanks given to the cowled men, no shouts at the speaker, not even whispered comments to a neighbor. Aelfhild had never seen a Thrym crowd so pliant.

"An age of darkness comes," said the old man. "A time of strife and toil. Brother against brother, father against son. The gilded halls will burn. Bonds of love and loyalty will fail. Old ghosts will rise. The omens speak clear."

The crowd churned up a space for Aelfhild as the sacrificers approached. Refusing seemed unwise. She was not the only one in finer cloth, but the odds were not in her favor if any hands were feeling restless. Best not to provoke those who were drawn so taut. She leaned forward. The blood was hot on her forehead. Twine scraped at her neck. Ranks closed around her again and she was hidden in the press.

"Pray. Make your sacrifices," the old one continued. "Listen for the words. The Gods speak truer than any of the highborn. You will know their works. The darkness comes! Hark! A doom upon the wicked!"

A shudder ran through the onlookers. It passed around Aelfhild. She wondered at that. The words should have scared her, as they did these people. Such prophecy made them stare unblinking, or rock back and forth on their feet, or made the mothers squeeze their children so close that the little ones would squirm and squeal. But for Aelfhild, it was as though a chain had snapped and a millstone fell from her back. Someone else felt it. Gnawing dread had dogged her steps for too long, born of the dreams and the rune and the endless plots before that, but for a passing moment it eased. To hear it spoken, to give it form, made it bearable. Let the old man shoulder the weight for a time, let the crowd spread it among themselves. She had carried it alone for months and countless leagues.

She looked down at the amulet. It was a stick of wood, the length and width of her forefinger, with a carved face. She could not tell if they were meant to be runes. The worksmanship was poor enough that they were just scratchings to her eyes. No one in the crowd could read, regardless, so it hardly mattered. But she could see folk clutching theirs. It seemed a paltry defense.

The sermon ended with another spit-flecked cackle. "A time of winnowing is upon us. There is no running from the Gods' judgment!"

3 4

"INDEED, I SEE what you mean," said Dunstan. He hunched and leaned forward to whisper in a way that irked Aelfhild. It was not any quieter, and the posture screamed conspiracy to anyone who cared to look. There were only a few other Earnfoldings in the room, though, so the risk was low. Jarl Harald had given Sabert and his men quarters in Herjarsborg. The two leaders had been spending a great deal of time together, planning. Aelfhild had met Sabert and worried that for all his many qualities he might not be Harald's equal when it came to schemes. The Eorling would learn bitterly that his father might have trained him well with the bow but had not prepared him for the world of court intrigue.

"The trouble is," Dunstan continued, "our Sabert seems to be quite taken with the Jarl. I think Harald has certainly turned his head, as they say."

"As you say, maybe," said Godwyn. He at least had the good sense not to hunch over. "Listen, the likes of us can talk all we want. A bookreader who never lifted a sword in his life, a fierce and handsome warrior"—he winked and Aelfhild groaned—"who has no standing at all, and some . . . girl. None of us can figure why you are still here, so what in the name of the Smith's swinging hammer can we hope to do about it?"

"There is really no need to speak that way to our guest." Dunstan tried to straighten from his stoop. His chin stuck out more than normal.

Aelfhild shook her head at him. Charming as it was how he tried to rise to her defense, now was not the time. "Godwyn is right. He will not listen to either of us. But you are clever, Dunstan, and Cuthbert trusted you for good reason. Maybe Sabert will listen to you. You have to talk to him straight. Tell him that the Thrym have their own plans for our lands. Harald does not have his interests at heart, no matter what flowery nonsense he might spout about blood ties and family honor and the like."

The thought of any sort of confrontation clearly pained the sage. He shrank back down. "Well, er, indeed, but what is the plan? What is our goal? Perhaps we should wait until things are clearer?"

"He needs to hear more than just Harald's voice so that he can make plans of his own. I would trust Cuthbert—"

"Eorl Cuthbert," Godwyn corrected.

"I would trust Eorl Cuthbert to be wise enough to master it, but not his son," Aelfhild finished.

"And the thing she is leaving out, why she cannot go directly to him," Godwyn said, "is because she hit him in the face with a bloody rock!" He hooted and slapped the table, but Aelfhild was actually surprised he had been that perceptive.

"Er, you did?"

"I did." *I also helped lead him in an attack on the Oescan boats to delay the legion and allow the Thrym to attack and free the prisoners.* Aelfhild did not say so, but she suspected that the credit for some of those plans might have drifted slightly in the time since they had left Norholt. Few men wanted to admit to following some girl, as Godwyn had put it, into battle.

"Besides," she said, "if Eyrun is right I may have to tell Jarl Harald some things soon. I need to focus on that." *And make up my mind if I will stay that long*, she thought. But someone had to see to the interests of Earnfold. Osric would not. Sabert could not, at least not without wise counsel. If she were going to let out, she had to know that someone would at least try.

Dunstan buried his head in his spindly hands. "This whole mess is intolerable. My lord Cuthbert never would have allowed this to happen."

Godwyn was still chipper. "And when they ransom back Eorl Cuthbert from Osric and those bastards, all will be as it should. Quit your bellyaching. The Eorl always knows what to do."

"Have you not been listening? Can you really be so simple?" Dunstan's despair turned to venom. "Why would Harald buy back what he means to take by force? Why would he throw away chests and chests of gold when Sabert is easily led?"

"Well"—the young warrior's brow wrinkled under strain of thought—"he must. He has to. For honor's sake, you know."

"Gods save us!" Dunstan cradled his head once more.

"Come now," Godwyn said, clapping him on the back. "None of that whinging. You are a warrior of Norholt even if you never did shoot a bow. Chin up! Let us grab a spot of supper and we will feel better. All this talking can wait. Next spring we may all be surprised for the better."

The young warrior dragged the sage off, promising all manner of revels that would build up his confidence. Aelfhild took her leave. She had planted the seed, and that was the best she could do. But perhaps not the best. It was one piece she could put in motion. Dunstan's conscience would urge him to do right, she was sure, whether she was around to push him or not. Eyrun's use of the word "queen" had put the rabbit in Aelfhild's blood, though.

She walked back toward the Great Hall. Supper would be tense. Maybe she could snag something in the kitchen and avoid the main meal. Sitting near Harald, Eyrun, and Kolbrun sounded like torture. The idea of sitting next to Eyvind made the tips of her ears burn.

You have to see him eventually.

Shut it, Aelfhild said to herself.

It was what you wanted, remember? You were almost brave enough to run away before, but you botched that, too. You let your own loins doom your homeland and your people.

"Go away," Aelfhild said. Aloud.

A tiny hand was tugging at the back of her dress. She spun, ready to flatten another cutpurse. She came face-to-face—or would have if the opposing face had been higher—with a sprite of a girl. The child had a shock of flaxen hair and a dress that looked exactly like Aelfhild's own but shrunken to doll size.

The girl's eyes bulged at the sight of Aelfhild's fist. "Beg pardon, lady," she squeaked.

As battle-hardened as she wanted to be, and as furious as she was at all thieving, snot-nosed children, it broke Aelfhild's heart to see the child flinch. She kneeled and took the girl's hand. "Forgive me, little one. My mind was elsewhere."

The clouds passed and the little girl was smiling again. "The man wanted me to find you."

"What man?"

"Gave me a copper." The child proudly displayed a green-edged coin that looked small even in her minuscule palm. It might have purchased half an apple or, at a stretch, a handful of porridge oats in the market. She was beaming proudly, though.

"He told you to find me?"

"Said find the troll killer from outland."

That was a specific enough description. "And then what?" Aelfhild asked.

"Saw you."

She had to think like a child momentarily and get specific. "What did he tell you to do once you found me?"

"Take you to him."

"Where is he?"

The child latched onto the front of Aelfhild's dress with one hand, the hand not clutching the coin, and dragged. Aelfhild followed. They twisted and turned through the back lanes and alleyways of Herjarsborg.

"Do you know who stole my purse earlier today?" Aelfhild decided to drop a lure. The urchins in Cynestead, in her experience, formed their own interwoven coterie of fences, lookouts, and pickpockets, and the better-off children were all too often willing accomplices. Ceolwen certainly had been. "I was in the market and someone grabbed my coins. Shiny ones, just like you have. You would not want to lose your coin, would you? Do you know what happened?"

The girl did not even turn to face her. She just pulled onward. "Never saw him."

As far as denials went, it was a poor one. But Aelfhild was not going to interrogate a toddler. There had not been that many coins in the purse.

Eventually they came to the city's southeastern gate. This was the farthest section downstream of Herjarsborg, and Aelfhild recognized her own people. Every tunic and dress was scrubbed spotless but patched thoroughly. No flat space went unused; there was either a chicken pen, sawbucks and worktable, a bubbling cauldron of wash, or a rack lined with drying trout. Thatched roofs were mended into checkerboards of scavenged materials—planks here, cast-off shingles there, fresh gold reeds next to aged grey. But the women were sweeping the dirt away from their stoops. The men paused to greet neighbor and passing stranger alike. They were making do.

On each side of the gates, out of kicking range of the guards at their posts, were the beggars. They lined the road, each with a bowl set out in front. Some were legless, others poxed, some bloated, others palsied. Passersby looked over or around them.

Aelfhild found herself wondering where they went when it rained. Or snowed, come wintertime. A few of them had the remains of coats or robes.

The little girl pulled her along toward the line of invisible folk.

The last thing Aelfhild wanted was to have another toothless madman dribbling over her and jabbering about prophecy. She thought about turning back. There was so much else to dwell on. But the child's grip was insistent. "Here"—the girl pointed ahead as she pulled.

From a distance it looked like carrion. Aelfhild thought a dog had died and been left alongside the pathway. But at the sound of the little girl's voice the pile of stippled fur unfolded. It was a man, and a good-sized one, wearing a whole bear hide. The bear's nose and eyeballs were gone, replaced by pale, leathery slits, but the claws remained and dangled down around the man's bare torso. He was a mess of scars and tattoos. The bear hide and some travel-stained breeches were his only clothing. His beard flowed freely into long knots of almost the same burned hue as the fur around his shoulders.

The child extended an expectant palm. The man put in another copper coin and the little girl vanished.

Aelfhild's hand was already on her belt knife. This was not a ranting beggar. There was no bowl out in front of him. Passersby did stare at this one. Not for long, though, when they saw his eyes. They were pure, bloodshot madness.

"What do you want?" Aelfhild asked. She made sure he could see her stance, see the hilt of her knife. He did not look armed, but he was large enough that it would still be a contest.

"You are the girl from Earnfold?" There was an accent when he spoke. He was Thrym, clearly, but not from Herjarsborg or Trollsmork. "My mistress wishes to see you. You will wish to see her."

"Who is your mistress?"

"You do not know of her. Here, those that know call her the Whisperer. She tells me to fetch you. I am here to fetch you."

Aelfhild took a step back. "What if I do not want to go?"

The bear hide shrugged. "As you wish."

"Your mistress would not be angry?"

"You will wish to see her. She tells me to carry this to you." He held out a lump of bone.

As soon as she saw the beak, saw the cruel, hooked point, Aelfhild knew what it was. The yellow-and-black coloring was the same. She took it in her hand, and the brittle weight was exact. Eagle, hawk, buzzard, which bird of prey she still could not say. There was a dark stain on the tip. The beak scraped her palm exactly as in the dream.

"I will wait," he said.

He made no move to rise or grab hold of her. Still she backed away.

"I will wait," he repeated.

Aelfhild turned. She looked over her shoulder with every other step. The man never so much as twitched. She sped from a walk to a jog, then a flat-out run. There were a few stares as she made her way back to the Great Hall, heaving for breath.

3 5

EYVIND WAS SLEEPING on a bench with a damp cloth over his face. The exposed skin looked queasy pale. He did not so much as twitch when Aelfhild burst through the door. Embla shot up and licked every exposed bit of Aelfhild's face and hands as though they had not just seen each other that morning. The hound even nibbled her fingers for good measure. Aelfhild ran her free hand through the fur on the dog's snout and hugged her closely. Her other, shaking hand still held the bird skull.

Whether it was her posture or the speed of her arrival, Jarngrim spotted that something was amiss. He lifted himself from his bunk onto his elbows. "What happened to you?"

"Someone knows about me. Someone knows something they could not know—my dreams! There is a man by the gate in a bear hide, said his mistress sent him." Aelfhild's breath was still ragged. She pulled herself onto a bench across from Jarngrim. "I never told anyone. No one could know that. But he had the skull and he knew who I was."

Jarngrim glanced at Eyvind, then glanced at the door. No one came to his aid. He sat up and spread his hands in front of himself. "What are you saying?"

She took a steadying breath. "There was a man by the downriver gate. He sent for me. He told me his mistress wanted to see me and that I wanted to see her. Then he showed me this."

Jarngrim's eyes widened. "What is it?"

"A bird skull."

"Birds die all the time." His eyes narrowed. He seemed on firmer ground there.

"It is the exact same skull!" She clapped a hand over her mouth. The words had erupted louder than intended. She said it again, softer.

Jarngrim stared. After some thought he asked, "What was his name?"

"I did not stay to ask."

"What was her name then—the mistress?"

Her thoughts were all crowding together and pushing one another out of line. She scrambled for a moment. "*Hvíslarinn* was the word he used. The Whisperer?" She raised her eyebrows and he nodded. She continued, "Something about those that know her call her that."

"Never heard that. It is a word, surely, but not *the* Whisperer. And I am pretty good with names and such."

Aelfhild fanned her face. "I think I am just finally going mad. It is all too much. This is the end."

"Did anyone else"—Jarngrim cleared his throat—"see him?"

"There was a little girl." That sounded no better. Jarngrim just nodded along.

There was a hole in the conversation filled only by Aelfhild's heavy breathing. Embla laid her head on the bench beside and looked up with plaintive eyes.

Aelfhild looked over at Eyvind. His naked chest rose and fell as he snored. There was the scar on his breast, a purple lump beneath puckered skin. And glowing. The bench skidded across the floor as she stood. Embla yelped. Aelfhild walked to his side. She hoped it was just candlelight playing off the sweat. She knew it would not be. As she moved, the glow remained fixed, a dim pinprick but undeniable.

Jarngrim coughed. "He made me swear not to mention it."

She pressed both hands against her face. The skull was somewhere back on the floor, irrelevant now. Part of her had expected this. All of her, really—she knew her own luck. The darkness was comforting. It was simple. She just wanted to sleep.

"I hoped," Jarngrim's voice came over her shoulder, "that it might be something good for a change. To have two marked by the Gods."

She turned to face him. His eyes did not rise to hers. He did not believe it any more than she did.

His tone was gentle as he asked, "You knew?"

It was her turn to look away, but she nodded.

"And you did not tell me." It was a flat statement and all the more brutal for it. Yelling would have made it easier to bear. "Can you fix it?"

"I do not know how," she whispered. Sleep, blessed oblivion, where no care could touch her and there was nothing for her busy hands to ruin. But dreams would come. There was no sanctuary.

"You will try?"

She looked him in the eyes. "With everything I have."

If she knows my dreams, she might know about this, Aelfhild thought. What other path is there? "I need to find out about this Whisperer."

"Maybe," Jarngrim began after a moment, then lowered his voice to a whisper, "Maybe it is a women's . . . matter." He waved a hand vaguely around his belt line. "Those that know her, as it were."

She stared back. It was the only good idea she had heard so far. Maybe the womenfolk would know. Not Eyrun or Kolbrun, not right now. But the ones who traded every rumor, the ones who heard every secret. They would be toiling away in the kitchen garden just a few steps away. She could ask the servants.

He must have taken her stare the wrong way. "Forgive me, it was foolish. It was rude. I never meant to—"

The door banged behind her as she left.

It was odd to be on the receiving end of that familiar stare. Aelfhild had to plant herself directly in front of the young woman and make it clear that she had no plans to move until there was eye contact before the servant would look up from the floor. It was a face that neither agreed nor disagreed, neither approved nor disapproved, did not judge or comment or even remember anything from any time. The maidservant's shield. Beneath all the blank innocence was a well of secreted knowledge and gossip that would put the town's Runemaster to shame, but inaccessible to outsiders. And Aelfhild was very much outside. Here was a foreigner that sat at the Jarl's table. She carried a man's weapons and hunted with the warriors. The Jarl's daughter talked to her as an equal. She had been seen kissing the Jarl's son—and no chance someone had not carried that juicy tidbit around. It mattered precious little that she had been a servant once. The girl from Earnfold was not now, and probably would not ever be again, one of them.

If the cook was peeved to be interrupted from her kneading, it did not show. Clumps of rye dough clung to her fingers as she looked up at Aelfhild. "Do you need something, lady?"

The other servants had all flitted off on various errands when Aelfhild appeared. This one was unlucky enough to have been sitting at her work and unable to escape gracefully.

"I heard a name and I was curious about it. I thought, *Who better to ask than those that know best?*" Aelfhild tried her most winning smile.

The mask never cracked. There was no response, because there had not been a direct question. Flattery never would have worked on her when she was a servant, and Aelfhild felt foolish for trying. She stopped smiling. The only way she would get through this wall of silence would be if one of the serving girls decided to let her through. She opted for honesty. "Someone told me that the Whisperer wanted to speak to me. I want to know who she is. I want to know what she is. Do you know?"

"No, lady."

"You have never heard the name?"

"Never, lady."

"You do not know who she is?"

"No, lady."

"Do you think anyone else would know?"

"I could not say, lady."

No wonder Ceolwen used to get so cross. There was not even any softening around the eyes. No recognition of shared humanity. Just a gulf, yawning and unbridged, between them. The servant was back to her kneading as though no conversation had taken place. Aelfhild stifled the urge to scream. She could feel the tears building, stinging hot and just a hairbreadth away. She squeezed until her fingernails bit into the heels of her palms. "I am very tired and very scared"—her voice cracked—"and I just want to know if any of you have heard that name."

The maid's hands ceased working. She did not look up at Aelfhild but stood and wiped her hands across the front of her apron. "I will ask. Wait."

Aelfhild did as ordered. She took deep breaths. Every nerve was raw, and her mind was cottony. Jarls and eorls with their plots and secrets, all wheels within wheels, thieves, headaches, and now dreams breaking through into the waking world. It had been a day of ills. She envied the women in the Jarl's hall. Baking bread would have been just the right sort of tedium. Just keep her head down, make her dough, and survive through to tomorrow. Then again the next day, and the day after that. Until some raving loon appeared and dragged you into affairs well beyond the scope of your safe, steady life.

Aelfhild could sympathize.

The serving girl reappeared. She crooked a finger at Aelfhild, but not before glancing carefully in either direction. They passed from the court-yard and summer kitchen through a few time-stained curtains. Casks were stacked ceiling high in the room beyond, the air thick enough to taste the acrid sweet oak of the firkins. Aelfhild's guide led her to a huddle of women in kerchiefs and speckled aprons but did not stick around herself. Not everyone had time for idle chat.

There were streaks of white in the hair that showed past the edge of their headscarves, and deepening lines from noses to lips. They did not give their names. They wasted no time on pleasantries.

"You are with child, my dear?"

Aelfhild took a step back and shook her head.

"You wish to be?" another asked.

Before she had a chance to reply, more questions. "A man spurned you? Betrayed you?"

"Harmed you?"

"No," she answered.

"Then you do not need the Whisperer, girl. Better to leave such things be." The women nodded in unison.

"No, you do not understand," Aelfhild said, finding herself off balance. "She sent for me. She is looking for *me*."

All around her there was a sharp intake of breath. The elders looked from one to another. Evidently this was not how it went.

"Who is she?" Aelfhild asked.

After a pause, and further exchanged glances, one of the women replied, "She helps women—"

"—and sometimes men," another interrupted.

"—and sometimes men with quiet matters," the first continued. "She knows things, she sees things. She is *norn*. You know this word?"

Aelfhild shook her head.

More looks from one to the next. "She knows of the old ways. For a price, she helps."

"Always a price." The third woman broke her silence.

"You do as the Whisperer says. And if she sends for you—"

The second woman cut in again. "Why does she send for you, girl?"

"—then you must go to her."

Aelfhild's throat was dry. She had to work to swallow. "Thank you," she said, and left the women staring. She was not yet through the second curtain before they were murmuring to one another. The rumors would be flying thickly through the back halls of Herjarsborg tonight, Aelfhild knew. Jarl Harald was going to be the last one to know of the strange happenings in his own city. There was some small justice in that. Aelfhild was glad there would be someone out there as befuddled as she.

3 6

WHEN JARL HAFDIS arrived, Aelfhild was watching the messenger. The man never shifted. He sat beneath his bearskin day in, day out. He did not stretch or yawn or so much as scratch. If he moved to find food or relieve himself, Aelfhild never saw it during daylight. Instead, the world moved around him. Foot and cart traffic down the road made a markedly wider swing past him than around any of the beggars. None risked speaking to the intruder.

Hafdis arrived on horseback, aglimmer in the sun. There were sapphires on her breast, and the pommel of her sword was polished to looking-glass sheen. The few beggars that could stand lifted their bowls overhead as she and her men trotted past. The Jarl tossed out a few coins as she made her way down the lane. Each of her huskarls wore a greatsword strapped across his back and bristled with other bolts and blades. Even a friendly visit, for the Thrym, was best undertaken while heavily armed.

She strained onto the tips of her toes. Aelfhild could not see Onund among the dozen or so faces. Some of the men were wrapped in their blue hoods to keep out the summer rays, but she would have spotted the old man's coiffed whiskers from leagues away. Maybe his absence was a good sign. Maybe Hafdis had other, more pressing concerns to raise with Harald. Something like fishing rights. The Thrym did love to argue about fish.

But then, surely, a girl with a glowing hand was worth at least passing mention. Aelfhild might not tell anyone else the whole truth, but lying to herself was not working. She looked back at the lump of bearskin by the gate. The hairs on the back of her neck prickled. Each time she had come down to watch him she had chosen a different hiding spot, and a good one. His eyes never turned her way. But she always got the feeling that he knew she was there. It was like watching a house cat—even when it looked to be napping, the ears twitched back and forth and never missed a noise.

She was going to go with him. She had made up her mind after hearing what the old servants had told her. But she had not told anyone else yet. The question of when had stretched on for a few days. It was the other questions that tormented her most. What if Eyvind got worse when she left? Perhaps her closeness was the only thing keeping the glow from spreading. How long did he have? He could die while she was wandering the wilds in strangers' company. Would he still know her, or if he did, want to see her once she returned? But Hafdis's arrival was going to force the hands of several people, not just Aelfhild's. Sneaking out before that seemed cowardly. Staying for what was certain to be a thunderous row seemed foolish.

Her bare arms were burning. She shifted back into the dwindling shade.

Jarngrim came sauntering down from the upper city. Aelfhild marked him as soon as he rounded the corner. Folk made way for his bulk, but Herjarsborg's residents seemed to long since have overcome any need to stare at his dark skin. The sheen wore off any marvel over a long enough time. Still, the warrior stood out. He was chewing some sort of seeds and spitting the husks into the dirt. And he was looking for her.

Since he had borne the brunt of her first panicked outburst, Aelfhild had been obliged to explain a few things to him. He knew the outline of what was happening and where she had been slipping off to. She had spared telling him her decision to depart. Jarngrim seemed content enough with keeping secrets, but she did not want to test his limits. She hissed as he swung his head back and forth, shading his eyes to peer into the shadows. He did not share her desire for stealth. Anyone spotting him would spot her shortly thereafter. She waved for him to duck out of sight, but he took it as a greeting.

"Ay-o, there you are." He gobbed into the gutter. "Eyrun sent me after you. She was wondering where you got off to. Calm yourself; I told her naught. They are all scurrying about up there and cranky, too. Glad to get myself away."

Aelfhild pulled on his sleeve. "Would you get out of the light?"

He grumbled past a cheekful of seeds. "Still watching that one?"

She nodded. "He never moves."

Another round of husks went flying. "I could go down there and give him the old boot here and there. Watch him move, then."

Having seen the man up close, Aelfhild was not convinced it would be that easy. And she did not want to anger this Whisperer, whoever she was, because even stripping away the usual embellishment you might expect from servants' gossip, it did not sound wise to cross such a one. "You leave him be," she said.

Jarngrim shrugged and offered her some of his snack. "Can we get back? Eyrun will have some words for me, otherwise."

"Only if we walk slowly," Aelfhild replied.

She dragged her heels through the dust. Rain had been sparse, and the once-muddy lanes were baked into cracks. They fell in behind an oxcart heaped with cabbages destined for the upriver market. The great beast plodded along in no particular hurry. Aelfhild matched its pace. She noticed a talisman hanging from the eaves of a passing house. It was a scratchwork runestick like the one around her neck. They appeared around the city more and more, over doorways or around wrists and necks. The doomsayers were hard at work in the back alleys.

Jarngrim spat. "You going to tell Eyvind?"

Aelfhild grunted.

"You cannot duck him forever."

She grunted louder this time; he seemed oblivious to her tone.

"If you really think none of us sees all the looks—"

"Jarngrim, you are one of my dearest friends in the entire world, but if you do not stop talking right now"—Aelfhild lifted her hand—"I will smite you with all the fury of the Gods."

He chewed his seeds.

There was everything else to focus on. Eyvind had to wait. His father was the question. And the bearskin sitting by the southeastern gate. And Sabert's gullibility.

By the time they reached the Great Hall, the last of Hafdis's horses were being led off to the stables. Aelfhild was not about to take the chance of walking in on a conversation between the two jarls that might or might not be about her, so she looped around to one of the side doors. Jarngrim grumbled about the grief that would befall him if she was not delivered in timely fashion but followed along. There was the normal shuffle of servants in and out of the side doors, and Aelfhild could pass through without a fuss. Gently she nudged aside a curtain to sneak a glimpse of the main hall. It was packed with bodies. Hafdis's huskarls stood on one side and Harald's lined the other. The two jarls stood together in the center, blue cloak and red cloak spooling together on the floorboards. Hafdis was embracing Eyvind. Eyrun hovered nearby. The girl stood as rigidly as the elm pillars holding up the roof.

"My heart sings to see you back and alive. Onund told me a tale the likes of which few have ever heard." Hafdis held Eyvind at arm's length. "Such a tale."

"What strength there is in my boy, eh?" Harald said, beaming. He put a hand on Eyvind's shoulder. Eyvind, for his part, looked as uncomfortable as his sister.

"And how is Onund, Jarl Hafdis?" Eyrun's voice was tender as birdsong. "He is not with you, I see. I hope he is well. I want nothing more than to thank him for his part in returning my brother."

Harald raised an inviting hand, and the royal crowd began moving toward the courtyard. Aelfhild had to lean into her curtain to hear the answer.

"He begged to take his leave for a short time. I granted it at once. Onund served my husband well for years and has been nothing but keen in my service. Few are more deserving of a rest."

The voices faded. Listening at the entrance to the courtyard would have been a sure way to draw the attention of servants or guards. Harald was leading them to his Council House, but there were no side passages there, no curtains to peep through. Jarngrim already looked thoroughly miserable. Any more slinking around and the poor man would break. Embla came trotting up and scraped at Aelfhild's knee impatiently. If the dog had found them, others would follow.

Surely enough, Kolbrun walked in on them huddled by the curtain.

Gods deliver us from true and honest folk, Aelfhild thought. As soon as she saw the set of the shieldmaiden's brow, saw the shame and anger and disgust mashed into that stare, she knew that there was no more dodging. If Hafdis had not already revealed all, Kolbrun was going to. Asking her to carry it this long had been cruelty. The shieldmaiden was purer than the rest of them. That was no blessing in the world they now inhabited.

"Kolbrun, I—" Aelfhild began. Excuses seemed worse than useless. Instead she said, "Forgive me."

The shieldmaiden kept staring.

"Skjaldmaer, we all agreed," Jarngrim said. He hung his head under that gaze, all the same.

"I cannot lie anymore."

Embla whined. The hound was used to her pack being upset, but not with one another. Her tail sank low.

One of the courtyard-facing curtains parted and Eyrun stepped through. "Good, here you are. All of you." A pair of scullery maids carrying stacks of bowls out to the feast tables ducked aside as the Jarl's daughter swept through. "Where were you?"

Aelfhild opened her mouth to reply but Eyrun was not looking at her. Instead, she cut straight toward Kolbrun. The pair glared at one another.

"I had to think." Muscles along the shieldmaiden's jaw bunched as she spoke.

Eyrun sniffed. "And much good that did, I am sure." She turned to Aelfhild and held out a hand. "Come now. It is time."

Aelfhild looked at her companions. "Both of you deserve better. I am sorry it came to this." Jarngrim shrugged. Kolbrun nodded, tight-lipped.

"They are waiting." Eyrun's hand was still outstretched. Aelfhild reached out. Both their palms were slick with sweat.

"Ready?"

Aelfhild nodded.

Time, indeed.

3 7

HAFDIS WAS ABSORBED in studying the troll bones. The beast's remains were laid out in full over the sawdust floor of the Council House, flensed and rinsed in a vain attempt to remove the smell. They had been forced to burn the pelt because it did nothing but attract wasps. A few of the daintier finger bones and toe bones had disappeared into passing pockets. Each would make someone a grand charm or totem, no doubt. For the moment, the skeletal troll provided a fine excuse for the visiting jarl to stand clear of an unfolding family squabble.

The central throne was ringed by tracks. Eyvind's hobnails dotted back and forth at the farthest edge of the circle. Eyrun's smaller footfalls traced a web of turns and stomps in the dust; from the look of it, she had been trying to draw her father's attention from her brother. Jarl Hafdis's feet had made a beeline outward at the first sign of strife.

Harald's feet had never budged. He remained on his throne when Eyrun led Aelfhild in. The Jarl sat tugging the patch of beard on his lower lip.

Eyvind turned to face the two women. Aelfhild met his eyes. They were resigned—a mirror, she imagined, of her own weariness. All the plans they had made, the fireside daydreams before crossing the mountains, had all come to nothing. The Gods laughed at their scrabbling pride. If only Eyvind had dodged that arrow. If only Aelfhild had slipped away a day sooner. If only Osric had never been born. The ifs did no good. Here they were. Aelfhild shrugged. Eyvind shrugged back.

For the first time, Jarl Harald saw her. He looked up from his stewing and took note of her, considered her face. She was more than a gap between more fascinating objects. The feeling was double-edged. Flattering as it might be to matter, there was a thirst in those eyes that passed beyond the physical. The muscles in her legs bunched in preparation for escape. Aelfhild had to tamp down the reflex. His voice was surprisingly mild. "I believed the whole time, did you know that?" He did not wait for any-one's answer. "All the fuss with young Ceolwen and Cuthbert and King Osred, there was always a practical side to it, yes. You do not get to be Jarl without learning how to turn any matter to your favor. My daughter knows this much."

Out of the corner of her eye, Aelfhild saw Eyrun nod.

"But I believed in the Oath-Stone. My faith in the Gods has seen me through many troubles. As much as some may scoff at it." Harald directed this last one toward his son. Eyvind did not flinch. "And now, when that faith is rewarded, it seems I am the last to know."

Aelfhild pushed down the rising lump in her throat. "My lord, it was my choice not to tell you. The others only did as I asked."

At that Harald actually smiled. "A noble heart, too. My children both claimed that they were the ones at fault. It does seem to me that there were many chances and many choices along the way, and more than one person who held back the facts. Many shoulders to bear the blame. Many necks." The smile faded.

"Jarl Hafdis is wise, though," he continued. "She said that a man brooks no profit from vengeance. Certainly not against his kin. Certainly not against one chosen by the Gods." Harald stood and strode toward Aelfhild. Sword and scabbard jostled against his hip with every step. "To all of you I say this. Your Jarl understands. Your Jarl forgives. As does your father."

"And now"—he stood before Aelfhild and reached down for her gloved hand— "let us see what signs the Gods have sent."

Aelfhild's fingers trembled as he pulled the cloth away. Focusing her every thought on steadying it only worsened the shaking.

Hafdis had finished her inspection of the troll bones and turned to watch Aelfhild's hand. Harald licked his lips as light began to glimmer around the edges of the cloth. "Glorious," he whispered.

The rune shone brightly in the shadows of the hall. The glow faded and pulsed and made the room appear to breathe, contracting and expanding in turn. Everyone stared. Light glinted off the tears brimming in Harald's eyes.

"All my life"—he began but had to stop and clear his throat—"all my life I have wanted a sign that the Gods heard me. This is the answer to years of our prayers. Not just mine—your people's, my people's. It is one thing to believe, but this is a sign. A wonder!" The Jarl clasped Aelfhild's hand tightly with both of his, leaving the rest of her to tremble.

"Aelfhild." He savored the name. "Aelfhild, you will help lead us on the holy path. Together there is nothing that can stop our cause. Trollsmork, Rifstrond, Norholt, even Thrymgard and Earnfold, what do these trifles matter when faced with the true will of the Gods?"

She would have preferred a tirade. She would have chosen a whipping, chains, and a dank cell. Instead, words such as "holy path" thundered inside her skull. The word "together" rang in suspect tones. And the madness was catching, judging by the rapturous look on Hafdis's face. Only Eyvind had the good sense to look ill. It was time to take the plunge.

"My lord," Aelfhild whispered, "I must leave for a time."

Eyvind's eyes snapped up from the floor. "What?"

"What?" Eyrun spun to face her.

Jarl Harald's jaw worked up and down for a few moments. No words emerged. This was not the divine message he had expected. Finally he strained out, "You must?"

"Only with your permission, lord."

Aelfhild had been wrong in thinking the look on Kolbrun's face earlier was the low point in the day. The immediate change in Eyvind's expression was the lowest ebb in weeks.

Here was the anger that she had expected from Harald. The color was rising in his cheeks to match. Usually, as much as a man might praise the Gods, he would obey the Jarl. The Gods were first and foremost, of course, but the Jarl's wrath was a good bit less figurative than the Gods' judgments. Dissent was simply not the done thing. And from a woman, no less. "What is this nonsense?"

"The Gods send me dreams, lord. They tell me things. And a man came to the city carrying something from one of those dreams. Something only the Gods could know." Aelfhild had never been entirely convinced her dreams were all to do with the Gods, but now was not the time for discussion. Harald had one very clear lever. "Now I must find out if she can teach me about my gift. She is called the Whisperer."

Eyrun was the only one who did not look confused. *So she knows the name,* Aelfhild thought. *She would. The woman hears everything.*

The Jarl did not look convinced. His brow rose and fell in time with some internal argument. "I . . ."

From behind Harald's shoulder, Eyvind watched her face. "We have to bide until the spring thaw, Father, before we can raid. There is time aplenty." He nodded to her, but his eyes had hardened.

The Jarl glanced back toward his son. He snorted. "A day of ambushes."

"Lord, I will return before springtime comes." *And before you can start your war,* she did not add. "I swear this to you. I cannot disobey the will of the Gods."

That last push seemed to work. Harald nodded. "I will grant it. You will keep me apprised of what happens, I trust. No doubt my children will see to that." He could not glare at both of his heirs at once, so he settled on scowling at Eyrun's carefully blank face.

Hafdis broke the silence. "We still have much to discuss, Harald."

"Yes." The Jarl nodded to Aelfhild. "Thank you, Aelfhild. You may take your leave now and make what preparations you see fit. May the Gods smile upon you."

"And you, lord." She curtsied. "Many thanks."

She could feel their eyes with every step as she departed. She closed the doors behind her, harder than intended. Her ears rang. Her cheeks burned. She waited to see if anyone would follow. No one did.

"This is my fault," Kolbrun said. "I knew I should have spoken up. If I had not lied—"

"—all of this would still be happening," Aelfhild broke in. She wrenched a leather strap tightly and clasped the buckle on one of her saddlebags. "None of this is your fault and you know it."

"What will I tell Eyvind?"

"Let me worry about that."

Jarngrim stuck his head through the open door. "Horses are ready when you are."

"I just need the one," Aelfhild replied.

That got a laugh. "Not likely. If you think we are letting you ride out alone, well, bad luck. It will take more than some shiny mark to stop us."

Kolbrun nodded. "We owe that much at least."

Aelfhild cinched the second bag closed. It would be a light load for the horse; Sorg would appreciate it. She looked around her little nest. There was a gap in the dust where her clothes had sat folded and a few boards where her bedroll had been unfurled. The rest of her world was slung over her shoulder.

"We will need some food."

"Already done," Jarngrim said. "I know a few of the kitchen girls."

Embla stood patiently by the door, tail wagging. The hound was ready for an adventure. It rent Aelfhild's heart to disappoint. She kneeled down and scratched Embla's ears. "Sorry, my girl, no room for you on this one." The hound licked her face.

"Ready?" Kolbrun slipped her axe into a belt loop.

"Ready."

Jarngrim nodded and they set off for the stables. The summer days were still blessedly long, so they had hours left for riding. They could leave Herjarsborg well behind before nightfall. Aelfhild was freed of her secret, which was a relief, and being shed of the city and its ruler would be further kindness. There was a time when she had wished, even prayed, for nothing more than clean blankets and a solid roof. That was the way of it, though. A new life might look preferable from the outside, but step into it and it could stifle.

Eyvind was waiting by the horses.

"You told him?" Aelfhild whispered to Jarngrim.

"It came up."

The two warriors set about saddling the horses and left Aelfhild to the hard work. She nodded at Eyvind. He nodded back.

"You left the old man in a state."

Aelfhild scoffed. All the tension she had carried around her midriff—for days, it seemed—bubbled out with the butterflies in her stomach. There was a new journey ahead. Just one parting, albeit a hard one, left. "I have to go," she said.

He nodded. "Do you mean to come back?"

"I have to at least try to fix this first." She put her hand to his tunic, right over the scar.

They locked eyes for a moment. He took her hand in both of his. "That arrow should have killed me. Every day beyond it is a gift, Aela, one you gave. Whatever comes, should I die or"—he inhaled—"change, is not yours to carry. Do not throw all this away for guilt's sake."

Aelfhild stared into the dirt. Embla settled atop her master's foot and keened. She shook her head. "If all else fails, I can find a high cliff and throw myself into the sea, like in the old tales. End everyone's troubles."

His hands tightened around hers. "Self-pity does not suit you. I know you better than that."

"I have to go," she repeated. She pulled her hand from his.

The horses were ready. Jarngrim and Kolbrun were in their saddles, and Sorg was kicking impatiently at the dirt. Aelfhild pulled herself up on the stirrups. She was getting better; it was nearly graceful, with a good deal less flailing and squawking.

"Take care of my dog!" she called as they turned the horses downriver. "Keep her safe!"

Eyvind replied, "You say that like she will listen to a thing I tell her."

3 8

THE MAN BENEATH the bearskin called himself Narfi. True to his word, he had waited for Aelfhild. He did not seem surprised when she arrived. He paid no mind to her companions. After a moment to retrieve his possessions from a nearby hole, they were off. They crossed the bridge to the Earnfold side of the river, then cut hard west.

Over one shoulder, Narfi carried a club. It was a wrist-thick branch inset with iron studs and made more imposing by its lack of artistry. Blood or rust or both flecked the protruding lumps of metal. The heft of it screamed broken bones; shield and chain mail could do little to stop that weight of oak. From his other shoulder hung a waterskin. He made Aelfhild look decadent with her saddlebags. Horses did not like Narfi. They kept a distance and turned fidgety if he stood too close. Aelfhild was fine with that. The farther they went and the more she stared, she became convinced he was not simply wearing the bear hide. It was attached to him somehow. She was not anxious to get close enough to find out the peculiars.

That was where the word *berserkr* came from, Kolbrun whispered. They wore only the hide of a bear into battle. It was all they needed; the madness protected them. Aelfhild made camp with Kolbrun and Jarngrim at a fair distance from the man. He did not protest. Small talk was not the reason he had been sent. As long as she followed, he seemed satisfied.

They had stars at night and could watch thunderstorms cresting the distant peaks. During the day they followed the river and stirred up blackthroat cranes picking through the shallows. The bees were fat and summertime lazy and came trundling through the tall grass to bump off horse and rider alike.

Narfi led them toward the mountains to the west and the river's source. They picked their way upward gradually, gaining elevation day by day. The towering spruces grew sparser and spindlier. They traded knee-high grass for stringy bracken and crowberry. The horses had to range farther to find enough to graze on. Rapids and falls broke up the Frostá's course through the hills; the water roared down the slopes deathly cold but mirror clear.

"Keep on the lookout for trolls now" was Jarngrim's half joke, but conversation was sparse. They were all content; Aelfhild could feel it. This was the nomadic life that her friends had chosen—home for them was more an ideal destination that turned stale as soon as they arrived. Wandering was their pleasure. Intrigue and lies were left behind in the city. If one of them spotted some humorous shape in the clouds or a lightning-forked tree, they might point it out. Otherwise the horses chattered back and forth more than the riders.

They came at last to a strip of land burned clear of vegetation. It stretched in a broad arc along one rock-strewn hillside to disappear around either shoulder of the ridge. Poles were driven into the ground at even gaps, fifty paces or so by Aelfhild's estimation. Each pole was festooned with feathers and bones and topped with a skull. Some of the skulls were farm or forest animals; others had a roundness that was uncomfortably familiar. Narfi stepped into the black scar without pause.

Aelfhild drew Sorg up short. Kolbrun and Jarngrim halted beside her. These were *nidstang* poles, ancient magic for cursing foes. Earnfolding mystics—the blacker-minded ones, at any rate—dabbled in them well as the Thrym. Most kings and eorls made it their business to drive out those that set about such dark work. Still, the old ways did cling on.

Narfi turned back and smiled at their hesitation. Or he bared his teeth—"smile" might have been too generous a word for it. "You two leave. Take the horse. We cannot feed it." He continued uphill.

"Do not tell Eyvind we would not cross," Kolbrun said. "He would poke fun."

Aelfhild dismounted and untied her bags. "Sorg will not tell a soul." She stroked the mare's forehead. As far as horses went, Aelfhild had grown quite keen on this one. She slung shield and axe across her back and lifted the saddlebags over a shoulder.

Jarngrim bent to take the reins from her outstretched hand. "Are you sure you want to go? No shame in riding back."

"I am sure." She walked around to the side of Kolbrun's horse. "Skjaldmaer, I should have been a better friend to you." She put her hand on the shieldmaiden's leg. "Forgive me."

Kolbrun was off the horse in a flash. She pulled Aelfhild close. "All is forgiven, and always." The hug was tight enough to drive air out of Aelfhild's lungs. "Now go, outlander, get your answers."

"And me?" Jarngrim asked as the shieldmaiden hoisted herself back into the saddle.

"Watch yourself, Jarngrim." Aelfhild grinned.

He snorted. "Watch yourself, Aela." Clicking, he turned the horses away.

There was a cave in the center of the scorched ring. A fissure split one of the granite plates that made up the hillside, though it was hard to see from any angle but straight on. Moss hung down from the ledge above, and the crack was narrow enough at the top that it looked no different from the streaks and stains left by trickling snowmelt along the cliffs. At the base it widened enough for a single human to pass. Rocks had been artfully stacked and scattered around to throw off any spying eyes.

Aelfhild followed Narfi in. Soot darkened the rocks around the gap. She could smell woodsmoke. The gentle downhill slope to the stone pulled her inward, where the cleft widened into a proper cave. Water dripped down one glistening stalactite to form a calcified puddle in the chamber's center. Each drop sent out perfect concentric ripples. A campfire burned just beside, untended and down to embers. Whoever had started the fire was nowhere to be seen. Folded blankets, jugs and jars in tidy lines, and a single cast-off shoe were signs of habitation. There were other gaps in the cavern walls that led deeper into the earth, but they were too small for humans and choked with dust.

Narfi laid his belongings on a natural shelf in the rock. There was a blanket beneath, along with a wooden cup and bowl. He pointed a finger to a stretch of unoccupied wall opposite. Aelfhild set down her things. She recognized a mortar and pestle next to the assorted clay vessels. There were bones and bundles of feathers and every manner of awl, chisel, and pick spread around the floor.

Aelfhild felt a pressure behind her ears. It had been building since they passed the ashen ring but felt sharper inside the cave. She tried working her jaw to make her ears pop, if it was the elevation, but the pressure persisted. For now it was mild enough that she could push it out of mind. Nerves, most likely. Her heart felt like it was knocking against her ribs.

"When will she return?" she asked.

"When she means to." Narfi settled into his blanket.

Wherever the Whisperer had gotten off to, she was in no hurry. Night crept in. There was a nook in the back wall wedged full of enough firewood to last several winters from the look of it, so Aelfhild kept the fire stoked. She chewed some of her trail rations, more as a distraction than out of any real hunger. The sunlight through the cleft faded. Narfi stayed curled up in his bearskin. He snored in fits.

Aelfhild had set about honing the edge of her axe on a whetstone just as Kolbrun had taught her. The ritual was good for soothing frayed nerves. She dipped the long, flat stone in the cave's puddle, waited until the last bubble disappeared, then sat before it with her axe. She pressed her fingers against the blade and tenderly slid it back and forth on the stone. From the toe of the bit to the heel, she took care not to miss a spot. The blade had not needed sharpening, but after her ministrations the edge would split hairs off a bloatfly's belly. She still had her axe to the stone when there was a stirring around the entrance. Footsteps sounded down the passage. Aelfhild stood.

A woman walked in. She was shorter than Aelfhild had imagined; in her mind the Whisperer had loomed as a horned, spindly crone. The real one was nearly eye to eye with Aelfhild, which made looming difficult, and wide around the hips. She wore a clearly self-made frock, no more than a leather tube with messy stitching down both sides, which revealed veiny, copper-tan arms and legs. There were no horns in sight. Instead, she was painted black from the eyes up, all around to the tops of her ears and the skin below her single, severe braid.

Aelfhild looked at the Whisperer. Her hand tightened around the axe haft in her hand. The other woman made no move. She stared back.

The witch held a brace of hares in one hand. Wordlessly, she turned away from Aelfhild and dropped the dead animals on Narfi's sleeping form. He grunted and rolled over. It took a moment's struggling for him to regain his bearings, then he collected the carcasses and fetched a knife. His mistress left him to his work. She turned back to Aelfhild.

"Step into the light, girl."

Aelfhild obeyed.

The Whisperer's voice had the timbre of long years to it, but her skin, the unpainted bits, showed no lines. There was a gap in their ages, but Aelfhild could not guess if it was ten winters or thirty. The woman's eyes were odd. They looked at first to be fixed in constant surprise, but on closer inspection it was just that the iris was such a deep silt brown that it merged into the black within and made it hard to judge her gaze.

"Show me your hand."

Aelfhild had not bothered to cover the rune for this journey. There had been no point. If her dreams were not secret, nothing was.

Front and back, the witch inspected. She pushed a thumb along Aelfhild's palm toward the wrist but did not look impressed.

"What do I call you?" Aelfhild asked.

"You do not care for 'the Whisperer'?" The woman gave what must have passed for a knee-slapping guffaw in Narfi's mirthless company—one single, barely audible puff through the nostrils. "Kalma is my name."

There were hundreds, thousands of questions. Aelfhild had gone through them over and over again on the ride into the foothills. She plucked out the one that nagged most. "How did you know about the skull?"

"You are not the only one with dreams."

3 9

HE RABBITS WERE gone. Narfi picked every morsel clean and set the bones aside. Doubtless, they would be used.

"Did you save some for Surma?" Kalma asked.

"Why would I?"

The two spoke like husband and wife. Not some bright, early romance; rather the flat, measured tone that said they tolerated one another's presence and had done so for a long, long time. Their body language was relaxed without being intimate. They did not touch, not even an accidental brush of the fingers. Aelfhild would have guessed against them having been lovers but would not have wagered money on the hunch.

"Where is she, besides?" Narfi asked.

Kalma whistled. Wheezing echoed through the cleft leading into the cave, preceeding the appearance of a squat little dog. Surma had bandy legs of mismatched height and bulging eyeballs. Her tongue slipped through a gap on one side of her jaw. The dog's labored breath could have melted a hole through silver plates. She was everything a master would not look for in a hound—next to Embla, it would have been hard to tell that the wad of awkward fur and overhanging teeth was a dog at all. Surma sat down and started gumming the leftover bones. Aelfhild must have been staring in visible horror, because Kalma came to her pet's defense. "She is old."

Aelfhild blinked. One of her ears popped at long last. It was just a background sensation, that pressure, but it was still a relief. She worked her jaw to try to make the other ear release, but without any luck. She heard, or felt as much as heard, a rustling in the back of the cave. Nothing was there when she looked.

Narfi and Kalma were both watching her when she turned back. Surma's grunting was the only noise in the cave. Occasionally a drop would build and fall into the puddle, one solitary plink.

Aelfhild cleared her throat. "Is it a real place, where I go in the dreams?"

Kalma nodded to her manservant, and Narfi left them. He went to hang a wispy cotton sheet over the gaps in the rear wall. It made Aelfhild wonder if there might be bats. The thought did not make sleeping in the cave any more enticing.

"*Real* is not useful," Kalma replied. "You cannot walk there from here. But you are not the first to step in those lands. Others can, that know the ways. It is a between place. One of many. Understand?"

In truth Aelfhild did not, not at all, but other questions jostled for position. "Is it the Gods that put them there?"

The witch sucked in a long breath. "There is so much for you yet to learn." She stood and went to her mortar. Her hands danced across the rows of urns. A crumbled leaf, a flaking mushroom cap, moldering berries, and tiny rounded grains she dropped into the bowl and ground down with the pestle. "Some things are better shown."

She dipped a cup into the still waters of the puddle, then poured the milled powder in to stir. She offered it to Aelfhild. The clear water was turned vomitous yellow and smelled violently fungal. Aelfhild hesitated.

Kalma grunted and took a draught of her own brew. A trickle ran down from one corner of her mouth. She thrust the cup toward Aelfhild again.

It tasted better than it looked, actually; sour with earthy notes, though it left a tacky mineral coating on the back of her tongue. Aelfhild passed back the empty cup. Kalma tossed it aside as she went to grab her blanket from the nest beside her little brewery. She wrapped herself tightly and settled down by the fire. Aelfhild followed suit. They stared over the flames and toward the hanging cloth.

"There are more than just Gods and men in this world," the Whisperer began. She swayed back and forth as she spoke. "There are *aettir*, the tribes of men, and there are *vaettir*, the spirits of the land. You know this. You have seen some of them."

Aelfhild thought of the troll. She thought of the *draugr* that had guarded the Oath-Stone, that had taken a friend from her. The potion was hitting her stomach now. A jolt ran down through her guts. The liquid threatened to return. She heaved once, but it felt too heavy to come back up.

"There are vaettir in all places and in all things. They were in these lands long before man came. They will be in these lands long after man goes. That is the way of things." Kalma exhaled. "You must learn of Trollmother. Has anyone taught you?"

"No." Something tugged at Aelfhild's memory, but her mind was starting to feel slippery. "Yes. The Runemaster in Herjarsborg. He said, he said something about Jarl Torfi killing the troll fathers or the mother of the trolls."

That was some joke Aelfhild had missed out on. Kalma lost herself in a fit of her silent, snorting laughter. "Stronger men than Torfi tried and failed, but always they tell themselves the same lie. Easier that way, easier that way. No, Torfi might have killed a brooding troll but he could not slay Trollmother."

"Listen, now. Every child can tell you how the Gods came and shaped the earth. But there is one thing that they do not know and that is what the Gods, too, forgot. Vaettir go everywhere. Everything has a spirit. Tree, rock, water. Fire and air, birds in the sky. And from the earth that the Gods themselves shaped rose Trollmother, firstborn but unwanted."

Aelfhild's stomach bubbled and foamed. She was trying to pay attention to Kalma's words, but the rustling noise from the back of the cave built and faded in her ears at random. It was a sound like dozens or hundreds of mandibles chittering away, like locusts swarming across fields. She caught movement around the cotton sheet out of the corner of her eye whenever she turned her head.

"The Gods saw it as their great task to order the land. They wanted straight lines and even rows. They wanted a place for everything beneath the stars and a comely order to their creation. But Trollmother was the untamed earth. She would not be bridled. Earthquake and volcano, storm and crashing wave were her answer. What the Gods bent to their precious order, she cast unto disarray."

"She has an old name. Before the Thrym came to these lands, before the Earnfoldings and the Oescans before them, my people called to her: *Tuonetar*." Kalma threw up her hands in front of the fire. "She is the worm that feasts on the flesh of kings and heroes. She is the root that works in to topple the highest walls, the wave that wears rock to sand, the palsy that turns strong arms feeble."

There were most definitely shadows on the cloth. They played across the pale cotton whenever the rustling built to a searing climax in Aelfhild's head. The part that rattled Aelfhild's admittedly addled mind most was that the fire was between her and the cloth, but she saw nothing pass between them. Now she found herself hoping it was only bats. She pulled the blanket tighter around her shoulders as the chittering rose and the shapes returned, tiny, nearly human figures cast in flickering shadow.

"Then came the Jotnir. Then came Man. The Gods needed help to subdue this unruly world. But Trollmother was there to whisper in their ears, to show them how the Gods did not see all ends. To teach them that there was more to their world than the seen. The Gods did not care for her meddling."

Aelfhild squeezed her eyes shut and cupped her hands over her ears. They did no good.

"In their wrath, they split the world with a great shroud. Trollmother and the vaettir were chained on one side, unable to cross. The Jotnir and Man were rooted to the other, unable to pass through. And the Gods rose up in their pride and judged their troubles ended. But every veil has holes. Every shroud has gaps. And every gap can be bridged—a place, a dream, a person."

Aelfhild tried to hum herself soothing melodies. Focus on each moment. The next breath. Master yourself, control your breath, grapple with the fear. Every lesson her friends had taught her. Jarngrim. Kolbrun. Eyvind. She should have listened.

"Aelfhild, look at your hand." Kalma's voice was insistent, but Aelfhild did not obey. She kept her eyes shut.

"Look at your hand, child."

She peeked under one eyelid. The rune on her palm still glowed, but her entire arm was stretched. Or rather her arm itself stayed the same as a line of spectral echoes of the arm stretched up and down and trailed away into space on either side. The rune was a glowing arc all along, a bright line marking out a ghost-lit path.

A bridge.

"Trollmother speaks to some louder than others. Look at me," Kalma demanded.

Aelfhild looked up. The witch blew fine powder off an open palm into her watering eyes. It stung for only a moment. That same fungal smell clawed up through her nostrils. She fell back through the earth, the weight of her body left far behind. She fell along the glowing line of the bridge that extended through her own hand. She fell through herself, through a countless number of selves that were identical but offset from the touchable, waking world. Her fall slowed and came to a stop.

It was a shadow world, like a fog bank or the unlit depths of the ocean. She could see but not far. She could breathe. She could move, though the thought of straying from the bridge made her shrivel. Being lost in the murk was a weight of pure dread in her chest. Pinpricks of light appeared around her. Some were closer, others distant. Each grew in fits and starts. It was like watching a flame kindle and writhe as more twigs were added. Firelight grew in the shapes of arms and legs, suggestions of human forms. Balls of light where heads should be. The glowing spirits were drawn to the rune bridge. They gathered around Aelfhild. Just as in the cave, she felt the sound more than heard it. It built behind her ears. And built. And built. She felt the voices.

Help us.

I wanted to be free.

They promised to save her.

Save us.

I thought I was chosen.

It was pride. It was vanity. It was sin.

They betrayed me.

Help us!

Save us!

Aelfhild screamed. The pain stabbed into the depths of her skull, bright white and urgent. She could feel something hot trickle down her earlobe and on along her neck.

Then there was silence. A hand on her shoulder.

"Aela." A familiar voice. An impossible voice. "All is well, Aela. They are gone."

She looked up at the suggestion of Ceolwen's face in firelight, a hint of the proud nose and the regal cheekbones cast as lines in the shifting glow. The feeling of her presence, though, was familiar from childhood and the voice unmistakable.

"Is it really you?" Aelfhild's eyes were already streaming. The physical pain was gone now and the terror with it. This new spirit stirred up fresh agonies.

"I cannot say," Ceolwen replied. "I think it is a part of me. A memory, maybe. All of us touched the Oath-Stone and all for different reasons. And now we are here."

The fire. Aelfhild remembered dancing motes of light and the drifting ash. She remembered Ceolwen's final scream. "Forgive me, lady," she whispered.

"What for, Aela?"

"I betrayed you. It should have been me that burned. This mark was meant for you. I never deserved it."

Ceolwen laughed. It was unfeigned, gentle, and soothing. Her flickering hand lifted Aelfhild's chin. "No, Aela. I was wrong. Every one of us here was wrong. Some sought glory. Others sought power. Some were forced, others bribed. All of us are failed seekers. You are not. And so you must go back home."

"How do I know what to do without you?"

Another laugh, this one entwined with a thread of melancholy. "It is not my world anymore, Aela."

"I do not want to leave you here."

"This place is not so terrible. It is . . . quiet. And I think this is just one piece of me. There are worse places, besides."

Aelfhild wept openly now. "I never said good-bye."

"So say it now."

"Good-bye, lady." Aelfhild sobbed.

"Good-bye, Aela." Ceolwen bent to kiss Aelfhild's forehead.

Aelfhild flew upward.

4 0

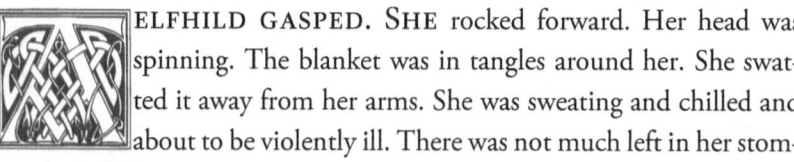ELFHILD GASPED. SHE rocked forward. Her head was spinning. The blanket was in tangles around her. She swatted it away from her arms. She was sweating and chilled and about to be violently ill. There was not much left in her stomach but it all came up on the grass beside her.

Either someone had been clever enough to move her outside the cave in preparation for this result or she had wandered out on her own. There was a gap in her memory after she had left Ceolwen but before sleep. The texture of the blankness was different, demented as that seemed. She looked down at her hand. It was normal, perhaps a shade paler than usual and beaded with sweat, but very much singular and not see-through.

Surma trotted past, if it could be called a trot with her uneven spindle legs. The dog had a bone in her mouth and paused to regard Aelfhild for a heartbeat. But the human proved boring, so Surma continued on to find a spot to bury her prize.

Aelfhild pressed against the sides of her head. She did not feel awful. This was not like having too much mead. Instead she felt floaty, untethered from her own body. Her mind had not made the full trip back and was still a half step outside her skull. It was profoundly disorienting. The pressure in her ears was gone for the moment, though there was a line of dried blood down her neck as a reminder. Part of her wanted everything to be the fault of the potion. It was a hag's trickery, poison herbs and honeyed words to make her see what the witch wanted her to see.

But the noises had started well before she had taken that drink.

She sighed. "I thought there would be answers," she said.

Surma did not look up from her digging.

"Who do you speak to?" Narfi's voice came from behind her. He had just come up over the lip of the hill.

"The dog," Aelfhild replied. She was beyond trying to preserve dignity. There was still sick crusted on the front of her tunic, and she could not even begin to imagine the state of her face.

Narfi grunted. "Fetch your axe. You are with me today."

"Where is Kalma?"

"Left."

"Where did she go?"

"Left."

Aelfhild sighed. "What are we doing?"

"Gathering. You want to eat?"

Swell, she thought. She ducked in to grab her weapon. All of her things were as she had left them. The saddlebags looked untouched. Someone had left slimy noseprints on the leather, but the straps showed signs of only a few halfhearted nibbles. Aelfhild hooked the axe through her belt and went out to meet Narfi.

There were snares set all around the cliffs and dells. Each one was empty today. Narfi had to prop up a few deadfalls or reset a rope here and there, but most of the traps went untouched. Animals were sparse in the high heather. The flowers were bursting out in sky blues and golden starburts, though, and that much was pleasant. Aelfhild savored the mountain air. It helped. They wandered on. Down among the trees were more empty traps but a scattering of footprints to go by.

Aelfhild followed one set of five-clawed, splayed-toe tracks down a ravine. The creature was small and leaped about frenziedly, most likely a stoat. It had been careless enough to track through the mud and leave a record of its passing. The tracks disappeared into a sandy burrow. Aelfhild was not about to stick her hand in to meet the critter's teeth; small did not mean harmless. She heaved herself onto a nearby boulder. A splash of sunlight would have helped with her malaise, but the clouds were not cooperating.

"Keep moving," called Narfi from the ravine's edge. "Rain is coming. The water will catch you down there."

"Should we get back?!" Aelfhild hollered.

"More traps to check."

A black tufted squirrel had met its end beneath a logfall. Narfi tied the carcass to his belt. Aelfhild helped him prop the log back up. Rain was beginning to patter off the branches overhead as a line of roiling clouds crested the peaks and came swirling onward.

"Now should we get back?"

Narfi's eyes narrowed as he peered up at the breaking front. "There is shelter closer by."

The storm moved fast down the mountain slopes and raced toward open forest beyond. Drizzle turned to downpour in a breath. The pair jumped among what cover the ragged pines offered. Narfi hunched into his bearskin. Aelfhild had dressed light. The rain was cold enough to tighten her skin into gooseflesh, though it did work better than a slap in the face to sharpen her mind. She felt alert for the first time all day. And it washed some of the mess off of her clothes.

Through the rain appeared the peak of a roof. Shingles had fallen away in places and a dozen branches wormed their way inside the hut, but it was shelter. Aelfhild followed Narfi in. There was no door left in the front frame. There were a few dry patches inside where the roof did not leak as badly. Aelfhild settled into one. She batted moisture off her arms and wrung it from her sodden hair. The walls canted steeply to the downslope side. Surrounding trees were crowding in and onto the hut, pushing it slowly sideways, and the framing looked as though it would soon surrender the battle. Moss came up through cracks in the floor and around the single window with its dangling shutter.

She wondered about the inhabitants. The rain did not appear to be slackening, so she decided to ask. "Do you know who lived here?"

"Homesteaders," Narfi replied. He was on his haunches in a circle of dry wood and vines. "They come this way from time to time. The Jarl has no use for the land, so he allows it. Settlers think they can tame the wild."

They hope they can tame it, Aelfhild thought. Hope is a bitter gift, in endless supply. "What happened to them?"

Narfi jabbed a finger at the knobby roots that poked up through split floorboards. "Trollmother. She tested. They failed."

"You believe in her, too?"

He nodded.

"If she is so real, why does nobody else mention her?"

For a while Narfi frowned. He was not swift in his conversation. Quiet did not seem to bother him; rather the opposite. "A few know but keep it hidden. Most folk want to believe easy things. The Gods are great. The Gods are masters of all. Easy. It is not so easy."

Aelfhild watched him. There was a mind beneath the scars and the bearhide. Not an eloquent or learned one, but the wheels clearly turned in those long silences. She settled back against the wall. She felt the drumming of the rain against the wood outside. "Who are you, Narfi?"

He settled down onto the floor, cross-legged. "I am an Ulfing."

Aelfhild raised her eyebrows. Jarl Harald would not have been pleased by that one. None of her companions would. The Leifings and the Ulfings were not the fastest of friends.

"I was born on Hrauney. A speck of land. No one has heard of it. My parents had a farm there. It was small but they managed. I had brothers and a sister." His eyes were fixed on the floor directly in front of his legs. "The thane came with his men. He said the land was his and wanted my father to pay to farm it. My father could not."

"The thane called it a debt. Every year, my father would pay. Every year, the debt grew larger. My brothers went to fight for the Jarl in Ulfheim. They promised to help but time passed and they forgot. The debt grew. One day my father tried to kill the thane. I think he knew that either he would end his trouble or it would end his. The thane took the farm after he killed my father. He took my mother and sister into his house. I was a danger. He cast me out."

"I sought my brothers but they were gone wandering far or dead. I fought for this man and that man to earn a few coins. It was a hollow life. One day, I heard talk of a witch."

"Kalma," Aelfhild said.

Narfi nodded. "It took a time to track her. The stories were all loose weave. Rumor on rumor, you know? But I had a bargain to make and she loves bargains. I found her." He grew quiet. "She laid a curse upon the thane. His entire line withered. His crops wilted and his fortune soured. The seas gave him no succor. The Gods were of no help to him. After a time, his own body failed. But slowly. He knew, in the end, what had befallen him. They say he sacrificed every animal he had, praying and praying to lift the curse. Sailors still keep clear of the island. Now it is an empty speck."

That was one way to get revenge. Aelfhild was leaning back now. The man's gaze was fit to bore a hole through the floorboards if he kept staring. But she was still curious. "What was your side of the bargain?"

"I serve."

And Aelfhild got the sense that the bargain was not short-term. There was a finality to the last word. That was the reason he and Kalma spoke as they did; they were together, forever, and not out of some storied friendship. "I am sorry," she said.

"I am not. My vengeance is done. That is all."

He clearly had no use for her pity. In his own way, he seemed content. Not happy; the word could not be more distant from a human, but content to merely exist.

They waited in silence for the rain to end.

4 1

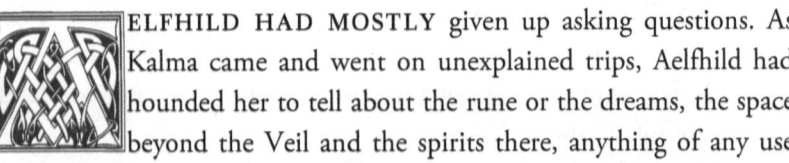ELFHILD HAD MOSTLY given up asking questions. As Kalma came and went on unexplained trips, Aelfhild had hounded her to tell about the rune or the dreams, the space beyond the Veil and the spirits there, anything of any use at all. The witch dodged or mumbled the cryptic nonanswers of every vagabond seer and palm reader, from the empty "time will tell" to the infuriating "you shall know when you are meant to know." When Aelfhild confronted her and accused her of being a fraud, Kalma had not batted an eye. She had pointed to the sunlight straining through the mouth of the cave. "Nothing keeps you here," the witch had said.

Aelfhild had stayed. Now she leaned in. There might yet be something worth learning.

"There is a place of power near here," Kalma said. "The Veil is thin there when the moons are right. You can hear the other side. Maybe even reach through."

"What will happen?"

"Who can say? Sometimes the spirits are eager. Not always. They are wild things." Kalma's black eyes stared unfocused into the water.

Aelfhild felt the rustling from the back of the cave again. She was convinced something lived back there, buried in the cracks. The others either did not hear it or did not mark it. But that something was trying to speak to her. It took on an urgent edge now. Perhaps it was to do with the moons, as the witch had mentioned, but there was a change to the sensation, a building pulse. Aelfhild had to grit her teeth until it faded. She asked, "Why?"

"A child's question," Kalma spat.

"What is to be gained?" Aelfhild raised her voice. "Why do you have me here? You were meant to teach me."

"That is what you wanted," Kalma snapped back. "I show you what pieces I know. Signs, dreams, visions. You want me to tell you what to do with all the kings and thrones and armies? That is of no matter to me. I can teach you to peek through the Veil. That much I know. The rest"—she waved a hand—"is yours to dwell on."

"But what—" Aelfhild began.

"Since you came here, always 'What do I do? What do I do?'" Kalma's lips curled into a sneer. "Trollmother does not deal in your plans and prophecies. If the Gods or anyone else have plans for you I will be last told. You want someone to own you, child. You are a whipped dog whining for a new master. That is not me."

Aelfhild's fists were balled. "You do not know me."

The witch spat. "I see you for just what you are, girl. I do not waste my time with cattle."

Aelfhild had to push her knuckles into her thighs to stop from lashing out. Her cheeks were searing. There was truth behind the words that bit deeper than any slur. "Show me, then." It came out a hiss through her clenched teeth.

"Speak up, girl!" shouted Kalma, eyes flashing.

"Show me the place!" Aelfhild screamed.

There was a pause. No rustling now; just silence. Surma, too, had departed, and Narfi was minding the remains of his meal. The women were left to stare one another down in silence.

Aelfhild's gaze did not waver. "Show me."

Kalma blinked. She said one word: "Follow."

The witch hopped like a billy goat over rockfalls and from tussock to tussock of shriveled leaves and yellowing grass. There was enough moonlight to help, but Aelfhild still had to pick her steps carefully. Kalma never stopped to look for a landmark or so much as sniff the air. She never backtracked or stumbled. The land belonged to her; it bent to her certainty. "This way, faster," she called over her shoulder.

Anything could hide in the mountains. The slopes were porous with caves and lined with canyons and ravines that crisscrossed or drained one into the other. During the spring melt each one would doubtless be roaring neck-deep with whitewater, but for now they were dry beds of gravel. Kalma led them along the edge of one canyon. The bottom was out of sight in the darkness and the pebbles they kicked over the edge took a long while hitting bottom. Aelfhild focused on her balance. They came out onto a plateau, high enough that their breath was misting, and Aelfhild was glad she had snagged her cloak. Walking was easier with solid rock underfoot rather than the loose moraine below. She could look up to take in the view. The stars were the best of it; everything else was cracked stone and sand glinting in the moonlight.

"Here," said Kalma. She pointed ahead.

Two inset rings of granite pillars broke from the flat shelf. They were clearly man-made, evenly spaced circles around a central bowl, but chipped down from their original angular shapes by long years of blowing wind and ice. They had once been earthen fangs bared skyward. Now the stones had a lumpy slouch to them, more like the nubs of aged teeth.

Time does its unstoppable dance. Aelfhild wondered what the builders would feel at the sight of their monument now. She followed Kalma toward the center. Her ears popped as she stepped through the first line of stones. A wave of nausea hit her. It was fleeting, gone as soon as she passed the threshold from stone to sand. She stepped out and back in. The same feeling washed over her.

Kalma was watching.

"Who built this?" Aelfhild asked. She stretched her jaw to ease the pressure in her ears.

"My people," the witch said.

Who those people were, Aelfhild still did not know. They were not Thrym, Earnfolding, or Oescan. If Kalma was not the last, she was one of few, and their language was long since forgotten. But there were traces. In her wanderings Aelfhild had come across paintings on cave walls and whorls and wriggling symbols carved onto rocks. She ran her hand across the standing stones. There were patterns beneath her fingertips. They were runestones but no runes the Aettir would recognize.

Within the second circle her foot slid into a low spot in the rock. They were mostly filled with sand and worn smoother than when first fashioned, but she could make out one channel branching out in each cardinal direction. They emptied into the central basin, filled now with nothing but dust and grit. Muscles around Aelfhild's stomach knotted. Ritual loomed over the whole bleak plateau, and she could imagine the dragging feet of chain-bound sacrifices stirring up dirt, smell blood filling the bowl.

"Yes," Kalma said. Her eyes followed Aelfhild's.

Aelfhild feared she knew the answer to her next question but held on to hope. "Humans?"

"Yes."

"Do you still?" She had not thought to bring her axe.

Kalma snorted her dry, mirthless laugh. "No." The witch kicked some of the sand away from the basin. "Those were old rites. Men. A sledge hammer when all that is needed is a needle." Her teeth glinted in the moonlight, which did not help Aelfhild to relax.

"What is meant to happen?"

There was no immediate reply. Kalma was busy kicking sand from the stones and staring up at the moons. The two orbs were a hair offset from straight overhead and nearly touching; Rymr and Valr were close to battle, and the tides would be surging. The witch was muttering about them being "not close enough" and how Narfi did not know nearly as much as he thought. She grumbled and glanced skyward as she stomped around.

"Should I do something?" Aelfhild asked.

"Hush." More skyward looks. Kalma lined up her fingers with the moons. Finally, a half-satisfied grunt. "Close enough."

"What do I do?"

"Wait." The witch hissed. There was a flash of moonlight as a knife disappeared under her frock. The witch held out her finger and let blood drip into the basin at her feet.

"Wait for what?" Aelfhild's temper was rising. There was never a straight answer. And if the old woman said anything about the Trollmother, she was going to headbutt her. Aelfhild craned her neck up to look for any

change in the moons. Another wave of nausea hit, and she rocked backward. Her heels slipped into one of the channels and she windmilled as she
fell. Dust flew up as her backside slammed down. She really hoped that
Kalma had not seen any of what had just befallen her.

But Kalma was gone. The moons were gone. Aelfhild waved the dust
away, but her fingers cut through fog. The night had been clear a heartbeat before. She righted herself with one hand. Beneath her palm the sand
was grittier. The few grains that stuck to her skin as she pulled away were
glassy black.

The ritual ring had changed. Obsidian fangs cut through the mist, not
at all touched by age, each one well above Aelfhild's head. They pointed
toward a sky without stars that swirled and rippled like the surrounding
mist. The only light came from the rune on her hand. Aelfhild looked
down at it, hoping to see a line connecting her back to the waking world,
but there was nothing more.

She was through the Veil, where she had met Ceolwen's spirit, and
she did not see a doorway back. She pushed down the panic that shook
her hands and legs.

"Kalma?" she whispered.

There was no answer. The air around her was dead; the mist strangled
sound. It swirled about her even though there was no breeze, as the slightest movement stirred it to dancing life.

"Kalma!" she said with a hiss. She did not want to yell—Gods only
knew what else could be in the darkness—but she had to raise her voice.

She held up her rune and tested a few steps forward. Sand crunched
underfoot. Outside the ring of fangs, the mist thinned but did not disappear; it clung around her ankles. Aelfhild could see contours in the dark,
shades of midnight blue, that looked similar to the mountainside in the
waking world, sweeping up and away from the plateau on which she stood.
This world appeared to be close to a copy of her own. There were specks
of violet light dancing ahead of her.

She stumbled once as her foot slipped into a hole. It was impossible
to watch every footfall within the mist, so she tested with her toes before
putting down her full weight. The lights disappeared as she drew near.

A few more tentative steps and she found black stalks protruding from the ground. On them, flowers with velveteen skin and delicate fronds that curled in around a bulbous pod. Aelfhild lifted her rune to examine the plant more closely. As soon as the white light hit the flower, the black skin began to blister and smoke. The plant shuddered and furled in on itself. Aelfhild gasped. She dropped her hand at once. She fumbled with her cloak and swaddled her palm in the thick linen.

Her breathing was heavy in the darkness. She waited.

Slowly, the violet glow peeked through cracks between petals. The fronds extended and fanned out. The flower bloomed, showing a luminescent purple bud within a shimmering pink cradle. Back and forth the plant slowly drifted. She stayed still and kept her light hidden, and slowly other blooms began to open around her.

There was life through the Veil, not just spirits. Entirely alien it was, but life nonetheless. Aelfhild boggled. She was not in a hurry to touch the flowers, but they put on a show of lights as spectacular as anything she had seen in the waking world. Her mind began to work through it, though. If there were plants, there might be something to eat the plants. If there were something to eat the plants, even larger things usually came along to eat them. She stepped back toward the ritual circle as quickly as she could without breaking an ankle.

There had to be a doorway back. Kalma could not leave her here. Back in the center of the pillars, Aelfhild spun around. The stones were cold beneath her fingers but perfectly smooth. There were no markings, no runes. No basin in the ring's middle for blood. No way back that she could spot.

Aelfhild screamed, "Kalma!"

There was a chittering noise behind her. She recognized it from the cave; this time it did not bite at her ears. She whirled to seek its source. A pair of tiny dots shone through the mist a few paces away near the base of a ritual pillar. They blinked and there was the noise again. Aelfhild took a step forward. The eyes disappeared.

Whatever it was, it was too tiny to hurt her. Or she hoped it was. And it, or they, had spoken to her in the cave. She remembered angular, demi-human shapes cast against the curtain during her previous sojourn. She kneeled. "Hello," she whispered. Nothing more useful sprang to mind.

The dots reappeared, two robin's-egg blue pinholes in the mist. More chittering. The eyes did not approach but they did not retreat.

There were copper beads on the end of the drawstrings of her cloak. Aelfhild had to fuss with one for a moment to pry it free. The eyes watched her the whole time, clicking away. She held up the tiny ball in front of her. "If you show me a way home, there are plenty more where this came from." She tossed the bead into the mist.

The eyes blinked out.

Aelfhild waited. She did not know what else to do. The idea that they understood her was madness, but she had fallen through to a world removed from her own, and that itself was beyond reason.

Two sets of eyes reappeared this time. They were not focused on her but where she guessed the copper bead would have landed in the mist. A third pair blinked in. Aelfhild swallowed. The disembodied eyes chittered back and forth. More eyes began to appear, and Aelfhild felt the sweat dripping down the small of her back.

A screech split the mist. There was no other word for it. It set the sand aquiver beneath her feet. Blue eyes clicked and scattered in every direction, and Aelfhild was left in the dark again. The screech had come from above. She kept herself low to the ground and scanned the sky, such as it was. Mist swirled and obscured her sight in every direction.

Another screech, closer this time. Aelfhild shuffled under the overhang of one of the stone fangs. She breathed through her nose and tried to let as little noise slip out with each exhalation as possible, though her chest was pounding. She pulled her swaddled hand close to her stomach. There could be no chance of spilled light.

Wings beat the mist into towering waves. The fog could not clear, there seemed an infinite supply, but it swept around Aelfhild in dense banks. Something massive slammed down onto a pillar opposite her hiding spot. Mist boiled up between them.

In the stillness, Aelfhild tried not to breathe. She did not see light from any sort of eyes. There was an intake of air, though, and the fog drew back over her. Something was sniffing. She had no way to mask her scent.

The creature snorted. Aelfhild ran.

4 2

S SHE SPRINTED, Aelfhild was left to hope that this land was indeed a mirror to her own. The ground was rough but she kept her balance and made for what should have been a ravine.

Massive wings swept over her, and she threw herself to the ground. The black sand bit into her skin; the grains were hard and scraped deeply. Another screech. Mist swirled as the monster wheeled to dive again. She was back on her feet. Every decision that led her hence she cursed. She cursed the Gods, she cursed Kalma and Narfi, she cursed Trollmother and her horrid realm. She cursed herself and the foolish girl that she was, playing at being a hero.

The ravine should have been close by now. The ground dipped beneath her shoes. She got up a head of speed, slid on her side, and braced for the fall.

She dropped maybe a step. What ought to have been a ravine was just a divet in the hard soil. Just as the pillars around the ritual circle were unaged and unweathered, it seemed there was no ice or rain to dig out the terrain here. She dragged herself down the slope of the ditch with her elbows.

The creature had been sniffing for her, which meant it might not need light. She did. She unwrapped the cloak from her hand and tossed it aside.

An impact shook the ground and tossed sand into her face. It had landed on her fluttering cloak. She heard cloth tearing. The creature shrieked in frustration and snuffled around.

Talons latched onto Aelfhild's foot and dragged her sideways. She scrabbled for a hold in the dirt as she was thrown aside. Air spilled from her lungs. Mist swirled as the beast sprang aloft. She could feel it bearing down on her. She threw her right hand up, fingers extended and rune shining brightly. She saw a massive beak, void black rippling in the mist, two massive nostrils, but no eyes. There was the impression of feathers along the shape, but the monster's body soaked in light and appeared only as vague outlines to the watcher. As the rune glow struck its skin, it screamed.

The screams continued back into the clouds. The dread raven circled. Burned, yes; chastened, yes; but not beaten. Aelfhild still had to run.

She held her hand toward the ground. The light gave her a hint of the land ahead. She tried to keep her course irregular in case the beast dove again. Its screaming had ceased and she could not turn her eyes skyward to watch for its coming. The mist ended ahead. She skidded to a stop in the sand. There was a sheer drop into blackness below. Whether this canyon existed in the real world and where she was in relation to her arrival point, she had not the faintest idea by now. The dark swallowed any sign.

Her breathing was ragged. Her legs burned. *Just a little farther*, she told herself. *Just a little farther.*

She jogged along the edge. She hoped for a narrow spot or a shallow place or any indication of depth. Flicking her hand from side to side, she thought there was more fog on the other side of the gap. It was hard to judge without stopping. It looked near enough. The other side was lower. There might be somewhere to hide down there. Other options did not present themselves. She backed off and lined up the jump. As she ran, she could feel air rippling behind her. The creature swooped in.

She leaped. Its talons cut the air, snapping for her back. They did not manage to snag her, but one claw nudged her akilter. She saw the wall of the opposite cliff approaching. Forests of jagged obsidian crystals, whence all the black sand beneath her feet, jutted through the fog. Razor edges gleamed in the light of her hand. She managed to throw her left arm in front of her face before she hit.

Pain lanced through her forearm. She slipped backward and felt flesh suck at the glass shard as her arm pulled free. She dropped into the canyon. Her back struck sand.

The wound was mortal; she knew without having to look. The spike had cut straight through the widest part of her forearm, scraping past bone. Blood was already steaming as it hit the frigid sand. There were some shallower cuts on her chest and legs, but the arm held her attention. She pressed as hard as she could. The pain was vivid starbursts across her vision and a tearing in her throat as she howled. More blood bubbled up between her fingers.

There was no way to rip bandages without letting it bleed freely. There was no one to help. There was nothing save the dark.

This is how you die, she told herself. *This is where you die. Unsung, unmarked, missed by only a few and not for long. One wrong step and you never see your friends again.* She missed Kolbrun and Jarngrim. She wished she had seen Onund again. She thought of Cuthbert, Eyrun, and Dunstan. She thought of Embla. War was coming and she would not be there to watch their backs, not be there to catch them when they stumbled. Instead, she had run off in pursuit of her own idle dreams. Selfish as ever, and to the last. She thought of Eyvind.

Her head was light. The easiest thing to do would have been to lie down. She was dizzy. Her limbs were heavy. It felt like well-earned respite, to settle back in the sand.

"No!" she yelled. She rocked forward and squeezed her arm tightly again. Pain burned away the haze. *I will see them again. I will.* With all her ebbing strength she focused on the wound. She pictured each of her friend's faces. She saw Embla running up to greet her. She imagined feeling sunlight on her face again.

She heard a song.

The rune seared and her arm glowed from within. Light burst out to drive away the mist on all sides and bounced from crystal to crystal up the surrounding walls. For a brief moment a beacon of radiant light cut skyward through the eternal night beyond the Veil. Aelfhild felt the heat more than anything. Charred flesh, burned hair stenches filled her nose. Her muscles writhed. Her ears echoed with the rippling thunderclap sprung from between her hand and arm.

She rocked back. Hitting the ground forced her lungs and heart back into motion. It was amazing Eyvind did not bear more of a grudge.

For a time, she drifted in and out. How long was impossible to know. No moon or sun spoiled the perfect blank of the sky. Mist flowed back in to fill the void around her body.

She stirred back to consciousness as the sand beneath her began to tremble. The fogbanks rolled in thicker. Aelfhild sat up. It took effort and her head spun as she came upright. She nearly toppled back over. Her breathing was slow and heavy. She was soaked in sweat from head to toe, and the skin she could see was as pale as untrod snow. Except for the patch on her left arm, where a handprint still glowed gold atop cracked, blackened skin.

The ground shook in every direction. The quaking swelled with the mist. Clouds swirled around her.

Aelfhild tried to stand but managed only to shift her back against the canyon wall. She got her knees up in front of her. There was no more strength in her arms or legs.

Then it was still. The sand went dead. The mist dropped. A whisper of noise was all that remained. It began to build. She had heard it before—in her dreams. She had at times hoped, at times dreaded that it was the voices of the Gods.

Thousands of whispers built into a single, writhing voice. It came out of the mist on all sides. *Little worm, so far from home, watch how it wriggles.*

Aelfhild's voice came out a croak. "What do you want from me?"

A thousand cackles echoed through the canyon. *It comes into our home and it asks what we want. What a rude and foolish thing it is.*

"What are you?"

That is not the question. It must ask the proper question.

Aelfhild pushed herself up onto her feet, keeping her back to the jagged obsidian wall. It sapped the warmth from her but the chill was least of all her troubles. "Just let me go. I want to go home."

Silence. The mist twitched as if impatient, waiting.

"Please."

Wriggle, wriggle, little worm. We do not give our gifts to prey. Be you hunter, or be you prey?

There was a screech high above. The raven creature had returned.

Run, run, little worm. Earn what we offer.

"What do you offer?"

Everything.

Another screech, closer. Aelfhild stumbled in the opposite direction. She propped herself against the rock with her good arm. The voice was gone for now. She hoped the canyon was too narrow for the beast.

Her feet barely answered. They scuffed up the sand. She could hear her own haggard breathing in the narrow space, not quite loud enough to mask the snuffling noises from above. Her head pounded. She seemed to lose consciousness every few steps; the world went dark and she lost time. She snapped back to awareness a few steps forward or a few steps back. The mist crowded in on her. She had to stop. She bent double to retch, but nothing came up. As she lifted her head from between her knees, she glimpsed a pair of tiny blue eyes down a fork in the path she had not noticed.

The eyes danced up and down, agitated. Aelfhild lurched after them.

They danced her down a path, blinking in and out, and she followed. She swayed heavily from step to step. More eyes blinked from nooks in the walls around her. The best she could hope for was that it would not be an ambush. Or that it would at least be quick.

Blue eyes danced around a hole in the rocks. There was a screech from overhead. The eyes chittered desperately. Aelfhild fell forward.

And kept falling.

She heard the thousand-whisper voice cackling as she fell.

Run, run, little worm. We are not yet done.

She hit snow. There were stars overhead now. Her eyes swam such that she could not pick constellations, but the air felt natural. It felt wide open. It felt freezing. The snow was ankle deep as she got to her feet. It had not yet been harvesttime when she had gone up the hill with Kalma. Aelfhild looked around for any landmark. There were mountains around her, but they were carpeted white and unidentifiable. She could have been a hundred paces from the witch's cave or a hundred leagues.

She spun a full circle. Blue lights downhill caught her eyes. Again, the robin's-blue pinpricks twinkled. She marched after them and rubbed her working arm against her shivering chest for any shred of warmth.

Her fingers were blue and her feet dead numb when she caught sight of thin firelight through the mouth of the cave. She had fallen out through the Veil not far from where she had entered, but somehow much time had passed.

She scrabbled her way through the snow and through the entrance. The air was warmer. There was bright light within.

"Did you hear that?" Kalma's voice came from within. "Check it."

Narfi emerged. He dropped his bowl to catch Aelfhild as she fell forward. "She has returned!" he shouted over his shoulder. He dragged her body back into the cave. She heard her feet scraping the floor but could not feel them.

"Get her by the fire." Kalma's voice.

"She is near gone." Narfi's voice.

Surma snuffled around her face. Even those bulging eyes were a welcome sight.

The familiar rustling sound came from the back of the cave. This time it did not rasp so harshly across her ears. Aelfhild craned her head back to get a look. She saw blue eyes peeking out from every crack in the back of the cave, two or three sets packed from side to side in some of the larger clefts. Blankets were draped over her.

"The *huldufolk* seem fond of this one," Kalma was saying.

Huldufolk, Aelfhild thought. "Hidden folk" was the translation from Thrym.

She shivered as more blankets were piled on. Then she was gone.

4 3

ELFHILD FOCUSED. SHE was trying to pick a leaf with her left hand. It still took concentration.

The snow was hip deep in places. To the south the sun struggled to heave its weak glow over the horizon. It was about as bright as it would get all day, and there were still hardly any shadows. Winter this far north was a misery; Aelfhild had decided she did not like snow after all. She had loved it back in Cynestead, when she had been able to watch flurries gusting off the lake from the comfort of the ever-blazing kitchens. Wading through it now, less so.

She had a coat of furs that Narfi had trapped and snug hide boots that kept out the damp, so she was as dry and warm as could be. The chill from the far side of the Veil had been hard to shake. She still felt it in her bones in idle moments and it would set her shuddering.

But now she focused every fiber of effort into her left thumb and forefinger. It took time and patience. She had cleared a patch of snow to reveal mountain sorrel beneath. The rusty stems and green leaves were spots of color on the otherwise monochromatic landscape. Even the spruce boughs were buried in white. There was a whole bundle of sorrel stems in a sling at her side, but those had been picked with her right hand.

It had been a long recovery. Days before she could even stand again, and that only with Narfi's aid. There had been more days spent walking short steps with long breaks until she could finally make it out of the cave on her own. Then even longer with the bandages and ointment—a lumpy paste that smelled of honey, one of the few things Kalma brewed that was close to pleasant. It helped soothe the scorched skin. Aelfhild had to learn to do everything one-handed in the meantime; the fingers on her left were a useless clump. With practice and pain, she was able to get her thumb and forefinger bending again. The other fingers remained stiffly stubborn. She spent nights coaxing them to twitch a little farther, flex a little tighter.

Her fingers, trembling now with the effort, locked under the plant's stalk. She pulled until the stem snapped, then carefully transferred the leaf to her right hand. She popped this one into her mouth. The sorrel had a sour, bright tang to it. At first she had not taken to it. Kalma had shrugged and said that was fine, as long as she did not value the teeth in her head. Since then, Aelfhild's tastes had improved.

She slipped her left arm back into her coat and made sure the sling was tight around her waist. After pushing the snow back over the remaining clump, she turned and waded homeward.

There was a feather on the snow along the way. Aelfhild spotted it only because of the touch of brown mottling around the otherwise per-fectly camouflaged plume. Gyrfalcon or white owl, she suspected. Either way, her friends would like it. Anything bright and beautiful was their delight. She pocketed the feather.

Surma met her at the mouth of the cave. The dog pressed her soggy nose against the back of Aelfhild's hand and snuffled at her pockets. "Nothing for you," Aelfhild chided, but stooped to scratch the proffered belly. Against her own better judgment, she had grown fond of the mal-formed mutt. She felt a certain kinship. At the current pace, she herself would be nothing but a ball of scars and welts before long. The handprint lingered on her arm even as the burn healed. The golden color had mostly faded, but the light would play off it at odd angles. It was one more thing to hide.

Surma whined. Aelfhild had stopped petting.

"Come on, then." Aelfhild clicked for the mongrel to follow. Instead she stayed out in the snow to snap at bugs. The dog was not deaf, as Aelfhild had once thought, but listened only when the mood took her. That made her as reliable a source of conversation as the others. Kalma was frequently absent and bizarre when present, and Narfi was always himself.

There was a new visitor in the cave when Aelfhild entered.

The witch did love to make bargains. Narfi had not exaggerated that part. Nearly every week someone from the outlying hamlets would come to strike a deal. Each one asked for a different favor and each one brought payment. Never silver or gold—there was little use for those in the wilds—but Aelfhild watched everything else pass through the mouth of the cave. Spun cloth, raw wool, turnips, cured pelts, firewood. A half keg of mead that both Narfi and Aelfhild eyed on the sly. Goats, a piglet, a raven in a wicker cage. One farmer's daughter offered a kitten but Surma would have no part of that and Kalma drove the girl away.

After a while it grew easier to tell which visitors wanted what. The noblewomen and merchants' wives, for it was almost always women, wanted potions and curses. They came on horseback wrapped in capes and asking for love or retribution. Peasants made the trek on foot to beg for a fat harvest or to cure an ailing sow. None of them ever knew where to look. They did not want to stare at the witch, or the wheezing dog, or the berserker, or the wounded girl with glowing marks, or the myriad bundles hanging from the ceiling filled with the Gods only knew what. Most stared at their shoes and stammered. But if the payment was fitting, Kalma sent them away with a tincture or charm or poultice.

No one ever returned to complain.

Today it was a terrified maiden whose otherwise pleasant face had sprung out in angry pustules. She tried, in vain, to cover them with a scarf. The girl whispered to Kalma through the wrapping.

Aelfhild found herself wondering if the pox was the fruit of a separate visit to Kalma, perhaps a rival in love. It would not have been a shock for the witch to trade a cure for some ill she had herself caused. Her approach to morality seemed to be that it was a complication best avoided outright.

She dropped the sorrel beside Kalma's nook. Neither of the whispering women looked up to mark her passing. She went to the back of the cave and laid out her feather. The chittering was distant today; the huldufolk did not respond to most strangers. There was the faint pressure behind her ears that accompanied the sound, but it was familiar enough by now that it did not bother her. The little gifts were always gone by morning.

Kalma's petitioner squealed in dismay. Surma had returned, nose still cold from outdoors, and apparently sneaked up on the newcomer from behind. The dog skittered away with equal surprise.

"Out!" shouted Kalma.

Aelfhild smiled to herself as she unspooled the wraps from her shoulders and wriggled her useless arm out of the furs. Every time the sleeve came off and cold air hit the scar, she winced.

The pox-covered woman hustled out of the cave with a pouch in hand. She tried to fasten her trailing scarf at the same time, but her haste to be clear of the place overcame vanity. Aelfhild's heart panged at the sight of oozing skin. That was a hard way to live.

"Will you heal her?" Aelfhild asked.

Kalma did not answer. She was busy sorting through the sorrel, frowning at each bruised stem.

Aelfhild sat outside the cave and watched the sun set. It had not been long since sunrise, and the lazy orb had not risen far into the sky. They were on the other side of Midwinter, though, so it would be getting better day by day. It seemed she had missed the holiday while trapped behind the Veil. She had asked Kalma about the lost time. The witch had shrugged. Aelfhild had not pressed her. Whatever wisdom the woman had, she doled it out only on her own terms.

To the southeast, smoke rose over Herjarsborg. It did on most days. Whenever she saw the plume Aelfhild wondered what her friends were busying themselves with. She tried to recall their faces, which grew ever harder, but it was nice to think of pleasant company.

There was, though, a far more somber reminder in that smoke. Harald's smiths were awork hammering and smelting and casting. The anvils rang, the forges belched embers and smoke. Sparks skittered off grinding wheels, steam curled up from the tempering vats. That was the might of the Thrym stirring. The smoke was a trickle from the sleeping wyrm's jaws that but hinted at bubbling ruin within. It was a reminder of what was to come and all the things she could not stop. But Aelfhild stood by her dying, or near-dying, resolution. She would see her friends again and take the rest as it came. Hiding in the mountains was not a plan.

Narfi trudged his way up the hillside, empty-handed from the look of it.

"No luck with the traps?" she asked.

The berserker hocked into the snow in place of an answer. He took a moment to catch his breath. He never bothered to look at the sunset, but his eyes followed hers to the smoke. An unpleasant smile spread his chapped lips. "The eagles will be well fed come spring," he said.

Aelfhild was long since used to his lack of manners. "You know they will be feeding on my people."

"The strong eat the weak, that is the way of it. There are not this people and that people," Narfi said. He turned and walked into the cave. Over his shoulder he added, "Only hunters and prey."

Aelfhild shivered. The feeling of that whispering voice inside her head lingered, too. From the first moment she had heard the whispers in her dreams, she had known she was mad. Known she was cursed. Now that knowledge was crystallized, and the madness had a name: Trollmother. The dreams came from her. The madness came from her. As sure as Harald might be that it was the will of the Gods made manifest in her hand, Aelfhild knew the truth.

There were two sides to Trollmother. There were the silly stories that Kalma told, naught but children's tales meant for the campfireside.

Trollmother stole mead from the Gods and gave it to foolish mankind. That was why strong drink forever bested men.

Trollmother whispered the secrets of life into the ears of the giants, but she twisted the magics and gave rise to the Thurse. Thus were the Jotnir undone by their own greed.

Trollmother hid away the stars. Trollmother cursed the tongues of man that they would never again understand one another. Trollmother this, Trollmother that. The trite little fables ran together until Aelfhild lost interest.

Then there were the bargains. About them Kalma said, "Drink of Trollmother's gifts and bear her burdens."

That was the voice Aelfhild recognized. The words sent lightning coursing down her spine. *Everything*, the whispers had offered behind the Veil. Even the wisdom doled out in pinches to her in dreams came at a cost—she thought of the blood rage, the fury that seized her in battle. It had not cost her, not yet. One day it surely would. And then there was Eyvind, never far from mind. *Everything*. He had said that he would accept whatever came from his scar. Aelfhild would not. She was sure there was a way to stop it.

But the spirits would come calling for their due.

44

T WAS HARD to know which was worse in the mountains,
the snow or the mud. Thigh-deep snow was a bother. Drifts
would mask the edges of the ravines and send an unwary
wanderer tumbling with one wrong step. It blinded, either
by the sun's reflection or by the blowing crystalline dust off the crusted
rime. Snow worked its way into the cracks between boot and binding or
coat and belt with eerie persistence, always finding a way to dampen a foot
or drip down a leg. But as the spring melt came, so did the mud thicken.
And oh, what mud.

Aelfhild followed Kalma uphill. They both wore snowshoes, more so
they would not sink into the softer tracts of soil than out of concern for
the snow itself. There was still plenty of gritty snowpack left, especially in
the shaded dells and overhangs, but the sun was rising more and more to
melt it away. The air was warm enough that Aelfhild's coat hung open.
Wind from the peaks made it flare behind her. At least the gusts pushed
the blackflies away. They were starting to swarm.

"Was it me that opened the way for the troll?" she asked Kalma.

They had barely spoken all day. The question was the continuation of
a conversation that had been rolling for a month or so. Kalma and Narfi
were not the talkative kind. What would have taken half a moment to talk
through with Jarngrim or maybe an hour to wheedle out of Kolbrun took
day after dreary day with the witch or the berserker. And with Kalma's

erratic trips out into the hinterlands, sometimes a single question would go unanswered for as long as a fortnight.

But the witch was used to it. "The dreaming is a soft place, same as the circle above," she said, nodding toward their destination. "Your passing sends ripples. Things fall through. Trolls are not clever enough to know better."

"I thought your Trollmother was meant to be trapped away."

"And she is. Mostly."

Aelfhild puffed sweat off the tip of her nose. The snowshoes were right cumbersome. "Why do the Gods allow it?"

Ahead, Kalma shrugged her shoulders. Apparently Aelfhild would have to put that question to the Gods themselves.

They crested the plateau toward dusk. The moons were straight overhead but appeared as washed-out orbs in the fading blue of the sky. Glacial ridges to the southwest hid most of the sunset, but shreds of burned orange and violet shimmered through and hinted that there was a grand show beyond.

"Pack." Kalma beckoned her forward. Aelfhild turned and allowed the witch to root around in the satchel on her back.

Not so much as a "by your leave," Aelfhild thought. And "thank you" would have been cause for wonder. Soon she would be gone and rid of the irksome pair, though. The rivers were thawing, the ice packs breaking, and the Jarls would be girding themselves for battle. Kalma had promised one more lesson and then Aelfhild would know all that she ought. Or so the witch said.

Kalma pulled out whatever she needed and walked toward the ritual stones. "Leave your things," she said.

Aelfhild left the bag with the snowshoes. She kept her axe and her belt knife. They might not be much help against vaettir, but they made her feel a damn sight better about the prospect of facing them. The circles of worn stone stirred up memories. Unbidden, her fingers were brushing across the scar on her left arm. She inhaled and followed Kalma across the ridge.

"Stay back until I call for you this time," the witch said. She muttered to herself, kicking ruts in the mud that now clogged the central channels.

Aelfhild thought she heard snippets about clumsy girls falling around the place amid the grumbling, but chose not to rise to such bait.

Kalma had a dead hare in one hand, fished from one of Narfi's snares, and a knife in the other. She made a few careful cuts and left the carcass in the central bowl of the circle. Then she paced out along each channel, marking her steps, and flicked blood to the north, south, east, and west. She looked up at the moons and measured with her fingers. Satisfied, she hustled out of the ring.

No more was forthcoming, so Aelfhild asked another question: "What am I meant to be learning?"

"Patience, for one thing, girl."

They waited through the gloaming. The witch kept her eyes skyward; the moons seemed to be key. Ever so slowly, Valr's smaller, bone-white face inched in front of the pale giant Rymr. As the orbs aligned in perfect sequence, Kalma sucked in her breath.

Aelfhild felt the pressure building in her ears. It swelled and swelled with each heartbeat. Her ears drummed against it but she knew working her jaw would bring no relief. Though, beneath it, was something new. There was a raw, thrumming energy to the ring tonight. It was a slippery feeling, impossible to draw out from the jostling background. This must have been the ritual Kalma had first intended but never finished.

"Approach now and be ready," the witch whispered to her.

"Ready for what?" Aelfhild hissed back as they crept forward.

Kalma lifted a finger to her lips. They paused at the edge of the outer ring.

The hair on her arms stood on end so close to the first circle. Kalma's braid was bound too tight to stir, but Aelfhild could feel her own loose locks spreading of their own accord. Her fingertips buzzed. Power pulsed out from the runestones in steady waves that crackled across her teeth.

Mist trickled into the central bowl of the ring. If Aelfhild squinted hard she could make out a tiny ripple in the air, a shimmer like the horizon on a blazing summer's day, from which the mist began to pour. Her hand drifted down to the axe handle in her belt. She checked the rune on her hand. It flickered in time with the pulsing energy. A distant shriek echoed through the rent in the air. It made Aelfhild freeze dead.

"Stop the ritual!" she said with a hiss. "Stop it! The beast can sense it!" Kalma waved her down. "Wait."

Again, the shriek. It was stretched and distorted through the tiny gap in the Veil, but it was coming closer. Aelfhild drew her axe. Maybe on this side, in the waking world, iron would be useful. The shimmering rift was spreading. Mist continued to spill through.

"Stand ready, girl," Kalma spoke. There was no fear in her voice, no hint of surprise. She had known. "It is here."

Aelfhild spread her feet. She hefted her blade.

As the dread raven beat its wings and launched forth through the portal, a ball of white light burst outward. Aelfhild was knocked back onto her heels. Even Kalma, who had braced herself against the ground, was thrown.

The spirit screamed. It was the same sound as when Aelfhild had burned it with her rune but was continuous now. She threw her arms up to cover her ears. The raw crackling was intense, slicing into her mind, and she could feel the creature writhing in the circle's center. She tried to steady her footing against the force rippling out from the ring. The nausea struck hard and her eyes watered.

"What did you do?!" she screamed at Kalma.

The witch did not answer. She looked ill herself. Some things maybe even she could not control.

Aelfhild pushed herself forward against the battering waves. The raven shook in agony. Mist swirled off the void-feathered wings as they beat in vain. Some force tethered it to the ground.

It had been a trap, Aelfhild realized. The ritual ring worked as a snare for the spirit world, either by design or by Kalma's own warping. The beast was caught inside. Aelfhild could feel the ethereal strands that webbed across the rings, from one pillar to the next, that cut into her thoughts and tore at the spirit's body. It was the feeling of metal wires stretched taut across sharp glass, creaking and cracking under vicious tension.

There was a keening edge to the spirit's screech now. Suffering tinged with resignation. The outline of jet black talons, as long and as thick as Aelfhild's own legs and wickedly hooked, clutched at the rock but could find no purchase. What little moonlight cut through the fog was enough to scald its wriggling form.

Kalma had worked herself up onto one knee. "Take it!"

"What?!" Aelfhild had to yell over the throbbing.

"Take it! Take its power! Feed!"

Whispers trickled up through the sweeping mist. *Feed! Take its power!*

And there was a stirring within her. Aelfhild felt hunger, not physical but a gnawing hollow buried deep in the recesses of her chest. The rune on her hand twinged. There was power here, trapped and vulnerable, such a glut that she could gorge on. The beast gasped as it writhed against its bonds, weakening. All that escaped now was a gurgling whine. The fight was gone from it.

Aelfhild's knees shook. The hunger surged up with alarming force. It had teeth to it, pricking at her heart and worming up into her throat. She wanted to bite, she wanted to feast. She wanted revenge. She could see the red flecks edging in at the sides of her vision. But she hesitated.

"Drink of Trollmother's gifts and bear her burdens," the witch had said.

Feed! She heard the voice, insistent in its urging. Desperate, almost. *If you would save him, you must feed!*

"Bear her burdens." The thought stuck up against her surging desire. *Feed!*

Aelfhild gasped. She drew in the crackling air deeply.

"No," she said.

She forced the hunger back, pushed it down, bound it within her breast. It was a wild stirring, but her life had been spent denying her own wants, suppressing her own needs. In that, she was a master. The strands vibrated around her. She could feel them scraping against the walls of her mind. She focused and reached forth. She imagined hooking a finger and plucking.

There was a snap, a shattering crack, an uneven ripple in the cascade of power.

Fool! Prey! The whispers swarmed up from around her feet. *Stop the mortal! Stop the prey!*

She reached out for another strand and tore at the web. The raven spirit shifted and cried out. There was an edge of hope to it now. Aelfhild's confidence surged.

Stop the fool!

"What are you doing?!" Kalma howled. She tried to grab hold of Aelfhild but could barely right herself against the invisible torrent pouring from the rings.

Aelfhild cast the witch aside easily. She could stand upright against the flow. She held sway over her hunger, not the other way around. She lifted her runed hand. The web was tattered, failing. Spectral strands scythed through the ring, their thrashing felt rather than seen. Her fist clenched. The snare screamed under the strain. One more piece gave way; she felt the snap across her eardrums and hot blood trickling down her earlobe. Then another gave, and another.

"Mother!" Kalma screamed.

The whispers rose to a wordless shriek.

The snare broke. A final wave of power burst out from the central ring, knocking Aelfhild off her feet and throwing Kalma clear past the outer pillars. One last sphere of hot light and shimmering air shot forth, slowed, then came sucking inward.

The spirit lifted its wings and gave an exultant cry. As the sphere crushed back in, Aelfhild felt the glow of recognition. Then there was silence.

There was no mist; it had been wrenched back behind the Veil. In fact, there was nothing left within the ritual ring at all. No snow, no dirt, just the bare rock of the plateau scraped to a mirror shine. Moonlight reflected back up toward the sky. The two celestial orbs were drifting apart. A bare circle extended twenty paces out past the farthest runestones, marking where the energy had reached its apex. Everything within had either been blown clear or sucked through the closing void.

Kalma lay outside the circle's edge, curled into a ball.

Aelfhild swallowed hard as she approached the prone figure. Her ears still rang. The sudden silence and still, cold air were jarring. At first she feared that the woman was dead. The body was completely still. Then she marked a gentle shaking around the shoulders. The witch was weeping.

Of all the responses, grief was not one she had expected. She did not know what to say. She stood at a distance and waited.

After a time, Kalma sat up from the dirt. Her braid was disheveled, her shoulder caked in dirt from when she had been thrown. Tears streamed down her face. The black eyes tore into Aelfhild. "Fool!" she spat.

It was Aelfhild's turn to shrug.

"What have you done?" the witch asked. The question was clearly not meant to be answered. "How could you be so ungrateful?"

The hunger had risen up so hard and so fast, a base, feral need lunging toward any glimpse of freedom. That had terrified Aelfhild the most. *Everything*, the whispers behind the Veil had offered her, but she knew within herself that the cost for that sort of power would be her very being, her soul. She spoke softly to Kalma now. "You said something to me once; maybe you do not even remember, it was just a passing insult to you. Lead or be led. I tire of being led."

"Stupid girl!" The witch spat in the dirt before Aelfhild's feet. "You have no inkling what is to come. You will not be strong enough to face it. You will suffer and you will die, and you will not be able to save your wretched little flock."

"Your god asks too high a price," Aelfhild said.

"You walk alone now. You walk unguided!"

Again Aelfhild shrugged. "My mistakes are my own."

Kalma scoffed. Tears continued to roll down her cheeks. "Oh, Mother," she whispered between ragged sobs. She snorted and drew in a long breath. "I want you gone. There is nothing left for you here."

Aelfhild nodded. She left the witch behind. At the edge of the plateau she tied on the snowshoes. The night sky was cloudless, a breeze was still blowing, and the moons lit her way back down.

THE WITCH WAS done. Whatever hold she had on Aelfhild was broken. There would be no eldritch bargains. There would be no mad power. If anyone was going to save her people, save her friends, it would have to be her. By her own strength, such as it was, and by the strength of her bonds. No tricks. No deals. Her stride was long and her steps rang out as she marched down the slopes. She struck eastward, toward Herjarsborg.

The journey back was not rushed. Avoiding the worst of the flies was the only real concern; otherwise she slept under open stars and walked in the long shadows of birch groves, black alder, and lanky spruce. There was food enough for those that knew where to look. There were fat roots and a few early blooms, scattered berries better left untouched, and trout still slow from the winter. Her skin was hardened to the icy water, and Onund had taught her how to snag the drowsy fish from among rocks and eddies along the riverbank.

In the late evening she caught sight of Herjarsborg's lights through the trees ahead. The city looked to be aglow; she quickened her step and soon was jogging down the riverbank. A spit of mossy bank cut out into the water, and she rushed out to look. There were fires down the length of Herjarsborg, raging up through gaps between walls and reflecting in orange bands across the river's surface. For a moment she worried that there had been some disaster or an Ulfing raid, but there would likely not have been so much dancing in either case. In the clear spaces between halls, Aelfhild could see spinning, jumping outlines cast in firelight.

The bridge that crossed the Frostá into Thrymgard and Herjarsborg was deserted. She did not meet a soul until she was already onto the city streets. She heard the clamor long before: every sort of drum beat, every cymbal clanged, every horn blew and in no particular cadence. It was just wild, and likely drunken, exhaltation.

The downriver bonfires thronged with tradesmen and common folk. They danced and beat makeshift drums, clanked pots and pans, and cast wooden effigies onto the flames. Aelfhild recognized the outlines of sea beasts and serpents made of sticks, leather, and cloth; she saw what were meant to be wolves and other unrecognizable shapes. One sprig of a boy tossed up some nearsighted craftsman's impression of a troll—likely a bear at the start, but with more branches tacked on as extra legs and horns. Aelfhild laughed as the gathered folk let forth a rowdy cheer. The din itself was intoxicating after so long in the solitude of the wild.

A long procession carried banners and more effigies for burning toward the Great Hall. Crowds lined the streets on both sides. Some symbols were hard to make out in the dark, and others she could see but simply did not grasp whatever meaning the locals put to them. No one in the press spared her a second glance as she passed through. There was much hide and feather in evidence in the ritual dress among performer and onlooker alike. Her rustic furs did not stand out. The procession was in full swing, the music rang out, and the mead had clearly been flowing.

"Aela!" A familiar voice rang out. "Come here!"

Jarngrim was already running toward her and did not slow. He lifted her clear of the ground, trappings and all, and spun her in circles. "I told them all you would be back!" he shouted. She laughed and returned the bear hug.

"I was always coming back," she said with some effort. His grip was fierce. As he set her down, she could see the touch of strong drink in his unfocused eyes. But he was merry and her heart swelled to see him, too. "Where are the others?"

"Here!" called Eyvind from up the street. He was perched atop a chest-high wall, Eyrun and Kolbrun settled beside him, and Embla at his feet.

The dog snapped at every passing effigy. All this merrymaking was not to the hound's liking. But as soon as she caught scent of Aelfhild, her tail was up and wagging. She pranced and whined as a familiar face approached.

Eyvind lifted a hand in salute. "Welcome home," he said. His smile caught the light. Aelfhild grinned back.

"Aela!" Kolbrun slurred. She gave a vigorous wave and nearly toppled backward off the wall. Eyrun caught hold of her and the two dissolved into a pile of heaving laughter. They were deep into their cups, judging by the sour honey smell, and Aelfhild had never seen Eyrun so free. The pair were red-cheeked, and their unabashed gaiety was nigh irresistible. Everyone in earshot grinned just to hear such joy.

Aelfhild squawked as Jarngrim's hands latched onto her back. He lifted her bodily onto the top of the wall beside Eyvind. "Up you go!" he cried after the fact. Hoisting himself took several attempts, with a break to steady his spinning head. "Pass the jug!" he bellowed at the still-giggling women once he was positioned.

She dropped her bundles on the far side of the wall and tried to make note of exactly where they were in the city. It was hard to see for sure in the flickering light and with all the commotion. Dancers with chalked faces were springing up the path now, pirouetting and twirling scarves and spinning torches. Behind them came a group of inebriated men balancing a massive wooden chair on unsteady shoulders. The occupant did not seem to mind the jostling. In the throne rocked a fool made up in paints and ornamented brocades to look the full caricature of a useless, preening noble; the man gesticulated wildly and shouted nonsense orders over the crowd to much amusement.

A wooden jug nudged against Aelfhild's arm and drew her back momentarily from the spectacle. "Drink up," said Eyvind, though he looked to have taken the advice a tad less than the others. His grin remained. "It helps."

Aelfhild took a swig and passed the container into Jarngrim's waiting hands. Whatever was in it was stronger than mead and put up a fight all the way down. She shuddered as her eyes watered. It felt like wildfire through her nose as she exhaled.

She squinted at the next figure that emerged in the procession. He was dressed in rags and wore a cap of woven straw. His face was dirtied with ashes, as were his clothes. He walked barefoot and swept the street with a reed broom. The face was familiar but Aelfhild scarcely believed her eyes.

"Is that . . . ?" she asked.

Eyvind nodded.

Harald looked as happy as could be. He danced a little jig as he swept. The smile on the Jarl's face was as broad and genuine as the fool's up in the high seat. His gait was light and the set of his shoulders said he had fewer cares than a newborn babe. The people loved the display; the crowds jeered at their Jarl as brashly as they had laughed at the painted fool.

Aelfhild gawped. No king in Cynestead would have debased himself so. Old Osred would rarely have gone without heavy guard among the commoners, much less alone and in such a state. But, as she reflected, maybe that was why Harald could be so happy. For one day, maybe just one evening, he was mocked and scorned and laughed at. For one day, he could set aside the weight of power and authority and just dance. Every other day of the year he ruled uncontested, while the people had that memory to cling to, to say, "now our Jarl, he does not turn his nose up like the rest of them." There were worse deals that she could think of.

"You missed the feast," Jarngrim said after a fragrant belch. "Best part."

Harald was disappearing up the street. The waves of laughter and insults followed him. Next there were maidens in white dresses, bedecked in dried flowers. Aelfhild lost interest and took the jug back from Jarngrim.

Embla barked at a gang of children that ran past with switches. The youths gave a good wallop to any adult that tried to stay their unruly course. Evidently the Jarl was not the only one who lost his authority on festival nights.

Aelfhild coughed. The second sip went down easier, but not by much. She passed along to Eyvind, who held it for himself. His sister and Kolbrun were still hanging off each other, laughing away at their own jokes.

He inched himself forward on the ledge. As he moved, the collar of his tunic flapped down below the nested braids of his beard, and Aelfhild saw the glow on his chest. The light had spread. Not far, but sunlight threads reached up toward his shoulder now. She did not bother to mask her gaze as he pressed his tunic back down. There was no accusation on his face as he looked at her. He asked neither guilt nor pity. She tried her best to banish them. He offered a hand down along the wall's edge, where the others would not see it. She wove her fingers into his.

"I am glad you came back."

"Me, too."

"So." Eyvind cleared his throat after a lull. "Did you find the answers you sought?"

There was another pause as Aelfhild considered. Horns and makeshift trumpets rang out from upriver and were picked up farther down. Somewhere, rites and celebrations were unfolding that would have to remain mystical to her. She settled on an answer: "Some."

4 6

ELFHILD PASSED SABERT the next morning as she went
to the Council House. He emerged from the grand doors with
shoulders thrown back and chest stuck out ahead of him, eyes
flashing in the morning sun. He nearly bumped into her. She
could only imagine what dreams of conquest and glory Harald's flattery
had put into his head, but clearly they obscured his vision. The eorling
graced her with a distracted nod. She doubted he would even remember
their crossing paths at this point.

Boy, if your father could see that greedy look on your face . . . Aelfhild
imagined Cuthbert was not above taking the rod to even his grown prog-
eny. She doubted Godwyn and Dunstan had been working at him as she
had asked. The pair needed firmer steering. Even if they had been, their
efforts had come up wanting.

A pair of huskarls loomed from the shadows within the hall. One held
up a meaty palm to stop her while the other turned to tell his lord of the
new arrival. There was a call from within and she was granted entrance.

Harald still had traces of soot around his eyes and nostrils that scrubbing had not removed; those, alongside his whitening locks, lent his face a
ghoulish, sunken cast. A waxen smile only worsened the effects. He spoke
from this throne. "Aelfhild, you have returned to us. And in time with the
thaw, no less. I feared I would have to send someone to fetch you back
from your travels."

"My jarl." She bowed. The old man's eyes had not dimmed in intensity. Suddenly she yearned for the days when he had not deigned to remember her name.

"Did this Whisperer teach you what you wanted to know?"

"It was that I wished to speak to you about, lord." She launched into her tale without preamble.

He tracked her pacing with all the concentration of an owl watching an unsuspecting mouse.

She tried not to be nervous in making her case, but feared that her restless feet gave it away. That only worsened matters. But she arrived at her point uninterrupted. "I have felt that cold behind the Veil. And I know that voice from my dreams. This is not the work of the Gods. The w-witch," she paused. Her tongue felt swollen and thick. It had been easier to get the words out with Eyvind the previous night. Perhaps the drink had helped. She could have used a nip about now, but the Jarl had not offered anything from his table. "The witch told me stories of Trollmother and I think she is to blame for all this. I think she has cursed me to bear this."

As she lifted her hand, Harald's eyes moved to her rune. He still had not spoken.

"They wanted this, wanted me, for something, the witch and her mistress. All the half answers and mystery were ways to keep me keen. I was meant to submit, but to what I cannot say." She rubbed at her chest. The scratchwork necklace still hung against her breast. "My dreams give me hints. Now it bleeds into the waking world. Trolls in the wild, doomsayers in the streets, I feel the shadow, too, lord, as I know you must. War against my people only wastes both our strength."

Harald steepled his fingers in front of his lips. He spoke softly. "Plans are already in motion. Promises were made."

Aelfhild cleared her throat. "Perhaps, lord, the other Jarls could be convinced to hear reason. I bear no love for Osric nor for his Oescan puppeteers, but surely there must be enough wisdom among us all to heed the warnings. Our world shifts beneath our feet. And to go laying siege to Haernmuth? Breaching Cynestead's walls? That is long, bloody work that we can scarcely afford. And we know the Oescans will not sit idle."

The Jarl clicked his tongue. "No, I do not reckon they will."

A ray of hope split dark clouds. Aelfhild perked up. "So do you think there is a chance the others would listen? Terms could yet be made. Alliances, even, if we can." Belatedly, she remembered herself and added, "lord."

His gaze bore down on her again. He lowered his hands to rest on the arms of his seat. "Aelfhild." Another click of the tongue. "Dear Aelfhild. Your kindness does you such credit. You have a mother's care, worrying for the safety of each of your kin. I understand it. I respect it. I cherish it. What a steward you shall make for them one day."

Harald stood and swept toward her. His ermine-trimmed cloak billowed behind. "To me, though, falls a father's responsibility. Children cannot hide behind their mother's skirts forever; they must be driven out if they are to grow and rise to mighty fame. This is my burden. I drive our peoples onward, through pain and tears, to achieve great purpose."

Aelfhild held her ground. She resisted slightly as he lifted her hands in his.

"And you must cast aside all this peasant nonsense," the Jarl said. He simpered down at her, ever the benevolent adult. "Trollmother? Just a story told to scare the poor and the unlearned into behaving. They cannot take in the full grandeur of the Gods' works, so they turn to vile talk of spirits in every loose stone and puddle. It is our duty to know better, to act better, and to correct their foolishness."

"I—" Aelfhild began, but Harald shook his head. Even the most indulgent of parents had only so much patience.

"It is a test of your faith, my dear child. We are called to meet our fate by the Gods themselves. I know this. You must learn this. And this path is not without its pitfalls. There are always snares to catch up the unworthy and the unfaithful alike. This Trollmother of yours is but one such test. Cast it aside. Pay no more mind to it."

His fingers crushed hers, but it did not seem intentional. His voice swelled, and his eyes shone with tears. The expression was not unlike Sabert's had been. It was a strain of ecstasy that filled Aelfhild with terror. Not out of any fear for herself, but for every man, woman, and child caught between that fanatical stare and its imagined destiny.

"Cast it aside, I say! You and I will stride out together and do bold deeds. All the world shall marvel at the wonders we work in the sight of the Gods. Thrymgard and Earnfold are trifles in the face of what we can create together."

Aelfhild's hands shook as she drew them away from his grasp.

He continued to smile. "Good. It is settled. Make yourself ready then, for we sail soon to Aldvik and to the gathering. You will have your place at the head of our fleet."

There was a map spread on the table behind him. The map was possibly the Jarl's most valuable possession, kept under lock and key in a scrollwork wooden case, bound with silver and wax to keep out the damp. The finger-thick vellum bore a detailed reckoning of the coastline from the Ormsund in the far north of Thrymgard down to the bays around Aculeo in Oesca, and all the inlets and channels along Earnfold's coast in between. Harald turned back to study the map, just as Aelfhild had found him.

She turned to go. The tips of her ears burned with shame. She had known her hopes were foolish. She had clung to them for the slightest comfort. But Harald's obsession was the perfect match to Osric's greed. There would be so much blood before the pair were finished with one another.

As she neared the door, Harald spoke again. He did not turn to face her. "You have sworn no oath to me. You remain free to do as you please. But remember, your companions have all sworn oaths to me. Their fates are mine."

Aelfhild slammed the door shut behind her.

She was trying to skip rocks across the river's surface, but there was hardly any space between the press of hulls. Her first stone pinged off the pleated boards of a knarr. She hooked the next one in a gap between the stubby boat and a neighboring longship, and managed to get a few bounces. That felt slightly better.

Herjarsborg's docks thronged with ships. Anything with a shallow enough draft to get up the river had been sailed or ferried in and was now being loaded for a seaward journey. The riverbank was a thicket of masts and prows bobbing in the current down the entire length of the city. Craftsmen lugged their tools to and fro along the piers, crews shouted at one another from their respective crafts, and enterprising merchants walked up and down the length of the river hawking blessed charms or sharpening stones or honeyed sweets.

Aelfhild hucked another stone that bounced off a serpentine prow. She sighed.

"What did you think he would say? 'I was wrong, call the whole thing off'? When was the last time you heard any man say that?" Kolbrun said.

Eyvind and Jarngrim were nearby, loading barrels of water and crates of dried foodstuffs into a longship with the aid of a few red-clad docksmen. The shieldmaiden had broken from the work when she caught sight of Aelfhild's face. She sat on the head of a piling at the pier's edge and watched the skipping rocks.

A flat pebble skittered through to clear water and left a trail of rippling circles. Aelfhild exhaled. "I should know better than to hope, anyway, these days."

Kolbrun chuckled. "Now you see right."

There were no more good stones in sight, so Aelfhild settled for kicking around in the packed dirt until one presented itself. She found nothing but more dirt. Her shoulders drooped. "I had to try."

"So you did." Kolbrun had her arms crossed in front of her. She rubbed her hands against her elbows. Pensive was not a usual look for the shieldmaiden, but she was clearly mulling something over. "You want to know how I look at it?"

Aelfhild cocked an eyebrow.

"You have to hope for what can be. Your trouble is you are always hoping for what should be. That is no help to no one."

"I like this side of you, skjaldmaer," Aelfhild said.

"Things are the way they are. We live a little while, we can only make changes around the edges. You take what little you can manage in your lifetime. Make the best that can be in that little piece. Leave the rest to gods and jarls and kings."

"It should not just be them that get to make those choices."

"There you go with 'should' again, Gods save us!" Kolbrun cried. "They do. Now, you either make the best of it or you go live under a boulder, because I do not see a third way."

Eyvind had turned to look at the sound of raised voices, but Kolbrun waved him off. He went back to helping Jarngrim with the ropes and knots. "If there were any *should* to this world, those two would be doing all this whining while Eyrun gave the orders. If there were any *should*, Jarngrim would long since be a *karl* and the old men on the council would not talk crosswise just for him being a shade darker. *Should*, and maybe Rolf and Geir and Vidar would still be here. *Should*, and maybe I would not have to hear the same jokes about what's in my breeches time and again."

Aelfhild nodded. "Yes, and that is what is wrong about all this! We cannot just take it."

"You are not listening, Aela! You try to carry that weight, it will snap your back. Hope for what can be, I said. Then you might get somewhere."

Kolbrun was everything she had aspired to be, as untameable and unswerving as the very tides. The pit of Aelfhild's stomach was suddenly hollow. She had fancied herself to be rising among the illustrious ranks of the Shieldmaidens. Now she could only stare. "I thought you were stronger than this," she whispered.

Kolbrun's eyes locked with hers. "Strong has naught to do with it. I lived this life, lived this world, long before you came traipsing along into it. I do not shy away from fights that come my way, but I know enough to pick only ones I might win."

"You know Harald will just throw your life away."

"I am oath-bound to the Jarl. If that is his choice, then that is my duty. I will fight the hardest I can and die the best way I know how."

There was a foul taste rising in her mouth. Aelfhild swallowed. "That is not how it should be."

Kolbrun snorted. She did not bother answering.

HE WEATHER SPOILED the mood of what Harald had likely planned as a grand departure. Banks of low grey clouds, the sort that press down from above and narrow the sky to a meager white line, swept in from the ocean and poured rain on those that gathered to see their Jarl and his warriors off. Many ships had already left to join the assembling fleet in Njallsfjord at the river's mouth, but the sleekest ships and the polished armor had been saved for last. The Jarl put on a brave face and gave his speeches, but rain thinned the crowds and made the warriors eager to get rowing. At least then they could get under cover in the boats.

Eyrun stayed behind to watch over Herjarsborg for a time. She would join them eventually, Eyvind said, but his sister was not one for the shield wall. There was much work to tend to. The city, and most all of Trollsmork, was emptying of men before the spring sowing. Plows needed to be set, fields tilled, seeds planted. Womenfolk, slaves, servants, all would be dirtying hands and straining backs while the raiders sailed south. For her part, Aelfhild was glad to be with the latter. The Jarl's boat had been filled, as there were plenty of men old and young who actually wanted his favor, and she got to sail with Eyvind and her friends.

Rain dogged their journey downriver. Sometimes they rowed, but mostly they sat beneath the ship's awning and took their ease. *Haf-söngur* was the name of the craft, *Ocean Song* in Earnfolding. The nimble longship brought back fond memories to Aelfhild, even though their last journey had not ended so well. Eyvind and Embla sat at the steering oar. Kolbrun and Jarngrim kept their sea chests to the front and side of Aelfhild, and the other Leifing warriors were pushed to the fore of the ship. The pair showed a pride in acting as her bodyguards. It was not that they did not trust their fellow warriors so much as she was precious cargo that needed to be kept secure. And likely their jarl had ordered them to do just that.

She caught glances here and there. There was always one set of eyes that snapped back to the river a touch too slowly when she looked up, or a back turned a little too quickly to be innocent. Sometimes a pair would screen one another's aftward glances with idle conversation and assume she did not notice. She did. Her hand was always carefully wrapped, but rumors spread. Talk of glowing hands, gods, and witches could do nothing but spread.

So Aelfhild did not mind being cloistered from the rest of the men. She was not eager for conversation. It left her free to make her own plans. Harald had been weaving his webs for years. She saw them in every burnished helm and speartip around her. She had only days. Her plans could not be perfect, but they would have to be enough.

Jarngrim's voice stirred her from musing one morning. Or it might have been afternoon. Grey hours slipped by indistinguishably accompanied by the constant, drumming rain on the canvas overhead. He hummed a jaunty tune, and was in the middle staves of some poem. "Spear asinging, at the dike he stood; swords abiting, the Oescans swarmed."

"Shields abreaking, before him they fell," Kolbrun joined in.

And they both finished off the bar with a rousing chorus: "As Norholt wept, her sons amourning."

"What song is that?" Aelfhild asked.

"You were worlds away again," Jarngrim said with a laugh. "'The Lay of Hengist,' that is. One of the Norholtings started spreading it around while you were gone. It caught a few ears. Halfway decent, that lot, as far as weaving a verse goes."

Kolbrun scoffed. "Not a candle to ours, mind."

It was a rare thing for a living man to earn his own song, but Aelfhild still felt the need to ask. "He fell at Wynnthwait, then?"

Jarngrim nodded. "Fell atop a mound of Oescans, if the story is to be believed. A worthy end."

I cannot say we parted on good terms, thought Aelfhild. But Cuthbert was right. Hengist had done his duty. He had helped in his way, as Aelfhild had strived to do in her own. She hoped that whatever eternal reward he had earned befit not the man she had known, but the one the Eorl had seen in him.

"Thinking of how we laid him out?" Jarngrim asked.

Aelfhild chuckled. "We? No. Something Cuthbert said that finally makes sense to me. It will be a time for Hengists soon."

"Aye." Jarngrim considered it for a moment, then laughed. "Aye, sure enough."

"It does make me miss Onund," Kolbrun said.

"Oars out!" cried Eyvind from behind them. From his higher perch he could see more than they, though it meant he did have to endure the wet. "Enough lounging, you lot, time for rowing!"

Embla barked to add her seal of approval.

Aelfhild smiled to hear Rolf's words coming from Eyvind's mouth. Some friends were not fully lost. She ran out her oar and waited for the familiar command.

"Pull!" shouted Kolbrun. She stood at the aft platform and kept the time. "Pull!"

They fell into rhythm. Aelfhild could drown out the voices once more. Her view into the outside world was the slit between the oarlocks and the awning ties. The riverbank was gliding away into the mist. Off to starboard she could see a ridge that ran out along the water's edge until it disappeared into the haze of rain, and glancing across to the port side she saw similar. They were coming out into the fjord now.

She caught the scent of salt air as the water changed from brackish to pure sea. The fjord sheltered them from the brunt of the waves, but there was more of a back-and-forth rocking to the hull now. It felt good. It felt right. She was not alone. Jarngrim hollered, "Seafall! Home at last!"

"Pull!" Kolbrun yelled.

Eyvind drummed a hand on the awning above. His voice soared

through the rain, "Seafall!" Jarngrim kept hollering as more voices, toward the prow, took up his wordless cry.

"Pull!" yelled Kolbrun.

Despite herself, Aelfhild let out a whoop. For a moment she could put aside all that was to come and be free. Through a tiny gap, she could see ocean. It was good to feel that endless possibility once more, wide open and inviting. She raised her voice to join the cry.

Kolbrun shouted, "Pull!"

"Aldvik, ho!" came a shout from *Haf-söngur*'s prow.

They had stowed the awning, so Aelfhild could pull herself up by the rigging ropes. Clouds still pressed down, but the rain had stopped. They had picked up a fair offshore breeze to bear them along. Crimson and silver bars rippled across the taut sail as the prow cut whitecaps. Sails billowed to all sides, some with similar bars, others with red whorls on white or half in silver, but all bore Leifing colors. More than a dozen ships of varying sizes were around them, and she could make out more masts ahead.

Njallsfjord was edged with sheer limestone cliffs on both its eastern and western shores, but the eastern wall had collapsed in scattered spots to create runs and gullies that spilled onto beaches of pearly white sand. Each of these strands sported a fishing village, though most were no more than four or five huts huddled against the shelter of the cliffs. Along the largest gorge, though, the Thrym had put more effort into carving out a haven. This was Aldvik. Barnacle-crusted jetties extended out past the tide line, and shingled longhouse roofs hedged all the way to the edge of the wharves. On the landward side the village hugged the contours of the limestone. Halls jutted precariously out along the sloping gully, and dwellings were carved out of natural shelves in the rockface. Ladders ran from one level to the next, and there was no wasted surface, lending the town an anthill appearance.

From the jetties extended a grand causeway of longships lashed together. Aelfhild had seen such before on the Leohtmere with the Oescan boats, but not of so great a scale. Those logging rafts and ketches had been blocks of unshaped wood compared to the artful curve of the longships ahead. More boats were anchored offshore, and some were pulled up along the thin strip of sand at the base of the cliffs. The masts were thick enough that a man could walk from one to the next and make landfall without getting wet as long as his balance held true, and Aelfhild could see green, white, black, and gold among the bundles of furled sails.

Jarngrim whistled at the sight. "How many do you reckon?"

"Father said that we, the Ulfings, and the Skjoldungs all pledged a hundred ships. Add the free spears to that," Eyvind said. "This is just our part."

Kolbrun breathed deeply. "Take it in, Aela. We shall not live to see another fleet like it."

Aelfhild knew the Aettir were split into four main clans in the current age; there were other bloodlines, but either too small to hold any sway or scattered during leaner times. Eyvind had mentioned three. She asked, "What of the Eldings? Are they not sending ships? I see some green sails here."

"Fishermen!" Jarngrim called.

"Jarl Runar will send a few," Eyvind explained, "but his fleet is mostly set for fishing. They will be bringing the food while we do the fighting. Less glory, but the Eldings are a queer folk that way. They prefer their dealing and trading. Lively now, stow the sails! Hands to oars and ready with the mooring lines!"

The Jarl's ship received pride of place at an empty pier. There was some innate order to the docking, as all the ships fell neatly in line, though Aelfhild would have struggled to tell one from the next. Whatever the ranking, *Haf-söngur*'s berth was close to the Jarl's and they were soon tied amid other bobbing hulls.

"Aela!" Eyvind beckoned her over. "Stay close to us here. Boats are coming in from all around. Who knows what sort of men they carry? Keep your axe handy."

She nodded.

There was barely space to extend her arms from the moment she stepped off the boat. Aldvik was full, in the realest sense of the word. If anyone had intended to do her harm, he would have had trouble finding room to take a swing. The narrower docks were a shoulder-to-shoulder jostle of raiders coming and going to their ships. There was a constant flow of barrels and sacks back and forth, as men traded in town for whatever they had forgotten or had brought in surplus. Curses abounded as men tred on one another's feet or knocked shoulders, but huskarls in their red cloaks swept down on any fights that threatened the flow of movement.

And as the streets widened ashore, the press was only slightly eased. Every house and hall was packed enough to spill out onto the street. Chickens clucked from the eaves, having lost their space in the street. Geese hissed from their pens as strangers bumped the fences.

Aelfhild stopped dead at the mouth of one alleyway. She sniffed. Buried among a dozen more pungent scents, she smelled mushrooms. It was an almost rotten, earthy smell that belonged to a breed of red-cap toadstool when dried. She recognized it immediately. She knew a man with a penchant for that fungus. On the tips of her toes, she peered down the crowded side street. There was a flash of bearhide slipping through the mass of woolen tunics.

"Narfi," she said.

"What?" Kolbrun hollered. The shieldmaiden pushed her along from behind, not fully by choice. It was impossible to hold back the shoving bodies for long. Aelfhild shook her head and they walked on.

If he did not want to be found, she would not find him. There was no use searching. But he was here. Watching. There were more than a hundred ships to catch passage on, more than a hundred crews to hide among, and most would not shun a good sword arm. She would have to keep her eyes open.

Smiths were grinding edges and hammering bent blades along the open lane. Sparks flew up with the smoke. A makeshift butcher's table took up half the street. Sheep bleated in an alleyway pen behind. Joints of mutton hung from a rack; men crowded around and pointed at their desired cut, while the butcher and his whole family grabbed up coins. Aelfhild stepped over a river of blood that ran from the tables and pooled in countless footprints in the mud.

"Which way are we going again?" she shouted over her shoulder as she squeezed between two massive, wool-clad backs. She saw Jarngrim's hand over the crowd, pointing to the right.

"Hard astarboard!" His voice struggled to overcome the shouting of fishmongers and gutterside shamans.

Aelfhild gave a stubborn back in front of her a shove. The man spun to face his assailant. He was as big as Jarngrim—taller, even—and dwarfed her utterly; the purple veins that stood out around his columnar neck said he was no more pleased with the crowd than she. Tattoos covered what little face poked from between his sprouting beard and sweat-plastered locks. Aelfhild gulped. She feared she had grown overconfident.

But instead of throwing a boulder-size fist, the man snatched the linen cap off his head with both hands. "Beg pardon, lady!" he shouted as he flattened himself against the nearest wall.

"What was that?" Kolbrun asked as she caught up through the press.

Aelfhild glanced back. The man was still staring at her. Not at them, not at Kolbrun or Jarngrim or Eyvind, but clearly at her alone. What he saw that rattled him so, only the Gods could tell. Well, she knew, but did not want to know. "Not the faintest," Aelfhild muttered. "Straight ahead here?"

Jarngrim nodded. They levered their way through the mob gathered outside one tavern and made for the tallest roof in the lower village. Most of the buildings looked to be knocked together from driftwood more than anything, but this one was different. A great longship had been flipped upside down and blocked in with stone and mud. It had clearly been expanded upon since, as a second, cedar-beam roof rose up out of the old hull, but the lines of the longship remained unmistakable. There was a low doorway covered with a curtain, leaking firelight and flanked by a pair of axe-wielding huskarls in scalemail.

They watched as Aelfhild approached and looked less impressed than the giant in the crowd. Jarngrim and Kolbrun were not worthy of note either, it seemed. Eyvind's arrival received a silent nod. One of the men lifted the curtain aside for them to pass.

48

NSIDE THERE WAS space to breathe, although the curve
of the old ship's hull forced those entering to bend at the
waist or risk knocking heads on ceiling beams. Aelfhild took
a few steps in to allow Jarngrim and Eyvind to straighten. She
looked around the room. Tables were arranged around a central firepit.
The smoke rose through a hole high above in the tacked-on roof. She felt
straw underfoot, but the light was poor.

"Who is that now?" Harald asked. The Jarl sat with his back to the
fire, facing an assembly of men wearing tabards and cloaks of all different colors. He shaded his face against the light. "I cannot see a thing in
this murk."

"Eyvind, Father."

"Step forward, my boy! Is the girl with you?"

Aelfhild cleared her throat. "She is, lord."

"Come along now!" Harald waved them inward. "You all know
my son."

There was a murmur of greeting. Aelfhild could see grey beards and
caught the glint of firelight off bronzed breastplates and chainmail, the
glimmer of precious stones. These were chieftains, thanes, men of import.
They did not wear the colors of the Leifings, so Harald did not necessarily
hold sway over them. But the free spears, as Eyvind had referred to them,
could apparently be bought.

"This is the one I was speaking of. She is marked by the Gods. They smile upon us and grant us their seal. With her at the fore of our fleet, we shall be unstoppable!"

"What new foolery is this, Harald? Make us your offer or leave off, there is drinking and rutting to be done before we sail," a hoarse voice called from the back.

"Aye!"

"Hear, hear!"

Some of the men chuckled. A few of the more cautious-minded kept their eyes trained on Aelfhild and the Jarl.

"Come now, brothers," the Jarl said, feigning offense. "Some of us can think with more than what's betwixt our legs." More chuckles at that. He placed a hand on Aelfhild's back. "Show them your hand."

She squirmed beneath his touch, but the fingers remained on her shoulder. With her left hand, she pulled the glove slowly from her right. It felt like a violation. Such things were not fit for public show. Sweat pricked up along her skin as the cloth fell away. The room went still; every man in eyeshot held his breath. Yellow light spilled out to dance off the planks and struts of the ceiling. It reflected off staring eyes.

Harald waited for a moment. His timing was masterful, as usual, and Aelfhild gave begrudging credit where due. "Foolery indeed," he said.

There was a longer silence. Logs settled in the fire, crackling up sparks.

The hoarse man spoke again. "What do you offer, Harald?"

"A fair price, brothers. Half weights of silver for every ship you bring, and a quarter weight more for those that stay to break the walls of Cynestead. I feed and arm any man that will bloody a spear under Leifing banners. And more, you get to march behind the chosen of the Gods."

"What price for ships lost?" asked a new voice.

"I am not your nursemaid. I do not clean up messes. Your ships are your own to care for."

"What share of plunder?" Hoarse voice again.

The Jarl was about to answer, but Aelfhild cut in first. "We go to free Earnfold, not to sack it. My people are not yours to steal from."

Harald's hand stayed on her shoulder. She waited for the fingers to tighten. Instead he said, "As Aelfhild speaks, so it is."

"Some fair price," a man scoffed.

The Jarl stood. "Wealth is a worry solely of this world, brothers. I urge you to set your sights farther than mere metal. Those with the strength and the courage to march with the Gods shall reap rewards far greater than any purse can hold. Who will join us?"

Muttering from the assembly.

One man stood. "I will." Aelfhild thought she recognized golden, bushy eyebrows beneath a fur cap, but it was hard to see through the shadows toward the rear of the hall.

"I will join."

"As will I." More began to stand. A few stubborn souls kept their seats.

"Then follow with us, brothers, and know that we go toward bright deeds!" Harald raised his cup in toast, then drained it. The standing men followed suit.

"Well done," Harald whispered to Eyvind and Aelfhild as he guided them away. "I have more to see to, but Aelfhild, bide here a moment. There are wonders in Aldvik that might not meet the eye. I shall lay them open to you." Then the Jarl swept off to make final arrangements with the chieftains.

Eyvind nudged her with his elbow. "That was quick thinking back there."

Aelfhild strained to peer over the milling crowd. "There he is! Thane Kjartan!"

Kjartan approached with his fur cap clutched in nervous hands. His golden hair shone even in the dim firelight, the grand eyebrows lifted in greeting. "Young Haraldsson, and lady, I feared you might have forgotten your old host." The braids in his beard waggled as he spoke. "I feared the worst when you never returned from the Ormsund, but I should have known better than to doubt. What tales you must have!"

"Never forgotten, my Thane." Eyvind clapped the man heartily on the back as they embraced. "Never forgotten."

"How is life in Oddsbaer, Thane?" asked Aelfhild.

"Songspinner smiles upon us, lady! I tell you, we have not seen such a harvest in years, and our flocks swell. Come to visit again and I shall put the grandest tables of Jarlstad to shame with my hospitality," the man said, beaming. His nerves seemed forgotten at mention of his steading. "There is enough put away that when the Jarl's call came, my men and I answered. It has been too long since these old legs felt the sea beneath them, far too long. Oh, Jarl Harald, health to you, lord!"

"Nonsense, Kjartan, no bowing today. My son told me of all your folk did for him. I shall bring your ship forward to the vanguard!" Harald cut in. "If I might steal Aelfhild from you for a moment? Many blessings, Thane!"

They left Kjartan speechless, stricken with a smile and wide, blinking eyes. Eyvind slipped an arm around the stunned man's shoulders and led him off for a drink.

"This is sorted for now," Harald said to Aelfhild. "Walk with me."

A wedge of huskarls, greataxes in hand, walked before the Jarl as they made their way through Aldvik. The crowd melted in front of them. Aelfhild felt their eyes as they turned, appraising just who this girl was that walked in such fancy company. She went to cover her hand again.

"Leave it!" Harald coughed. "If you wish, I should say, you might leave it. Faith is a powerful tool, Aelfhild."

She wiped the sweat off her palm onto her breeches as they walked. It reminded her of nightmares in her youth where she walked through the King's halls in Cynestead, laughter echoing along the corridors, only to look down and realize her shame. This time, though, there was no laughter, and that was decidedly worse.

The huskarls led them up the streets and toward the limestone cliffs. They emerged at the edge of the gully that ran to the ridgetop. Aelfhild marveled at just how steep it was. Steps were carved out of the stone in a few places, flat against the cliff, then there were runs of grass so bright a green that it seemed painted on. It was a hike to get to where they were going. Ladders shot off the path every so often, leading to caves that had been fitted with ramshackle doors to make homes or sheds or larders.

There were a few more of the inverted longship buildings along the cliffs. Evidently when the boats got too battered to be patched, they were repurposed as halls and hutches. Goats chewed straw under one such domed pen.

"Is it this one? I can never remember these blasted caves," Harald said. One of his men nodded. "Lend an old man a hand, my child."

There was nothing frail about him, but Aelfhild felt a slight hesitation as the Jarl stepped up onto the rungs of the ladder. It was his knees, from the looks of it. A lifetime of beating the waves came with a price. He gritted his teeth as he climbed. She steadied him and lifted his cloak, then followed up the steps.

They came out on a landing chiseled into the limestone. None of the huskarls followed. Harald seemed to know the way now and led Aelfhild into the mouth of a cave. He lifted a torch from a bracket on the wall. "A right, a left," he muttered to himself as they wound through branching passages. "Straight ahead. Left."

The caves had started as natural, judging by the smooth contours of the rock, but had been chiseled and knocked through to form a labyrinth back into the cliffs. If strange sails ever cropped up on the horizon, the entire population of Aldvik could hide away within the hollows. There were a few damp spots, but it was actually quite homey. Aelfhild spotted several alcoves hung with curtains and set with rugs, benches, and beds.

A man in the long robe of a priest passed them with a torch of his own. As soon as he spotted the Jarl, he bowed out of their path and motioned them onward.

"This way it is, then," Harald whispered. Then to her, "Even in a town like this, there are some things worth seeing."

They came into a great cavern, jagged with every size of stalactite. Torches guttered along the walls and at the feet of four statues. Titan columns of stone, where ancient stalagmites had risen to meet their hanging partners over aeons, were carved into the likenesses of the Four. Solveig Songspinner and Ivar Hammerswinger stood proudly in the center. Halla Beasttamer kneeled to one side, looking over some sort of carcass, but the dripping limestone had swallowed the beast's form. Hakon Runecarver, to the other side, sat crosslegged with a runestone upon his lap.

Chalky water dripped from the ceiling, adding a glistening white shine to the statues. Aelfhild could feel Harald watching her. "What do you think?"

"Beautiful," she whispered. And it was. The Gods' faces were delicate enough, and the eyes caught the light just so, that they seemed ready to reach out to the supplicants.

Something cracked beneath her foot. She looked down and saw, too late, that she had tread on a wooden stick. It was carved and marked with childish, crude runes. She stepped back. The statues had held all her focus and she had not noticed the gifts. Ribbons, coins, clay pots, whittled statues—there were piles of offerings at the base of each statue. There were carved sticks in abundance, hundreds of them, each with their own little message. Countless candles had burned down to congeal each tribute pile into a solid mass.

"This is what our Gods can inspire." Harald spread his arms to take in the whole cavern. "Think of all the muck below and then see this. Even the roughest men can be raised to something greater with faith."

Aelfhild kneeled and tried to put the two halves of the broken rune stick back together. She gingerly placed the reunited whole atop the wax-bound pile of offerings below Ivar's towering figure and hoped the Smith would not look too closely.

"Do you mark the difference?" the Jarl asked.

She shook her head. "What do you mean, lord?"

He pointed at the piles of offerings. Ivar's was clearly largest. "The Smith, you would call him in your homeland, he is a god for the common man. He forges, he thunders. He is all strength and fire and raw will. That strength is easy to grasp. Every warrior comes here and leaves something for Ivar before he sails."

The second biggest pile was below the Weaver's statue. "Solveig gives us the waves, she gives us the harvests, then the frosts. Her wheel spins and spins, and her circles never end. She claims the elderly in their time but she grants children. You see how the womenfolk come to lay down ribbons and bright trinkets. Fishermen leave a coin to sate the hungry sea."

"Then Halla." This was the most rustic of the tributes. Bones, feathers, dried blooms, and arrowheads were mounded around the Huntress's knees. "Shepherds and hunters come to her. Farmers, trackers, woodsmen. Rough hands and muddy shoes bring these offerings."

"But here" said Harald as he knelt before Hakon, whose tribute was the most meager by some margin. "Here I leave my gift." He lifted a golden chain from around his neck and draped it over the Runecarver's stone foot. His fingers remained on the statue as he muttered a prayer.

The Jarl stood. "Hakon speaks to the likes of us. He tells us that our deeds echo down through history, that our names can be carved to endure for all time. And that, to my mind, is worth more than the strongest of shield arms or the wildest of hunts."

Immortality. Aelfhild finally understood. It was not more power over men or wealth in silver and gold that the Jarl wanted. He wanted such fame as to grant him life eternal. He wanted to join his august ancestors among the annals of the runestones in Jarlstad. Most men feared death in the immediate, physical sense. Harald's great fear was oblivion. That was his weakness. Aelfhild made note.

"I will leave you to make your own gift. But Aelfhild, think on this. The Gods have much to offer if we are willing to faithfully serve." Harald stepped out of the cavern and left her on her own. By the flickering of the torch she could see he had not gone far.

She looked on the faces of the Gods. The rune on her hand felt dirty in such a sacred shrine, what with the taint from behind the Veil and the filth of Trollmother's snares. She tucked it away under her other arm. There was nothing in her pockets worth giving. Her left hand went to her trollbone necklace. That was too dear. Even for the Gods.

"I have nothing to offer you," she whispered, "save for my words. But I swear before you all that I will do whatever is in my power to save the people of Earnfold and Thrymgard both. What strength I have, I will spend to protect them. What gifts I have, I will use to uplift them. And what wisdom I have, I will use to teach them."

"I know I cannot save them all." One face in particular popped to mind; her fingers clasped the stone around her neck. Her cheeks were wet. "I pray instead for the courage to save the ones I can."

"Forgive me my misdeeds. Forgive my presumption. Punish me as you must. I beg only the time to do all I might."

The cavern was silent. No God answered, but Aelfhild stood resolved.

4 9

"READ THAT. WHAT does that say?" Godwyn pointed at runes carved into the siding of a nearby hut.

"*Þróndr var hér*," said Dunstan. His patience was wearing thin with the game.

Godwyn cackled. "What does that mean?"

"Thrond was here. Really, you fool, it is just the same as in Earnfolding!" Dunstan's voice cracked as he shouted.

But the idea of reading seemed to hold no end of merriment for the young archer. He pointed at another scrawl. "What does this one say?"

"Shut it, Godwyn." Aelfhild lifted her hand. "You said Sabert has been planning with the Jarl, Dunstan, but that is useless. I know that much, but *what* is he planning?"

"Er, indeed." The scholar tried to hobble sideways so he could look at her as they walked. The bundled kindling he carried was too unwieldy for his thin arms, though, and he nearly dropped it. "But he has only said that the Jarl is very generous and that his father will be well pleased with him for what he has won us. I could not get more! And you see what sort of help I have had while you were away."

"What about this one?" Godwyn peered at a suggestive woodcarving. "Oh, it is a picture." That set him chortling.

"Keep as close to him as you can. I need to know what he says." Aelfhild cinched the strap around her shoulder tighter. She had needed an excuse to talk to her Earnfolding informants and had bought a sack of barley cakes that were, she suspected, as much weight in weevils as in barley. Embla would eat them if worse came to worst. "And try to talk some sense into him before he gives all of Norholt away to the Thrym." She left Dunstan sputtering. One last exchange followed over her shoulder.

"Indeed, lady. Er, it is good to have you back. Oh, she is gone."

"Look at this one, Dunstan."

"No, Godwyn."

Aelfhild cleared the alley, took a hard right turn, and flattened herself against the wall. She peered back around the corner in the direction she had come. She waited. No bearhide appeared. After a few more moments watching, she cursed and spit into the dirt.

Either Narfi was too good in his shadowing to be caught, or she was losing her mind. She was sure he was around. Almost sure.

A townswoman in apron and kerchief, stepping out to empty a pot into the gutter, watched her from a nearby doorway. The woman's expression said that Aelfhild looked about as crazy as she felt.

With a grunt, Aelfhild hefted her sack and walked on. Drums beat along the main street as two teams of painted warriors pushed shield wall against shield wall. Their boots churned up the mud. The mob screamed and shrieked oaths at both sides. Coins changed hands as one team broke through, to a mixture of lamenting and raucous cheers from the onlookers. Aelfhild pushed her way past the stragglers in the back.

Then there was a fight in between her and the *Haf-söngur*'s mooring. It did not look like anyone had drawn a blade yet. A free spear swung and broke the nose of a Leifing. Blood flowed freely, but the Leifing was still in the fight. They grunted and bobbed. In contrast to the earlier crowd, the circle of bare-chested raiders gathered around made no sound. They seemed to be there only to assure fair play, and had no stake in whatever was unfolding. One of the judges must have caught sight of Aelfhild waiting.

"Here she comes. Break, you two! Enough! Clear a way for her." There was an extra force to the words "she" and "her" that made for no confusion as to who was coming. Word was getting round.

The men shuffled into two lines and made a gap for her to pass. Pinching the bridge of his nose, the Leifing dripped blood onto the planks of the dock as he made a little bow. Aelfhild still did not like the way space was cleared for her almost everywhere she went. Men parted to either side. They watched her pass. Some snatched off caps, some seemed to feel the need to raise knuckles to brow in salute. She wanted to grab them and shake back some sense, but that would have sparked chaos. Ignoring them only served to make her more regal in their eyes. There was no winning.

The fight started back up after she passed. She heard meat strike meat, and there was a groan from the onlookers.

"What is in the bag?" Kolbrun wrinkled her nose at the oily sack as Aelfhild swung down into the ship.

"Dog food," she answered.

The shieldmaiden shrugged. "Fair enough."

"When do we sail?"

"Some of the outer ships are breaking already," Kolbrun said, pointing into the harbor, "but we will wait for the Jarl to leave. I thought you would be with him."

Aelfhild shook her head. She could take only so much, and it was easy to sneak away. Aldvik abounded in ears that he could spout his talk of bold deeds and faith into; hers could be spared for a time.

"He will want you and Eyvind at the front when the time comes."

Aelfhild nodded. "When the time comes."

"I see you making plans, girl. Remember what I said. Work where you can." Kolbrun clucked her tongue.

"I am trying," Aelfhild said. "And about that." She coughed. "I never said that I was sorry for what I said. Back in Herjarsborg."

The shieldmaiden waved the apology away. "Takes more than that to drive me off. I am with you till the end."

The end, Aelfhild thought. Goose bumps started down the back of her neck at the words. "I can feel it coming," she said, "bearing down."

"Aye!" Kolbrun's wolfish grin said that she felt it too, but rose rather than shrank at the thought. "Soon now."

The drums picked up back in town. They were distant, but Aelfhild's heart quickened with the sounds.

Embla howled as they hit another swell. The crew roared. Aelfhild shouted. She hung down from the rigging and whipped her fingers across the foaming crown of the waves. Aldvik was an odorous memory. Now they were out on the open ocean, though they were far from alone.

To every side of *Haf-söngur* there were dozens of ships, and the number swelled daily. A handful of the longships, such as the Jarl's, were large enough to carry sixty warriors. Others were small enough to fit eight if packed tightly. The crews varied just as much. Some had full cheeks that suggested greed was their southward lure, or the heavy brows and dead eyes that hinted at more brutal inclinations. Others had taut, sallow skin that said returning home empty-handed was not an option for them or their village.

Thane Kjartan's crew was one of the latter. As much as he bragged about their fat harvest, his sailors looked to be on the boney side of lean. But they had scrubbed the rust from their armor, and their ship gleamed with fresh resin. Saeunn, the Thane's fair wife, had worked with the other women to sew a gleaming, gold-threaded band of stars upon their sail. As promised, their ship was ahead with the Jarl's. Kjartan was a decent man and deserved as much.

Aelfhild saw Dunstan's head emerge over the railing of a neighboring ship. Again. He and Godwyn had not yet found their sea legs and took turns to be violently ill overboard. Her heart went out to the wretched pair. She remembered holding back Ceolwen's tresses through similar trials. Times did change. She snagged another handful of seawater and flicked droplets back at Eyvind.

"You fall, Aela, and nobody is diving in after you," he called.

She stuck out her tongue as she hauled herself back aboard.

A horn rang from the head of the fleet. Steersmen picked up the call and passed it along. Eyvind raised his own brass-bound horn to his lips and blew.

"What is it?" Aelfhild asked.

Eyvind beckoned her up. She stepped onto the raised platform in the aft of the ship. There was not much space. She had to stand overtop of Embla and lean back against Eyvind's shoulder. He lifted his other arm and pointed.

"See that?" There was a flicker on the horizon. "Fornhofn. That's the Pyre, always burning up on the horn of Rifstrond. Now we make the turn south."

Aelfhild swallowed. It grew ever more real. "How long?"

"Three days? If—"

"If the weather holds, I know, I know," she finished.

He shifted to the side to make a little more room for her. They watched the shore, which at this distance was no more than a few bumps frequently lost behind the waves.

"I will need your help with your father," she said.

Eyvind nodded.

"It could get bad," she said.

He kept nodding.

"Sails!" cried the watch on a boat to their starboard. "Sails to the south!"

Aelfhild craned to see. Hafdis's fleet ran under blue canvas, which made one of them hard to spot against the water, but there were enough sailing out to meet them now that it was impossible to mistake. Just a rough count said there were as many in the Skjoldung fleet as in the Leifing's, and still more to come from Sindri and the Ulfings.

"Bad," Aelfhild whispered under her breath.

Eyvind was close enough that he heard. He squeezed her arm as they watched the distant sails.

5 0

"ELA." IT SOUNDED like Eyvind's voice but it was muffled by the dream, as if deep underwater.

The chill air was familiar, and the dim amphitheater. She sat atop marble steps, with her toes in bone-strewn sand. Aelfhild stood and walked out into the middle of the pit. The heart was gone. There were traces of the old vines—hoary fragments of bark that crunched in the sand underfoot, trails of crusting brown sludge along the pale stone where veins had crawled. But only empty space where the glowing knot had been.

In the shadows outside the ring, something sniffed. Aelfhild snapped to a halt. She was not alone.

A gap in the darkness stirred. Spectral feathers shifted as void-black wings spread. The dread raven stepped forward from the darkness. Light in the dreaming did not seem to scald it as much as the glow of the moons, but the spirit shimmered around the edges as it moved into view. There were no eyes, as Aelfhild had guessed behind the Veil, only a pair of scaled nostrils set on either side of the hooked beak. Talons carved ruts in the pit. It inhaled deeply of her smell, then let out a trumpeting snort that riffled her hair.

She stepped back. There was nowhere to run. The beak was large enough and sharp enough along its serrated ends to cleave her in half. Ancestral memories told her to turn tail, but she dug in her heels.

The spirit showed hesitation of its own. Perhaps it remembered her hand. Aelfhild tucked the rune behind her back as a gesture of goodwill. It gave another snort, softer this time.

She reached out with her free hand. Shadowed wings splayed out onto the sand as the beast lowered its massive pinioned head to meet her fingertips. A raven was hardly an apt comparison, she realized. It was the closest thing her panicked mind had been able match to the form. Now she saw that there were two sets of wings, one nestled below the other, and shimmering jet horns swept back from behind the crest of its head. Smaller, similar pairs of spines descended down its back, disappearing between the forks of the tail.

A spark cracked between them. Aelfhild's hand snapped back and the beast cringed.

She exhaled. She steadied her hand and reached out once more. Slowly, the beak shifted forward. Whether it was a growl or more of a purr, Aelfhild could not tell, but a low noise vibrated through the glossy chitin of the beak as they touched. A mind stirred within, perhaps not equal to a human's but of some rudimentary intelligence and made itself felt. It thanked her for her mercy. And it bound itself to her. The vibrations spread up her wrist, arm, and into her chest. She could feel a tether fastened between her heart and the spirit's, thrumming just out of earshot. It was a spidersilk thread of warmth, unseen but palpable against the chill.

"Aela." Eyvind's voice again. A hand shook her shoulder. "It is time."

She snorted and rocked back out of his grip. Her eyelids were crusted and heavy. She rubbed at her face with the crook of her arm and blinked hard against the dawn. Phantom vibrations still ran up through her shoulder but faded with each waking heartbeat. Loose hair was in her face; she puffed it aside.

"Time," Eyvind repeated. He sat down in front of her and offered a wooden bowl.

She mouthed her thanks and took a gulp of water to rinse and spit over the side. The rest she downed. There was a wicked kink in her back from where she had somehow wormed her way between the ship's hull and her sea chest while she slept. She got to her knees first and groaned through a stretch. It was far too early.

"You were thrashing about," Eyvind said. "It took some doing to stir you. Nightmares again?"

Aelfhild mulled it over as she pulled herself up on a halyard. "No, not this time."

"Kinder omens, then, some might say. Gird yourself. The fleet stirs." He clapped her on the shoulder, which made her wince as her back shifted, and went to relieve the night watch at the steering oar.

There was a studded leather jerkin in her sea chest, with bracers and leg bands to match. Tightening some of the buckles around her sides and down by her ankles without wrenching her back any further was a challenge, but she worked through it. A little pain helped clear away the morning stupor. She pulled her belt tightly and slipped her axe through the loop at her hip. Her shield and helm could stay where they were for now. Eyvind was waiting for her on his perch with breakfast. Embla drooled as food changed hands.

"Hardfish." Aelfhild pulled a face.

He shrugged. "Barleycakes, too. And I give you the bugs for free."

She flicked a weevil into the sea. By the time they had finished their silent munching, she felt restored and almost awake.

"Ready?" Eyvind asked.

"Ready," she answered. *Ready*, she assured herself.

Harald's ship glowed amid the shadowed hulks of the fleet. Its hull was wide enough that it could fit a sand pit in the center and still carry four oarsmen abreast down its full length. They could kindle small fires, though the flames were always kept under close watch. Even surrounded by the sea, wooden boats and untended fires were sore companions.

Haf-söngur drew up alongside. The Jarl's men tossed ropes across, and Jarngrim and Kolbrun drew them together. There was a gentle bump as the hulls touched. They layed down a gangway and tightened mooring lines. A huskarl stepped across the plank. He gestured to Eyvind. "Jarl says bring your chests. We will take this little one."

"You heard him," Eyvind said as Jarngrim and Kolbrun lifted their sea chests from the deck. When Aelfhild hesitated, he grinned. "No time left for stalling."

She followed the others across, shield over her back and chest in hands. They passed a group of huskarls headed in the other direction who did not look overjoyed at the demotion, but the men left without words. Aelfhild set down her things next to Kolbrun's and tied off her shield along the railing.

Kolbrun settled against the hull. The shieldmaiden patted Aelfhild's knee. "Good luck."

"And take no nonsense," Jarngrim added from his seat behind. He was scratching Embla's belly as she rolled her scent over the fresh patch of boat.

Aelfhild stretched. She checked that the glove was pulled down around her hand, though she could not have said why. She thought of her raven friend. Hopefully, the spirit was watching out. Then she took a deep breath and turned to join Eyvind.

Jarl Hafdis's ship was drawn up on the other side of Harald's. More gangways ran back and forth. This was neutral ground, or as close to it as the long feud between the Leifings and the Ulfings was concerned, and the Jarls were holding a council. A table and benches had been set up in the center of the Skjoldungs' flagship. Hafdis sat breaking her fast and Harald stood to the side with hands clasped behind his back. His foot tapped the deckboards. The Jarl said, "He comes late. You know he does this to spite me. And I do not think he brought the full count of ships we agreed, either."

"Peace, Harald." Hafdis spoke around a mouthful of gruel. She threw down her spoon and raised both palms in surrender. "If you cannot rein in your pride for even a moment, then this whole effort is doomed. Eat something, for Gods' sakes, just leave off stirring yourself up before he even arrives. There will be plenty for you boys to fight over then."

Harald did not look calmed. He nodded to Eyvind and Aelfhild as they arrived, but the grimace was dug deeply into his features.

"My lord." Aelfhild bowed. "My lady."

Hafdis smiled. The Jarl of Rifstrond was geared for battle; her white-gold tresses were drawn into a comely topknot, and her ultramarine cloak, drawn tightly against the ocean air, showed the lines of pauldrons and jerkin. Mail was tucked away for the voyage, so only leather and cloth were on display today. If anyone took a spill into the waves, they did not want to be hung with a suit of iron rings. "Hafdis to you, Aelfhild. And to you, too, boy!" The Jarl had a soft spot for Eyvind, it seemed, and Aelfhild set her mind to ask him the story sometime. It was not jealousy. She told herself it was not jealousy.

One of Hafdis's blue-cloaks leaned over and whispered into his jarl's ear. She pushed away her bowl. "I told you not to fret, Harald. He comes."

Every Ulfing ship was hung with strings of bones. Each prow bore a wolf's head carving, showing grotesque tongues curled through bared teeth. Their jarl's ship was the grandest and grimmest of all, and its bone garlands clattered as it drew up to moor. Someone had once told her that the Thrym collected the ears of their foes to make necklaces. She had not believed it fully even then, and the Thrym she had come to know were more civilized. Sindri's men, though, made a great show of their savagery.

Eyvind, who had seen it all before, had a somewhat different view. "Makes you wonder what they are making up for, I think."

"Crude as usual," Harald said with a sniff. "But my son has the right of it. Any common animal has violence in it. A wise leader raises his men to be something nobler than they are. It is a lout, and a poor excuse for a jarl, that prides his men for being as base as they can be. I liked his father better."

"You killed his father, old man," said Eyvind.

"But I respected him." Harald looked past his son to Aelfhild. "Remember that lesson well, Aelfhild. Cruelty and fear are beastish things. Leaders may harness them but ought not revel in them. Respect, especially from your foes—now, this is true power. Queens must think on such things."

That made Aelfhild swallow. After a moment's recovery she asked, "May I make a request, my jarl?"

"Of course," said Harald. He watched her face.

Hafdis met Sindri and his guards at the gangway after the ships were tied off. They embraced rigidly and exchanged a few words out of earshot.

"Send them away from the fighting, lord, as far as can be. He will not spare my people. I beg that you do."

Hafdis was leading Sindri down into the ship.

Harald sniffed. "The thought had crossed my mind. He will not agree."

"We must try," whispered Aelfhild.

"Hmm." Harald stepped forward. He seemed to be in a rush to get in the first word. "Jarl Sindri, I hope the day finds you well," he lied.

Sindri knocked his heels together as he bowed. Silver chains hung off his neck and glittered beneath a wolf-hide cloak. "Jarl Harald, I am glad to see you in such robust health," he lied back.

The ritual was done. They all gathered around the table. One of Harald's men produced the map case, and the Leifing jarl drew out the scroll with reverent care. He spread the vellum on the table. "Haernmuth sits here, on the southern side of the inlet. We have had no word from our watchers that Osric has been building any boats, and the Oescans have sent nothing northward by sea. They know, I think, that it would be folly to meet us on the waves. But they also know that we will come this way. They will be digging in with the Oescans."

Sindri picked at his teeth. He made no attempt to hide his boredom. "Some of us know the coast well enough that we do not need maps, Jarl Harald. With respect, of course."

"With equal respect, I wonder if Jarl Sindri knows also that the Oescans have been building walls of their own outside of Haernmuth," Harald said, the picture of patience.

"I do."

"Then surely he is wise enough to know that the attack shall not be such an easy one. My suggestion is that we divide our fleets and attack from three sides at once. The Leifings sweep in from the north and attack the gates of Haernmuth proper." He touched his finger to the mouth of the river, Swiftea. "The Ulfings land along the coast due east and make for the Oescan fortress." The fingertip traced a line down. "And the Skjoldungs land farther south to catch the southerners in a pincer as their attention is drawn."

"You give yourself the lightest work, Harald," Sindri replied.

"Perhaps I fear that some other warriors might lack the discipline to keep their mind on fighting instead of pillaging, Sindri."

Hafdis spoke up. "The Skjoldungs do not shrink from a fight. We will breach from the east, even if it means taking the brunt for the Ulfings."

Handsome as he was, the Ulfing jarl had not been blessed with a pleasant manner. Even the way he stood, shoulders thrown back and legs spread to take up as much room as possible, grated. "That is not—" Sindri began.

But not before Harald cut in. "Splendid, we are agreed. My fleet from the north, Jarl Hafdis's from the east, and the Ulfings from the south. They have no hope of besting the gathered might of the Thrym."

"Aye" and "Hear, hear" said all the red- and blue-cloaked huskarls that stood behind their lords. The Ulfings remained silent. Sindri's mouth was drawn into a puckering frown. He shook his head. "The Ulfings came to this table in good faith. We raised our fleet to sail as equals. There is far better plunder to be had on the southern coasts, but still we joined. If this is the vote, we accept it. But be warned. We will not suffer long being treated as lackeys. The best of dogs will snap when ill handled."

"Indeed," said Harald. The men stared each other down.

In the silence, Aelfhild prepared herself for the plunge. She took a breath. "If I may speak to the Jarls."

Harald glanced in her direction. Sindri seemed to notice her for the first time and looked around with amusement. But Hafdis said, "Of course, Aelfhild, your place is here."

"I would ask for the chance to speak with Hauld Caelin before we rush in to the fight. I remember from old that he is no good friend of Osric's. There is a chance that we can avoid some bloodshed in this, at least among the Earnfoldings," Aelfhild said. She tugged at the glove on her hand.

"A fair point," Harald said.

"It is not!" Sindri had a smirk on his face as though he still thought that having some servant speak among the Jarls was a most impish prank. The Ulfings had not been with the fleet long enough to hear rumors, nor were their men quick to mix. "We give away our advantage of surprise, and for what? Harald, the girl wears red. Why does she speak in your place?"

"If we truly come to free Earnfold, lord," Aelfhild locked eyes with him, "and not only despoil it, then we must be willing to treat with its people."

"Agreed," said Hafdis.

Sindri recoiled. "This is a farce. Why should we even be here? Why should this little bit—"

The word never made it out of his mouth. Eyvind stood just behind his father by the table, and so was within arm's reach of Sindri. He grabbed a handful of the chains around the jarl's neck and slammed the man's face down into the table. The beams creaked with the force. Eyvind had his belt knife pressed against Sindri's right eye in a flash. "Watch yourself."

Ulfing blades flashed and Leifing huskarls drew axes. The grey-cloaks could not move closer without risking their lord's life, but if Eyvind cut he would be first to die. The red-cloaks looked to Harald for instruction. Hafdis's huskarls formed in front of her, hands on hilts. Hafdis spoke calmly: "Everyone breathe."

"Your orders, lord? Lord!" shouted one of the grey-cloaks. Sindri's hand waved him back. Evidently, Eyvind's grip on the chains was tight.

"Words were spoken in haste. Still, there was no cause for blows. Both sides overstepped." Hafdis brokered the peace. There were eyes lining the boats on either side. Leifings and Ulfings stood ready for the call, and her ship lay between them. "Jarl Sindri, if young Eyvind withdraws his blade, will you let matters lie?"

Sindri squirmed on the table. It looked like a yes.

"And Eyvind, will you make an apology?"

"I will, my jarl."

"Are all sides agreed?"

Blades wavered as the Ulfing huskarls glanced at one another. Sindri's hand flicked again. They lowered their weapons.

Harald tipped his head to his men. The red-cloaks backed down.

Eyvind sprang back and Sindri pushed himself off the table. He fussed with the ruffled collar of his cloak; it appeared the clasp had broken.

"A thousand apologies, Jarl Sindri," said Eyvind. He almost sounded sincere.

"Accepted." Sindri brushed away a thin line of blood where Eyvind's knife had pricked. He glanced across the table. "But not forgotten, Harald."

"My son is burdened with temper." Jarl Harald did not appear concerned.

Sindri spat onto the deck. "We will sail to the south, as asked. But do not ask more of me." He turned and stalked over the gangway to his own ship.

Hafdis watched them go. "If you had told my husband that I would spend my late years playing peacemaker, he would have laughed you out of our hall."

"Forgive me, Jarl Hafdis," Eyvind said. This time it was genuine.

"Save it, Haraldsson. Neither you nor your father ever learn, and I have no more patience for teaching," she said. "Rein in your men, Harald. Rein in yourself. The Gods will not conjure two thousand extra spears for you. You need Sindri. And he needs that land. Work it out." Blue cloaks swirled as Hafdis and company turned away. "Now get off my ship."

As they went back to the Leifings' vessel, Aelfhild asked, "What land?"

"Bargains must be made, dear Aelfhild," Harald replied. "You have your meeting and the Ulfings move to the south. Take victories where you can find them." The old man went to join his council of greybeards in the prow of the longship.

Eyvind tugged on her cloak as she made to follow him. He shook his head. They walked back toward where their friends waited. She said, "It would have been easier if you had not done that. I have been called worse."

"I know." Eyvind rubbed at his bruised hand. "But sometimes I just cannot help myself."

Aelfhild scoffed.

5 1

CAELIN'S SHIP APPROACHED. Haernmuth was just visible across the estuary, a thin stripe of wood and thatch. Aelfhild stood under a tent on the beach near where the Swiftea's waters met the sea. Harald, Hafdis, and Eyvind waited nearby with a rank of axemen. The Ulfings had not deigned to send anyone.

The Hauld of Ealdorscir came under heavy guard. They were mostly Earnfoldings, marked by tabards bearing the scythe emblem of their shire, but several Oescans were mixed into the band. Their crested helmets and sunbursts set them apart. There was jostling among the men as the Hauld disembarked that suggested the alliance might not be such an easy one. Aelfhild took note.

Caelin did not look to be sleeping well. She had not been overly familiar with him in Cynestead; he visited rarely and kept his own quarters and servants. Rumor had treated him kindly enough. What vices he had did not raise any eyebrows among the gossiping classes. But his eyes sank in heavy rings now, his face was drawn and blotchy. The chestnut hair in his beard was without luster even under the sun, and she suspected he kept his helm on to hide losses along his scalp. His guard halted a few paces from the tent. The Oescans stood apart from the Earnfoldings, and the southerners watched the Hauld more closely than they watched Aelfhild.

There were two stools and a small table in the shade. As Caelin approached, Aelfhild lifted a jug from the table and poured mead into two cups. She had left her hand uncovered. The rune strained to match the sunlight. Stepping into the shade of the tent, he blinked as though it might be some artifact of the glare.

She stepped back from the table and bowed. "Hauld Caelin, I greet you. Aelfhild is my name. We crossed paths in Cynestead years ago but there is no reason you would know me. May I offer you a drink?"

The Hauld stepped forward and lifted a cup. He kept it pressed against his breastplate until she took up her own cup. She sipped, then he did as well. "Aelfhild," he muttered. "I expected another."

"Ceolwen was my mistress. She is gone."

"Did those Northmen kill her?"

In a way, Aelfhild thought. *But then again, so did I. In a way.* "No," she answered. "I fear it was an accident. Will you sit?"

"No. So now you lead them. A maidservant from Osred's court in Cynestead." By his tone he struggled to believe it as much as she still did.

"I do not lead them, my lord. They granted me a chance to speak with you that I might try to save Earnfolding lives. I hoped to sway you to see reason and join us against Osric and his Oescan masters. He sits unlawfully upon the throne and we would gladly have allies to cast him off."

"What trickery is that?" He pointed at her hand.

"No trickery, I assure you. I was marked by the Oath-Stone in Aettirheim. That is where Ceolwen fell, on that journey. The Jarls believe I am marked by the Gods themselves for this noble purpose," she answered, and hoped he would not notice her skipping over what she herself believed.

"So that is the excuse," Caelin said, more to himself than to her. He looked her up and down. "You look pleasant enough, Aelfhild, but I cannot reckon it. Why would you turn against your own? What did they offer?"

"The truth, lord?"

"As though I can trust aught you say."

"Fair." She nodded. "I am troubled by dreams, lord."

"I should not wonder, with the company you keep."

That remark she let pass. It was hard to fault his lashing out. "Visions, then. I fear greater enemies shall fall upon us as we spend our own blood. Our world changes for the worse. You must feel it as surely as I do. Join with us against Osric. Bring a quick end to this fighting. We must buy time to make both our realms strong. Earnfold can stand with Thrymgard against whatever comes. Our shared past binds us together. We both know this."

His tired eyes gave no hint of belief. "What are your terms?"

"Fight with us against the Oescans. Keep your title, keep your lands, follow the Jarls and the one they choose to rule."

"You?"

"If it comes to that, lord."

"You have not even thought this through."

"Thought what through, lord?"

He barked a laugh but one bereft of any shred of merriment. "You think Osric did not know this might happen? You think he has sat upon his hands while you and your mistress traipsed about the Northlands? He has my oldest. My firstborn. Did you know that? Did you think of that, Aelfhild?"

She could not meet his gaze now. She shook her head.

"He came when he knew I would be away, if that does not tell all you need to know about the man he is. My wife, she was raised loyal to the crown. He said he wanted to take the boy to Cynestead to be schooled so he could be a great leader for our people one day. What could she say to that? Fool that I am, I left them alone. I blinked. And now an Oescan legion is dug into my back. Those men?" He pointed a thumb back through his chest so none of the onlookers could see. "They guard Osric, not me."

Aelfhild's cheeks were red. She knew there was nothing for her to say, but felt guilty remaining silent.

"Yes. You see it now. This world is not yours. Run. Hide. Shed your conscience however you can. Saw that hand from your arm if you wish to help. But leave us men to our work, because that work is all that is left to us."

"There has to be something we can do," she said.

"Then work your magic, girl. Cast a hex. Weave a spell and make Osric disappear. Otherwise, from where I stand, my only choice is to die fighting you. Then at least my family will be safe from Oescan knives and my son will be safe from Osric's noose."

Aelfhild looked into the eyes of a man truly cursed. She had thought her rune an incomparable burden. She had not fully known the depth of the waters she swam. "Then forgive me for what I cannot do," she said.

Caelin stared. "Know the price of that crown when they put it on your head. No king's—no queen's hands are clean. Enough of this chatter. Tell your masters to come with everything they have. The blood of Ealdorscir has some fight left in it." As he turned, he saw the riders perched atop a knoll to the north. The men had shadowed the Thrym fleet south along the coast, ensuring that no invader stepped foot into the borders of Blaedscir.

"What was Eorl Hlothere's price, I wonder?" Caelin did not wait for an answer. He spat into the sand. "Coward. He farms and takes his blood money while others suffer. Long may it last him. Blessed to rule a town that no one cares a whit about."

The Hauld returned to his guard. He snapped at one of the Oescans when questioned; Aelfhild could hear shouting but could not make out what was said. They left the way they had come.

"Anything?" Eyvind asked, stepping up alongside.

She shook her head.

"You tried."

His hand tightened around her shoulder. Her hand went to the empty loop in her belt where an axe would soon hang. Trying would not be enough.

"Could have been done with this hours ago, if not for all these damned nobles wanting to jabber on!" shouted Jarngrim over the waves. He sat beside Eyvind and hauled back on the oar.

Kolbrun kicked him in the back between pulls. "Shut it, oaf. She had her heart set true, even if they were too foolish to listen."

"Sorry, Aela," he called back over his shoulder, "just raring for the push is all."

Aelfhild grunted. He was not wrong. The result was the same, maybe worse. She had given them more time and warning and gained nothing.

Maybe an extra reason to hate Osric, but ample cause to turn that hate back on herself as well. There was one thing she stood by: saving one life, that would be enough. A start. Kolbrun had been right after all. What *can* be done.

A massive hide drum boomed out the rowing rhythm from the aft platform. Aelfhild could see Harald there by the steersman, clad in his oiled ringmail and hidden behind his helmet's gilded faceplate. His sword was in its scabbard, and he carried a long bronze spear with his silver-runed shield. Everyone around her was similarly furnished, if with simpler arms. Her shield was on her back and the axe in her belt. Spears were stacked in the center of the longship to be snatched up as they came ashore.

She focused on pulling the oar. The drum boomed out and she bent her back in time with Kolbrun. Buckles on her armor bit into the soft flesh below her ribs, but the shieldmaiden had insisted that every clasp be double tight. It made the difference, she said.

"We follow the Jarl's banner up the center," Eyvind said now. "Stay with Jarngrim and Kolbrun no matter what, Aela. They will keep you safe."

"Sure enough," said Jarngrim as he drew back the oar.

"Aye," said Kolbrun and nudged Aelfhild with her knee. "Stay close. You remember."

Aelfhild nodded. Her tongue was numb; she could taste nothing. The entire world was washed out; the sunlight bleached everything of its color. Every heartbeat throbbed up to shake her collarbones. The drum boomed. She kept her grip on the oar and pulled. There were red sails and scroll-work prows to either side of them and she could see more in their wake as they crested each new swell. The Thrym had come to Earnfold's shores at long last.

The waves began to ease. They were coming into the inlet now. The drum boomed. She pulled her oar.

"All hands, ship oars!" the drummer screamed.

Aelfhild shoved her oar along and down onto the deck.

"Helmets!" Eyvind called.

The helm focused her world down to the two half-moon slits. Aelfhild hammered it onto her head to make sure it stayed snug. There was a dreadful stillness as the boat drifted into shore.

"Shields to the fore!"

They were on their feet, unslinging shields and grabbing up spears. Aelfhild followed Kolbrun. The boat lurched forward as they moved toward the prow. She felt hands on her back. Embla barked from the ship's rear. She was tied to a bench and furious at being left.

Jarngrim's voice by her ear. "Breathe, Aela. Steady." He sounded so eager.

A grinding noise underfoot as the keel hit sand. "Shields ashore!"

She followed the line of men over the port side. Her feet sank deeply into water, and she toppled hard against the back in front of her. Shorter legs were a weakness; she bogged down in the lapping waves. Jarngrim and Eyvind bore her up from behind. Her feet hit solid ground.

"Form rank!"

They clattered into a shield wall. Kolbrun was on her right, Jarngrim her left. She vaguely recognized the spot. They were on the northern edge of the docks, near where she had once watched Bercthun try to sell their little riverboat. It was a lifetime ago. Now it seemed like it had passed in a breath. Madness. Just as then, no one seemed to mark their arrival. No arrows came down, no bolts or boulders, not so much as a challenge issued.

"Forward!" cried Harald from within the nest of shields and spears.

They marched into Haernmuth.

5 2

THEY HAD TO shrink file to fit down the narrow streets. The tramp of booted feet and the clatter of shield against shield were the only noises. Not so much as a chicken stirred; outer Haernmuth was emptied of life. Aelfhild kept her shield over the man's head in front of her. She was in the middle of a column of Leifings marching toward the gates of Caelin's stronghold. Her left shoulder ached already.

She waited for the clatter of arrows or the screaming countercharge. It did not come. They paused at the mouth of every alley and crosscut. No defenders appeared.

A palisade encircled the inner town, the Hauld's fortress. The beams were too tall to climb and bristled with nails at the top. Jarl Harald pushed them on toward the gate. The great doors were barred from within. Shields shifted to guard from above. Two of the huskarls, clad head to toe in iron scales and wielding greataxes taller than Aelfhild, lunged forward to work at the doors.

Aelfhild caught glimpses of the roofs above through gaps between shields. She expected the ambush at any moment, but there was no movement. Her breath rattled past her face guard.

The logs that made up the gate were almost matchwood. Hinges groaned under the assault.

"Stand ready!" Harald yelled.

The doors quivered with each blow. Wood screamed, nails popped.

"Ready!"

The bar snapped. One huskarl gave the gate a mighty kick and melted back into the shield wall.

"Brace!" the Jarl yelled.

They piled forward with their shields. Aelfhild gritted her teeth.

Nothing. Stillness. Silence.

"Forward," said Harald.

Caelin's Great Hall rose up in the center of the stronghold circle. They passed by temples, inns, barracks; none spit forth attackers. Harald waved a hand at each building as they passed, and a few men would break off to batter down the door. "Nothing!" the men shouted from behind.

The Jarl waved a hand to the left of the column. Eyvind led Jarngrim, Aelfild, and Kolbrun with him to check a high-eaved longhouse with ornate doors. Where there had once been filigree and stones set into the carvings, there were now empty holes and discolored lines. Someone had pried off anything worthy to keep it from grasping hands. Eyvind leaned against the iron-bound door.

"One, two," he counted them in, "heave!"

They all rammed forward with shields and shoulders. Wood gave way and the doors buckled inward. Aelfhild's eyes took a moment to adjust to the darkness. There was nothing inside. A table lay on its side, knocked over in the previous occupant's haste. There were bales of hay and stacked barrels, lines of barrels, but no one inside.

Back in the street, she pulled up beside Kolbrun. "Where are they?"

The shieldmaiden shook her head. Eyvind and Jarngrim formed up beside them.

Another column of Leifings had broken through the eastern gate and moved to join Harald in the center of the palisade. The Jarl stood outside Caelin's seemingly empty hall. He was in whispered council with some of his men.

From the south, Aelfhild glimpsed fire. Lines of smoke rose in high arcs. Dots of orange, flickering light grew. They came from the direction of the Oescan fort.

"Down!" she screamed. She yanked at Kolbrun's and Jarngrim's shoulders as she dove.

The first wave of fireballs hit Caelin's hall and the buildings nearest the center. Thatch crackled as the missiles broke roofs, then flames roared up as whatever was in the barrels ignited. Doors gouted forth fire, walls splintered with the erupting heat, dry straw and reeds kindled immediately.

More fireballs rained down. Aelfhild raised her shield overhead. Some exploded in the dirt of the streets and sent up clouds of choking dust. Others found unbroken roofs and added to the fire.

"Fall back!" The Jarl's horn blew. "Back to the river! Back!"

Jarngrim's hand was on her shoulder. Aelfhild pulled Kolbrun up with her as they ran. They kept shields overhead and stumbled through smoke and searing heat. A blazing wall collapsed into the street ahead. Her shoulder slammed into another warrior as they sprinted around it. Flames spread with unholy speed. Oil, spirits, or some Oescan alchemy made the buildings burst up in blue-white pillars, and the fire itself seemed to stick to any dry surface.

"To the river! To the boats!" Harald was yelling.

The Oescans seemed to predict their course. Fireballs continued to rain from the sky as they ran north. The rest of the town was slower to catch, but Haernmuth was but a giant tinderbox. Every roof touched at least three neighboring buildings. Smoke spilled out ahead as they ran, and the heat bit at their heels. Toward shore the walls gave way to open sand. The air was smoky but finally breathable.

"Get the boats into the water! *Drengir* onto the boats, steer them into the channel!" the Jarl called over the din. "Freemen and huskarls with me! To the south!"

"Where do you want us?!" shouted Jarngrim to Eyvind.

Eyvind called back, "Stay with Aela! On me!"

Embla bayed from the Jarl's ship as men pushed it back into the waves. The longships were more valuable to the Thrym than anything else, Aelfhild knew that, but Harald was giving up what looked to be half his men to get the boats to safety.

"With the Jarl!" Eyvind yelled.

Harald's horn blew. "Forward the ranks!"

Aelfhild pushed against a line of jogging backs. Her legs moved without thought. Her breathing was still wild, but her body felt impossibly weightless. The nerves would not carry her forever, but now she was flying. Her friends pressed in on either side. "Forward!" The cry echoed up and down the line.

To the left, Haernmuth fortress was a tower of yellow twisting amid a shimmering haze of black smoke. The heat was enough to bake Aelfhild's bare skin, and she could feel her hair curling away. Acrid, bitter air tore into and out of her lungs.

A field opened up in front of them. On the far side, to the south of Haernmuth, was the Oescans' siege camp. No more fireballs spouted forth, but Aelfhild could see archers on the ramparts. Most were facing eastward, toward the shore. The Skjoldungs had made it across the beach, but at cost. Blue-clad bodies and arrow-filled shields lined the sand and the path inland. Hafdis's men were hunkered down behind their shield wall outside the far side of the fortress, trying to find a gap in the defenses. On the northern walls, archers were taking aim at the emerging Leifings.

"Brace!" Harald yelled.

Aelfhild lifted her arm. She heard arrowheads thudding into wood around her. One shaft slipped through the shield wall, screaming into the lines behind. A man fell gurgling.

"Sabert, put your bows to them!"

The Norholtings came up from behind, sheltered by Thrym shields. Bowstrings thrummed, and fletching whispered overhead. More bolts came rattling in. Aelfhild took one on her shield; her arm wrenched and an iron point emerged through the boards over her face. She yelled at the distant enemies without words.

"Forward, step!"

"Ho!" the shield wall yelled, lunging forward in time. Whenever arrows made it through chinks in the wall, fresh arms rushed in to fill the gaps.

"Forward!"

"Ho!" Aelfhild screamed with the rest.

Voices rang out from her right. "Riders to the west! To the west!"

"Spears west!" Harald shouted.

The shield wall spun on its axis, leaving the Norholting archers to scrabble for cover. There were howls as boards clattered and moved. Some men kept their shields up to the south against Oescan arrows, but it left their line bent and vulnerable. Aelfhild, Eyvind, and the rest were just up from the curve.

"Plant your spear in the dirt and lean on it!" Kolbrun screamed into her ear.

The Thrym presented a thicket of spear points as Oescan cavalry broke through the sawgrass cover and charged in. Aelfhild saw crested riders, a few officers with purple cloaks whirling behind them, sweeping in with swords raised.

"Hold! Hold!"

The horses hit in a wave. Screams rent the air on both sides, human and equine alike. Aelfhild felt the shaft of her spear snap as it drove home into something, but she could not see what through the helmet slits and the shields over her head. The line had held by her, but broken between them and the Jarl.

"Leifings re-form on me!" Eyvind yelled. "Square!"

Men looped around to raise spears. The surviving riders were circling back, free of formation and attacking where they found holes. Aelfhild cast her shattered spear aside and drew the axe, but it was too short to reach out of the shield wall. She flung curses at an approaching horseman. An arrow ruffled her hair from behind and took the man from his saddle. Some of the Norholtings yet lived.

"Rally on the Jarl!" Eyvind called. "To the north, step!"

"Ho!"

Their square shifted, crablike and awkwardly. Blood slicked the ground underfoot. Aelfhild stumbled over a stricken Leifing corpse.

"Step!"

"Ho!"

A band of horsemen galloped between them and the Jarl, dancing between spear tips and swinging at helmets.

"Hold!" cried Eyvind. "Hold! We break when they come through next!"

The band turned and bore down on the square. Sword points hovered in the air, but they could not match the reach of the spears. They pulled their mounts aside at the last moment.

"Now break!"

Jarngrim and Kolbrun lunged forth. Aelfhild followed with them. She swung at the leg of a passing rider but hit air and stumbled forward. Beside her, Jarngrim impaled an Oescan with his spear point. Kolbrun got her spear between a horse's legs and sent beast and rider to the ground. More Leifings leaped in upon the fallen horseman.

"Re-form!" Eyvind was calling, but a moment too late. Aelfhild saw another wave of horsemen coming. A sword arced down. Kolbrun fell. The shieldmaiden's helmet went flying with the blow.

"Kolbrun!" Aelfhild howled. She dodged out to grab hold of her friend's body.

"Aela, back!" Jarngrim cried from behind. He threw his spear to skewer an approaching rider. The man toppled, his dangling foot pulling the horse in a circle.

"Help me with her!" Aelfhild called over her shoulder.

Jarngrim's hand grabbed Kolbrun's left arm, and Aelfhild seized the right. They dragged her back to the circle. The shieldmaiden's face seeped blood and chunks of scalp.

Harald inched his men down to join Eyvind's line. The Oescan fortress was alight now, and no more arrows rained. The Skjoldungs had breached. Soldiers and siegemasters poured out of the far side, pursued by blue-cloaks.

The cavalry rallied for one last, desperate charge against the Leifing wall. "Spears up! Hold!" Harald yelled.

Aelfhild was forgotten along with Kolbrun. Aelfhild tore away the sleeve of her tunic and pressed the cloth against the side of the shieldmaiden's head. It was hard to tell the full extent of the wound, but there was at least one long, gaping slash from cheekbone to the top of the skull. The right ear was mangled; maybe the eye would be lost as well. Aelfhild dared not try to use her rune on her friend's head. It had nearly killed Eyvind to heal his chest. She knew it would end Kolbrun at once. She pressed down hard to stanch the bleeding as best she could.

The Jarl's line was moving forward, hemming the surviving horsemen between them and the Skjoldung force.

Sindri had never come up. Damn the coward!

She heard hoofbeats and turned to look behind her. Not all the

Oescans were on the far side of the line. Three horsemen galloped toward her. She dropped Kolbrun's limp body and stood across it. She raised her shield and axe.

The men lifted swords. Firelight glowed along the blades. The smoke from the burning town and fortress had turned day to night. Only orange light flickered through the dark.

Two of the riders split to pass on either side of her. The third looped off to the side, no doubt to circle back and finish whatever the others did not. Aelfhild could not split her attention three ways. She focused on the rider to her left.

His blade swept down, and she caught it on the edge of her shield. Wood cracked. She swung her axe. It bit home through his hauberk, but the horse galloped on past and yanked the handle from her hand. The second's rider's sword sliced across her back. Aelfhild reeled to the side.

The point had cut through her cloak and torn through the armor beneath, but no farther. She was still alive, though she had no weapon and the third rider thundered in upon her. She rolled as he swept past and threw up her shield. His sword split the loose boards away from the iron boss. Scrabbling about in the mud and flattened grass, she could find no new weapon. There was a broken spear shaft. She hefted it like a club. Her broken shield dangled uselessly off her arm.

"Come on!" she screamed at them. Red flecks danced into her vision.

The men kicked their horses in.

A foot hit Aelfhild's back. A bear-skinned form launched itself overhead.

Narfi took the nearest rider from the saddle. The berserker landed overtop of the Oescan and his club swung down, once, again, three times. Blood sprayed up across the scrabbling horse. The second rider turned his attention for a moment. Aelfhild took her opening. She slammed her spear shaft into the man's arm and felt bone crunch. She howled her challenge to the sky as the man tumbled down.

Narfi joined in the howl. He was speckled with gore as he ran past her; he trailed sweat and bled from a dozen gashes. With a heave of his studded club, he stilled the writhing of the man Aelfhild had downed. Firelight glinted off his eyes. He nodded in her direction, then went off to join the rout of the remaining Oescans.

Aelfhild cast aside her club and the remains of her shield. Her whole body heaved. She sat and pulled Kolbrun's still form onto her lap. With two fingers she felt for the shieldmaiden's pulse; it was there, but faint and fading.

She gasped a few more breaths. Her muscles were drained. She could not shift Kolbrun's weight on her own.

The Leifings and the Skjoldungs cut down fleeing Oescans. There were likely Earnfoldings in the mix, too, Caelin's men. Aelfhild watched her own people fall. She watched Thrym raise shields to bash stricken foes. She watched spears fly into Oescan backs. The Northmen raised axes over their heads and cried out to the Gods in the bloody thrill of victory.

She clutched Kolbrun close. "I will save them. Next time I will save them. I promise," she whispered into her friend's ear.

The Oescan fort crumpled into flames before her. Bodies lay strewn, broken and riddled with arrows, from the eastern beach all the way to the western weald beyond. Sunlight struggled to break patches through the haze. Behind her, Haernmuth burned.

Aelfhild had come home and carried ruin with her.

AUTHOR'S NOTE

Thank you for reading!

This is a self-published novel. Self-published novels (and their authors) rely on word of mouth and reader reviews to succeed. If you enjoyed this book, please consider taking a minute to post a review on whatever website you purchased your copy.

If you would like to receive a notice whenever I release
a new book, click here to join my mailing list:

http://eepurl.com/da0ZCf

This list will only be used for notifications of any new titles I publish.

NOTE ON PRONUNCIATIONS

The language of Earnfold is based (loosely) on Old English. The stress in all Earnfolding words will always fall on the first syllable. Here are some of the names with a guide to pronouncing them:

Aelfhild – ALF-hild

Bertwald – BERT-wald

Ceolwen – CHEH-ul-wen

Cuthbert – COOTH-burt

Cynestead – COON-eh-steh-ud

Ealdorscir – ALD-ur-shir

Earnfold – ARN-fold

Hengist – HEN-jist

Leohtmere – LEH-ot-mer-eh

Osric – OS-rich

Sabert – SA-burt

Wynnthwait – WIN-thwayt

The language of Thrymgard is adapted, again liberally, from Icelandic and Old Norse with simplified spelling. Stress will always fall on the first syllable of the word.

Eyrun – EY-roon

Eyvind – EY-vind

Hafdis – HAF-dees

Herjarsborg – HAIR-yars-borg

Jarngrim – YARN-grim

Jotnir – YOT-neer

Kjartan – KYAR-tan

Leifing – LEYF-ing

Narfi – NARV-ee

Saejunn – SIGH-oon

Skjoldung – SKYOLD-ung

Ulfheim – ULF-haym

Oescan names, places, and words are adapted from Latin. They are heavy on vowels and should be a little easier for speakers of English to read.

Oesca – oh-ES-ka

All errors and inconsistencies, in any language,
are my fault and mine alone.

ACKNOWLEDGEMENTS

Once again, many thanks to Andy Meisenheimer for his valiant editing. He salvaged something from the wreckage of the first draft.

Thank you to William Drennan for his eagle-eyed copyediting.

Much love to Mike, Teresa, and wee Torin. He'll be old enough to read it before you know.

As always, I thank my parents for their love, their support, and their patience.

I could not have done this without y'all.

ABOUT THE AUTHOR

Ander Levisay writes fantasy stories featuring faraway worlds that still, somehow, have Vikings in them. He has lived in Iceland and Russia, but currently resides in Virginia with his dogs and cats. Whether it's writing, reading, or gaming, Ander can always be found in front of a computer screen. He probably should get out more.

Oaths and Old Gods is his second book, and the second entry in the *Queenmaker* series.

You can learn more about the author and his novels at:

www.anderlevisay.com